David Sterling lives the suburban lif   e for
fourteen years and they have two da   hind
the Sterling's picket fence looks perfect, and in many ways it is—save for
the fact that David carries a burdensome secret...one that he has guarded
well since he was a teenager.

David's life is unravelling and he cannot carry the burden any longer. To
make peace with himself and his world, it is time to tell the truth, a gamble
that may lose him all that is precious. But he needs to be released from the
shame, the guilt, and the fear.

In the pain and hurt of the aftermath, this deeply personal journey is driven
by David's desire to hold on to those he loves, while at the same time revealing who he really is to them and the world.

UNSTRAIGHT

John Thurlow

A NineStar Press Publication

www.ninestarpress.com

Unstraight

First Edition, September 2022

ISBN: 978-1-64890-538-4

Also available in eBook, ISBN: 978-1-64890-537-7

CONTENT WARNING:
This book contains sexual content, which may only be suitable for mature readers. Depictions of death, a deceased family member, homophobia, infidelity, pedophilia, religious shaming, sexual assault (recounted), bullying, cheating, and grief.

For Rudi, who gave me the courage to own my truth.

They tell us from the time we're young,
To hide the things that we don't like about ourselves,
Inside ourselves.
I know I'm not the only one who spent so long attempting
to be someone else,
Well I'm over it -
I don't care if the world knows what my secrets are.

—Mary Lambert, Secrets

CHAPTER ONE

DROPPING THE BOMB

23 June 2013

MY HEART WAS beating in my throat. I was terrified and while time seemed to stand still, the digital clock on the opposite end of the room carried on counting the minutes. I planned to drop the bomb at around eight o'clock. It was now heading for nine and the evening was running away. Oblivious to my fear, Carrie was engrossed in the movie—unaware of how her world was about to change.

As the clock jumped from fifty-four to fifty-five, I knew I needed to seize the moment. I sat up straight—too quickly almost. Adrenaline pumping in my veins, everything seemed to go into slow motion.

"Carrie," I sputtered—my voice quivering, "please turn down the TV, I need to talk to you." I turned myself around and sat at the foot of the bed facing her. I looked into her startled eyes and I felt the tears welling up in my own.

"What is going on?" she asked. I took a deep breath and I began to babble.

"You know things haven't been great between us lately?" I asked and stated at the same time. "I think you might suspect that I've been having an affair," I continued, "... I'm not... I would never." The colour ran away from Carrie's face and her eyes were frozen. "I feel so bad, seeing that you don't look happy," I explained. "I know you're hurting... and more than anything in the world, I don't want to cause you any more pain. I've tried hard to fight this, but it won't go away." My babbling came to an abrupt halt and I took a deep breath. I knew I had rambled on for too long and what I had wanted to say hadn't come out as I had planned. Carrie looked stunned; she didn't say a word.

I took another deep breath—I needed to get the words out, they were strangling me from the inside. Then, somehow, they escaped hurriedly and with some trembling.

"Things are not as they should be because I'm gay." The air in the room felt heavy and dry. I had just dropped a secret... my secret! One which I had harboured in my head for at least 30 of my 44 years. A secret I had carried, protected and nurtured—and a secret I was ashamed of.

I said the words with both a feeling of liberation and a huge sense of fear. I felt unshackled because the secret was out of the dark and it had no more power over me, but I was also afraid because it was uncaged and I was no longer its keeper. Equally, I was terrified at how Carrie would respond to the unexpected revelations. I had no idea of what awaited me on the journey that I had just begun.

A few moments of silence followed and staring directly at the confusion and pain on Carrie's face bore no comfort.

"How long have you known this?" she asked. Anger and bewilderment were evident in her eyes. I hadn't anticipated the question, but I knew I needed to speak the truth.

"Probably since I was teenager," I spluttered, clenching my hands tightly together.

"Then why the fuck did you get married?" she barked. The f-word and a raised voice always meant I had crossed the line with Carrie. She didn't use it often, but I guess I had crossed the ultimate 'line'—there was no going back now. I also needed to be cognisant of the fact that this was an issue I had been processing and mincing in my head for the better part of my entire life. In a few moments, I had thrown it all at her... she needed time to un-pack it.

I looked over my shoulder to make sure that the girls hadn't stirred and made their way to our bedroom door. Why had I gotten married?

"I married you because I love you, Carrie." My trembling words were calm and sincere. I hadn't planned to launch into this detailed explanation, but it seemed appropriate and I had spent many of the fourteen years we had been married trying to make sense of the journey in my head. "When we got married, I believed I had overcome this sexuality issue," I took a deep breath, feeling clumsy, "I honestly did." She seemed disorientated and who could blame her. "I loved you and thought—and hoped—that those urges would be gone forever."

"What urges?" she scowled.

I didn't answer the question and continued.

"At the beginning, I thought they were gone, and I have fought them really hard for many years." Carrie didn't seem convinced by this answer and a few minutes of silence followed. The torturous still felt like a lifetime. Carrie's anger broke the quiet:

"Why did you choose me to do this to?" she scorned. A relevant ques-tion, but there was so much else I needed to say. It was difficult not being in control as my secret took flight, but I knew I needed to let her lead the process. I had already given up the control.

"I didn't choose you to do this to," I replied. "This was not planned, nor premeditated—I love you and I love everything that we have created and established. I know that you don't feel loved and cherished because it doesn't come naturally to me. I can see that you hurt every day." Carrie's eyes were distant in the aftermath of the shock.

THE REALITY OF what I had told her started to hit her hard. The anger turned into pain and the tears began to flow. I instinctively leaned forward to hold and comfort her. I was nervous. Would she want me so close to her given that I was the source of her pain? Would I be the comfort and security she always wanted me to be? I knew I had a responsibility to console her if she would allow me. She held me tight and she wept. I wept too. There were no more words. Her wet tears on my shoulder were a stark reminder of the flood gates that had been opened. After what may have been a few seconds, I leaned back, looked at her and spoke.

"I NEED YOU to know that I will always look after you and the girls," I promised. "I am not going to abandon you overnight. We're going to work through this together. I want to preserve our friendship." I had rambled on way too much again. 'Less is more,' I told myself. Carrie said nothing, she looked dazed and bewildered—almost immediately exhausted. "I am going to do whatever I can to look after you," I affirmed. She nodded, tears running down her cheeks. It was obvious that she was not convinced.

I knew it had taken 14 years to build what we had, and that it might take just as long to recreate the trust which, with only a few words, had ceased to exist. The truth was that those words had always been there, lurking and hiding—waiting to escape and cause the pain they had already begun to inflict. My heart was heavy, laden with guilt and a shared grief.

"Right," I asserted, turning into operational mode, "I think you need to switch off and deal with this in the morning." I offered her a sleeping tablet—something she usually never took except on long-haul overnight flights. She didn't hesitate at the offer. I rifled through my bedside drawer for the tablet and I got her a glass of water. She swallowed it, and once I had given her a peck on the cheek, I told her I loved her. She didn't reply. She lay on her side with her back toward me and a few minutes after she was breathing deeply.

I turned off the light and lay on my back for some time. My mind racing... sad for Carrie, concerned about what this meant for us and our children, excited at the possibilities that awaited me, and anxious about the journey that lay ahead. Although I was proud of myself, I still felt laden with guilt and shame. I felt dirty. We all needed a journey of healing. I closed my eyes, but I couldn't switch off. I quietly climbed out of bed, made my way to the kitchen, boiled the kettle, poured a coffee, and sat down on the sofa in the dark. The curtains hadn't been drawn and I could see the bright moon in the distance. It looked like it was starting to wane—a reminder of the movement away from the reality of my world as I knew it. I drew in a deep breath and held it for a while. I didn't quite know how I felt, but terror and excitement were in the mix.

As I exhaled, I reached for my phone. There was somebody I needed to speak to.

CHAPTER TWO

HE'S A FUCKING POOFTER

13 May 1980

IT WAS THE week before half-term and I was playing on the playground before the morning school bell. We were playing Chinese jump rope—which we called *elastics*. It was an unusually cold morning for that time of the year and there was a soft drizzle. In my school uniform, I was over-dressed for this game which combined the skills of hopscotch and some hand motions. A group of girls were chanting: *"England, Ireland, Scotland, Wales. Inside, outside, puppy dog's tails."* As the chant grew louder and louder with each repetition, I was jumping and completing the sequence inside and outside the elastics that were held in place by Lucinda's stubby legs and Lisa's skinny ankles. I was hot and sweating, but there was adrenaline pumping inside me. I was enjoying the sequence, how good I was at it, and also all of the attention.

I noticed a group of boys move closer. Not exactly the group I would have chosen to spectate my jump rope skills. It was Michael Carlson, Gerald

North and Anthony Milligan. These boys thought they owned the playground and they had a reputation for being troublemakers. I was mostly scared of Michael. He was devilishly handsome, and he knew it. He looked like a boyish Tom Cruise, only taller. I always found him nice when he was alone, but as soon as he had his posse with him, he became mean and nasty. It was always so hard to understand how he could be these two different people. Gerald was square and burly and he had a massive mop of curly, auburn hair. He was an interesting person, because despite being big and bulky—there was definitely something effeminate about him. His large frame and the fact that he played rugby and hung out with Michael Carson made him a misnomer of sorts. I didn't find him attractive at all—but I could see why others might. I preferred the look of boys who had dark hair and continental features. Boys like Michael Carlson and Tom Cruise. The final of the horrible trio was Anthony Milligan. He was more of a hanger-onner, than anyone to be afraid of. He was a leech who wouldn't have had much of an identity if Michael and Gerald hadn't given him some kind of space in which he could belong. He was their bitch—he did what he was told and he knew his place in the pecking order.

"He's a fucking poofter!" The words hit me like a cricket bat to the back of my head. Michael smiled smugly at the words he flung across the playground.

"Yeah, he is. He's a queer!" Anthony tried to make himself sound tough, but it didn't work. By now the chanting had stopped and I felt like I was in hell rather than in 'England, Ireland, Scotland or Wales'.

"No, he's not," retorted Lisa, who was unravelling the elastic from her delicate ankles. She may have been the shortest girl in the class, but she was a fireball. Principled and direct. Lisa continued, "How dare you, Michael Carlson? You're just a bully!"

"Oh, really Lisa Prestwick—I may be a bully, but he's a poofter!" Then it was Gerald's turn to enter the conversation. He looked at me with an air of cool calm intimidation and then he spoke.

"A shame you have to play with girls. Not cool enough for the boys," he sneered.

"I guess that's what Nancy-boys do," Michael added.

"Damn right!" interjected Anthony. I tried to speak, but my mouth was dry, and the words wouldn't come out. To be honest, I didn't know exactly what to say. Lisa walked up to him, stood right before him and looked up at his handsome face.

"Just get away from here before I report this all to Mrs Lumsden," she threatened. Mrs Lumsden was the intimidating Year 6 teacher at Forest Primary, and everybody was terrified of her and her quick tongue—except for, it seemed, Michael Carlson.

"Oooh scary, scary," Michael responded sarcastically. Lucinda was now standing next to Lisa and she was uncharacteristically mad.

"Listen to me, Michael Carlson—you and your sweet little gang don't scare us—or David for that matter. Why can't you just leave us alone?" she instructed. There were a few seconds of silence and then Gerald jumped in before Michael could respond.

"There is no place for poofters in this school." He was sticking his chest out in an effort to make himself look bigger than he actually was. Suddenly my throat felt clearer and I found my voice. I was calm but clumsy:

"You're entitled to your opinion, which isn't the same as mine—or Lucinda's or Lisa's," I rebuffed. "I don't think I'm a nancy, or a queer, or a faggot, or any other name you want to call me."

"Oh, shut up," Anthony interrupted, trying to assert his intimidatory position in the gang.

"I'm not finished, Anthony," I continued—shocked by the attention I had gained from the other two and also by the silence on the entire playground. "You can call me whatever you want, but I know who and what I am—so I really don't care." The girls, and one or two boys, beside me and behind me, started to clap and cheer. I felt like a hero—a humiliated one, but still a hero. Michael flung his middle finger in the air as the three of them turned and walked away in a perfect v-formation. It was flawless and almost looked rehearsed.

'You can call me whatever you want, but I know who and what I am— so I really don't care.' These words echoed in my head. They were my words—but they were all a lie. I had no idea of who or what I was—and I cared a lot about what other people thought. A lot more than I should have. I wasn't as brave as I would have liked to have been.

THE TORMENT OF the bullies never actually goes away. This kind of event evaporates away until the next. You forget the humiliation and the pain until the next time. There's always somebody who thinks it acceptable to point out that you are different while at the same time mocking the essence of who you are. I know this all too well—I am embarrassed to say that I did it too. It was a deflection technique—a way to keep the focus off me. A way to keep the secret hidden and a way to mask the pain. It was a way to survive—but it perpetuated a toxic cycle, because I brought pain to my tribe. If only I could go back and undo all of it.

MANY YEARS LATER—a few years after Carrie and I were married—I was standing around a barbeque with a group of friends. It was couples' evening and all of the women were inside. Somehow a conversation started about a recently released movie called *Brokeback Mountain*. The movie, which is about two cowboys who find physical and emotional love, created controversy and debate when it was released in 2005. The incredibly handsome Heath Ledger and Jake Gyllenhaal played the very masculine and sexy cowboys. At the time of the barbeque I hadn't seen the movie—but I was well aware of it. The conversation was slightly homophobic in nature and the discourse was typically macho. I was uncomfortable.

"I can't watch that kind of thing, it grosses me out," commented Miguel, who was himself rather gross to look at. He had a pot belly and a face that was staring squarely at the ugly end of gravity. Nicotine and a dozen beers a day had made him look a lot older than his actual age.

"Yes, it's so unnatural," Peter interjected, "and besides, who wants to watch two fags touching each other anyway?" As everybody laughed at his question, I remember thinking 'actually, I wouldn't mind watching that'—but it didn't seem appropriate to say it out loud to that audience. I was sure Peter was possibly also gay, in the closet, fighting a similar battle to me. He was married—as was I. He had a loving wife and children—and so did I. He was a gay-shamer—and I was good at that too. My gaydar told me he probably wished he was one of those cowboys. His naturally pink cheeks, his effeminate voice, and his awkwardness around me gave him away.

My friend, James—who was the host of this gathering and who had been the best man at my wedding—was standing away from the others with me.

"What do you think of this kind of stuff?" James asked as we made our way toward the others.

"Makes me quite uncomfortable—I wouldn't like to watch it." I felt my face glow, as I told the lie.

The words were hardly out of my mouth and I wished I could recall them. I had had the opportunity to be an ambassador for equality, fairness and gay love—an ambassador for my people... but I blew it. Again, I had become like all of the bigots I had met on the way. In simplest terms, I had missed the opportunity to be principled, objective and enlightened. I was so disappointed with myself. Instead of being a pioneer, I had injured my own people and their long and painful struggle.

CHAPTER THREE

FIRST HOLY COMMUNION

1 June 1980

JUST TWO-AND-a-bit weeks after being called 'a fucking poofter' on the playground by Michael Carlson, my sister and I had our First Holy Communion. This was a big event for the Catholics in our family. Not so much for dad or grandad—but more so for mum and for gran who made the trip from Zimbabwe. Grandad had come along too, but church wasn't his thing—his thing was whiskey or beer—which made my dad, his son-in-law, great company.

The preparations during the week were relatively calm. Holly, my younger sister by nearly two years, and I were at school and gran used the time to make Holly a white dress—angel wings and all. She had also made her a white Amish-styled scarf and had bought her some white sandals. If my memory serves me correctly, there was a splash of regal purple somewhere in the ensemble, but I don't remember exactly where. I was kitted out in a white shirt, white pants, white shoes and a chocolate brown tie that matched my hair perfectly.

Before we knew it, it was Sunday morning, and it was time to head down to the Church of the Holy Rosary. Holly and I emerged from our rooms—white, like snow in the summer. We were white all over. Gran smiled as she tilted her head sideways as if to get a better view of us. She looked incredibly proud.

"Tuck your shirt in properly," she commanded in her Polish accent, "and Holly, you need to pull your scarf forward." Holly grimaced a little and did what she was told. I was generally more compliant and did what I was instructed to do. Gran ran through a quick practice run with us: "Body of Christ" she prompted.

"Amen," we responded, immediately sticking our tongues out as if to receive communion.

"That's how you do it," Gran praised, "and don't forget to bow your head and say a prayer afterwards." Holly and I smiled.

"I'm so proud of you two," she added. Dad and grandad were outside having a smoke and it seemed we were all ready to go.

I checked myself once more in the bathroom mirror. 'Not bad', I thought, 'in fact—somewhat handsome—maybe I could actually have a girl-friend.' I guess the truth was that I would have preferred a boyfriend, but that was so far from my reality and I wasn't sure if that was what I really wanted anyway. I felt confused because I knew I wasn't mainstream.

Driving to the church, I found myself thinking about a bible verse I had once read. I forget exactly where I had been when I read it, but it terrified me. The verse was from the book of Leviticus, which is, still today, commonly quoted and paraphrased by anti-gay Christian fundamentalists. The bit that unnerved me so can be found in verse 20 of chapter 18. It read something like: 'if a one man lies with another it is an abomination.' I re-member having to use my dictionary to find out what 'an abomination' was. I had no idea, but it didn't sound good at all. It turned out I was right. I discovered that it meant: a disgrace, a horror, an atrocity, a violation, a crime and an evil. I read the verse over and over again, feeling more and more afraid each time: 'if one man lies with another it is a disgrace, a crime, an evil!' I wondered if it was also an abomination for two men to hold hands, to say 'I love you', or to kiss?

Going to church and participating in sacraments like the First Holy

Communion made me feel like a devious imposter in the church.

As our car turned into the church parking lot, I was afraid by the realisation that my natural attractions were either sick or evil—or both. I suspected that I needed some serious help. Maybe I was ill, maybe I was demon-possessed. Something was wrong.

"Are you excited?" gran asked.

"Yeah, sure," I answered, not sounding convincing.

"Today is the beginning of an exciting journey for you and your creator. It is time for you to walk with Jesus and be everything God designed you to be. Don't forget the sacrifices Jesus made for all of us." Gran's words: 'be everything God designed you to be' resonated deeply. I said them again to myself and I felt like there was a glimmer of hope.

I felt excited and scared... it was all so confusing. Mum smiled at me reassuringly as I got out of the car. I smiled back.

"Enjoy every moment," mum encouraged with love and sincerity in her voice. "All those years of Catechism have taught you a lot. I'm very proud of you and Holly." Mum smiled, pride shining from her eyes.

"Thanks mum," I replied and anxiously added, "We better hurry because we need to meet Father Ryan at the side of the church." Dad and grandad had already found a bench close to a statue of the Virgin Mary where they were firmly seated and puffing away.

We all met Father Ryan at the side of the church where he gave us a thorough briefing in his charming Irish accent. He was a man of medium build and he had soft eyes. He exuded warmth, but you could see he liked things done in his particular way. He was a well-respected member of the community and my mum and gran held him in high esteem. Even though gran lived in another country, she had made sure that she and Father Ryan had stayed connected. I had once overheard my gran say that Father Ryan was 'way too friendly with Sister O'Brian' who was from the neighbouring parish. At the time I thought that this was probably a good thing—it was always good to be friendly, wasn't it? Then, I had also, at some point, overheard my dad—who didn't have the greatest amount of time for the Catholic Church—talking about priests being overly friendly with altar boys. I had also thought that that was essentially good and kind. Priests were supposed to be friendly. I had always wanted to be an altar boy, but the secret I carried in my head made me scared to spend more time at the church than was absolutely necessary.

"All right, follow me now you wee ones, we have some important business to get done." Father Ryan's voice lilted in the morning sunshine. You could listen to his soothing and gentle pitch for hours. We followed him into the packed church, single file—girls first and then boys. We filled the front two pews. The congregation was largely Portuguese and Lebanese, hence the other boys—all equally kitted out in white like me—were all pretty much my type. I learned that I found Mediterranean and Middle Eastern men easy on the eye. Dark hair and dark eyes made them beautifully handsome.

Father Ryan began the service in prayer and then a song. The first hymn selected for the service was: 'Suffer little children to come unto me.' As we sang the second verse, I felt a feeling of peace and hope in my heart:

For I will receive them, and fold them in My bosom;
I'll be a Shepherd to those lambs, oh, drive them not away!
For if their hearts to Me they give,
They shall with Me in glory live:
Suffer little children to come unto Me

IT ALL SOUNDED so simple. Give your heart to God or Jesus—I always got those two guys confused—and you will live in glory. No more abomination. Maybe the secret would disappear? Maybe I could be cured. Feeling hopeful, I looked up and saw the life-size crucifixion statue that hung behind the altar. Father Ryan was standing right beneath it preparing the communion. He looked somewhat insignificant beneath Jesus's nailed and perfectly manicured feet. I looked up at the pained face of Jesus with thorns on his head and the nails in his hands and feet. I felt pity for him, but I felt pity for myself too. I wondered if he had secrets. What was in his head? Were there any things he wanted to do—or did—that he shouldn't have? He was, after all, a human being with flesh and emotions and carnal needs.

Dad had once mentioned that Jesus had done things with Mary Magdalene which ten to one weren't befitting of a so-called celibate messiah and that the Catholic Church had not published the Gospel of Philip because it didn't tell the story of Jesus that they subscribed to. I looked down at Father Ryan and wondered too, if he had any secrets in his head. Had he thought of—or done—things he shouldn't have? Maybe with Sister O'Brian or with any one of the many priests or altar boys who had passed through his many congregations?

ANOTHER HYMN BEGAN and I glanced back up at Jesus. The depiction of him on the cross was not comforting or peaceful in any way, but I did find myself feeling a bit envious of his life and times. He got to hang out with twelve apostles—all day, every day. Twelve Middle Eastern looking men who Bible illustrations always depict as handsome and mildly buff— each with their own air of mystery about them.

Just before communion, all of us first time communioners were called to stand at the front of the church. We queued up as we had rehearsed, and one-by-one we took our places. Standing at the front of the packed church, dressed all in white, repeating the words of Father Ryan, I felt like I might be at a wedding. My own wedding, saying my vows. A wedding at which I was marrying my religion. I didn't like to think it, but with only the glimmer of hope provided by the words of the hymn 'suffer little children to come unto me', I felt uneasy that this marriage may end in divorce. I didn't want it to, but the odds were against us.

CHAPTER FOUR

A QUEER WEDDING

19 September 1981

MY DAD WORKED in retail for a large clothing chain. He was well respected, worked hard and loved the social aspects of his work. His socialising meant two things for us—either we didn't see him much, or we were dragged along to the many events he attended. We enjoyed going, it was always fun, and we met many interesting characters in his circles. Driving home wasn't always fun—it was always directly proportional to the number of beers he had consumed that day.

One cold and chilly Saturday afternoon in September 1981, we attended the wedding of Kai and Chris. It was an interesting wedding. There was no church service and so instead we arrived at a house in leafy suburbia. The impressive perimeter walls were painted pure white and were strobe-light bright in the early afternoon sunlight.

"Grab this for me please, Son-Son." That was my dad's nickname for me. I quite liked it. I leaned over and took what was an unexpectedly heavy present from his hands.

"Just be careful with it," he cautioned. "It's heavy, but its fragile... the queers are going to love it." He was jovially confident.

"Queers?" I asked, scrunching up my face.

"Yes," dad replied, "Kai and Chris, silly!" I wasn't completely sure what a queer was—but I was eventually to discover that I was one too. Kai and Chris were kind of unisex names—I expected one to be a man and the other a woman. I wasn't sure which way around.

As we approached the door to the garden, it flung open.

"Welcome, welcome, welcome Nick and family!" It was Kai—flamboyant and animated in a white suit that matched the walls of his house. "Hello Laura, great to see you," he said to my mother and then welcomingly turned to me. "You must be David—pleased to meet you, you handsome young man." I shook his hand and smiled. Squatting down a little, he turned to my sister and animatedly whispered, "And this must be Holly, daddy's little treasure." Holly hated the limelight, but she smiled sweetly as she glowed a tinge of red.

Kai was the overly flamboyant manager of the retail displays section of British Home Stores where dad worked. He looked a bit like a caricature. His complexion was slightly chalky and he had big eyes and a perfect nose. He was short and stocky with dancing hands and he walked with a pronounced waddle that would have made Daffy Duck envious. He had the perfect gay voice and he curled his lips up on the left side when he spoke. He synchronised his lip curling with the rolling of his eyes and it made for entertaining conversation.

"Let me introduce you to Chris." Kai gestured for us to follow him and we pretty much followed him in a straight line to where Chris was talking to some other guests next to a large fountain at the bottom of the garden. "Let me introduce you to Nick and his family." Chris turned around and that was when I lost track of what Kai was saying. Chris was incredibly handsome. A mop of well-groomed dark hair, worn back to his shoulders, Prince Valiant style. He had a perfectly chiselled face, deep brown eyes, and the shape of his crimson lips was perfect too. Chris smiled sweetly, greeted and welcomed us warmly and then immediately returned to his conversation. "He's immensely nervous about the nuptials," Kai explained. "His family is coming and they don't support our lifestyle—they're excessively religious."

"Religion will put a spanner into any spoke it can," my dad added supportively. Mum, with her Catholicism and her kind, gentle and accepting heart remained quiet, so you never quite knew where she stood on the topic.

"It's been very stressful over the last few weeks," Kai explained, "and we nearly didn't get to be here today."

I WAS SOON to be thirteen and my hormones were awakening. What I was becoming aware of was that I was more attracted to boys than I was to girls and I found this somewhat disconcerting and confusing. It felt oddly comforting to be in close proximity to these queers.

Many years later, I came to realise that Kai and Chris's wedding was never actually a legal wedding. Gay marriage was illegal in 1981, so the celebration we went to that day was simply a personal endorsement of their love for each other, and it was shared with close family and friends who would not inform the authorities.

"BLOODY RIDICULOUS THAT we have an Elvis-style priest hanging around here today, and not the real thing!" my dad exclaimed at the table once the beer was flowing.

"Damn right," responded Bev who was one of dad's work colleagues seated at our table. "It's so unfair that love can't just be celebrated and acknowledged," she added sincerely—and maybe slightly raucously. It was too early in the day to have the booze flowing but it was too late to stop it. The formalities hadn't started yet, but the party seemed to be well on its way—at our table at least.

MY DAD WAS an interesting character, complex and confusing, but easy to like. He was always the life and soul of the party. He had had a difficult childhood and this seemed to cause deep and difficult emotional scars. In public he wore a brave face. At home we experienced his pain—sometimes annoyingly and sometimes abusively. Somehow, we all survived, but we loved him immensely and his charisma was as appealing to us as it was to others.

It did surprise me that he could, after a few drinks, express his support for equal or homosexual love. I remember once watching the 1980 British mystery movie *The Mirror Crack'd* with my family. The movie starred Rock Hudson as a character called Jason Rudd. I recall my dad making a comment about Rock being a 'bloody faggot.' The messages were confusing—on one hand being a homosexual was fine, whilst on the other 'bloody faggot' didn't sound like something I might want to be.

Even from this early age, I felt like I had to be on my guard: try to be more of a boy, try to be tough, avoid saying things like 'those flowers are beautiful,' hang out with the boys, say cool things like 'don't you think Rock's a fag?' Later I realized that by deflecting, you sacrificed others cut from your cloth. You had to protect yourself.

Maintaining my cover and hiding any possibility of anybody knowing my inner thoughts was paramount. I had no idea how tiring and utterly exhausting wearing this mask would become. As a young boy of 12, I would never have predicted that 32 years down the road the mask would eventually crack. The phantom would emerge and I would finally need to define who I undeniably was.

SOMEBODY STARTED BANGING a large xylophone—I couldn't quite make out the tune. It may have been *Edelweiss* from the *Sound of Music*, but I wasn't sure. It was tremendously loud and slightly baritone in its pitch, but it certainly stopped the buzz at each table and the garden fell quiet. As the song ended, a flamboyant young man with olive skin, blue eyes, and short shaven hair stood up toward the main table. He was wearing a rust-orange suit and his wrist was dangling at his side like the pendulum of a clock.

"Good afternoon everybody, my name is Alexi and it is soooo wonderful to have you all here to celebrate the marriage of my amazing friends—Chris and Kai." He took a deep breath and seemed to look somewhat emotional. "It's been a long and bumpy road for us to get here," then turning to

Kai and Chris he continued: "you are brave my friends... you're making a stand for love and you are doing what you know your souls are here for."

Everybody clapped and cheered except for a middle-aged woman who looked a little like an Airedale Terrier at the table to our left. There was something weird happening around her mouth... I couldn't quite make out if she had naturally crazy jowls—or if she was pushing her jaw forward and pulling her face in disgust. I could have sworn I heard her mouth the word 'faggots' while Alexi was talking. It turned out that the Airedale lady was Kai's aunt—his mother's sister. She was a fundamentalist Christian who had no time for this 'homosexual fad' which she had declared 'evil and sick' at a family luncheon earlier in the year. She was not a welcomed guest—an enemy on the inside. Her big problem was that her son, Martin, who was Kai's cousin, had also recently revealed he was gay. I noticed a young man, two seats away from her. He was tall and slightly awkward. I remember thinking to myself that that was probably him: Martin, the queer son. I felt sorrow for him, but I didn't know why. A family of gays. I should have felt entirely at home here... and strangely I did. To be honest, I found some of the overtly camp behaviour overwhelming and it made me uncomfortable— but I was dealing with my own elephants. In all likelihood, I was disliking something about myself that I saw in these brave and honest men.

The applause and cheering settled and Alexi took control.

"Welcome Reverend Presley," he proclaimed, inflecting his voice upwards at the end. "He's not a real priest, but he's the best we can do given the circumstances and the laws that don't allow us to marry who we want to." There was another applause from the guests. "Does he meet with your approval Aunty Val?" We all looked around trying to find Aunty Val. It turned out she was the Airedale Terrier that I had spotted earlier. Her pronounced jowls glowed crimson and she scrunched her mouth tightly.

"He's ok," she replied in a heartbeat. Everybody laughed. There was obviously some deep stuff happening there, but I have to give the old bitch some credit—she took it well, even though she was dealing with her own pain on an uncharted journey. A journey like that could end in a multitude of ways: pain, hate, rejection and tears or love and acceptance—also with some tears.

The 'priest' took over and he tried valiantly to be Elvis-like, entertaining the guests right down to speaking with a southern drawl. My mind wandered and I drifted in and out of my head. The picture of two men standing up front, declaring their love to each other was intriguing and comforting to me. It helped that Chris was beautiful. Those two men had no idea of how they impacted me and how their special day would live in my head for years and years to come. It gave me some hope.

MAYBE ONE DAY I would marry somebody as strikingly kind and handsome as Chris. I wasn't yet as brave as Kai and Chris and Alexi and Martin. These men—and many others like them—were pioneers for people like me.

CHAPTER FIVE

FIRST KISS

4 April 1982

JESSICA DAVIES WAS a popular girl—sporty, friendly and loved by most. She was a year older than us, although also in our year group. Apparently, she had repeated Year 5 after the emotional trauma of losing both of her parents in a car accident. She was an only child and was sent to live with an aunt and uncle who had placed her in boarding. Despite her tragedy, she was a positive and happy-go-lucky person, and although slightly tomboy-ish, she had petite features and plaited tails that would have made Pippi Longstocking envious.

Jessica and I were both in the school's athletic team which was how we became friends. We travelled together on the bus to many sporting events and spent many hours on the grandstands between the events. She was a long-distance runner and I was a high jumper. Somehow, we had decided we were 'boyfriend and girlfriend'. I'm not quite sure how that happened. We would openly hold hands and were happy to let everybody know that we were an item.

Jessica was also friendly with Gerald North who had moved to the same high school as me. This was a little tricky because Gerald and I had a history and I honestly didn't want to be his friend. I'm sure he didn't want to be friends with the poofter either. Gerald was also in the athletics team and he competed in the under 14 shot put events. This meant I got to spend a lot more time with him than I really wanted to. I know it may be prejudiced, but I always found shot putters to be a slightly dim-witted. Gerald North fitted my prejudice perfectly. Burly and handsome—although not my type—and just a little dumb. Truthfully, he was rather nice to me when it was only me, him, and Jessica. It was almost as if he had washed the primary school poofter playground incident from his head. Or had he? I certainly hadn't. I could still see him standing there on that May morning, with his windswept curls, singing to Michael Carlson's tune.

Thursday the 25th of March was to be my 13th birthday. Jessica had been granted permission by her aunt, uncle and house mistress to join me and my family for dinner. It was a weeknight, so she needed special authorisation to leave the school grounds. We went to a local restaurant called *The Bonanza* where the ambience was dull, but the food was always good and the manager was comical and entertaining. He had taken a shine to my parents who dined there often. The evening was uneventful, except for the cringing I did while everybody sang happy birthday to me. Later, dad started to tease us on the drive back to Jessica's boarding house.

"Time to separate the love birds," he commented. I wanted to die. Jessica laughed. She was kind of embarrassed.

"Dad, please stop," I demanded, cringing a little. Holly giggled.

"Nothing to be embarrassed about," dad reassured, "we've all been there." I could see he felt awkward as his joke had gone pear-shaped, but mum came to the rescue as she often did.

"Nearly school holidays, are you going away anywhere, Jessica?" While Jessica answered, I thought, 'Good one, mum.' I probably should have joked back with dad, but it was too late now—the moment had gone.

ON THE NEXT Saturday, I took part in a show jumping competition. Holly and I had been keen horse riders for at least four years and show days were a great time for the family to get some fresh air and just have some fun together. Jessica accompanied us to the show. I was excited. Excited to have her around and excited to show her my talents.

My only event was scheduled for after lunch, which meant we had most of the morning free. I suggested we go for a ride—tandem—onto the neighbouring field. I helped Jessica up first and then I got myself up. She was wearing flip flops, which were not the most practical for riding a horse. We rode bareback. I was behind, holding her firmly between my chest and the reins that were coming up from Spruce's mouth. Spruce had been my horse for the last two years. He was palomino in colour, with a slightly darker mane and tail. His face was squarish and he had a slim white abstract splodge, that ran from between his eyes to halfway down to his muzzle. He was placid and gentle and always wanted to please.

We moved from a topsy-turvy trot—where Jessica nearly slid off to the left—to a smooth canter. It felt wonderful. Jessica spooning with me on Spruce and the wind in my face. Free. No Michael Carlson. No Gerald North. No Anthony Milligan. Just Jessica, Spruce, the wind and me.

"I've lost my flip flop," Jessica shouted. I brought Spruce to a screaming stop.

"Oh dear, how far back?" I asked.

"Not sure," Jessica answered. I turned Spruce around and we started our flip flop surveillance exercise. It was at least 15 or 20 minutes before I spotted it. Green and face down on green grass, it was not easy to find. We both dismounted Spruce. Jessica picked up her flop and put it back on her naturally brown feet. We sat on the grass for a while. I was holding Spruce's reins and he was using the opportunity to eat as much of the green grass as he could. I had my other arm clumsily around Jessica's shoulder.

"I enjoy being with you, David," she volunteered. The words sounded like magic to my ears. I didn't know how to reply, so with a huge amount of courage, I moved cautiously in toward her lips and she, too, came closer. It was all going to plan, the game was on. Our lips met. The kiss was open-mouthed and clumsy. It felt unnatural. We fumbled our way through at least 15 seconds which felt much longer. The kiss ended, we hugged and we both knew it certainly could have been better than it was, but it was, none-theless, a start. I wasn't sure I wanted to do it again. It didn't make me feel any sense of 'wow' and it was memorable for all the wrong reasons. My relationship with Jessica was a short-lived and I don't recall how it ended. After Jessica, I entered many girlfriend-free years. The next one would be Charlene Barnes when I was 19.

IN MY EARLY twenties, I bumped into Jessica in a supermarket aisle, whilst shopping at Sainsburys in a neighbouring town. It was good to see her. Her Pippi Longstockings plaits had unravelled to form shorter free flowing strands of auburn hair that was brushed backwards from her weather-chapped forehead. Her eyes looked a little tired and it seemed like life may have beaten her a bit—it was as if she was burdened. She told me she was happily married. She had a babe in arms, a toddler, and a bun in the oven.

"Looks like you have your hands full," I joked.

"Sure do," she laughed. We spoke fondly of our happy days at school and of our antics on the athletics bus and at the many athletics meets.

"Did you hear about Michael and Gerald?" she asked.

"Carlson and North?" I questioned, seeking clarity.

"Yes," she replied.

"Don't think so," I responded.

"Apparently, they had been romantically involved since our last year at school—and when Gerald went off to work as cabin crew for British Airways, Michael used all of his free time to be unfaithful." I was shocked—not at the infidelity, but rather at the revelation that the playground bullies were themselves fags.

"Are you serious?" I asked somewhat flabbergasted. Jessica carried on as if she hadn't heard my question.

"Gerald was devastated, tried to take his own life...I haven't been able to get hold of him for a few months now. Seems he's gone into hiding," she explained. This was a lot to take in: Michael, although a mean person, was delicious and he was gay! Gerald was also gay but I had always suspected that. Jessica was talking about homosexuality in our circles like it was normal. I needed to digest all of this.

"Terrible," I retorted lamely. Not entirely sure exactly what I thought might be 'terrible.' I needed to do some processing. It was hard to feel sympathy for my bullies, but I did. They, like me, had used deflection tactics and had persecuted their own to cover and protect themselves. I was as guilty as they were.

Many years later, Jessica and I connected on Facebook. Her life had moved on. She looked younger, less pained and generally happier. She seemed less drawn and haggard. She had since come out, divorced her husband and now had a wife and a modern blended family. In a brief exchange, she wrote:

"It's been a roller coaster for us and it was difficult to blend the family—but so far so good. I've been with Sandy for 9 years and she's the love of my life." I remember smiling contently when I read this message. I was sure that that first kiss had been as uneventful for her as it had been for me.

Who would ever have thought that in our year group at school there were so many homosexuals? I wondered how many others there were still hiding in the woodwork, too scared to reveal their authentic selves.

"Well done, Jessica…you have done good," I said quietly to myself after reading her message for a second time.

CHAPTER SIX

HIDEAWAY

14 February 1983

AS I MOVED into puberty, I began to vehemently dislike Valentine's Day more and more. It was a day for straights. It was a day where straight love, boy-meets-girl love, was celebrated. Well, it certainly was in Chelmsford where generations of my family had lived. Even Rodney Daimler, who was the queerest boy in the school, right down to his pigskin man-bag and fake eyebrows, pretended to be straight on Valentine's Day. He sent—and rather oddly received—some of the many red roses that were delivered anonymously to eager teenagers across classrooms at Manor Hill School. I often suspected Rodney probably sent some of those flowers to himself and I wouldn't have been surprised if he also sent a few to some of the good-looking boys ...boys like Michael Carlson and another boy called Wayne Evans who was delicious to look at. Given half the chance, and with anonymous protection, I would have happily sent long-stem red roses to the likes of those two. Receiving roses—or even a card—from either of them would have been equally satisfying. Alas, it was never to be. Adam and Eve, not Adam and Steve! I felt pretty sure that on this particular Valentine's Day, I had seen Michael Carlson receive a bunch of cherry-red roses with a card—the handwriting on which looked a lot like that of Gerald North.

Valentine's Day of 1983 was on a Monday and it was some 5 weeks before my fourteenth birthday. My face was blotchy with pimples—all attributed to, as my dermatologist had told my mum, 'very oily skin and an active T-zone'. My frame was scrawny and out of proportion and my voice could move at least three octaves in any given sentence. I was a late developer and I felt unattractive and completely out of place.

The Valentine's Day before had been built around some excitement, Jessica and I were 'boyfriending and girlfriending', and while it was as much a fraud as my vows to Carrie were to be later in my life, I believed in it all very strongly at the time. Jessica had bought me one of those musical cards—it belched out the tune of Elvis Presley's 'Love Me Tender' each time you opened it. She had written kind and loving words in it, possibly similar to the ones Father Ryan might have sent to Sister O'Brian at least once a year—anonymously, maybe? She had also bought me a large limited-edition mint flavoured Toblerone chocolate from the One Pound shop in Ilford. I didn't even like mint, but I didn't let her know. I had made her a fairly big card, too big for an envelope. It had an asymmetrical red heart across the front of it. On the heart, I had stuck some cotton wool under a large plaster, and I wrote the corny words: 'Thanks for mending my heart.' Totally ridiculous, outlandishly gay and just a little bit sad! I delivered the card to the boarding house at school, accompanied by a bowl of two goldfish that together we named 'Hercules' and 'Emerentia'. I knew Hercules was a Roman god and a hero—the son of Zeus. It was only years later that I discovered that Emerentia was the name given to the Virgin Mary's mother...Jesus's grandmother, I calculated. There didn't seem to be any escaping from the church.

Time had moved on—and so had Jessica, who was now dating Pierre Viljoen. He was French, not bad looking—just short. She seemed happy, and I hoped for her sake that he kissed her better than I did. I noticed she was carrying a teddy bear and at least two roses at lunch time. I should have felt happy for her, but I didn't. The whole day had me feeling uncomfortable and unnerved. At break time, I found a quiet spot to sit where my empty hands might not be noticed.

"God," I muttered to myself, "can today just be over." I looked up and noticed my sister, Holly, and a group of her friends standing outside the tuck shop. I was happy to see that she was carrying a card, a rose and a big smile. That made me smile too. Before I could begin to feel sorry for myself, my friend Dean came over.

"All good Davey-wavey?" he asked in his usually friendly way.

"Yip," I replied and faked a smile that concealed my frustration and pain. Dean chatted with me for a while and proudly showed me his Valentine's card.

THE NEXT FOUR Valentine's Days were all written from the same script for me. Painful, tiresome, and just a real drag. The build-up to each of them was agonizingly exhausting, and pretending to participate and to be attracted to and hungry for the opposite sex was both tedious and harrowing. It made no sense to me as to how and why the execution of two men—both called Valentine—by Roman Emperor Claudius II in the third century had evolved into an annoying commercial frenzy. Somehow, the Catholic Church had then also canonized one of them in 500 AD—making him Saint Valentine, the patron saint of love. Patron Saint of which love? Straight love, gay love, *all* love. Or only some love? I needed some answers from this canonized martyr. I wondered if Father Ryan might be an approved and appointed spokesperson.

I thought long and hard about approaching Father Ryan to talk about my pain and to try to gain some answers. I liked him, and I trusted him—but it was all too close...way too close. Our town was small, our congregation smaller and some people's views on equal love were tiny.

At the end of March—only five weeks after the uneventful Valentine's Day of 1987—I celebrated my 18th birthday. As usual, my family made a fuss of me, but overall the celebrations were relatively unexciting. I might have gone out with some friends, but I don't remember. My life at that time was hazy, as it often was—I missed out on so much of the present as I grappled with my sexuality in my head.

A week after my 18th birthday, I bumped into Dean at the local supermarket. He, like me, was completing his A-levels and he had turned out to be a good guy who worked part time as a DJ. He never did find out who the mystery 'V' was—and that was probably in his favour.

"I remember you once told me you like the music of Depeche Mode," he stated out of the blue.

"I do," I replied, slightly confused about where this was all going.

"I'm not sure if you know of a group called Erasure?" he continued. I shook my head to indicate that I hadn't. "Well," he progressed eagerly, "they had an album out a little while ago called *Wonderland*. It wasn't that great—but they've just released a new album called *The Circus*, and the songs are a-m-a-z-i-n-g."

"Cool," was all I could muster.

"I'll tape it for you and give you a copy at college tomorrow," he offered.

"Thanks, looking forward to it," I answered, and we said our goodbyes.

THE NEXT DAY, true to his word, Dean handed me a cassette labelled '*The Circus*—by Erasure.' As soon as I got home, I popped it into my Walkman and I played the album over and over...the songs were indeed 'a-m-a-z-i-n-g'. I found myself rewinding and playing one song repeatedly. It resonated deeply with me. It was a song about me, or it could have been about me. I wanted it to be about me, but not all of it. Some of it was happy, some of it was painful. It was called "*Hideaway*", something that I was incredibly good at doing. I couldn't listen to it enough.

I didn't want to be rejected by the people that I cared for, I didn't want my mother to breakdown and cry, I didn't want my father not to speak to me—but I did want to let people know how I felt inside, I did want them to still be proud of me, and I wanted love to mend my broken wings. The words of the song spoke to me.

I started to find solidarity in songs that were being sung about people like me. I found myself on a mission to find them, and I did: 'I want to break free' by Queen, 'True Colours' by Cyndi Lauper, and 'I will survive' by Gloria Gaynor were just a few. There were many more. Every night with my Walkman plugged into my ears, I would lie on my bed and listen to 80s gay liberation music...always comforted and inspired by it—but too scared to take the bold steps they encouraged me to take.

CHAPTER SEVEN

THE MORMONS

19 August 1983

FOR AS LONG as I can remember the Mormons were always there: at school, at the front door and then in my family. The suburb I grew up in was disproportionately populated with many Mormons and even more Germans—and some people were both. How that all happened nobody knew. The Church of Jesus Christ of Latter-day Saints was situated on Baddow Road close to *The Star*—where Mormons were forbidden to drink alcohol.

The many Mormon families in the area hosted numerous young Elders who travelled from the US to complete their two-year missions. These young Elders were always kitted out with bicycles that they rode from house-to-house and door-to-door, selling the gospel of Jesus. Not the same gospel I had learnt from Father Ryan or in the many Catechism classes I'd attended. This was the gospel where Jesus travelled to North America and a convicted criminal called Joseph Smith was supposedly commissioned by

God to interpret the book of Mormon. Then immediately after he had completed his task, he destroyed the golden tablets somewhere in upstate New York—and they were never to be found again.

It was always exciting to have a young Elder at our front door. Sociable dad would always invite them in and try to convince them to drink some beer. I always imagined them back at their digs in the evening declaring how Satan had tempted them that day, and delighting in their retelling how they had resisted him. The longer my dad tormented them, the longer they stayed. The longer they stayed, the more I got to look at them. Those young men were always lovely to look at and their Salt Lake City accents were kind of sexy. They were always clean cut, with navy style haircuts—always brushed to the left with no fringe. They had buff arms that strained the seams of their white collared short sleeved shirts and their fingernails were always cut a tad too short. Most were blond, but that was okay. Their black ties, black shoes and black name tags completed their look. Their skin was perfectly toned and they had whiter-than-white teeth that they showed off beautifully with the whites of their eyes, in what my irreverent Uncle Dave called the 'Mormon murder stare'. I never quite understood what Uncle Dave was referring to. I had decided that Mormon men must all have the handsome gene—and if they didn't, there must have been some missionary selection criteria that excluded you if you were not pin-up boy gorgeous.

Wayne Evans was Mormon and he had been in my class since before I could remember. As I became sexually aware, he was probably my first crush. He was tall like me and he had a pretty-boy face with soft features and a thin protruding nose that turned up slightly at the end. As I grew older and matured a little, I came to realise that I found large and interesting noses as appealing as I found dark-haired continental looking men. I'm not sure why, I just did. Wayne's nose was definitely the trigger. He had dark hair, with natural highlights—not traditional missionary Mormon blonde. He wore it combed back in an 80s-style middle path. His prowess on the sports field also made him more attractive. He was somewhat friendly with Michael Carlson and Gerald North, but not mean and awful like them. Wayne was handsome and kind...the other two were only half the package. I spent a lot of time with Wayne when we were younger, playing in the park, exploring forests and streams and going to the shops. My softness and his robust straightness were certainly the cause of us drifting apart in our teenage years.

ONE WEEKEND, A group of us were at Wayne's house. Wayne, Jason, Brandon, and I emerged from the end of the back garden where we had been making MacGyver inspired home videos on a video camera that my dad had loaned from work. It was exciting and innocent 14-year-old boy fun. As we approached the house, Wayne's dad was standing at the back door smiling at us.

"I worry about this one," his dad divulged to the others—in front of me—as he handed us each a glass of blackcurrant Ribena. It was Friday, and the day before Wayne's birthday on August 20th. I'm not sure how, but I always remembered that day because Wayne was special to me. I still remember it.

"Why are you worried about David, dad?" Wayne looked puzzled. His dad responded to him as if I was invisible, a deaf visitor perhaps?

"He's soft and likes the softer things...flowers and paintings...those kinds of things." Wayne squinted at his dad. I did like flowers, I appreciated nature and I also liked to draw and paint. I couldn't deny it.

"Maybe he's a fag," Jason joked. Brandon laughed—too loudly.

"Maybe he's not," Wayne jumped to my defence. Even though I was humiliated, it felt good to have Wayne protect and defend me. I blushed and Mr. Evans tried to salvage what he had started.

"Why don't you guys go and finish your movie," Mr. Evans proposed. We headed off to the garden and I frantically looked for an excuse to leave.

YEARS LATER, WHEN we had finished uni and poly, Wayne did the Mormon mission in reverse. He headed to Boston, Massachusetts in the US where he too was given a bicycle, a white shirt and a navy cut. It was his time to evangelise the prophecies of Joseph Smith. We had grown apart since his father's warning some ten years earlier. Something must have transpired after that and I can only assume it was the Mormon anti-gay warning. I knew he was straight, but I missed him. I knew he probably didn't miss me and I was okay with that. I wasn't obsessed or desperate, I just found myself still mildly infatuated with him—maybe more so as his existence was only in my head.

IN 1994, I did a short backpacking stint to Boston after the summer camp where I met Avery, a crazy Canadian woman who was fun to be around. While in Boston, I arranged to meet Wayne, and Avery came along too. We met in a diner under strict missionary rules. He was chaperoned by another Elder and it was as if an egg timer was watching over us—every word a grain of sand through the hourglass. It felt like I might be visiting a friend in jail. Elder Evans looked handsome, his sporty arms dangling from his snow-white shirt and his name badge giving him an air of authority. We reminisced about the good old days and it was slightly awkward with our two spectators close in check.

"Is Avery your girlfriend?" he asked without any embarrassment. Avery laughed from the bottom of her stomach.

"Are you fucking crazy?" she shrieked. I kicked her under the table and Wayne's chaperone flinched and blinked simultaneously.

"Sorry," I explained, "that's how Canadians speak." Avery laughed.

"Not all of us, just the fucking rough ones," she bellowed loudly and animatedly. I could feel my face getting hot and I knew we had to leave.

"I'm sorry," I mouthed, "was great seeing you again, Wayne." He smiled.

"And for me too...maybe next time it will be at one of our weddings," he added. We shook hands formally, following the cue from the chaperone and we left. I so wanted to give him a hug.

"Fucking odd!" Avery was never one to mince her words. "Strange looking bunch!" she groaned, pulling a face.

"Don't you think Wayne's handsome?" I asked.

"Uhmm, no!" Avery offered without hesitation. "Why, do you?" she came back promptly.

"He was always the school heartthrob," I tried to cover my tracks. The truth was that he had been the school darling—he had possessed sex appeal; he was handsome; and he was a nice person...the perfect triple cocktail. Sadly, the Mormon mission seemed to have killed some of his spirit.

Three years later, I received his wedding invitation in the post, I RSVP'd to say I wouldn't be able to attend and that was the last contact we ever had.

SHORTLY AFTER MY trip to Boston, my cousin, Kacey, surprisingly announced that she was leaving uni to marry her Mormon boyfriend of 6 months. Aunty Clare was not impressed at all, but Uncle Hamish was excited at the prospect of free-flowing alcohol at the wedding—except it was a Mormon wedding and central nervous stimulants were not invited. The wedding day arrived and everybody wore a happy face. I was pleased to see a few visiting Elders had also been invited. Mr. and Mrs. Evans were there too—and vaguely distant when I greeted them. The Mormons in Chelmsford were tight and insular and I felt like I might have been identified as an outsider, a threat maybe.

"At least she's wife number one," was the most positive thing Aunty Clare managed to spit out while we were waiting for the newlyweds to return from the tabernacle. Kacey's new husband, Robert, could never have been a Mormon missionary—he was simply too ugly and out of proportion. Within a few years, Kacey and Robert had produced their pigeon pair but there were some deep cracks in their marriage. I was sad for Kacey who had made a bed she didn't want to sleep in. They both wore masks, a lot like mine, and the outside world was oblivious to the mess hidden behind the neatly painted white posts of their impeccable picket fence.

A few months before their marriage collapsed completely, I was invited to their home for a meal. The dinner *sans* alcohol was a little stiff and there was definitely an elephant in the room doing its best to chase away the delicious food. The dessert plates had hardly been cleared when Robert began.

"David," he said, "you are very special to us, and one day when we all arrive at the pearly gates, we don't want to be guilty of not telling you about Angel Moroni and the Latter-day Saints. We want you to spend eternity with us." Everything seemed to grind into slow motion as Robert pulled out a dark and unpleasant painting of Angel Moroni. I felt a little vulnerable—it was all so unexpected. Is this what Elders did? Is this what Wayne was doing on his mission? Had they spotted the secret I was hiding? Did they think Joseph Smith and Angel Moroni were the right cure for me? I didn't need them. I didn't need Joseph Smith or Angel Moroni. I had found my peace elsewhere.

CHAPTER EIGHT

AN ACCIDENT AT THE STABLES

24 July 1984

IT HAD BEEN two years since I had gallantly salvaged Jessica's flip flop and kissed her clumsily in that field, Spruce smiling at my inexperience as straight-faced as a horse is able to. There were other girls at the stables who I tried to show an interest in: Samantha, Debbie, and Tracy to name a few. I say tried, because I really had to try. I tried the hardest with Debbie Roach and she played along too. All we did was flirt, and that was enough for me.

I was more interested in Henri with his long and lean body and tight jodhpurs that hugged his powerful thighs. His whole body stood attractively in his sleek Dublin equestrian boots which he wore with elegance and grace. He had thick middle-parted hair, somewhere between noirette and chocolate brown and it was always shiny, hanging perfectly above his beautiful brown eyes that sparkled against his olive brown complexion. He was handsome, with sex appeal—and only two years older than me. Henri had kissed all of the girls at the stables, including Debbie Roach, Samantha, and

Tracy. I had secretly fantasised that he might actually be attracted to me, but it was just a game I played in my head. It fed my daydreams.

One Sunday afternoon, after a few beers, dad volunteered Henri to give Holly and I some driving lessons in his company car—a 1982 yellow Golf GTI. Dad had always taught us that the only car that went 70 miles an hour in reverse was a company car. By volunteering his car keys to a 15-year-old to teach his 13 and 11-year old children to drive, he was affirming his lack of respect for company vehicles. It was fun having Henri teach us to drive. He was calm and patient, which made him even more attractive. I only saw him flustered twice: once when I reversed into a tree, and on another occasion when Holly accelerated far too expeditiously into a barbed wire fence. On both occasions, but less so the second time around, Henri was a bit of mess, his beautiful bangs flat on his forehead from his sweat as he surveyed the damage to the car.

"Don't you worry yourself," dad told Henri after the barbed wire incident, "this is not our problem—tomorrow I'll fill out a form and then it becomes a British Home Store irritation...nothing for us to worry about." Each of his words seemed a little unfinished from the beer in his cheeks.

ON 24 JULY, the first Tuesday of the summer holidays, we were all at the stables where we loved to be as often as we could. There were at least 25 of us there on that day despite the fact that the weather was dreary. It had been raining lightly in the morning, which had made the ground slightly mushy, but the sun had come out for a while before midday. We had hoped that it would have dried up enough for us to practice some jumps for the show scheduled to take place on the following Sunday.

"Saddle up," boomed the voice of Wendy, the stable caretaker, giving us all permission to ride. The curfew was over. Halters and harnesses, saddles and girths and heaving and pushing...and in a few minutes we were all ready to ride. The last of the riders were hardly out of the stables, when the accident happened.

Henri was first into the arena and first to start jumping the course that we had set up in the rain. At the third jump, a triple combination, Henri's horse, Onyx, tripped and went careering into the red and white painted poles at the middle of the three jumps. Onyx was fine, but Henri was not. Onyx, alarmed and certainly in a lot of pain, bolted for the stables, but Henri lay on the ground, crying from the pain in his leg. Wendy was the first on the scene. We all dismounted our horses which were dotted, obliviously and happily grazing, across the arena. All the focus was on Henri.

"Are you okay, boy?" she asked. I couldn't help but think that it seemed odd to call somebody so strapping a 'boy.'

"I'm not sure," Henri managed, tears running down his clenched cheeks.

"We're going to get you some help," Wendy explained calmly and confidently, trying to allay any of his fears.

It must have been some 40 minutes before the paramedics arrived. One gentleman and a lady. The young man was handsome and attractive in his white and blue uniform.

"Let's check you out, young man," he consoled.

"Young man", I whispered to myself thinking that it sounded better than 'boy.' It took a few minutes of pushing and prodding, with Henri flinching and squirming in-between.

"It's definitely broken," the paramedic announced after his assessment. "Your lower femur has a clean break, and there might be some damage to your kneecap." I watched the paramedic's manly hands dance across Henri's thighs, and I wished those thighs had belonged to me. "We need to cut your jeans off," he explained to Henri, "and we need to get your leg stabilized with a splint, before we try to move you." Henri nodded his head in appreciation, the tears still flowing slowly. I wished that I could hold and comfort him to try to alleviate some of his pain.

The lady paramedic began to cut his jeans right to the top. As she flapped the fabric open, she exposed the muscular definition in his broken leg, and also his tired, soft blue briefs, with their frayed elastic waistband. They looked like their time might be up. Things are never as they seem below the surface, in places where nobody gets to see: certainly not in my head, possibly not in Sister O'Brian's bedroom—and evidently not beneath Henri Viviers' jeans.

The male physique was something that I have always been drawn to, it was something that I lusted over—but it was a desire I could never admit to. I rarely got to observe the lines of man's body, except on Sundays when

Jesus peered down at me from above Father Ryan's head—but he always looked sad and vulnerable, a little like Henri had looked on that fateful Tuesday afternoon.

IT'S STEREOTYPING, I know, but my observation has taught me that horse riding, like disco dancing, attracts the gay boys. But not Henri, he was an exception to the rule. Many years later I reconnected with him on Facebook. Sadly, he hadn't aged well like a full-bodied Merlot. Instead, rather disappointingly, he had aged more like a rough Russian vodka. His bangs were gone and in their place were deep receding hairlines, that contained remnants of thinning hair. His cute and slender nose that had turned up slightly at the end was replaced with something a lot stubbier and much less attractive. His worldview had become unattractive too, his Facebook wall was full of bigoted, narrow-minded perspectives. It was at the time of the Australian Same Sex Marriage Referendum in 2017. He had papered his wall with what amounted to hate speech, not quite Leviticus, but the message was the same. So, I did what I have become very good at—I pushed the 'unfriend' button and in an instant, Henri was gone...just a fantasy on my journey, and I am grateful for the role that he unwittingly played—but his place was now redundant. Even after I liberated myself from him, I did find myself wondering about him and his sexuality. He was rugged and straight looking, but then again maybe his style and his grace were telling tales of an internal closeted fight. Maybe he was dealing with his own demons, I don't know. I do know from my own journey, that deflection is a cool strategic game when you want to hide secrets. Religion is a tremendously large shield—a master prop in that game. I wondered if James's friend Peter might also have plastered Jesus and fear across his Facebook wall? If I cared enough, I would check—but I simply don't anymore.

My journey has taught me that not everybody sees the world in the same way that I do, and I have come to realise that this is okay. I have also learnt that it is difficult to change perspectives, especially when the dogma of the Bible is involved. And to be completely frank, I have neither the inclination, nor the energy to fight any of it, ever. I have wasted far too much time in this precious life caring about what others think and trying to modify myself for acceptance. Those days are done. 'Unfriend' and 'block' just take a whole lot less energy and help to keep me focused on what makes me happy in the irreplaceable time that I have left. The same could be said of the likes of Wayne Evans's dad, Michael Carlson, and Gerald North. I guess in some sort of way, I had also unfriended those Mormons and those playground bullies many years ago—only without the convenience of social media.

CHAPTER NINE

BODY OF CHRIST

15 August 1985

FIVE YEARS HAD passed since my First Holy Communion and I was back at the Church of the Holy Rosary, this time for the sacrament of Holy Confirmation. Gran was back from Zimbabwe, this time without grandad—he had gone to the other side some four years earlier. Nothing much had changed since, save for the fact that I was taller, spottier and sporting a Duran Duran fringe that would have made even the likes of George Michael and Andrew Ridgley envious. For the big day, I donned a silvery-grey double-breasted suit that gran had specially taken me shopping for, and I wore a pair of patent leather winkle pickers that my parents had bought for me. A thin, stylish black and white paisley tie, which had been my dad's work tie in the 1960s, completed the look. The tie was a good finish to my ensemble and paisley patterns were all the rage at the time. I thought I looked incredibly cool, but it would have been impossible to look any gayer. The truth was that many popstars in the 1980s were closeted gay men, who either emerged willingly or accidentally from behind their guises. They created a culture and look that came to be synonymous with the 80s. The fact was that many of them looked gay and I aspired to look like them. I made a brilliant Boy George lookalike—but he was a self-declared queer. Obviously then, I didn't really want to be his lookalike. Too close to the bone.

By the time of my confirmation, Father Ryan had been replaced by Father Finnigan, who had recently arrived from Ireland. Father Finnigan was much older than Father Ryan and he liked the bottle more than he should have. I wondered whether after his appointment, Myrtle, the church bookkeeper, noticed some kind of an escalation in the communion budget. Father Finnigan could have been the perfect drinking buddy for my Dad and my grandad, but it was a non-starter because my dad had nicknamed him 'Father Fiddle-again'. Perhaps a sly dig at the trauma of his own unspoken school day secrets?

The Confirmation service was routine and uninspiring, and it was clear that Father Finnigan just wanted it over—and he did get it over as hurriedly as he could. I was standing between Miguel Dos Santos and Manny Khoury—one Portuguese and the other Lebanese, both handsome and both straight. Also, both with not much style. They were the same two people who flanked me at the front of the church for my First Holy Communion—only they were on opposite sides of me the last time around.

Being in church, a sacred space where God and whichever Father it was at the time were in charge, always made me feel extra guilty about my homosexual thoughts and desires. It was as though I was in a place where the spotlight shone brightly from above—into every corner and under every pew. There was no place to hide any secrets and, even if you tried, that spotlight would catch you out. It made you feel exposed and vulnerable. The light always exposed what lurked in the dark, and for this reason I needed to be extra vigilant.

Being around handsome boys like Miguel and Manny always made me feel awkward—especially at church. I felt awkward looking at them in case they worked my inner thoughts and feelings out. For this reason, I always kept conversations short and breezy. I needed to be cool and calm and I needed to hide any interest I might have been feeling. My wandering eyes needed to be policed. It was a full-time job. On some occasions, I felt uncomfortable looking up at the life size statue of Jesus on the cross. The sculptor had made Jesus to be a beautiful specimen. His chiselled Middle Eastern face looked a lot like Manny Khoury, and his well-defined torso rippled with an impressive six pack. His manly forearms were muscular and attractively veiny...disturbingly inviting. His modesty was only just concealed, and from beneath his creased and crumpled robe extended beautifully defined and elongated thighs. On many Sunday mornings, sat beside my mother and sister, I would guiltily cast my eyes downwards... ashamed and tormented by the beauty I recognised in the body of Jesus. It wasn't specifically that it was Jesus, but more so that I was secretly aroused by the naked body of man. Ironically, church became my place of temptation, it was the only place where I was ever exposed to the naked physique of a man.

"Body of Christ," Father Finnigan repeated for the umpteenth time as I stood before him for my turn in the communion line.

"Amen," I mouthed, remembering gran's practice drill from my First Holy Communion some years before. I stood to the side and bowed my head. "Please forgive me for my evil thoughts," I prayed silently in my head. I kept my head down, steering my eyes firmly away from the real 'Body of Christ' and I returned to my place in the second row of pews. Miguel was already seated, and Manny wasn't far behind me.

Father Finnigan's haste to get the service over was helpful for me. He gave me less time to look at Jesus—suffering, yet beautiful—and he helped me escape the intensity of the sacred spotlight where nothing could hide. The final hymn, as it usually was, was "Go In Peace", which the congregation sang with gusto. Father Finnigan remained at the front of the church and with an inebriated smile across his face, clutched the chains that suspended a well-used pewter thurible. He swung it about rigorously, effusing incense smoke across the church. Smoke that confirmed the resurrection of Jesus and that also reduced visibility—making it easier to hide and more difficult to breathe.

WE WERE HOME first after the service because mum and gran needed to heat the food before the family arrived for dinner. There was great excitement in the air. Mum was proud and gran was even prouder. Holly and I were entertaining our young cousins with a hand clapping routine we had learnt many years before at primary school:

"*...eighteen, nineteen blueberry street, this is what you say when you get into a fight...,*" we were reciting the words and demonstrating the hand actions. They were engrossed and loving it. My Uncle Bob was unaware that I was eavesdropping on the conversation that he was leading on the opposite end of the room.

"David seriously worries me..." I heard him say. I missed the next bit because the little ones burst back into song:

"*...girls go to college to get more knowledge, boys go to Jupiter to get more stupider...*" As the song and clapping ended, I could pick up some more of what he was saying.

"...he's too perceptive and caring, he should toughen up a bit." At that point, gran joined them and the topic of conversation abruptly changed. Uncle Bob continued, now directing his attention to gran.

"So nice to see you mum, it's time you came back to England." Ever since grandad had died, all four of her children had been pressuring her to return to Blighty. It would have been so good to have her near us, but she wasn't ready. She told us that her arthritis didn't like the damp and the cold. I was hoping gran would leave Uncle Bob's conversation so that I might hear if he had any more to say about me. I wanted to hear—but also didn't. Gran moved away and if Uncle Bob had said anything else that night, I missed it.

Gran approached me and the little cousins, with a small and delicate silver box.

"Which one of you are going to help David open this special present?" she asked. Young Alison eagerly volunteered. She excitedly opened it and pulled out a shiny silver chain and an even shinier St Christopher pendant.

"Always wear this, my boy," gran insisted with sentimental tears in her beautiful eyes. "He will always guide you. He carried Jesus across the river, you know." I smiled and thanked gran and she helped me put the chain around my neck.

IT WAS THE innocent and unnecessary observations of people like Uncle Bob and Mr. Evans, who years before also expressed concern for my perceived weakness, that pushed people like me deeper and deeper into the closet. The words they expressed were unnerving and they exacerbated the exhausting guilt and the unrelenting shame. Those comments were as cruel and unkind as the ones that closeted gay people, like me, made about the gentleness that they recognised in other gay men—whether they were out or not.

These were all in contrast to one of the few encouraging opportunities I remember receiving on my journey. It came from my friend Georgina on a cool and crisp April morning in 1995. I was visiting her in Edinburgh where she was living and teaching. We were lying on the grass in St Andrew's square, reminiscing about our chance meeting while on holiday in Egypt a few years before. We were jabbering about our aspirations and dreams and about anything from politics to religion. Talking to Georgie was always easy and we seemed to see the world through similar lenses. She was more like my sister from another mother. Then, out of the blue, with her assertive voice, her kind heart and love all over her face, she gave me an opportunity.

"Davey," she announced, "it's okay to be gay." Her sincere and caring blue eyes, framed by a multitude of charming freckles that sparkled like stars in the early evening sky, made me want to spit it all out—but the words wouldn't come. Her words were soothing, but way too premature and somewhat overwhelming for where I was at in my head. Years of conditioning couldn't be undone with one expression of acceptance, love and hope.

"Thanks Georgie," I replied, "but I'm not gay," I lied. She smiled and she squeezed my hand.

"I really do love you, Davey," she reassured. I loved her too, and I had missed an opportunity.

CHAPTER TEN

THE AUCTION

7 December 1985

WHEN GEORGINA HAD been backpacking in Argentina, a year or two after we met, she had stumbled across an antique telephone at the *San Telmo* Antiques Fair in Buenos Aires. Somehow the phone had had my name 'written all over it', and she had bought it for me and then lugged it some 7000 miles across the globe to perch it on my mantlepiece. She was nearly as eccentric as I was gay, perhaps that's why we had bonded so well since our first meeting. We were both a little on the periphery of what was mainstream, but we embraced it. For me, eccentricity was the mask that helped me survive—it kept me undercover. Georgina's telephone remains a lovely display item in my house and if it could talk, it could probably tell some interesting stories from the many years that it has peered down on my life from its elevated position above the fireplace. Its receiver covertly listening and the holes in the circular dial, like ten eyes, sneakily observing, always.

Georgina liked things pristine, clinical and shiny, so when she had first visited me in my bachelor digs, she didn't appreciate the non-linearity of my ancient artefacts. That's why I had been surprised that she took the time to visit an antiques market whilst on her travels, let alone actually buy something from one of the dusty bric-a-brac stalls.

MY LOVE FOR old things was something I had learnt from my dad. He loved the smell of old wood, especially those that oozed scents like linseed and beeswax. He got excited about old and tired pieces of wood that sparkled and came to life with the right treatment and some tender loving care. He loved artefacts that told stories of bygone times and places: ornaments, bank notes, registry deeds, padlocks, models of ships, lamps...you name it, he was intrigued by them.

One of the things he liked to do was visit an auction every Saturday morning and, much to mum's horror, he would always return with some new treasures—or displeasures. Some of the finds were sold in job lots which meant that you had to take the good with the bad, and sometimes you had to pretend you didn't see the ugly.

Holly and I used to love to tag along on Saturday mornings, especially the first Saturday of each month because that was when all of the antiques came out. The auction was held on the tarmac in a local car park and the items to be sold were laid out in straight lines, starting at the end where the cash office was. It was run on a first come first serve basis. If you had goods to sell, you laid them out and the auctioneer would sell your items in whatever combinations and packages he decided. The first to be laid down, would be the first to be sold. The auctioneer was himself an intriguing individual, he looked a bit like JR from the TV series Dallas—Stetson hat, big metal buckle and big fat sausage fingers. He spoke with an accent, which may have been Dutch, but it might also have been Greek. I think he made it up as he went along, swinging and merging the sounds into his speedy and dramatic auctioneer lingo.

The morning of 7 December was cold and icy. One of those mornings where you can see your breath and you can't feel your fingertips. Dad had bought us all some coffee and Holly and I had our gloved fingers wrapped around the paper cups trying to steal as much warmth as we could from the hot beverage inside. My dad started to chat with an elderly gentleman. He had soft skin, a kind face and his grey hair was thinning. It turned out his name was Mr. Eggleston. He seemed nice enough.

Mr. Eggleston regaled us all with interesting stories of the war, his failed printing business and of a fiancé whom he had shaken off because she was 'too controlling and possessive.' He made us laugh a lot. You couldn't help but like him, he had charm and charisma—nearly as much as my dad.

"Come on Son-son," dad called, pointing out that JR was about to auction off the gramophone that I had been eyeing out. It was a more recent model than the old horn versions, but it was still branded HMV, and it smelt old and looked touched by time. It was built into a black wooden box with its speaker concealed inside. It was well used—and it even included two small triangular shaped metal tins, branded 'Heart Needles', that contained hundreds of small replacement needles. Whilst waiting for the auction to start, the seller had played an Elvis track on it and the tinny and amplified sound was somewhat mesmerizing. I was desperate to own it. Bidding opened and dad initially helped me, and then halfway through he gave me the reins.

"Now you take over," dad instructed. The bidding finished at £14.50, and I had myself a bargain. Dad was praising me when Mr. Eggleston joined us again.

"Good buy," he exclaimed with a smile. "I have a couple of long-playing records and some spare boxes of needles that you're welcome to have," he added.

So, the following Saturday, Mr. Eggleston picked me up at the auction lot and he drove me through to his house, which was somewhere close to Great Notley. He had agreed to meet my dad at a service station just outside Chelmsford at 5:00 p.m. that afternoon to take me home. Mr. Eggleston's cottage was intriguing. It was packed with old keepsakes, but it felt sad—it may have even felt desperate. There was sadness in the walls and the old lace curtains in his kitchen even looked tired and confused. They swung aimlessly above the AGA whilst he made us a pot of tea. They, like him, seemed to be lost and without focus and purpose...present but not actually adding value.

"So, are you retired?" I bravely asked.

"Sure am young man, and I'm single." It felt like he was offering too much information, but he continued: "It can be lonely, but you know I was engaged to two women and I got rid of them both. The first was bad in bed, and the second was too controlling." I wasn't sure how to respond, so I replied by asking him if he had ever had any children. This question seemed to open the door for him to try to promote himself some more. He rambled on for some time about how he was like a father to many young men, but that he had never had his own.

"One time," he regaled, "I picked up a young military hitchhiker who was trying to get home to his girlfriend for Christmas. This young chap told me that he was so horny and that he had a big dick, and that he wanted to fuck his girlfriend when he got home." I wanted him to stop, but he was so enthralled in his story. "He asked me to touch it," he continued. I was sure I looked shocked but there was no stopping Eggleston. I was starting to see the evil in his face and the grooming in his eyes. "I was driving," he continued, "and so I leaned over and touched him down there...and he was so big, very big and so hard." Eggleston was animated and turning himself on with his own story. I felt myself swallow with panic. "I had hardly touched him," he went on, "and he ejaculated all over the place. I had to bring him home to clean him up, and to clean and iron his clothes. Later, I drove him to his girlfriend."

As he poured the tea, I filled the awkward silence.

"Sounds embarrassing," I offered.

"Not embarrassing at all, it's quite natural," he smugly retorted. "Do you have a girlfriend?"

Before I could answer the question, he was delighting himself in another story about a young man who he had brought to his home. This one he explained, had had family problems and he needed to be jerked off to feel better about his life. I was becoming terrified and I wasn't sure what to do next.

"Have you got those records and needles?" I asked.

"Sure," he replied, "come with me, they're in my bedroom." I needed to respond smartly and with haste.

"It's okay," I replied, "my parents have taught me that it's rude to go into people's bedrooms...they're personal and private spaces." I was surprised that he didn't push anymore. I fled outside, where I felt safer and he returned a few minutes later, true to his word, with three records and two tins of needles. We sat outside talking for the remainder of the time and I tried with all of the skill that I had to steer the conversation away from male genitalia. At around quarter past four, he told me that we should probably get on the road to have me back in time for 5:00 p.m. Driving home, things were somewhat silent and prickly in the car, I was frightened, and he must have felt unsure himself. I was relieved to have survived the ordeal and I just wanted to get home. Halfway through the journey he started his nonsense again.

"Is your dick as big as that military boy?" Eggleston's question was flippantly direct. Before I could muster an answer, he stretched his left arm over the handbrake and grasped at my groin, manhandling me in a way that shut down my senses. Horrified, I was too afraid to speak or move. "Not bad," he critiqued. "You should get a girlfriend."

A few minutes later he dropped me off with my dad at the service station as was agreed. Eggleston immediately returned to the persona of the man we had met at the auction the previous week: smiling, friendly, entertaining, soft-faced and generally a kind-hearted old man.

"Your son is a real gentleman," he told my dad, and dad looked proud at the compliment. I didn't breathe a word of my ordeal to my family because he had been a kind predator and I didn't want anything gay associated with me—besides, I was 16, and therefore almost an adult. I was baffled as to what Eggleston had recognized in me. Was he just taking a chance, or did he see the gay in me? My conclusion was that I needed to hide harder. He was a wolf in sheep's clothing—but good at his game, that's what he was.

CHAPTER ELEVEN

WAITING ON A MAN AND HIS DAD

15 August 1987

IT HAD BEEN six months since Dean had introduced me to Erasure's "Hideaway". I had been playing it secretly on the Sony Walkman I had received for my eighteenth birthday. Listening to the song still gave me a rush. I felt like I was illegally smuggling and gaining pleasure from something that I shouldn't have had. It was a kind of contraband and I was living on the edge.

"What are you listening to?" mum asked.

"It's a new band that Dean told me about, it's really nice," I hadn't lied. Dad joined in.

"Probably one of those get into the grass and pull your pants down kind of songs," he complained. I laughed and reminded him that he was talking about the Tiffany song called 'I think we're alone now'—and that it was actually a remake of a 1967 song by Tommy James. Mum laughed and I managed to escape any other questions about the gay themed music I was listening to...the music that gave me comfort and solace in the straight world in which I lived.

AUGUST 15, 1987 was a Saturday and I was working the evening shift at The Bonanza. My dad's social dexterity had helped secure Holly and I a part-time job waiting tables at his and mum's favourite restaurant. It was my second job. My first had been at the service station close to the Holy Trinity C of E. I didn't last there long because my hands were soft and the environment too hard for what my friend Anna described as my 'metro-sexuality'. If only she knew. The restaurant was great fun; we worked with good friends and I liked interacting with the diverse customers.

James, who would later be the best man at my wedding, and I became great friends at The Bonanza. Our friendship grew steadily over time. We became like brothers. I enjoyed being with him. James had many girl-friends and I didn't. For the first time since Jessica, I tried again—this time with Charlene Barnes, but I didn't enjoy the taste of her. She was my second girlfriend—the only one after Jessica and the last one before Carrie. James was Spanish and, like Wayne Evans, he oozed sex appeal and was charm-ing, kind, and clever. My mum had always told me that a girl who is kind and clever is better than one that looks like a beauty pageant winner. I al-ways wondered if the same logic applied to boys, but I was always too afraid to ask. Either way, James was never an option. The older and more mature version of me had worked out that to crush on a straight guy was like look-ing for rain in the desert. James was my friend and I didn't want any bene-fits from him, unless of course he did.

At around 8:00 p.m. a man, who I later learnt was 31 years old, and his father came in for dinner. They were seated in James's station, but he had asked to leave earlier that night, so I offered to serve the table. The younger man was tall and lean and he had a large and slightly skewed nose—some-what disfiguring, but also appealing. He had blonde hair, blue and deep-set eyes, and a soft and endearing face. His hands were long and sleek, and he spoke with them as much as he spoke with his mouth. His father on the other hand was short and rounded with a chicken skin neck and a balding head. I did find myself wondering how faithful his wife might have been:

how was it possible that this man could produce this slender and fairly attractive male specimen? The dad and son were quick to order and eat. Then after, they drank—and then they drank some more. Beer, then wine, then whisky and then more. I lost count. The restaurant had emptied and they were the only table left. It was getting late. Our dad usually collected Holly and I at around half ten after our shifts had ended. It was now nearly eleven and, deep in conversation, they were nowhere near leaving the restaurant. It felt awkward to ask them to pay the bill and leave. We arranged for my dad to pick up Holly, and Felicity, the dykey assistant manageress, offered to drop me at home later.

Finally, at around quarter to twelve, they settled the bill and left me an amazingly generous gratuity. I had learnt during the course of the evening that the younger man's name was Graham, but I didn't know what his dad's name was.

"I'm sorry we're leaving so late," Graham was drunk but sincerely apologetic.

"It's no problem," I replied. "It was great to meet you." As we approached the main entrance, Graham asked me how I was getting home. I explained that the manageress had offered to give me a lift.

"Nonsense!" he demanded, the alcohol fuelling his words. "I'll take you." It felt safe, I had worked out that he worked with my friend Marion's dad. My gut told me that he was a good guy.

Graham said goodbye to his dad and we made our way to the carpark. We climbed into his car in the basement and he turned on the radio. The Communards' hit, "Don't leave me this way" was playing quietly.

"This is gay," he blurted. I was confused, assuming that he was saying that the radio in his car was gay. I wasn't sure if he was just more drunk than I had thought and not articulating himself properly, or if the mention of the G-word sent me into an unnecessary spin. I was doubtlessly foolish to have gotten in his car, but for somebody so inebriated he seemed to be in control.

"You're a damn good-looking boy," he slurred, "you're my type." I found myself scared, but excited. Apart from Jessica—who, by no fault of her own, possessed a vagina, two breasts and lots of oestrogen—this was the only other human being who had ever shown some physical interest in me.

"Thanks," I retorted, "but I'm not sure that I'm gay." He leaned across the gear stick and squeezed my thigh, briskly pulling his hand back.

"That's ok," he said, "but if you change your mind..." I so badly wanted to entertain him, but the truth was that I was terrified. He knew Marion's dad, he lived in Chelmsford and it all just felt too close for comfort.

"What were you and your dad talking about tonight?" I asked, trying to hastily change the subject.

"We're both having marriage problems," he divulged. "My first marriage and dad's third."

"Three marriages...your dad doesn't sound like marriage material," I joked.

"I'm not sure I am either," he was quick to add.

Graham seemed to sober up substantially on the short drive to my house. The tightly tucked and sorted boxes that contained the secrets in his head had been disturbed by the booze that was flowing through his veins. He was hungry for me and I should've been flattered. We pulled up outside my house. The house was in darkness, except for the light outside the front door that my parents always left on for me.

"Let me kiss you," he kind of asked and stated at the same time. I really wanted to, but I was petrified and I was also worried that I didn't know how to. I shook my head to show that it was a no-go.

"All right then, let me hold you or touch you," he bargained. I smiled nervously. "Only your leg," he added. I was so tempted—more tempted than I had ever been in my life, but I was terrified. I was also aroused and excited. Physically my body was ready for whatever it was Graham had in mind, but I wasn't ready. There was movement in places that he could not see. I fought the urges as he pleaded with me to share some intimacy with him. I resisted. He may have been drunk, but it could have been safe and innocent fun...I just wasn't ready. AIDS was all over the news and I was a risk averse closet dweller. We sat in the car for at least two hours, and it was as though he was too scared to leave. He had unleashed something he probably shouldn't have and he was staying close to me to guard it.

"If I change my mind, I'll be in touch," I told him as I got out of the car. In bed, only minutes later, I fantasised for hours about Graham, his slender body, his crooked nose and also of the parts of him I had not seen.

TWO WEEKS LATER, I was working an early evening shift at the restaurant and Felicity came over to me at the soda fountain.

"Somebody to see you at the door," she sneered. "You know the rules about visitors at work." Scolded and confused, I walked to the entrance. There stood Graham, a little drawn and pale. His beautiful blue eyes filled with terror.

"I need to see you, please can we arrange a drink." Compliantly, I told him that I shouldn't be talking to anybody while on shift. He scribbled his number down on a restaurant flyer and he left. His gate was hurried and frantic. I hated the responsibility of carrying his secret, especially since it was enticing me. There was every chance that his fear might send him deeper into closet. At the time, I didn't understand the extent to which the events of that night may have weighed him down. I was tempted to gay-shame him to divert any suspicions from me, but somehow, I didn't. I didn't tell anybody...not James, or Marion, or Holly. Dykey Felicity may have worked it out for herself. Telling somebody like Father Finnigan at a secret confession might have helped Graham with his healing. Penance was always a temporary and satisfying cure. I did it once as an anonymous attendee at the Catholic Church in Stratford. Fifty Hail Marys for some dirty thoughts and a naughty phone call and I was good to go.

FOUR YEARS LATER, after tracking Graham down by making a few phone calls, I gave him a ring at his new work.

"I need to see you," I said. He took a few seconds to place me and when he had worked it out, he enthusiastically replied.

"When and where will work for you?" he asked. I had waited four years to make this call.

"How about tonight?" I asked knowing that I was taking a chance. A small silence followed. He told me that his dad was in hospital and that he needed to travel across town to see him.

"No problem, I'll call you in the week," I told him. I never did.

CHAPTER TWELVE

BOARDING DUTIES

5 September 1988

WHILE I WAS at uni, I was fortunate enough to get a student boarding master position at Redhill Boys, an esteemed Grammar School in Reading. Redhill was steeped in history and provided weekly boarding to 60 boys from Year 1 to Year 6. The boarding house was two blocks from the school and school was a 15-minute walk from the uni where I was studying teaching. It couldn't have worked out better—I lived rent free, I had limited living costs, I could walk to uni and into town, and my food was cooked for me from Monday to Friday. In return, I had to provide some of my time. I assisted the boys with homework for three afternoons and two evenings each week, and I was on duty most mornings where I had to make sure the boys were ready and decent for school. With the help of the matron, I supervised the breakfast serving every day.

Redhill's junior boarding house was a happy place and I loved my interactions and engagements with the young and impressionable boys. Their innocence and youthful determination was refreshing. The world was their oyster and they were ready to leap from the clams that held them, to conquer and shape the paths that lay ahead of them. I used to read Dr Seuss to them and I would relate those nonsense rhymes to bigger personal and social issues: *What was I scared of?* teaches us to love ourselves and overcome our fears; *The Lorax* teaches us to love the world and to prepare for a sustainable future; and *Horton Hears a Who* teaches us to love and respect all people.

I had three incredibly happy years at Redhill, and I enjoyed acting as something somewhere between big brother and teacher to all those boys. I was young and it was a big responsibility, but I tackled it with love and dedication—I know I didn't always get it right. In many ways, I think those young men taught me more than I actually taught them.

When I arrived at Redhill, I worked alongside two other housemasters. The Senior Housemaster was a young teacher named Desmond Bradford. He wasn't a teacher at Redhill, he taught at neighbouring Millside Primary and performed the housemaster duties at Redhill parallel to his job at Millside. Desmond, or Dessie as he oddly liked to be called, was in his late twenties, of medium build with an unfortunate Boris Johnson type complexion. He had fine silky white hair that was parted to the left and it hung oddly low into his face. His piercing eyes, slightly obscured by his hair, were like welding arcs that were difficult to look at. His pursed lips scrunched downwards toward his pointed and dimpled chin. He was mildly flamboyant, a little uncomfortable in his skin—and he seemed to have a bit of temper on him.

One morning during breakfast, Dessie told us how he had put Jonathan Marsden, a Year 5 boy, into the sickbay the previous evening. Jonathan—or *Jonno* as he was known—had reported to the matron with a sore head and an upset stomach after the previous night's homework session. The matron had consulted with Dessie, who made the decision to isolate him in the sickbay.

"So," Dessie continued, "last night, I went in to check in on Jonathan at about eleven, I could see he seemed to be sweating with a fever."

"I could see he wasn't well before bedtime," the matron interjected. Dessie ignored her.

"So," Dessie continued, rolling his eyes, "I decided to take his temperature and when I touched his forehead, he told me to 'fuck off' in his sleep." The shock of his expletive words seemed to punch everybody's faces—especially the matron's. Her saggy chin seemed to tremble. We hadn't seen the f-word coming. Once the initial shock was over, we all had a bit of a giggle.

"He must have got a fright," the matron offered. Maxwell, an elderly teacher who was generally miserable with life didn't look impressed.

"I'm just shocked that boys of this day and age even know words like that," Maxwell scowled with an unimpressed face that made the corners of his mouth point downwards.

As the boys were leaving the dining room, and whilst our plates were being cleared away, Jonathan passed our table as he was heading out. He looked straight ahead, avoiding eye contact with anybody at our table.

"Hey Jonno," I called, "come over here quick." Jonathan made his way over to us. He still looked a little green around the gills and he seemed uncomfortable.

"You okay big guy?" I asked.

"So, so," he answered, tilting his head from left to right.

"That's great news," I offered, "I hope you feel better than you did last night." After which I jokingly added: "And why did you swear at Mr. Bradford last night when he was checking up on you?" I was expecting him to have no recollection of the incident, instead his reply was perplexing.

"I just wanted to sleep sir," he groaned. Everybody laughed, except for Dessie and Maxwell. Jonathan left us and he headed back to his dormitory.

A FEW MONTHS later, we were told that a certain Mr. Alexander had been appointed to teach mathematics in the secondary section of Redhill. We were also told that Mr. Alexander needed accommodation and, as maths was a critical subject, he had been offered the senior housemaster position at the junior boarding house. There was no loyalty to Dessie, as he taught at a different school. Dessie left within three weeks and Mr. Alexander moved in immediately after. I felt incredibly sorry for Dessie as I knew that he was very fond of the boys, and it seemed that they liked him too. His abrupt departure seemed to significantly affect him, and I knew that if I was in his shoes, I wouldn't have been happy at all. Working with those boys was a hugely emotional experience. So, if the opportunity presented itself, I would invite Dessie over to the boarding house in the afternoons or early evenings and he would be received as a welcomed guest by many of the boys. The only people who didn't seem happy to see him were Mr. Alexander, Maxwell and the matron.

One evening after he had left, I was summoned to Mr. Alexander's office. When I entered the office, it looked like I might be about to face a tribunal disciplinary. Mr. Alexander, Maxwell, and the matron were sitting along one side of a long table and I was invited to sit in the middle opposite them. My heart was in my throat and I felt quite terrified.

"What have I done?" I asked as I shuffled in my chair. Mr. Alexander continued in a stern and monotone voice as if he hadn't heard my question.

"Mr. Bradford was removed from this establishment due to numerous allegations of sexual misconduct." I felt myself gasp and then swallow. The neon light in the room was intoxicatingly bright and their three faces looked shadowed against the stark white wall behind them. "Now," Mr. Alexander continued, "you've been under surveillance for three and a bit months." I felt my eyes stretch wide open, and then he continued: "We are pretty certain that you are not involved or implicated in any way, but you need to understand that Mr. Bradford is banned from these premises. This matter is in the hands of the police." I was stunned.

"I'm sorry," I rebutted, "I had no idea."

"That's what we've worked out," Mr. Alexander continued. "My advice to you, young man, is that—for the sake of your reputation and for the sake of your career—you break ties with him immediately." I nodded my head to show agreement and willingness, but also contemplation as I tried to process what I had just been told.

"I certainly shall," I replied.

"Do it from right now," he cautioned with care and authority in his voice. "In the short time that you have been here," he continued, "you have earned huge respect with the boys, the parents and the staff—both here and at school—don't let this predator take you down."

I left that meeting feeling shocked and somewhat dirty. Shocked at the news and at discovering that what I had only read about in the papers was virtually happening before my own eyes; and I felt dirty that I was somewhat of an accidental accomplice.

BRADFORD WAS NO different to Mr. Eggleston who had preyed on me some years before. I was disappointed with myself. Albeit mildly, I had previously experienced the claws of a predator—but I hadn't been smart enough to recognise similar actions whilst they were happening right under my nose.

When the court case started to unfold, it was reported on widely in the local press. We had been instructed that we were not to talk about it and that we may not offer any press interviews or comment. The main complainant was Matthew Marsden, on behalf of his son Jonathan. He led the fight with a huge amount of energy, having done his homework thoroughly. He had managed to get five other alleged victims to speak up. It looked like Bradford was going to sink. Bradford had tried to call me a couple of times during the trial, but I heeded Mr. Alexander's warning and I didn't respond to any calls or messages.

Bradford's parents had found and funded him a solid solicitor who managed to get him a suspended sentence due to 'lack of physical evidence'. It was a disappointing outcome for the plaintiffs, for the school and for moral justice—but the lesson for everybody was to be cautious, Dessie Bradford included. The last we heard was that he had taken up a teaching position at an independent school in Margate. It was sickening to know that he might be continuing his antics, but in the same vein the rule of law needed to be respected.

I felt particularly vulnerable during the Dessie Bradford ordeal, because of the truth that I was hiding behind my own eyes. It was so easy to confuse homosexuality—especially closeted homosexuality—with paedophilia. As homosexuality has historically been such a social taboo—an illegal act and a devious act, it has unfortunately been bundled into a basket of sick sexual acts.

Some people would suggest that all gay people must be paedophiles. It's as if they think that gay people don't understand sexual or personal morals, let alone the law. I have always known that I was gay and, as a teenager, I had crushes on other teenagers. As a man of 50 plus, I find men of my own age with silver and receding hairlines handsome and attractive. It is unfortunate that the likes of Bradford and Eggleston skew lines and the reputations of people who are simply gay—not paedophiles, not predators...just normal people looking for real and authentic love with somebody who is a mutually consenting adult, and who might happen to be of the same sex.

I HAVE TAUGHT and nurtured many boys over the years. I have never been physically or sexually attracted to any of them. I might have been an undeclared homosexual, but I am certainly not a paedophile. My relationship with these young men has been that of caregiver, guide, teacher, confidant, friend and mentor. These are roles and responsibilities that require love, dedication, commitment and trust. My work has required my professional and humanitarian skills.

DEVIANT SEXUAL ACTIVITY transcends all genders and gender combinations. The issue with homosexuality is that the deviance has prospered because of the guilt and shame—ingredients constantly fuelled by the dogmatists, the homophobes, the religious, and the gay-bashing closets.

CHAPTER THIRTEEN

AN IMPULSIVE PHONE CALL

8 December 1993

MY FIRST TEACHING job was at Nightingale Primary School. Two years in, I had become totally absorbed in my work, and it was a good distraction. I loved teaching and I loved the interaction with the children. They were so fresh and innocent and revitalizing for my soul. Their enthusiasm and joy made every day worthwhile. I couldn't help but feel overwhelmed by the trust and worship they had for me. This was contrary to how the headteacher, who we called *Madam Draconian,* viewed me—although I did suspect that deep down, she may have actually had some respect for me. She just wasn't ever going to show it.

My obsession with my work had kept me distracted and it helped me ignore the issue of my sexuality. To be totally honest, it hadn't bothered me for some time and the gay demon inside me seemed to have gone into hiding, a hibernation of sorts, perhaps. I didn't quite appreciate it at the time, but it was rather liberating to be unconsciously agamic.

"MAYBE YOU'RE ASEXUAL," my friend Mary-Jane had once commented. 'Wouldn't that be nice', I had thought—but instead, I deflected.

"Possibly," I replied, "but I'm not interested in a relationship for now, at least." Mary-Jane's brother Dane was overtly gay and she adored him. I should have recognised her as an ally but I wasn't yet ready to disclose anything to anybody. I guess I didn't have the desire to unpack what I had neatly and securely packed away somewhere deep in my brain, many years before.

I WAS HOUSE sitting for my good friend Mandy whose new beau, Mario, had taken her off on a Caribbean cruise and an extended South American adventure. Mandy was an amazing person, who didn't always make the best choices in men. Her latest selection was no better.

"At least this one has got a decent bank balance," I joked. "Make it work for you, honey," I advised. She laughed, but I knew she was desperate for my approval. I wanted to give it to her, but I simply couldn't. I had seen her hurt way too often.

On a fateful Wednesday, a lot went wrong. On my return from school, I discovered that the fridge had packed in. I checked the mains board and wiggled the plugs—but it looked like the motor had given up the ghost. By chance Mandy called me early evening from the Bahamas to check up on her kitties, Tom and Beatrice. Strange names for the duo I had thought.

"They're all good," I confirmed, not revealing Beatrice was clearly in a sulk at the disappearance of her human mother. Tom seemed unphased. I explained the situation with the fridge and asked her what she would like me to do.

"There's an old local paper in the broom cupboard under the stairs," she explained, "check out the classifieds...I think there's a place in Chelmer Village called *The Appliance Doctor*, I've used them before—their service is great."

After we ended the call, I found the paper, located the advert and made the call. Benny from *The Appliance Doctor* would come around at half-four the following evening. I continued reading the paper and as I paged aimlessly through the classifieds I stumbled across an advert that I certainly wasn't looking for. It was unexpected and it ripped me right out of my so-called 'asexuality'. It read: 'House share wanted with other gay people. Call Mario'. I read it repeatedly. A gay person who was accessible—and only a phone call away. Should I, shouldn't I? I was in a conundrum and my brow was damp with the sweat of uncertainty. Scared and excited all at the same time. I made myself a coffee and pondered over what to do. 'Just make the call,' I told myself. 'He can only be better than Mandy's Mario," I tried to convince myself.

I waited a few minutes before I dialled.

"Hello, may I speak to Mario please?" I inquired, polite and confident. The lady on the other end of the line had a foreign accent—Spanish maybe or possibly Portuguese?

"Mario isn't home from work yet" she answered, sounding more Portuguese than Spanish. "Would you like me to get him to call you?" she continued.

"That's okay," I responded, "I'll call back later." I'm sure I sounded suspicious or terrified.

"He'll be back in about half an hour," she told me before we ended the call.

I made another coffee to pass the time and was ready to abort the entire idea. Thirty-five minutes had passed since I had dialled Mario's number the first time. I dialled again and this time it seemed to ring for longer.

"Hello, Mario," came the deep voice from the other end.

"Hi Mario," I responded.

"Yes, who is this?" came the reply.

"You don't know me," I explained. "My name is David, I found your details in the advert you posted looking for a house share." I paused, and he interjected.

"How much is it and where is it?" he asked. His tone was abrupt and it took me by surprise.

"I don't have a house to offer you," I explained. "I'm just keen to talk to another gay person." I hoped I hadn't sounded desperate.

"Tonight?" he asked, taking me by surprise.

"If that's okay with you?" I answered. We agreed to meet, and just over an hour later, I was sitting opposite Mario in The Plough on Duke Street.

ON MEETING HIM, I knew I probably shouldn't have made the call. He was quick to tell me I was physically attractive to him and he explained, in great detail, what he wouldn't mind doing with me. Whilst I was shocked, I found it incredibly exciting, tempting, and flattering. It was somewhat erotic. Mario looked like life had been tough, I realised he may not be looking for the kind of house share I had had in mind. His hands were manly, and it looked like he may use them to earn his daily bread and butter. He was stocky and trim and he looked very fit. I didn't find him as attractive as he had said he found me, but he did have mesmerising eyes...gunmetal grey, with a dash of blue.

"Let's get a room, where we can talk a little more privately," he insisted. It sounded sensible and enticing. I hesitated because I wasn't sure if I wanted to do it, but I caved quickly.

"Don't panic," he reassured, his Portuguese accent more pronounced than it had been earlier. We put on our jackets and I followed him into the unknown. Brave and stupid, intrigued and terrified.

Mario knew exactly where to go for a cheap room. I should have identified this as a red flag, but I didn't. My adrenaline was flowing. The side street B&B was shameful and dingy. As he closed the door of room 18 behind us, Mario grabbed me in a way I had always hoped to embrace Wayne Evans or Michael Carlson. He was rough and hurried. I was slightly afraid, but I found myself enjoying his hands on my body. It felt good to finally be desired by a man.

"Let's talk some more," I suggested. Mario looked alarmed at my suggestion and his hands suddenly slowed and came to rest across each of my glutes. He pulled me closer to his body.

"Sure," he grunted, standing right in front of me, chest on chest. I could smell his manliness as he held me captive against his body. I would be lying if I said I had wanted it to stop. "Tell me what you want to talk about then," he asked with a firm and seductive smile—his lips uncomfortably close to mine.

"About being young and gay," I offered naively.

"Let's lie on the bed and chat then," he suggested. I sat on the corner of the bed and Mario probed his tongue into my left ear. It was nicely erotic for starters—but this was moving far too swiftly for me...I wanted to talk. As much as I tried to resist him, I wasn't convincing enough to send out a clear message. I guess I didn't actually want it to stop. I was afraid, but not terrified, I was intrigued and not yet ready to run. He aggressively moved his tongue into my mouth, which felt prematurely intimate—and exciting. I went along with it. I had waited the best part of 10 years for this. It's a pity it had to be with a stranger down a grubby side street. Father Ryan would have been so disappointed. Gran would not have approved. The only consolation, I guess, was that no money was exchanged.

An erotic tumble ensued, and I found him pulling the clothes from my body with my every twist and turn. It was an unknown game of cat and mouse. I was in unchartered territory with a man I had found in the classifieds less than two hours earlier. I knew nothing about him, save for him being Portuguese and a wannabe house sharer. In the frantic tumble, Mario had removed everything that clad me, except for my underwear—and even that seemed to be in danger now. It had been adrenaline-filled, but I was becoming afraid. I didn't want any more of this.

"Please slow down," I pleaded with some authority. He stopped.

Sitting in my underwear on the edge of the bed, I watched him undress himself. If I hadn't been so panicked, I may have enjoyed his physique, and the personal strip show he was delivering. He stepped toward me, his naked glory protruding.

"Give me a blow job," he demanded.

"I'm sorry," I quavered, "I can't...I need to go." Not wasting any time, I pulled on my clothes and quietly closed the door of room 18 behind me.

I never saw Mario again. My Catholic guilt went into overdrive. The following morning, I found myself in a psychologist's room and much to gran's dismay, I quickly progressed to the evangelical 'tent'. I needed to be punished and I needed forgiveness.

CHAPTER FOURTEEN

A NEW TEACHER

6 January 1997

IT WAS A new term and there were at least three new teachers, all looking slightly nervous, at Nightingale Primary School. Carrie was one of them. She was a new Year 1 teacher, replacing Mrs Copeland who had retired before Christmas. Mrs Copeland was hugely loved and respected, so Carrie had some big shoes to fill.

This wasn't the first day I had laid eyes on Carrie. I recalled her visiting the school a few days before the Christmas break. She had popped in to meet Mrs Copeland for a handover and to orientate herself to the school. She had probably also finalised the paperwork for her appointment too. When I saw her in the staffroom, I remember being taken by her soft and gentle presence. She had striking blue eyes that were calm yet intensely piercing. Her medium length blond hair was elegantly styled and it wrapped her pretty and petite face. She seemed the sporty type, but I wasn't sure. She was dressed in a classic college-style sports jacket that was smart and casual at the same time. It was baby-blue in colour and it made her azure eyes shine bright. She seemed to be kind and beautiful—inside and out. Like my friend Rupert would have said: 'this one is from the top drawer.' After having spotted her, I remember saying to Lilly-Rose, the much-loved school secretary, that the new Year 1 teacher, "was pretty nice to look at." Lilly-Rose had laughed and agreed:

"Just be careful, it sounds like she has a serious boyfriend," Lilly-Rose cautioned. "She mentioned temporarily staying at her boyfriend's aunt's house until she sorted herself out with local accommodation."

'Local accommodation?' I contemplated and wondered where she might have hailed from. Not only was she pretty and gentle, but she also had an air of intrigue about her.

I didn't talk to Carrie for the first few weeks that she was at the school. I taught in the upper grades and she in the lower. It was obvious that we had become aware of each other, but a natural opportunity to talk didn't arise in those early days. Once or twice, we made eye contact and exchanged the odd awkward smile. I was heeding Lilly-Rose's gentle warning.

I found Carrie utterly lovely, and having recently found peace with God, my head was fully compartmentalised. My gayness was dead and buried. It hadn't shown its ugly head for at least two and half years. My few hours with Mario in that dingy hotel room had set me down a path where I found religion. This time it was not Catholicism, it was reborn evangelical Christianity. It gave me comfort and false hope.

My phone call to Mario and the evening that followed had let my homosexuality almost spill out completely. It had scared me so badly that I needed God to fix me. I ran to the church for forgiveness and healing. I attended home prayer meetings, had demons cast out of me and I could quote Biblical chapter and verse for most topics and subjects. I was cured— or so I believed.

BEING CURED, FIRMLY straight and attracted to women, I needed to get on with it. I hadn't had a proper girlfriend since Charlene Barnes when I was about 19 years old and I was now 27—soon to be 28. So many wasted years—but I believed the confusion was all behind me. I felt free and liberated. It felt as though I didn't need to be concerned about dropping my guard and forgetting to wear my mask. I felt convinced I had nothing more to hide. As far as I was concerned, the gay in me had been defeated.

Carrie did indeed have a boyfriend—so that was a little problem, but not one that couldn't be overcome with time and hard work. A few weeks after she started at the school, there was a parent function in the school hall. After the function, it had been arranged that many of the staff would stay on for a few social drinks and a chat. Partners were welcome to join too. Rather disappointingly, Carrie's boyfriend, Jim, also came. I did however have the opportunity to talk to her and another new teacher, Debbie, before both of their partners arrived. I had had a glass of cheap box red wine, so I was feeling braver than I usually would.

"Hi," I said to both of them, "we've not officially met."

"No, we haven't," Debbie replied, putting out her hand to shake mine. "Great to finally meet you, we see you're quite the social butterfly in the staffroom." I felt myself blush a little. By this time, Carrie was also putting her hand out to shake mine.

"Good to meet you properly," she replied as we shook hands. Those words were comforting and I wondered if they were loaded—or if the wine, which was flushing my cheeks, made them feel like they were.

"So, are you ladies settling and happy at Nightingale?" I asked.

"Yes, it's been great so far," Carrie replied.

"It took a bit of adjustment but, by the grace of God, it's all working out," Debbie offered.

'By the grace of God', I thought, 'this one is also religious—good to know, an ally perhaps?' Although I gave God and the church the credit for curing me of my thoughts and desires that amounted to 'an abomination', I wasn't hugely religious anymore. I was happy and content in my 'straightness' and felt strong enough to pursue the journey on my own.

When Jim arrived, Carrie made a point of introducing him to me—he seemed friendly enough. In the conversation I learnt he had been around for at least three and a bit years before. He was a young successful lawyer and he made a lot of money, which I assumed would make me less attractive. I was a teacher and my pay check was humble—as humble as hers.

Over the coming weeks and months Carrie shared more details with me. I learnt he was devoutly Anglican—a factor that impacted their relationship negatively. I knew what it was like to be raised in the church—the good and the bad. I also learnt things weren't as rosy as they seemed. Jim was consumed by his work and his religion. He was not willing to make any long-term commitments and Carrie was frustrated. She desperately wanted a family and she would be 27 in a few months. She was clearly panicked that her three-and-bit-year investment in Jim may amount to nothing. It seemed she loved him, but I wasn't sure how deeply.

Over the weeks and months that followed, Carrie and I began to develop and grow a solid friendship. It was platonic, but there was something unspoken that we were both aware of—but didn't want to acknowledge. I didn't feel like a fraud, because I had nothing to hide. We would chat at school, sometimes we would meet for coffee in the afternoons after school and then we would also socialize in the same circles as the other teachers. Sometimes Jim was there, and other times he wasn't. It all depended on his work and religious schedules.

"How did you and Jim meet?" I had asked at one of our coffee meets. She seemed taken aback by the question and became a little flustered. Jim was never a topic we spoke about and my question clearly took her by surprise.

"We met through a mutual friend," she replied vaguely.

"And how did you come to be at Nightingale?" I asked, trying to change the subject.

"Same mutual friend," she answered.

"Sounds like a useful friend," I joked.

"Yes," she smiled and continued, "Nicky who teaches Year 4."

"Nicky Thomson?" I asked.

"Yes, Nicky is Jim's cousin and I was at uni with her." I usually had a knack of knowing the finer details, but I had missed this one. Come to think of it, I often noticed Nicky and Carrie chatting in the staffroom, but I wasn't aware of their history.

"Great friend to have," I commented jokingly. "She found you a man and a job." We both laughed. Carrie then paused before answering, trying to be a little guarded.

"She did," she offered, "but it's complex when one of your best friends is family to your boyfriend...you can't always share everything...and it's hard when you need advice."

"So, do you and Jim have problems?" I asked bravely.

"Like most couples," she answered flippantly. The moment felt clumsy, and I recognised I may have pushed too hard. "Only time will tell," she offered to fill the silence. It was a cliff-hanger moment, but the conversation was getting way too serious. "I need to get to the vet before it closes at six," she explained. "My cat has not been well, and she stayed in overnight."

"Sorry to hear that," I responded. "I hope it's not too serious. It's twenty to, you better hurry—don't worry, I'll sort out the bill," I offered.

"Thanks so much," she said as she stood up and put on her brown and white pinstriped jacket. It was not from her standard palette, but it worked, and it fit her perfectly. It made her look ultra-sophisticated. We exchanged a hug and a smile and she left. She hurried out, looking rattled. Sophisticated and pretty—but clearly rattled.

The room felt empty. Had I chased her away or was the story about her cat a legitimate one? I hoped I hadn't scared her off. I was enjoying her friendship, I was enjoying the thrill of the chase and also the attention that I was receiving. It was becoming clear that I wanted what Jim Winterton had—and he didn't seem to want her as badly as I did.

CHAPTER FIFTEEN

SWOONING A MAIDEN

21 July 1998

IT HAD BEEN a year and half since Carrie Durham had come to teach at Nightingale. She had equalled—if not bettered—the benchmark set by her predecessor, Mrs Copeland. She was highly rated by the draconian head-mistress, who nobody liked. That, itself, was a massive feat. Her classes, unlike mine, were always orderly and calm. She had created a happy place for her daily wards. It was clear that she had settled in—and settled in well. She had won over the hearts of the staff, the parents, and the children. She may also have won me over.

The distraction she had created for me had kept the boxes in my head firmly in place, and I had no need or desire to move or fiddle with them. They were stacked neatly and perfectly, just as I liked things to be. Our friendship was growing, and I became aware of Jim being a little uneasy around me. Jealous perhaps. He had no need to be. I was everybody's fa-vourite—the well-loved joker and the clown. The person everybody knew, but I was also the person they really didn't know. Not for now anyway, because I was rowing in the straight lane. Cured by my religion for what must have been at least four years, I was Nightingale's happy and most eligible bachelor.

AT THE BEGINNING of May, I made a decision to tender my resignation for the end of June and to spend the next six months teaching English in Barcelona. Madam Draconian seemed indifferent to my news, all she managed to mutter was, 'how inconvenient'. I assumed she meant for her and not for me. She did manage to add, 'put it in writing'. So, I did. I started to spread word of my departure, firstly cascading it to my nearest and dearest. I started with close friend Vicky Goldberg, she took it well and was quick to suggest that she drag her husband Josh there for the half term in October. Next, I told Avery Nixon, my crazy Canadian friend who had come to teach in the UK for a year. Avery and I had stayed in touch since we had met in the summer of 1992 while working at a holiday camp in the US. I had paved the way for her, convincing *Madam Draconian* of her brilliant teaching abilities. Let's just say the two of them were not a happy match.

"No time for any grass to grow under your feet!" Avery said with a smile. She had no room to talk—she was the same—an intrepid traveller with itchy feet. The third person I told was Carrie. I made my way to her classroom, stood at the door and got her attention. She stood up from her cushion on the reading carpet and walked over to me. I told her my news and her response was totally unexpected. As soon as I spurted the words out, her beautiful blue eyes frosted over, and tears ran down both her cheeks.

"Sorry, excuse me," she choked, as she turned and walked away to the administration block.

'That was totally unexpected,' I exclaimed to myself. I was confused. At break time, we found ourselves, alone, at the urn in the staffroom at the same time.

"I'm sorry about earlier," she offered, "it was kind of unexpected."

"I'm sorry too," I offered. "Had I known how you might have responded, I would have been a little more sensitive about where I broke the news to you."

"It's fine," she replied, "I can be emotional at the best of times." A slightly uncomfortable silence followed. I needed to fill it.

"Should we do a coffee after school?" I asked.

"Sounds great," she immediately responded.

"Where would you like to go?" I asked. She replied with what may have been a naughty grin.

"Why don't I come to yours?" she suggested.

Afternoon came. It was a Friday, my favourite day of the week. Carrie arrived slightly after 4:00 p.m. and I had had just enough time to arrive home before her. On my way home, I had made a pit stop at the local off-licence to pick up two bottles of wine. I was straightening and puffing up the cushions on the sofa when the doorbell rang.

"Come inside," I proclaimed. "Nice to see ol' blue eyes is smiling again." The cringey words left my mouth too soon. She smiled and that dissipated some of my embarrassment. We drank the bottle of wine I had bought— and then we drank another. The afternoon was both slow and fast. It was full of wine and a lot of Carrie's tears. While there were some moments where everything was lucid and clear, there were others where it all felt a little blurry.

"I can't imagine life at Nightingale without you," she declared.

"Oh, you'll be just fine," I told her. "I have no doubt that Jim will take good care of you." I regretted those words almost before they left my mouth. Somehow, I had openly endorsed my competitor—or whatever he was.

I ALWAYS FOUND alcohol to be a destabiliser of the boxes in my head. Somehow it weakened the walls of the compartments and made them all unhealthily fluid. It mixed things up. It wasn't helpful. God had fixed me, and alcohol always undid some of His work. Her work? Maybe the Mormons were right—central nervous stimulants were ungodly. None of this made sense. My guard was down, and I might be losing the control I always needed to maintain. Wine was swirling all over my body and it was squirting around and in-between the neatly stacked boxes that contained my secrets in my head. After Carrie left, I lay on the sofa wishing I could kiss and cuddle Wayne Evans. He was a Mormon. I wondered if he might be another one of those woodworm fags from my long-gone school days. He was a looker and he had some serious sex appeal. He also had the church keeping him in check. The following morning, I was sober, back in control and ashamed of my alcohol induced gay fantasies. The secrets were packed back in their boxes and stacked neatly in my head. God was again at the steering wheel and I was happy to ride shotgun.

I ARRIVED IN Barcelona on the evening of Tuesday 30 June and started working at the language school in the *El Raval* district the following morning. It was a small and cosy facility—just as I had expected and hoped for. I have always been a firm believer that we create the realities that we wish for. This seemed to be one of them. A good one.

By pure chance Jim Winterton had to attend a weeklong work conference commencing in Barcelona on 20 July. Since it was half term, they had decided Carrie would come along for the adventure. 'How convenient for me,' I smugly thought. After work on the Tuesday night, Carrie arranged a clandestine meeting with me. We met at a tapas bar down at the waterfront. I chose a table neatly tucked away to be as private as possible. It was silly, as we were in foreign city far from all that was familiar. It had only been three weeks since we had said goodbye, but it was so good to see her again. In between my new adventures, I did sporadically feel the distance from her.

"Great to see you," was my opener.

"You too," she replied. We ordered a bottle of wine and we seemed to pick up smoothly from where we had left things before my Mormon fantasy, some 7 weeks earlier.

"Jim just seems so vacant and distracted," she complained.

"So, what is your plan?" I asked without much emotion or expression. Carrie scrunched her forehead and brought her hand up to her face.

"I don't know," she kind of whispered.

"You need to look after your own happiness," I told her. Uttering these words felt a little fraudulent. She nodded in agreement.

"I know," she contemplated, "I have some important decisions to make in the coming months.

"Just make sure you put yourself first…that's what I've learnt," I offered. I squeezed her left forearm and she put her right hand tenderly on top of mine. It was warm and gentle but lacking some *joie de vie*. Her nails were perfectly painted in a light pearly turquoise.

"Thanks, David," she smiled and subtly squeezed my hand back. "Getting through this without you close by is going to be tough." I walked her back to her hotel which was adjacent to the *La Rambla* district, and not far from my new workplace. We took a back route and whilst walking down *Carrer Nou de la Rambla* toward her hotel, we passed *Palau Güell*—a striking mansion and the work of Antoni Gaudi. It was considerable, playful and undefined, also confusing and alluring…all a little like what was happening between Carrie and me. We stopped for a while and admired it. It was sprawling with tourists and young lovers under the early evening sky. A while later we reached her hotel.

"Stay in touch," she said, as we brushed each other's cheeks and kissed the air. It was better than nothing.

Over the months that followed, Carrie became my penfriend, or penmistress—I wasn't entirely sure, and neither was she, I think. It was in the days before email had taken off fully, so it was letters with licked envelopes that were splashed in cologne or perfume—dependent on the direction they were headed. The letters were flirty, open to interpretation and I'm not sure how it happened, but they took on a traffic theme:

Dear David

I'm at a traffic intersection and I don't know whether to go left or right.

Love

Carrie

Dear Carrie

You might want to turn around. Find a new route if there are road-works.

Love

David

It was a long way to send such a few words at a time, but limited words or not, the game increased in intensity and it was fun. Some letters were bold, some silly, others confusing—but it was clear something was brewing. You better watch out, Jim Winterton!

CHAPTER SIXTEEN

EXPEDITED LOVE

4 December 1998

MY TIME IN Barcelona seemed to fly by. I enjoyed my work and I had become quite friendly with another guy who taught at the school. Lorenzo López, or 'Double L' as I like to call him, had the benefit of being both Spanish and English—Spanish dad and English mum. He had grown up in Tunbridge Wells in Kent and had attended a posh grammar school. He never had any urge to go to university and his parents had basically forced him to complete a course in teaching English as a foreign language. It was a no-brainer for them to send him to Spain to learn some independence and to earn some of his own money. He was soon to be 26 and I was fast approaching 30. What Lorenzo lacked in ambition he made up for in good looks. He had sharp features, hazel brown eyes and jet-black hair that he wore in a middle parting. It was good to have an English-speaking friend whilst on my self-declared sabbatical. We shared many happy times, and I'd be lying if I said I had never wanted to grab him and pull him close to me. When he drove me to the airport on the morning of 4 December, I felt a bit of a wrench, but I was excited to get back to Carrie.

"Really good to have a friend these last couple of months." Double L was sincere in his tone.

"Yes, and for me too," I responded, "it's been fun." He smiled and he looked forlorn. "Come and visit," I told him. "There's always room on the sofa." He told me that he may return to London in February for his mother's 50th birthday. "So, it's not goodbye," I offered, "it's just...see you soon." I turned away and wheeled my suitcase into the airport terminal.

When I arrived at Heathrow a few hours later, it was chilly but mild. I used the underground to travel to Liverpool Street and then took an overland train to Chelmsford. Holly picked me up at the station and she drove me home. During the 10-minute drive, it was so good to catch up with her. I updated her on my feelings and thoughts on Carrie, on my time in Barcelona and I also managed to share some reflections on my new friend, Lorenzo. It was always good to be with my sister. She was OCD and hyperactive, but she was a good listener and she was never judgmental. We stopped at Tescos to grab a few groceries, and she came in for a quick cuppa when we arrived at the flat. Sitting opposite me, I was amazed at how grown up, mature, and happy she looked. She was a far cry away from that white communion dress—wings and all—and that Amish scarf she had so happily adorned that had made gran so proud. She looked like she had it altogether. She had recently ditched her boyfriend of six years and she was being wooed by another young solicitor at the practice where she worked. His name was Xander, and I had yet to meet him. I liked him so far, because my sister looked happy.

Later, Holly dropped me at the Pizza Express close to Nightingale school. It was the day of the unofficial staff Christmas lunch. It was unofficial because Madam Draconian didn't see the need for a party. Nicky Thomson had organised it entirely on her own and everybody had chipped in. I was to be the mystery guest. Avery had kept me up to date and managed somehow to secure an extra place for me. She arrived early and kept me a seat right opposite where Carrie had seated herself. I would have made the plans with Nicky but I think she suspected that there may be a spark between Carrie and I. She needed to be loyal to her cousin, Jim. It just felt tricky. After the excitement of being reunited with everyone, I sat down opposite Carrie. She was clearly happy to see me but she looked slightly unnerved. I guess I hadn't learnt from my resignation announcement earlier in the year that she didn't respond well to surprises.

"Are you going anywhere when school closes," I asked as I sipped a glass of Merlot.

"Jim and I may spend a few nights in Edinburgh over Christmas," she offered.

"Sounds nice," I muttered, not thinking that at all. I tried to keep the conversation going, but Carrie was uncomfortable and distracted and I sensed Nicky was eavesdropping on every exchange. Without any explanation, Carrie moved herself to the far end of the long table—as far away as she could get from me.

"That went well," Avery shrieked in her Canadian accent.

"Sure did," I laughed, as I took another sip of my wine. I wasn't laughing on the inside. The rest of the afternoon was fun and apart from Carrie's fleeing from me, pretty uneventful.

As early evening came, people started to leave. There were small pockets of us left, and we were scattered along the table. As the crowd thinned out, some of these pockets merged together. It was only when Nicky left that Carrie allowed her pocket of party goers to merge with mine. People continued to leave, until it was only Avery, Carrie and I left at the table. We did a quick autopsy of the afternoon.

"What's up with Nicky?" Avery was never one to mince her words.

"Family politics," Carrie answered.

"Oh, really...do tell," Avery was quick at the opportunity.

"It's about me and Jim," Carrie offered freely, then after a big breath, she continued. "We're on a knife's edge." She sighed.

"Are you going left or right at the T-junction?" Avery asked insensitively with a piece of information she shouldn't have had. I blushed like a beetroot. Carrie seemed to let it go. Avery left soon after and it was just me and Carrie. We had drunk too much wine and it was certainly home time. I walked her to the bus stop which wasn't that far away.

"I'm going to spend some time with my folks in Devon after Christmas, would you like to come for a bit of a break?" Her offer took me by surprise.

"Sounds great," I pondered. "Can I check in with the family to see what their plans are for Christmas?"

JUST AFTER 7AM on Boxing Day, I set off to Torquay in Devon. It took me 5 hours with two short stops on the way. Carrie's parents were warm and welcoming, and I felt right at home in their seaside home. Maybe I felt too much at home. It was comfortable and easy. Carrie's parents were lovely people. Carrie was in frequent contact with Jim which annoyed me. I was, supposedly, nothing but the ex-colleague and visiting friend who had recently returned from a working holiday. I couldn't believe that Jim would have bought this version of the story. I tried to put myself into his shoes and I knew I wouldn't have been happy with the situation. He must have seen it as a recipe for disaster. I didn't know the full details of how badly things may or may not have spiralled between the two of them. Carrie was relatively private on this front and didn't divulge too much; maybe she too was hedging her bets. I didn't want to pry. I hoped to be on the same side of the hedge as her in the not too distant future.

The holiday remained platonic until Old Year's Eve, when it unexpectedly took a change in direction. After devouring Carrie's mum's delicious home-baked shepherd's pie, Carrie and I went out for some drinks at the Torquay Marina. There was a band playing live music in one of the pubs, and the atmosphere was festive. Nobody seemed to mind the tinny sound of the music and the slightly off-key lead vocalist—who had absolutely no idea how bad she was. We had a lot of fun there, we drank more than we should have, and we danced a lot better than the lead singer in the band could sing. We joined in and counted the seconds down to midnight, and 1999 was welcomed by the sound of the drummer attempting a dramatic circus-style drum roll. We were partying like it was 1999, and I hoped I would be Carrie's prince. Her straight prince. I think we kissed during the cacophonous belching of Auld Lang Syne by the band, but I can't remember exactly. Booze was flowing through my blood, but strangely the boxes in my head were all still neatly placed. The evening ended with us on the beach; we were still there when the sun rose. We kissed numerous times as the small waves broke just inches from our feet. It was freezing, and we were freezing—but we delighted in the warmth of each other.

The following morning, my head hurt, but I was thoroughly impressed with myself. Carrie was clearly disappointed in herself. It was likely she also had a throbbing head and she struggled to make eye contact with me. The easy conversation ceased and the atmosphere was instantly uneasy.

"What time shall we leave in the morning?" was all that Carrie could muster.

"We better leave early to avoid traffic…is six fine?" I offered.

"Sure," she answered, "breakfast at half five." That sounded more like a midnight snack to me, but I complied. Our drive back to Essex the following morning was slow and awkward. Like the passing of a baton, I dropped her at her flat shortly before one in the afternoon.

"Your turn, Jim Winterton," I muttered under my breath as I drove away. Carrie looked a wreck and I felt guilty for her pain.

Luckily for me—and in hindsight maybe unluckily for Carrie—she and Jim decided to part ways a few weeks later. It was a painful parting, and I was in the wings: listening, supporting, and trying to hold back on making any kind of advance. It was heart-breaking for her. She had been with Jim for quite some time with nothing to show for it.

With Jim out of her life, Carrie was sad, but she seemed less tense and anxious. It was as though her soft blue eyes were coming back to life. The playful flirting naturally found its rhythm between us again—and Old Year's Eve was now a celebration, rather than an embarrassment. It was 1999 and things were going to happen. Valentine's Day was to be my best ever. I was showered with love and appreciation and I reciprocated it all. Carrie gave me chocolates and a teddy, while I delivered six long-stemmed roses to her at Nightingale. We dined that evening, we drank red wine, we kissed, and we uttered the magic three words to each other: *I love you.*

Wayne Evans didn't cross my mind, neither did Michael Carlson—I didn't think of Double L either. It was all about Carrie. We decided to spend Easter with Carrie's parents in Torquay. We arrived in the early evening of Maundy Thursday. After dinner, Carrie and I went for a walk on the beach. It was tumultuously windy and restless clouds were racing to-and-fro in the sky. I reached into the money pocket of my jeans to check if it was still where I had securely placed it before we left the house. It was. Fumbling and trying to be inconspicuous, I carefully took it out and nervously held it discreetly in my right hand—between my thumb and index finger. Once we had cleared the side of the estuary and were firmly on the beach, I raised my hand through the hefty wind. The diamond sparkled in the scattered moonlight.

"Will you marry me?" I asked bravely, my heart in my throat. I could see Carrie was surprised—but delighted.

"There's no doubt about that," she answered. With pride, I slid the ring onto the ring finger of her left hand and we both stared at it for a while. It felt surreal. We held each other. She cried tears of joy; I was happy. She was to be mine.

We made our way back to the house and broke the news to her parents. The news was welcomed with joy. The champagne was popped and the wedding date was set for 11 September.

CHAPTER SEVENTEEN

A WEDDING TO REMEMBER

11 September 1999

EVERYBODY'S ATTENTION WAS focused on the preparations for mine and Carrie's big day. It had been dubbed 'Nightingale's celebrity wedding' and Carrie delighted in giving me daily updates on staffroom discussions about the wedding. It seemed everybody was excited about the event. I missed not being there—but not seeing Madam Draconian everyday was a consolation.

Nathan and Emily, the children of the school secretary, Lilly-Rose, were to be the page boy and flower girl. Carrie's best friend, Hayley was appointed matron of honour, while Nicky was asked to be the bridesmaid. The choice of Nicky was a surprise to me, but Carrie explained that while Nicky was Jim's cousin, she was still one of her closest friends and she wanted her to be included in our special day. I'd be lying if I said I didn't find it slightly uncomfortable having Nicky in the bridal party, but some-how we all survived just fine. I asked James, my Bonanza friend and pseudo-brother, to be my best man, while Dean, my schoolfriend and wannabe DJ, was appointed my groomsman. I never quite knew what a 'groomsman' was, but all of the bridal magazines that Carrie's mother bestowed on us suggested that we should have one. It was a big ensemble, befitting a 'royal wedding'. My big fat gay wedding?

THE TRUTH WAS that in the months leading up to my engagement and then on to the wedding, I had had absolutely no gay thoughts at all. I had found Carrie, and it was as though I had been cured. I wanted to be cured and I believed I was. Love and a beautiful woman had spared me the trauma of an unwanted life. I wanted Carrie. My head was sorted.

To be honest, I loved the build-up to the wedding, it satisfied my creative flair and I enjoyed planning some of the fanfare. I had to be careful, I needed to tame my extraversion and allow the day to belong to Carrie. We agreed on most things and I was willing to let her make a lot of the decisions. What we did fight about was the guest list, and this is the one battle I did win—our final list sat at 192. Two nights before the wedding the tensions burst and the guest list became the catalyst for a lot of other niggles and nags.

"Nearly two hundred people!" Carrie complained. "It's ridiculous."

"The wedding is the day after tomorrow, what do you want me to do, uninvite some guests?" I retaliated. I thought that my response may have sounded slightly bitchy and maybe a tad queenie. Carrie didn't seem to notice.

"You always get your own way, David Sterling," Carrie was peeved.

"What are you guys fussing about?" Dean had arrived to pick us up for the final church rehearsal. "I think we should just stop and focus on 'the rest of your lives'...I think it's eternity that you pledge to each other on Saturday?" Dean was slightly serious. Carrie was quick to respond.

"That sounds like a hell of a long time," she joked. We all chuckled, and the guest list was forgotten, at least for a while.

We were also unable to agree on the choice of service. My side of the family would have preferred a Catholic service, while most of Carrie's family would have opted for Methodist—some others in her family would have pushed for the tent. So, to keep the peace we chose a non-denominational service which worked well.

CARRIE ENTERED THE chapel and she looked beautiful, dressed in a slightly off-white dress with rich lace and beadwork across her chest that tapered down toward her navel. Short sleeves fell off her shoulders and hugged her modest cleavage with a style and classiness that embodied her. Her back was mostly exposed, and it was framed by beautiful beads with a sophisticated bling that crept backwards from the pattern at the front of the dress. The train that hung from just above her hips was long enough to be classy and contemporary, but short enough to not be pretentious. Her veil was long and chic and it concealed her beautiful face ever so slightly.

As Carrie made her way down the red carpet toward me with John Craddlestock belting Wagner's wedding chorus on the grand piano, it felt surreal. My life was beginning. The bridal party dressed in white, emerald green, and aubergine purple looked as majestic as one would expect at a royal wedding. Once the bridal march was over, Carrie's dad 'gave' her to me with a smile and a strong handshake. I felt honoured and over-whelmed—I was now firmly a straight man at the driving wheel, entrusted with another man's precious cargo. The scene at the front of the chapel must have been spectacular—it was a well-orchestrated show and our friend Vicky Goldberg had done an amazing job with the flowers and the outfits. The men's waist coasts complemented the bridesmaids' dresses and the palette was rich, exciting, and pleasing. Carrie was flanked by her bridesmaids and little Emily, while I was flanked by James and Dean—looking deliciously dapper in their dress suits—and young Nathan looking like a miniature adult as he clutched the ring cushion tightly.

Carrie cried through the vows as did I, although just a little. If this was a charade, it had gone too far—but it wasn't. In that time and moment, I was committed to every vow I made. Pastor Steven concluded, looking at me.

"... and forsaking all others, promise to love Carrie Megan Durham, as long as you both shall live." I smiled at Carrie as she squeezed my hand and looked up at me with adoring surrender.

"I will," I said with sincerity, love and conviction—and I meant it.

"You may kiss the bride," the words were hardly out of Pastor Steven's mouth and Carrie's mouth was on mine. The kiss was cheered and the energy in the chapel was alive. After the service and photos, we made our way to the reception venue.

The venue was beautifully decorated and Carrie had taken great care to attend to the smallest of details: individualised name tags and place settings, detailed menus, well thought out gifts for all of the guests, elevated flower and candle arrangements on each table, a sentimental dance playlist for the DJ—who happened to be one Dean's apprentices. It was all perfect: gentle lighting, white tablecloths, green and aubergine overlays, soft white backdrops scattered with dainty fairy lights, delicious and colour-coded food, and a classic tiered cake that carried, as its top tier, a stainless-steel pot containing miniature white and red roses.

The speeches were wholesome and rather uneventful, and there was a real sense of love and of two families uniting. To anybody who was there it looked perfect—and it was, and it would be...unless the unthinkable was to happen and the secret manifested itself. It seemed like that was nearly impossible given how I had found love and brought sexual control and order to my life.

Dean, who always had a song for every occasion, suggested that he and I sing 'We go together' from the musical *Grease* as a surprise for Carrie after the speeches. I stupidly agreed and we spent a good few evenings practicing the item before the wedding. We tried to incorporate the hand and dance movements that we had learnt for the song when we had sung it in a school musical some 15 years earlier. After my speech, where I took a lot of the traditional abuse from the guests, Dean and I pounced. If the song hadn't been playing loudly, I would have thought that Dean and I were doing a different routine. He was singing the wrong words and his hands and feet and anything in-between couldn't have been more different to mine. At one point I could have sworn that he was emulating the movements of doing the hoola-hoop. We must have looked like two real fools. The guests laughed and so did Carrie. I was wholly embarrassed.

"That was ridiculous," my Uncle Hamish roared across the room. He had had too much to drink...again, "you looked like a bunch of Mormons!" Everybody laughed. He had meant to say 'morons'—but it was too late.

Cousin Kacey, his daughter, and her husband Robert were already offended. His wife, Aunty Clare, clobbered him over the back of his head and everybody, except him, laughed again. After dinner we all danced, the Catholics, the Mormons, the Jews, the other gentiles, the agnostics and anybody in-between.

We danced with Dean's brother, Kevin, who was the only invited gay at our wedding. He unexpectedly bought his new boyfriend whose name was Martin—and who therefore didn't have a name tag assigned to him. He looked so familiar. I was sure that he was young Martin—Aunty Val's son from Kai and Chris's wedding. Only he had aged by about 15 years. I was sure it was him. He had matured into a lovely looking and gentle person. I was intrigued, but I dared not ask if it was him, it was too close to a place I didn't want to go.

CARRIE AND I left for Spain on our honeymoon the following day. We chose to go to Barcelona because it held happy memories for us. It was where we had silently affirmed that we had a mutual interest in each other. This time, we would be able to walk the streets displaying our love overtly— without guilt and safe in knowing we had no chance of running into Jim Winterton.

We walked *Carrer Nou de la Rambla* again—this time in reverse and we revisited the tapas bar on the waterfront where we had clandestinely met the previous year. I was certain that I had spotted Double L at one of the tables on the mezzanine level with an extremely good-looking and somewhat animated man who spoke with his hands a lot. I wasn't sure if he was a relative, a friend, or a partner. I was too nervous to approach him and besides, I hadn't told Carrie who he was and of the friendship that we'd shared.

This time, Carrie and I were one of the young couples at *Palau Güell,* those couples that kissed and hugged and asked other tourists to take pictures of them. We visited the Olympic stadium, built for the 1992 Olympics Games, and I felt like I was carrying the gold medal for the decathlon. She was at my side and she filled my heart with joy. She was my medal and my trophy.

After the honeymoon, we headed home to the small house in Moulsham, near Chelmsford, that we had bought together. It was a terraced house with a modest lounge and diner—both with Victorian features, a kitchen that needed modernisation, three small rooms upstairs and a tiny postage stamp garden outside. It was an end-of-terrace home that allowed for access to the back garden down a narrow path. It was a perfect first home, all it needed was the proverbial picket fence.

On the last day of our honeymoon, we arrived at the airport slightly before 10:00 a.m. for our return flight at midday. After breezing through immigration and security, we had some time to kill so we found a restaurant and sat down for a quick sandwich and a coffee.

"David is that you?" The loud and distinct voice was easily placed. It was Double L. "I can't believe it," he exclaimed. "What are you doing here?" There were so many gaps to fill.

"I'm here on honeymoon," I gloated. "Meet my wife, Carrie." He looked surprised but he proceeded unperplexed.

"Lovely to meet you Carrie...lucky girl," he commented. I blushed, and Carrie stood up to shake his hand.

"This is Lorenzo," I told her. "I worked with him at the language school while I was here last year. He was a great friend to me during my time in Barcelona." Carrie smiled and told Double L that it was a pleasure to meet him.

"Meet my fiancé, Stefano," Lorenzo offered proudly. "He and I have been together for five months." I couldn't help but think that that seemed pretty hurried for an engagement, but then I had absolutely no room to make any judgement on pacing. A year ago, Carrie and I weren't even an item, now here we were, married.

"Lovely to meet you Stefano," Carrie and I said almost in unison. He was the gorgeous man I had seen with Double L at the tapas bar three nights earlier.

"We're heading to Las Vegas," Lorenzo explained with a naughty grin, "and maybe we'll find a drive through." We all laughed, but I had a pang in my heart. Why was the universe determined for me to bump into Lorenzo whilst I was in Barcelona on my honeymoon?

CHAPTER EIGHTEEN

A NEW ARRIVAL

31 October 2001

NOT TOO LONG into our marriage Carrie became pregnant. I may have been a closeted fag, but I clearly had lead in my pencil. Even though we were planning to have a baby, we were surprised at how rapidly the home pregnancy test returned two red lines indicating a positive result. We were excited, but it was also a shock. We became the all too familiar over-the-top first-time parents who believe that they are the only parents in waiting— ever. Baby books, baby fairs, nursery planning and antenatal classes all formed part of the madness.

It was an exciting time. Carrie was the model of motherhood in waiting. She glowed in her pregnancy and she did it all by the book. I accompanied her to all her scheduled check-ups at the gynaecologist and we felt confident in Dr Schreiber's abilities. He had a long track record to prove that he knew what he was doing. Dr Schreiber must have been on the slope downside of 65. He was the sort of person you might expect to find at

Jerusalem's Wailing Wall. He always wore a black suit and a white shirt. He had a grey beard and curly payots that hung from the front of his ears to the top of his shoulders. His tortoise shell glasses were oversized and were always perched at the end of his nose. His blue-green eyes were as kind and as gentle as the words that he uttered—only quietly and always with total calm.

ON THE AFTERNOON of 30 October, Carrie and I attended what came to be our last consultation with him—for baby number one, at least.

"Now," he whispered to Carrie, as he always did, "if your contractions haven't started by 6:00 a.m. tomorrow morning when your husband wakes up for work, I want you to take this tablet." And with these words he handed Carrie a small and insignificant looking chalky white tablet in a clear hard plastic wrapping. It seemed incredible that that little thing could trigger something so enormous—not only would I be a husband at this time tomorrow, but I would be a father. The thought of being a father was quite overwhelming, but more than being a father, I wanted to be a dad. A father is somebody who gives you life, but a dad is somebody who steps up and makes your life worth living. My own dad had sometimes just been a father, and sometimes my father had been an amazing dad. He was more a dad in my early years and seemed to become more of a father as he got older and became more and more consumed by his own secrets and demons. So far, I had passed the first test, I was going to be a father. Now I needed to prove that I was worthy of the title 'dad'. This was such a small word with big demands and untold expectations.

Later that afternoon, we returned to our flat at Stanton Boys, where I was teaching and where we received accommodation in exchange for Carrie and I acting as boarding house parents to a number of secondary aged school boys. At first, I thought I was fine and then rather embarrassingly, I started to steal the limelight from Carrie who deserved to have all of it on that eve of our parenthood. A massive, and highly unusual, thunderstorm hit Chelmsford late that afternoon and it brought with it lightning, torrential rain and an unexpected spell of nausea for me. My head was hot and cold and my stomach became ungrounded. I was so poorly that I couldn't sit or stand, or even talk. I was drowning in nausea and I was causing Carrie unnecessary stress.

"Are you all right?" she asked me with both concern and irritation. And she had every right to be annoyed with me.

"I'm not sure," I replied, as I lifted my head from the toilet bowl. "I'm going to call your parents and ask them to come over to be with us," I suggested, trying to put some contingencies into place as I had no idea where all of this was going.

"Are you sure that's a good idea?" Carrie asked as she rubbed her tummy and screwed her eyes into a flinch, in what might've been the first signs of the beginning of labour.

"It'll give us both peace of mind," I suggested. Carrie's parents had travelled up from Torquay and they were staying with Abby—Carrie's sister—for a few nights to be close to us for the birth of their second grandchild. I called Carrie's mum to explain the situation and, within the hour, they had arrived by taxi with their overnight bags. They were amazing and dependable people.

As my attack of nausea escalated, so did Carrie's early contractions. I had to fix things right away. I needed to find the strength and the energy required for what awaited in the coming hours. It was my responsibility to comfort and support Carrie through this, the single most significant event that had happened in our lives up to that date. I was off to a shaky start. I was already failing the parent test. This child, waiting patiently on the other side of the birth canal, might already be deciding that I was more a father— and less a dad. By 9:00 p.m., I had arranged for one of the other boarding masters to take me down to the emergency rooms at Chelmsford Hospital. I was triaged on arrival and immediately put onto a drip. How appropriate, I had thought...'a drip for this drip.' I lay on the hospital bed for at least an hour, my veins sucking in the sodium and chloride from the saline solution that would send me home rejuvenated, ready to be the perfect husband and a worthy dad. While I lay there, a doctor came to see me.

"Any idea why you might be feeling like this?" she asked.

"Not sure...it might be a bug," I lied, too embarrassed to tell the truth.

"Seems to be more than a bug," she continued.

"I've been on the coffee in the last few days, and probably haven't drunk enough water," I offered. It was half true, but not convincing.

"These kinds of extreme dehydrations are often linked to something more severe, like stress," she cautioned. "You probably need to slow down a bit."

There was no time or space for slowing down—in a few hours, I would be a dad and life as I knew it would never be the same again. Together, Carrie and I had created something enormous and there was no going back. The truth was that my nausea was a guttural reaction to two things. Firstly, I was terror-stricken at the overwhelming responsibility of becoming a parent—I had only recently taken some kind of control of my own life, and now I would need to provide stability, order and focus to the life of a vulnerable and dependent little sprog; and secondly, I was petrified of the blood, the guts and the gore associated with the physical act of childbirth. I have been incredibly squeamish my entire life. One video that Louise, the antenatal nurse, had shared with us at our classes had scared the holy bejesus out of me. The latter of these fears was soon to be faced and surely overcome—the former would be one that I would carry for my lifetime.

"You should be fine to head off now," the nurse confirmed at around half ten. The tubes and needles were removed from my arm and I headed immediately home to try to pick up the pieces. I was on the verge of becoming a dad, a straight dad—and I needed to toughen up and step up my game.

WHEN I ARRIVED home, Carrie's contractions had gained momentum and I could see that I was in some degree of trouble. I did my best to support and comfort her through the flexing and tensing of her uterus. These weren't Braxton Hicks—these were the real deal, and things were looking imminent. The truth is that I was so delirious with anxiety that I wasn't as present as I should have been that night. This was to become the *status quo* for much of my marriage and for a lot of my time as a parent—physically present, but somewhere far away in my head. I was always dealing with demons from either the present or from the past.

Time seemed to fly once I got home from the hospital, and by around 4:00 a.m. we were on our way to the maternity ward. As we left the flat, Carrie's mum calmly gave us the hospital bag that we had packed—just as Louise had instructed us to, at least four weeks earlier at our final antenatal class.

The maternity staff were welcoming, patient, and sensitive. Carrie was assessed and we were told that she was 4 cm dilated. There was still some time to wait. Carrie was determined to have a natural birth, but as the contractions and the dilations increased, so did the pain. I could see that she was struggling and it hurt to see the agony that she was in. Just before she was too far gone for a pain relief option, Carrie gave in and requested an epidural. Fortunately, an anaesthetist was immediately available to administer the procedure. Then, almost instantly the pain abated, albeit temporarily, and Carrie looked like she could breathe again. She remained more composed for the remainder of her labour—our labour...although I didn't feel that I had fully earned the right to co-own it.

Shortly after half nine that morning, Carrie's labour pains and contractions peaked. Dr Schreiber was in the ward. There had been no need for his chalky white pill. He calmly made his way over to Carrie and straddled her up clinically for the birth. I was seated on a chair next to Carrie and was holding her hand, supporting and encouraging her. My misgivings of the hours earlier seemed to be forgotten—or at least, forgiven. With just a few pushes and a pair of forceps—that looked like a pair of giant salad servers—at twenty to ten, our baby Jane arrived into this world. Her entry was not a quiet one, she quite literally arrived screaming and shouting. She was whisked up, in a wave like motion, from the birth canal and out of Carrie's vagina and then into Carrie's arms.

"It's a girl," Dr Schreiber calmly announced with the minimal expression we had grown accustomed to. He handed me an odd-looking pair of scissors and instructed me to cut the umbilical cord which was as tough as old boot leather—a strong lifeline between mother and child. The experience was gory, but it was also incredibly beautiful. I was excited and I was terrified. I knew a lifetime of responsibility awaited me, but I felt up for the challenge. Carrie and I were building a life together and the demons weren't hounding me for now. They had been blocked out. They were not welcome.

Jane was taken away speedily for her Apgar test which she passed with flying colours. She was promptly bathed and then the nurse on duty dressed her in a soft, pure white sleepsuit—especially, gender neutrally chosen for our new arrival. It had been a gift from James and Becky at Carrie's baby shower some six weeks earlier. Jane was cautiously passed to me, I cuddled her close to my body, still feeling Carrie's warmth emanate from within her. She was flawless, save for the salad server bruise across her left cheek. It was overwhelming to hold this perfect being in my arms. She had an angelic face, a mop of brown hair, innocent hazel eyes, ruby red lips and tiny fingers. She looked like me, I thought.

I stared at her in awe for a few minutes and then she yawned, kind of opening one eye at the same time.

"Hello you," I said, speaking unrehearsed—and probably prematurely—sporting a massive grin across my face. "I'm your dad," I continued, "and I'm so excited to have the honour."

CHAPTER NINETEEN

A QUICKER THAN PLANNED ARRIVAL

28 May 2003

LIFE WAS BUSY and eventful, and the weeks and school terms seemed to fly by. I periodically tussled with the secret in my head, but Jane was an exciting distraction for both me and Carrie. Our decision for Carrie to stay at home to look after Jane seemed to have been a prudent one. Jane was thriving and Carrie was happy, enjoying every moment of motherhood. She was good at it and it was easy to see that the apple hadn't fallen far from the tree. I could see that Carrie's mum was also an amazing parent, calm and caring and always interested—dedicated fully to her three daughters: Carrie, Abby, and Chloë.

ON THE WEEKEND after Jane's first birthday, James and Becky had hired a guest house, not far from Bath, for Becky's 30th birthday celebrations. There would be nine couples and between us there would be 10 children ranging in age from 3 months to 4 years. Eighteen human beings in total, all gathered in a huge converted stone barn in the village of Trowbridge for a weekend sounded like fun. Becky always knew how to entertain in style, and her ideas were always fresh and unique. The old barn had nine bedrooms, all with *en suite* bathrooms and downstairs it had a massive open plan living area which housed a medieval dining table that could seat up to 20 people. The table glistened with stories of countless meals and conversations—I guess some good and others less memorable. Numerous baroque sofas dotted the room, filling the blanks spaces and providing areas for separate gatherings.

As Jane had just turned one, Carrie had recently stopped breastfeeding her. This meant we were acclimatising to the world of bottles, disinfectant and baby formula. We had also decided that Carrie would stop taking the mini-pill because the time had come to start to sow the seeds for baby number two. Becky's birthday weekend couldn't have been better timed. It was a time to let our hair down, and Carrie could drink alcohol for the first time in nearly two years. We needed a break from the routine of what our life as parents had become. Despite the fact that most of us at the gathering had the responsibility of children, the atmosphere was chilled, and everybody engaged in the loud merrymaking. Mulled wine flowed and its strong cinnamon aromas flooded the medieval downstairs area, soaking more memories into the rough surface of the imposing mahogany table. Carrie and I both had too much to drink, but it was good to reconnect and the only worry for us on that weekend was Jane's next bottle and her nappy change. All very straightforward. No demons and no distractions. Except maybe for James—but definitely not his irritating friend Peter, who was still in hiding. Hiding like me in any shadow he could find.

Four weeks later, we decided to do a home pregnancy test to see if our efforts of the last few weeks had been successful. To our surprise they were. The test reflected two red very clear lines and we were mildly shocked.

"I really do have lead in my pencil," I joked with Carrie to which she cleverly replied:

"Or my field is just super fertile." We both laughed. On Monday morning, Carrie called Dr Schreiber's rooms to make an appointment to see him to confirm what the home test had told us, and to get the ball rolling for round number two. The appointment was scheduled for Thursday morning. On Thursday morning, I left for work as usual, and Carrie and Jane left shortly after me because they had to get across town for Carrie's appointment at 9:00 a.m.

My morning at school had been particularly busy and because I was distracted, I hadn't realised that I had left my mobile on silent in the pocket of my jacket that hung across the back of my chair. After the lunch signal peeped loudly through the school corridors, the school intercom sounded, and Mrs. Hopkins from the front office was talking through her nose—as she usually did.

"Mr. Sterling, please report to the office for an urgent phone call...Mr. Sterling, please report to the office for an urgent phone call...urgent...thank you." My heart sank, and immediately, a million scenarios crossed my mind. None of them were good. I grabbed my jacket and ran toward the office. While I was running, I checked my mobile and saw that I had missed six calls from Carrie.

"Oh, my God," I chastised to myself. "What has happened?" When I arrived at the office, Mrs. Hopkins handed me the phone.

"It's your wife," she announced. I grabbed the phone from her, forgetting my manners in my distress.

"Is everything okay?" I asked frantically, forgetting to say hello to Carrie.

"It's all fine," she answered cheerfully.

"What's the urgency then?" I asked. "My nerves are finished." There was a small pause before Carrie spoke again.

"They might be totally finished after this call," she declared with a mischievous laugh.

"Okay, what is it then?" I asked, becoming impatient as my adrenaline was subsiding—and I was starting to feel my legs again.

"I AM pregnant," she stated with obvious joy in her voice. I felt excited and relieved all at the same time.

"We sort of knew that—but how far?" I asked knowing that four weeks had been the extent of our efforts.

"Are you ready for this?" she teased.

"Go on," I replied, slightly irritated.

"Four and a half months...we're halfway there." I was stunned into temporary silence.

"Are you sure?" I asked somewhat dazed.

"I'm as sure as the scans Dr Schreiber took this morning," Carrie's tone was cheeky.

The surprise news called for a celebration that evening. It was difficult to go out for dinner with Jane, in the cold December weather, so I arrived home with Chinese takeaways and some Lindt slabs. I greeted Carrie with a big hug, and she was somewhat teary. Carrie was always a little emotional with sentimental life events. We sat down to eat and I tried to explain to Jane that her world was about to be rocked.

"Sort of like when there are suddenly two suns in a solar system," I told her. She didn't appear to be fussed, let alone interested.

"Take a look at these," Carrie demanded, putting the prints of Dr Schreiber's scan down in front of me. "Look especially at the third one," she instructed with a mischievous smile. The image showed a fully formed head with an outstretched arm and five perfectly formed fingers at the end of it. The fingers were tilted slightly, as if they might be waving at us.

"How did we miss this one?" I asked.

"Have no idea," Carrie replied, almost giggling.

Lying in bed that night, it dawned on me that there had actually been 19 people at Becky's party in Trowbridge. The youngest was hiding inside Carrie and pilfering the mulled wine that she had so freely drunk.

"This one might be a bit of a party animal," I chuckled as I turned over to cuddle Carrie. She had had a rollercoaster of a day. I felt honoured that the universe was allowing me to have another go at this parenting thing, I must have been getting something right, secrets and all.

IN THE MONTHS leading up to the birth of baby number two, the boxes in my head did not want to be contained, they were spilling over everywhere on the inside of my head and behind the picket fence. For some reason, I struggled immensely with my secret as it danced around my head like a serpent without a master. It had been 10 years since Mario had given me my first taste of men, and probably 15 since Graham had tempted me with the offer of his body while we sat in his car outside my parent's house. Apart from the distant memories associated with people like Michael Carlson,

Wayne Evans, Manny Khoury and Henri Viviers, I was in the desert of my true desires and sexuality. I was thinking about people like Lorenzo López a lot more than I should have been.

I was also finding colleagues like Stephen Tyler and David Long increasingly more attractive—and they were beautiful specimens, especially Stephen, whose heart was shattered when David ran off with his wife. While consoling Stephen and wanting to kiss away his pain, I stupidly quoted him the words from a popular M People song.

"Search for the hero inside yourself," I told him.

"That could work" he said reflectively, "but I would replace 'hero' with 'Jesus'."

"Oh Jesus!" I groaned under my breath. I had forgotten that he was a full-on reborn Christian. Rumour had it that his wife had left him because she was tired of Jesus coming between them. This Jesus guy seemed to come between a lot of people.

Jesus also came between Carrie and I—as if he hadn't caused enough trouble already. In the buildup to baby number two, we began talking about a Christening for both of the children. As with our wedding, Carrie wanted a Methodist orientated ceremony. I would have opted for Catholic if I had had to make a choice. Ironic, I know—but better the devil of religion you have slept with, than the one in sheep's clothing. Following similar arguments to those we had had 5 years earlier for our wedding, we agreed on a simple non-denominational dedication service. Gran wasn't impressed.

"You can't call it a christening when there is no water," she grouched, dissatisfied with our feeble attempt at preparing to wash away their original sin.

IN THE WEEKS before the birth of baby number two, I managed to pull in my reins and focus more on the upcoming big event. I was in love with Carrie, I was in love with Jane and I was ready to love baby number two.

For the birth of Kate, I was much more in control—I had survived the blood and gore of Jane's arrival; and I was much calmer, because I had proven to myself and to Jane that I might not be such a bad father, maybe even a pretty good dad. Number two had to be easier.

As with the birth of Jane some 18 months earlier, we arrived at the hospital in the early hours of the morning. Things with Kate were different. As she had only been discovered late in the pregnancy, she showed us that she was going to hang on in there for as long as she could. Finally, at around half three in the afternoon, Dr Schreiber announced that we needed to get this little one out. Carrie's waters had broken about half an hour earlier and they were coloured with meconium. Dr Schreiber instructed one of the nurses to immediately attach a heart monitor belt to Carrie's bulging belly.

"We need to check that baby is fine," he explained calmly, "meconium often indicates that the baby has been in distress...we need to be sure that there is no damage to his lungs." Carrie and I were a little panicked about the condition of the baby, but we were also digesting the fact that Dr Schreiber had just announced the gender of our soon to be born baby.

"Did he say HIS?" I asked Carrie.

"That's what I thought I heard him say," she answered in a whisper. Her epidural of one hour earlier was taking effect and she looked like the pain she had been experiencing all day was subsiding.

"The good news," Dr Schreiber said calmly and confidently, "is that baby is all fine and it's time for it to come out." Was he playing games with us, or did he make a point of using pronouns interchangeably because of the nature of his work?

"It?" I questioned quietly, looking at Carrie and pulling a face. Dr Schreiber straddled Carrie up and then got busy.

"We're going to need to do a small episiotomy," he explained, as if quietly not telling us everything. I could feel my squeamishness squirm in my shins. The thought of Carrie's vagina being sliced with a scalpel was too visual for my tired and anxious senses. Dr Schreiber began to tinker away.

"Ooh...the umbilical cord is wrapped around its neck," Dr Schreiber was calm and composed. Carrie looked stressed and I squeezed her hand, I was becoming concerned too. Then Dr Schreiber made another exclamation, only this time with more emotion than we had ever heard from him. "Twice!" he exclaimed. His words echoed in the room and bounced off the big spotlight illuminating Carrie's compromised womanhood. Instinctively, I leaned over to see what all of the fuss was about, and I could see the baby's bald crowned head and two thick pieces of leathery umbilical cord wrapped around its neck like a lasso. The image was grotesque. "Pass me a scalpel Maria," he instructed the midwife with a panicked and urgent voice. Maria was quick off the mark and after that things unfolded rapidly. "It's a girl," he announced, and it sounded like a bit of a throwaway line given all the drama. Above Kate's loud screaming, reminiscent of her sister's arrival, Dr Schreiber told us, "Her cord was wrapped around her neck." He was focussed on and talking mostly to Carrie. "And that's why she wouldn't drop, as much as you pushed," he explained, "she was being pulled back—there wasn't enough give."

Kate was rushed away and cleaned and Apgar'd and then incubated.

"She's doing just fine," Maria told us reassuringly. Carrie had fallen asleep, and I stood at the incubator staring at our tiny creation through the glass. She looked cherub-like, alone, and vulnerable. She was with us, but she was still out of reach...still on the other side, a little closer but not quite with us yet. It looked like this one liked to do things in her own sweet time. I was amazed at how instantly I could find more love for this new arrival— it was like I suddenly found a double-dose of love. Another amount, equal to that which I had found for Jane when she arrived into this world. Like a bottomless well, it comes from somewhere inside and it just keeps flowing. It never runs out of stock, it never needs to be filled up or serviced—it's like a Busby vacuum cleaner with a lifetime guarantee, only it has a reverse action...it doesn't suck, it pours. I was grateful for having found more love, but I felt robbed of not being able to cut her cord, for not being able to hold her and for not being able to tell her I was excited to be her dad. Our latest addition was gorgeous and I was eager to get to know her.

Kate recovered quickly from her shaky entry into this world and within three days she was at home. Jane was excited to meet her new sister, and Kate seemed equally happy with the sibling she hadn't specifically chosen. We were playing picket fences again and we were happy, the only irritation was this thing in my head. It was distracting me, chasing me further inside myself and distancing me from the three girls I loved most in the world. Kate was the biggest casualty because it was early days for her, days where bonding was paramount.

CHAPTER TWENTY

THE VICAR

23 June 2003

THREE MONTHS AFTER Kate had bravely entered this world, the boxes in my head seemed to come crashing down and the serpents that held my secrets were dancing all over the show. I'm not sure why or how—but they were, and I was out of control.

I don't even remember how I found the dating platform called datingbuzz, but the urges in me were obviously intense enough to encourage me to proactively inquire. I needed to talk to somebody. I needed to find things out.

My *nom de plume* was *Keith Foster*—the surname borrowed from a young man I once taught. I was always super impressed with his bravery and his drive. He, like me, was also slightly eccentric and when he was a teenager he publicly stated and owned his own homosexuality. Such a brave thing to do in an all-boys school environment. How different would my life have been, had I been as brave and determined about my own truth as that young man was. He, also like me, was bullied by his peers—but he held his head up high and remained true to himself in the face of painful and unnecessary adversity. He turned the biblical other cheek, and never rose to conflict or confrontation. He didn't seem to have any gay anger or fury in him. He was an old soul.

On datingbuzz, I was extremely cautious. I would chat online and also on my down-low email address. If I thought that the veiled person on the other end could add value to my journey by having asked and answered the right questions, I would then agree to meet them for a coffee. I was always incredibly discreet about my identity until I was sure that I was willing to meet them. Some found this frustrating and others found it amusing. After numerous requests, and as many negative responses, one guy from Brighton had asked me:

"Are you a celebrity?"

"That depends on who you talk to," I remember replying.

How difficult might the down-low have been for people like Phillip Schofield, who live under bright celebrity lights where secrets have no room to hide? Coming out as *Joe Public* would be difficult enough—but the interfering media could make the transition a lot more traumatic. In my searching for answers, I met many interesting characters, some valuable to my journey and others who were scary or sad. The down-low is a lonely and frightening place.

Every thought, every message and every meeting that I had on my journey was more energy cast into the universe, leading me toward an unplanned meeting with the real me who hid in my own shameful shadow. The person I needed to meet and get to know; that person I had been abusively hiding in the dark beneath my own floorboards—that deprived and confused person who was actually, despicably me.

One meeting was with a big burly Dutchman. He had been mildly appealing, but when he tried to kiss me at the end of the McDonalds meeting outside his car, I didn't want to see him again. Then there was Carl who wheeled and dealed like Del Boy in *Only Fools and Horses*. He was so nervous that I did wonder how he managed to sell anything as he did an awful job of trying to sell himself. A few coffee meets led me to Gary. He was an intriguing character who wasn't hugely gorgeous—but he felt safe: a little bit like a Sainsbury's donut...nothing extra special, but it's going to fulfil a purpose and it's not going to make you ill—it might even give you a short-term rush.

"So, what kind of work do you do?" Gary asked, looking over his rim-less glasses, his hair probably greasier than it should have been.

"I'm in education," I told him, trying to be vague.

"Like a teacher," he asked bluntly. I could feel myself fluster.

"Yes," I answered, and then trying not to offer more information, I immediately flipped the attention to him and asked him what he did.

"I'm a vicar," he proudly declared and then he offered what I thought was too much information: "I look after a congregation near Harlow." These kinds of overshares were welcoming in that they demonstrated openness and initial trust, but they were also worrying because discretion was the name of the game that we were playing.

"That's not far from here," I noted. He ignored my comment and fired his next question.

"So, when did you realise you were gay?" he bellowed much too loudly for the rules of discretion.

"Not sure," I answered, "I think it's always just hung around the back of my head." He wriggled in his chair and it was clear he was pondering what I had said.

"I can relate to that," his voice was still booming, and his tone was un-relaxed and academic, "I have struggled with this since I was a teenager," he explained, "I thought a career in the church would heal me, but it clearly hasn't. Now I have a wife and three beautiful daughters, but I'm still not satisfied. So, I'm looking for somebody to experiment with, and would prefer a married guy who also has children. That's why your profile was perfect. Basically, I'd like to hook up with a regular fuck buddy and see where it goes."

Once his soliloquy was over, I leaned forward and affirmingly squeezed his left wrist. "Please can you lower your volume? I requested. "I think by now the whole restaurant might know what you're looking for."

"I'm sorry," he explained, blushing. "I'm a little deaf and background noise is not good for me." I explained that the idea of an affair with a man wasn't in my planning, but that I would think about it.

A week later, I was sitting in the office at St. Agatha's church in Harlow.

"Would you like a coffee or tea," Gary asked.

"Tea please," I answered.

"With or without a kiss," he joked. He made the tea which was strong and ghastly, and we spent the afternoon talking about our journeys and our needs. The room was freezing, despite the fact that summer was around the corner. The ancient stone walls were cold and damp and they filled the air with a chilly uncertainty. There was an underlying lustful electric energy in the room, and we were kind of circling around what the next step might be.

"I'm sorry," I said, "I'm not sure I can do this." He looked disappointed, but he remained upbeat.

"Perhaps you just need time," he replied with the pathos befitting of a clergyman. "No pressure," he added jovially. I gave him an awkward hug and left. Up close against his body, he smelt good, not Paco Rabanne good—manly good. Mild testosterone wafting from his pores.

A week later, same time, same day, I was back at St. Agatha's. This time, we had a plan of action—or rather we kind of did. We knew that we were ready to touch each other, we were ready to experiment and to take things further. This would be the first time in my 34 years that I was in a willing buyer, willing seller situation. He was swift. I was hardly seated in the chair on the opposite end of his desk, when he hastily closed the curtains, locked the door and lunged toward me. He leapt onto my lap, straddled his legs, and looked into my eyes as he rested his palms on my chest. His hairy face was neatly trimmed and his honest and daring eyes were mischievously calming. He still smelt of mild testosterone.

"Can I kiss you?" he blurted, speaking a lot more quietly than he had on the day that I met him.

"I don't think that's a good idea," I bantered, my face serious. He looked a little taken aback, and then before he could speak, I leaned forward and brought my mouth to his. It was intensely satisfying and his hands cupping my face felt mildly erotic. He leaned back and released my jaw, moving his hands to the back of my head.

"I really enjoyed that," he whispered as he released himself from me. "Let's do it again." We kissed a few more times, speaking reassuringly to each other at each pause. We met a few more times at St. Agatha's and each time we got braver and braver, taking our hands to new and uncharted places of exploration. I had been right. He was a safe choice and we taught each other honestly and with care as we blindly navigated this new and intoxicating space. He was certainly not my type, and to be honest, I found him mildly annoying in the way he tried to theorise and intellectualise absolutely everything. His booming voice made his words more irritating than they probably were, and when he uttered the three forbidden words in week 6, I was totally freaked out.

"I love you," he announced as he kissed me goodbye behind his closed office door. That had been too much for me so early on in the game. The guilt of my adultery was eating me from the inside, and I decided that I didn't want to love anybody else. Carrie, Jane and Kate were all I needed, and all that I wanted. But then why was I at St Agatha's over and over again?

Just over a week later, I called Gary.

"Hi, it's me," I announced realising the stupidity of the salutation after I had said it. "I need to see you urgently," I told him. Within an hour we were seated opposite each other at a pub in Birds Green which was about halfway between where we both lived.

"Hi, nice to see you...what's up?" he asked, looking slightly ashen. I took the bull by the horns and decided to get the business done straight away.

"I can't do this anymore," I declared.

"Why?" he sounded shocked and looked immediately forlorn.

"My conscience is killing me," I explained, "and I want to seal this all up and pretend that all of this never happened." I sighed. Gary looked devastated. "It's nothing to do with you," I reassured. "You're a great guy and I've enjoyed our chats and explorations, but I can't carry on with this." The room was silent and the air was still, I was waiting for him to speak. He looked frozen. Finally, I spoke again. "Please understand, Gary," I urged. His gentle eyes looked sad and he seemed terror stricken.

"Please don't do this to me." he pleaded. "I am in love with you." This was new territory to me, I wasn't sure how to respond, I needed to complete my exit and this meant I needed to get tough.

"I'm sorry Gary," I confirmed, "I'm really sorry. I hope you find your happiness. I cannot offer you what you're after." I stood up and patted his shoulder. "Take care," I said awkwardly and then I walked out of the door and out of Gary's life.

A COUPLE OF years later, I felt intrigued and curious about what had become of him. I went to Facebook and learned that he had a new partner, a man called Andrew and the photos indicated that they were happy: holidays, building projects and photos that showed both of their feet in the sand at the beach. I could also work out from his posts that he seemed to see his daughters quite frequently, but that they seemed to live with their mum. Andrew's Facebook wall also revealed that he had previously been married with children, three teenage boys—possibly, but I wasn't sure. He was tall and handsome, and a calm energy emanated from the images of him. He was much better looking than Gary, and he looked like he took better care of his hair.

I couldn't work out if Gary still worked for the church or not, so I made a call to the Church of England's headquarters.

"I wonder if you can help me?" I asked with some degree of authority. "I'm looking to find out at which parish I might find one of your clergymen, his name is Gary Beltham-Smith."

"Just a second," came the swift reply and I could hear the lady's long fingernails tapping onto a keyboard rather furiously. It took some time before she came back to me. "Mr Beltham-Smith was removed from our roll in 2004," she retorted very matter of factly.

"Any reason why," I quizzed her.

"I'm afraid I wouldn't be at liberty to disclose that," she replied with an officious bark. 'A Leviticus dismissal', I thought to myself as I put down the phone. I felt happy for Gary and Andrew and for the love that they had found. But I also felt responsible for the wife and children and the love that Gary had left behind. I had been the trigger for that. I wondered if Gary had been a trigger for Andrew and how their story had unfolded. At that time, I wasn't ready to be as brave, or as foolish, as they had been—but I did long to also live my true and authentic life.

CHAPTER TWENTY-ONE

A CLASH OF CELEBRATIONS

30 October 2004

WITH THE VICAR out of the way, the joy of parenting distracted me more than anything ever had—and it was a joyous distraction. It was hard to believe that these tiny human beings, who some time before hadn't even existed, could capture my heart and my soul so resoundingly. It was so out of proportion that these tiny bundles could exude such warmth and light and be so positively all-consuming.

Carrie and I enjoyed every second and every dimension of the new responsibilities that the universe had bestowed upon us. We were proud parents, fumbling our way through this new chapter of our lives, with Jane and Kate as our willing, smiling, and none-the-wiser guinea pigs.

"I can see you." Carrie was animated and, on all fours, towering over Jane as she lay belly up on her baby cushion on the living room floor. Her mobile of bright African animals swaying over her, gaining its momentum from Carrie's big breaths. "I can see you," Carrie did it again and again, and each time, Jane would laugh and squeal. It was a picture of happiness. Carrie was enjoying her time away from school, although I could see that some days she was lonely and desperate for some adult company. Nurse Louise had warned that antenatal depression was something to look out for.

The day after Jane's seven-week birthday, Carrie had decided to venture out for what would be Jane's first outing. She was going to meet Nicky, Debbie, and Avery, her Nightingale friends, at a new coffee shop in Springfield. She left the house just after three with some bounce in her step. It was clear that she was excited to escape the house, which had become like a cabin to her. She was also eager to show off her latest asset. It was the Friday before Christmas and the day that schools closed for the Christmas break. This meant that everybody was in a festive mood—even Jane it seemed. Carrie dressed her in a green and red Christmas sleepsuit with matching mistletoe patterned blanket. Once Jane was safely strapped in, Carrie struggled to get the pushchair into the boot.

"Just let me work it out," she insisted, "I'm going to have to do it when you are not around later." With a few more pushes and shoves, and turning it slightly onto its side, Carrie got the push chair in and she closed the boot.

As the VW Polo got smaller and smaller in the distance, I felt a pang of separation. This would be the first of many, and my learning that as much as I felt the need to protect this little creation, I needed to trust more. The truth was that she didn't belong to me. She belonged to us and she belonged to the universe. This was somewhat like my secret: although hiding and dormant, it was also sadly common property—jointly owned by us—and also by the universe. When Jane was born, James and Becky had visited the hospital and had given us a card welcoming her into the world. A quote, by somebody called June Stone, was embossed across the front of the card in an old typewriter type font. The words have come to mean so much more over time and are imprinted in my head: 'Making the decision to have a child is momentous. It is to decide forever to have your heart go walking around outside your body.'

And like the words in our wedding vows, forever sounded like a mighty long time.

Carrie returned earlier than I expected. I was relieved that they were both home—but Carrie looked exhausted and beside herself with worry. Jane was screaming and crying, pulling her legs up and down, clenching her fists and moving her arms in jerky actions as if she was in serious pain. The frenzy lasted until just after 9:00 p.m. that night when Jane fell fast asleep. Carrie and I were shattered. Oblivious to the trauma that she had caused us, Jane looked peaceful and happy.

"Might have been something she ate," I suggested.

"Unlikely," Carrie sighed, reminding me that Jane was being breastfed. "Maybe something, I ate," Carrie added with a cheeky smile.

We all slept in the following morning as it was highly unusual for Jane to wake up after 9:00 a.m.

"She must have been exhausted from yesterday," Carrie commented.

"And us," I joked. We both laughed. It was a lazy and peaceful day at home on that last Saturday before Christmas. Then, at 4:00 p.m., almost as if by clockwork, Jane started again. This time, it seemed worse. Jane displayed the same symptoms of the previous day, but she was now also furrowing her brow, holding her breath and scrunching her eyes tight and then opening them wide open again. It was distressing to watch, and it was frightening to see Carrie looking helpless. I called the hospital to ask for some advice.

"Dr Schreiber is doing his rounds in the wards now," the nurse on duty told us. "Why don't you pop down to the hospital right away for him to take a look?"

Carrie and I arrived with Jane shortly before 5:00 p.m. and Dr Schreiber was ready and waiting for us.

"What can I do for you today?" he asked in his usual soft and dull monotone. Jane was still screaming and squirming from her pain and Carrie was rocking her tenderly, fighting back her tears as she did it. Dr Schreiber smiled reassuringly, and I took over:

"Thank you for seeing us at short notice," I got the pleasantries out of the way. "We're really concerned about Jane," I continued. "She is six weeks old and yesterday at around this time, she started with the same symptoms that she's demonstrating now." I paused for breath and carried on. "Yesterday was the first time that she left the house since she was born, so we're not sure if it could be the cold? It's so confusing, because then at around nine last night, she stopped—almost instantly—and she slept until nearly ten this morning." Dr Schreiber closed his eyes as if he was thinking and as he was about to speak, Carrie jumped in.

"Do you think she has colic?" she asked. Dr Schreiber's eyes opened and he spoke a little louder than usual.

"That's probably all it is," he said, "prepare yourselves for six weeks of this, you might want to buy some earmuffs," he joked. Carrie and I were instantly relieved. "Hold her close, comfort her, rub her tummy really gently and soak her in warm water," he suggested. It all sounded easy enough. "Nobody is totally certain what causes colic," he added, "just stay calm, it's all going to be ok."

The next six weeks were taxing and exhausting and they taught us that perfection didn't exist. Our picket fence was no different to anybody else's. We kept it clean, we painted it and we treated it, but what happened behind it was only our business. Behind it we grew, and we learnt. We got a lot right and we got a lot wrong. We loved each other and what we had created, but we damaged each other too—not intentionally, but we did. We did this only because we often hurt those we love the most—and not because we want to, but because deep down we know that they will not desert us. Their loyalty gives us a licence to verbally and emotionally assault them. They become a space for us to dump our insecurities.

JANE'S THIRD BIRTHDAY was marred by family politics. Carrie's younger sister Chloë had decided to arrange her hen party for the same day as the closest Saturday to Jane's birthday, which was the day before her actual birthday. She sent out her invitations a week before the event, even though we had sent ours out one month prior. It was typical of her, selfish and self-absorbed. It had always made me angry and I always aired my opinions, not because I was hugely hurt or inconvenienced, but because it made me angry that the family tolerated her persistent self-indulgence. She had no consideration for anybody else in the family and she repeatedly hurt her sisters and her parents. I had decided that she wasn't going to steal the thunder from my princess.

Just as was the way the family usually dealt with Chloë, Carrie wanted to take the path of least resistance—but I wasn't having it. Carrie was prepared to change the time or the date of Jane's party to accommodate Chloë, but I wasn't entertaining it.

"I don't fucking care if the bridesmaids made this arrangement or not," I scowled, "she can fucking tell them to unmake them." I was irrational and out of control. I was mad with Chloë, I was mad with Carrie, I was mad with Abby and I was mad with Carrie's parents for allowing this to happen. The truth was I was going mad in my head. My secret was tormenting me more than ever and I was, no doubt, also mad with the universe. I was dying on the inside and I had only needed a trigger like this to set me off.

"Please David," Carrie pleaded, "let's not destroy the fibre of the family for something so trivial." I shook my head in disbelief. Sometimes Carrie was so very English—perhaps being calm and diplomatic for the sake of peace is not such a bad idea. But, when you carry a serpent in your head, it's hard to control your rage.

ONE OF THE biggest burdens that I carry is not the pain that I caused Carrie by telling her my truth, but the daily pain I caused her on the inside of our picket fence. The pain that I inflicted during those times when the boxes in my head rattled and I was scared and terrified—pouring my insecurities out, all over her. The truth is that even when I thought I was in control, I wasn't. I was constantly looking over my shoulder, trying to find a cure or forgiveness for my thoughts and desires. Constantly wondering how I might be able to fix the mess that I had made. Carrie was an innocent casualty. It was exhausting for both of us.

CHAPTER TWENTY-TWO

GOODBYE TO GRAN

26 September 2005

IT WAS ONLY after gran bowed out gracefully at age 78, that we started to unravel a lot of her secrets. She carried them well and she carried them proudly. She used Jesus and the Virgin Mary to help her hide them. They were the source of her strength. Pope John Paul II might have also have harboured some of them for her—she was a dedicated admirer and supporter of her Polish Pope. I always knew that she was a strong woman, but I only realised the magnitude of her strength after she died. Secret keepers wear brave faces that can be curiously deceptive.

Gran's secrets all stemmed from the trauma that she and her family had suffered during the Second World War. Disturbed and aggressed in rural Poland in the middle of the night, she, along with her parents and brother, were packed into rail cars and transported to a prison camp in Siberia. While in the camp, gran's mother died of typhoid. This fact was commonly known family history, but her broken heart and the tears that she couldn't tap when the topic was broached meant we never knew the details. It was too painful for her.

Toward the end of the war, along with her father and her brother, they were transported with many other survivors to Persia, now Iran. From there, her father was enlisted into the British army and she and her brother were shipped, as 13 and 11-year-old orphans, to separate refugee camps in Africa. Gran to Zambia and her brother to Tanzania. Early life for her had been rough, but somehow, she emerged strong, determined, and a worthy matriarch to our family.

AFTER GRAN DIED, I embarked on my personal journey that brought with it unexpected findings and honourable posthumous rewards. As much as I was interested in learning about gran's past and in uncovering family secrets, I had also learnt how to manage myself—the best way to tame the monster in my head was to keep myself focussed and preoccupied. I always needed a mission to keep me on the straight and narrow. Not having a focus meant that I might waver, creating havoc in my wake. The vicar had been my last mishap and I didn't want to relapse again. So, soon after gran died, investigating her family history became my mission. The journey was long and intense; whilst being incredibly sad it was also satisfying. I learnt that gran's big secret was the loss of three other siblings, also to Typhoid; and that for much of her life she had pined to have a relationship with her father, who was so damaged from the war that he simply didn't know how to be a dad.

It always astounded me that even though she was robbed of her childhood and her parents and her siblings and her grandparents and also of her culture, she still managed to pour love from that bottomless chalice that we keep somewhere beneath our ribcage. Gran was beautiful inside and out, and as much as her narrow religious viewpoints sometimes drove me crazy, I understand better now how they held her together, trapping her secrets inside, nourishing her soul. When she saw Jesus hanging above Father Ryan's head, she didn't see what I saw—she saw hope and love, she saw her rescuer and her redeemer. And I think, as the first-born grandchild, I represented so much of the family that she never had. That is what bound us.

She was the driver of the faith in our family, and rather than despise her for it, I am instead incredibly grateful for the strong moral values I learnt through the teachings of the church. It wasn't all bad, if I ignored my personal conflicts.

IT WAS SO good when gran returned to live in England to be close to her ageing dad. She arrived two years before he died. It had been her last-minute attempt to find some healing and closure for them both—and it seemed to work. She visited him often and she even learnt to tolerate his wife, who would never be a worthy replacement for her mother, and who she referred to as *the woman*. *The woman* died a few months before gran's dad, who we only ever called 'gran's dad'. It was a bit odd, but that's who he was. *The woman's* passing meant that gran had her dad to herself in the months before he died. She seemed to enjoy that—making the most of everyday.

One day, while I was still at uni, I stopped by her flat where she speedily fried up some delicious pancakes before I arrived. She was always trying to fatten me up. My gran glowed with love and grace, and this radiated from her beautiful thoughts and intentions. Roald Dahl had written that those good thoughts shine out of your face and they always make you look lovely. My gran was lovely. Her gentle eyes were as soft as her skin which time had scribbled on kindly—its gentle pen seemed to have spent more time above her top lip than it had around her eyes. Her grey hair was always perfect, her make-up was soft and sensible, and she always smelt like 4711 perfume.

I was scoffing down pancake number three, when gran took me by surprise.

"You know David, the way you behave with women, you should become a priest." She was calm and direct. English wasn't her first language and I think she may have meant to say: 'when are you going to get a girlfriend?'— or had she identified the fiend that was hiding inside me. It might also have even been that the thought of her second-generation progeny becoming a man of the cloth would signify a job well done, a life well lived and a mission accomplished. I don't know what it was she was trying to say, but it terrified me.

A FEW MONTHS before she died, Gran gave us a massive fright which resulted in the removal of her gall bladder. We had thought that she was on the mend, but toward the end of September she took a turn for the worse. It was her stomach; she couldn't hold food down, and she was nauseated and in pain.

"I'm afraid it's cancer in her stomach and it's quite advanced." Dr McNab was sincere and caring as he spewed those painful words across his desk at my mum, my aunt and I. Horrible words—sour and curdling and positively repugnant. I didn't want to hear them, and I didn't want to own them. Their odour clung to us like bleach in a toilet bowl. Mum and Aunty Em welled up and so did I.

"How long have we got?" I choked. I didn't want to know the answer, but we needed to.

"I don't know," Dr McNab, continued "it's hard to tell, maybe a week...maybe two...maybe less." The silence in the room was cold and his words became sourer than before. "It's important that we keep her comfortable for now," he added.

Mum and Aunty Em returned to the ward and I went outside to have a chat with God. I was clutching the St. Christopher that I wore around my neck. I had worn it for the 20 years since the day gran had given it to me on the evening of my confirmation. The tears were rolling down my face; I prayed to God and to Jesus and anybody else who would listen to please heal her from her pain and the disease and to please give us a few more years. I bargained and I begged, but it all fell on deaf ears because five days later, gran closed her soft hazel eyes and she was gone. Soaring home, soaring to her mother and to her entire family who had gone before her, to Jesus and the Virgin Mary and to Pope John Paul II. What a privilege to have known her and to have shared life, love, and joy with her. She was a worthy matriarch, self-taught, and she had excelled.

CHAPTER TWENTY-THREE

THE PICKET FENCE

30 September 2005

SEVEN YEARS INTO our marriage and four days after gran went to fly with the angels, we moved into a new home. It was to be our forever home...and forever is a mighty long time. The house had previously belonged to a friend of my mum's, so I had known it since childhood. It was the kind of house that I would never have imagined that I would be able to own. It was detached, in a cul-de-sac, and the sloped terrain that it lay on meant that it was designed to be twisted and layered, oozing with character as it hugged the contours of the land it sat on. It was cradled by trees that made it feel secluded, its high hedges kept the neighbours out. It was like living on a farm in suburbia.

Carrie and the girls loved the house too. The move hadn't been planned, but the property's fortuitous coming onto the market seemed too good for us to let pass by. The house wasn't only a house, it swiftly became a home that eclectically bought together both mine and Carrie's tastes. For me, it was traditional with a colonial feel, and for Carrie it was cottagey and quaint. It boasted high ceilings, Cotswold-green cottage-pane windows, and rough rendered and whitewashed walls. Below the walls were diamond laid terracotta tiles that sprayed innumerable shades of dark rust and chocolate brown into each room. These shades seem to warm the spaces, despite the tiles being cold and echoey. The four character fireplaces were well positioned, and they easily heated up the entire house during the cold winter months. The garden was delightful and a migrating maze of colour. Different flowers popped up at different times of the year: Petunias and Busy Lizzies in the summer; Asters and Nerines in the autumn; Pansies and Viburnum in the winter; and Primula and Wisteria in the spring. It was beautiful. To the outside world the picket fence was perfect, right from the curb-side to the furthest boundary wall.

And, in many ways, things were perfect, I was pretty much in control of my secret and had only had that short three-month stray with the vicar. I recovered from it quickly, wallowing secretively in my own guilt. I was an excellent keeper of secrets, especially my own. I was fighting the demons within me as best I could. I kept those boxes in my head as clean and organised and as tightly packed away as possible.

SHORTLY AFTER CARRIE and I were married, we did a short stint abroad. We had decided, for sentimental reasons, to spend a year teaching in Barcelona. Somehow, I ended up in an administrative role at one school, which I quite enjoyed. Carrie did a number of short-term covers at a few city schools. We stayed in a small and bright apartment opposite *Museu Egipci de Barcelona*, which was almost slap-bang in the middle of what is known as the *L'Eixample District*. In the LGBT community, this district was affectionately called '*Gaixample*'—a play on words, combining the word *gai*— the Catalan word for gay, and the name of the district. I should have felt tempted by the numerous gay bars, discos and shops that were the backdrop to my daily morning and evening walks to and from work but I wasn't—I was a married straight man, totally in love with the maiden I had courted. I was happy and I had overcome that evil voice in my head. We created many happy memories in Spain. We travelled to the Costa del Sol, we visited Malaga and Gibraltar, and we even made a short trip to Madrid.

"Thank you for bringing joy and light into my life." Carrie was earnest as we sipped our second glass of wine at a quaint restaurant we frequented close to our flat in Barcelona.

"I should be thanking you," I retorted with a massive smile across my face.

"It just all feels like a dream," she sighed.

"It really does" I concurred. We leaned across the table and shared a gentle kiss. She was wearing a stylish azure blue catsuit that accentuated her eyes. The subtle diamonds that dangled loosely on each of her ears danced in the evening candlelight, almost in tune with the band on the opposite end of the room. I had made an outstanding catch, and I was grateful. It all felt like a dream but the problem with dreams is that you can awaken from them without any warning.

Living frugally in Spain gave us a financial kickstart and we returned to Chelmsford with some savings. Carrie returned to Nightingale, while I was lucky enough to secure the teaching and boarding master position at Stanton Boys Catholic Independent on the outskirts of Chelmsford. The position required after hours pastoral care, but it also came with a lovely flat that allowed us to save for bigger and better things to come. Carrie decorated the flat beautifully and we were very happy there. We were slowly building our picket fence.

Behind the fence, we had brought our two beautiful daughters into the world. Carrie had given up work to give the girls the best we could. It felt like we were living the perfect dream, not without its day-to-day frustrations and irritations—but what we had was close to perfect.

I would often find myself feeling grateful for what I had found in Carrie. She was an adoring and caring wife, and I was a loving and faithful husband—mostly. A few years into our marriage, I did feel the boxes in my head slip and slide around. The three-month secret liaison that I had with a vicar broke the picket fence rules and it damaged the fence somewhat. I had surreptitiously slid another person through the rungs of the fence, I had shifted the energies behind it, bringing with it some unexpected and inexplicable pain. I realised what I had done, and I didn't want it. I wanted what Carrie and I had in the heteronormative world I chosen to clothe myself in. I wore it well, albeit slightly fraudulently and deceitfully—but with love and the best of intentions. I carried it off almost as comfortably as the gorgeous blue catsuit and shiny earrings that Carrie had worn on that beautiful night in Barcelona. I was in too deep now, there was no going back. I believed in the happiness.

DURING THAT TIME, I often wondered about the likes of my cousin Kacey and her Mormon husband. Their picket fence looked so perfect: children, Joseph Smith, and Angel Moroni. Somehow none of us saw that fence slowly break and then come crashing down. Then there was Graham, the good-looking man with the skew nose who had hit on me after my late shift at the Bonanza on that August night in 1987. Where had his life gone, was he still on the down-low, had he come clean with his wife, or was he braving it all in the name of traditional conformity?

My good friend James and his wife Becky looked like their picket fence was more robust than ours, but I guess we would never know what played out in its shadows when the guests were gone and it was just the two of them. Then there was Peter, the barbeque bigot; was he on the down-low and pretending to maintain and paint his picket fence? I remained convinced he was gay. Also, there was Jessica; she looked happy. She had two little ones and one in the oven, she looked like she was good at picket fencing, but as it emerged she also held a secret. Picket fences are complicated, nice from afar, but often far from nice.

CHAPTER TWENTY-FOUR

THE WEDDING ANNIVERSARY

11 September 2006

MY MUM AND dad, just like Carrie, enjoyed celebrating the sentimentality of small and big everyday events: birthdays, holidays, anniversaries, death days, and happy days. My catholic upbringing had also instilled in me a strong sense of tradition and ritual.

In our little family, I had made every effort to continue some of the traditions we had learnt from my parents, but I also made an effort to introduce some new ones as we went along. For example, we burnt candles on the birthdays and death days of people we loved, we slept together in a giant bed on Friday nights and we sang happy birthday as many times as we could squeeze it in when it was somebody's birthday. All in the name of fun and love and eccentricity.

One of our big traditions, one which Jane and Kate had come to love the most, only came around once a year. It was mine and Carrie's wedding anniversary. On 11 September every year, we would play loud wedding march music and we would all dress up—Carrie and I in our wedding clothes and Jane and Kate in Disney princess dresses. They were our modern traditional flower girls: Sleeping Beauty in fake fur and blue, and Cinderella in red crimplene and plastic clogs. We would sing and dance and make up our own vows and then we would sing and dance and make it up some more.

"Swing me around again daddy," Jane would roar with excitement.

"Let's say that again," Kate would shriek.

"One more dance please, daddy," they would both nag—almost in unison. I loved the sound of the word 'daddy' and I loved those two girls more than anything in the world. Those evenings were such fun and if anybody had been peering through our picket fence, the world they would have seen would have appeared perfect and, in many ways, it was. It's ironic that I physically re-enacted aspects of our wedding annually, which could have been interpreted in one of two ways: either I was trying hard to convince myself of the life I had chosen, or it was that I treasured what I had so immensely and the ritual of repeating bits of it made me comfortable and happy. Then again, it might also just have been good, spontaneous and eccentric fun.

The new rituals we had started to institutionalise in our family provided us with the opportunity for love, bonding, reflection, and contemplation. The candles we burnt for people like gran to honour and remember the days they entered and left this world brought us healing and hope. For gran, we usually burnt rose scented candles, because she loved them—probably because they smelt a lot like 4711. As the flames of those candles danced and shimmered with the breeze, infusing their aroma around us, it reminded us that she was still near—watching and certainly also the force behind the gentle wind.

The wedding anniversary eccentricities reminded us of the joy of our union and pointed to the origins of our amazing family unit. The zip at the back of Carrie's wedding dress pulled up less and less high each year. My forehead was growing rapidly in length, but strangely my suit seemed to hang looser on my troubled frame. Times had changed, our bodies were changing, and the girls were morphing into miniature adults. Nothing was ever meant to stay the same. Time was the agent of change. 'Forsaking all others, until death us do part', that's what I had promised Carrie some seven years ago—but strictly speaking, I hadn't followed through. My truth was changing, my lies were shining brightly, and my conscience was burning.

ONE OF THE other rituals I developed had proven to be a strong and powerful one. It was a sensible one and one that allowed the four of us to bond and thrive. The mechanics for this ritual were simple and straightforward. This ritual involved me meticulously cleaning and sorting my head on a daily basis. I had to keep it fine-tuned and focused and distracted from temptation. For nine years I followed this powerful ritual. It ensured the protection of my marriage, the nurturing of my children, and the temporary restoration of my sanity. But it was not sustainable. I kept it going for nine solid years after the vicar left and returned to his manse. My respectful duty to the ritual of burying my gayness brought with it nine years of relative sanity, until the pressure valve finally burst.

During those nine years—between June 2003 and July 2012—I still periodically fought my secret, but somehow it was more easily tamed. I didn't give the secret much credence, because I had more important rituals to perform. I needed to build relationships with my daughters and with Carrie and I needed the secret to take a back seat. As much as I loved Carrie—and I was certain I did—there was a space between us. It was rooted in the physical, or rather the lack thereof, and this I own fully. The negative impact of our lack of intimacy infected our spiritual and emotional connections too because Carrie would shut down as a means to protect herself. It was confusing to all of us. Our arguments became about irrelevant and unimportant things. The stress of the absence of physical intimacy, lust, and desire were taking its toll on us.

My most significant rituals during these nine years were around the kinds of routines I built with Jane and Kate. They became and remain my world. Two baby girls who loved their mum and their dad and on whom Carrie and I shared a mutual doting. I had to work extra hard with Kate because for the first three or four years of my ritualistic and clean nine years, she was a mummy's girl—focussed solely on Carrie, with very little time for her dad. I attributed this gap between us to two events: the first was the fact that we had not bonded at all on the day of her birth, and secondly it stemmed from me going briefly AWOL with the vicar and then again into my head, shortly after she was born.

For Jane and Kate, I have had the privilege of, amongst other things, being able to be there to show them how to dress in the mornings, to drive them to school, to teach them to bathe and to wash their hair, and to read story after story after story every night.

"Please read us one more," they would always plead. Usually, we would climb into one of their beds, me in the middle and their heads huddled into the hollows of my shoulders, their hair tickling my neck and cheeks. My long-outstretched arms, which held the book from either side above our faces would curl up around them like an octopus's tentacles and this would pull them in snugly toward me. Their warmth and proximity were the perfect ingredients for ever-lasting bonding. I would read with expression and annunciation, with pause and with dramatic effect, and they would squeal with delight—sometimes humorously and sometimes with suspense. Kate would choose the same books over and over, and Jane would get annoyed with her for the repetition. Even I had come to dislike *Duncan's Shorts* and *Not Like This, Like That*, but not Kate—she wanted them more and more. These were Kate's rituals. I was happy to read Dr Seuss over and over again and I taught them to appreciate Julia Donaldson's rhyming books, especially *The Gruffalo*—which was one of the many favourites. Often, I would read until one, or both of them fell asleep, and then I would carry one, or both of them back to their beds. I always liked to carry them in my arms, and I did so until they got too big for the weak joints in my lower back.

I would tuck them in, and I always kissed them in a criss-cross kite pattern: first on their lips, then on each of their cheeks and finally on their foreheads. There is something magical about a forehead kiss. I still kiss them on their foreheads whenever I have the opportunity. Seated behind the forehead and lodged somewhere centrally between the two brows is the sixth chakra—an energy point and intuition centre, the place where we continuously evolve and balance ourselves. For me, when I kiss them on their foreheads, I am kissing their souls and creating a universal and eternal connection. I am telling them I love the core of who they are and of who they might evolve to be. These are two souls I want to know and love forever. Two souls I need to protect from the guilt and the shame of my secret.

CHAPTER TWENTY-FIVE

ISLAND ISOLATION

27 January 2009

WHEN YOU ARE scared, you are always on the run. For much of my life, I had been on the run—continuously running away from myself, never actually getting anywhere. 10 years into our marriage and some 6 years after the vicar, I made the decision to run some more. This time, I ran with what I loved, what I valued, and what I treasured most in the world. I didn't want to ever lose Carrie, Jane, or Kate.

I had seen an advert in the Times Educational Supplement. It was posted by the government of the British Overseas Territory of Montserrat in the Caribbean and they were seeking to recruit an education adviser. I perused the job specifications and while it seemed to be a bit of a stretch, it seemed like a good career growth opportunity and an exciting adventure. A small volcanic island of 11 miles long and 7 miles wide—with a population of 5000 odd—was a stretch...but I was intrigued.

"Take a look at this," I said, pushing the newspaper advert under

Carrie's nose and on top of her laptop. "It's a job I've found on the island of Montserrat," I noted. She pushed her laptop back slightly and seemed annoyed as she glanced over at the advert.

"Where exactly is Montserrat?" she asked with some flippancy in her voice. I grabbed an old atlas from the bookshelf on the opposite end of the room. It was a little dusty and when I opened it up it smelt of age and damp. It reminded me of the smell of the vicar's office where the damp always made the room colder than it was outside. I used the world map on the first double page spread to point out where Montserrat was to Carrie.

"There it is," I pointed with some excitement in my voice.

"Not interested," Carrie replied, pulling her face to show her disapproval, and she pushed the atlas and the newspaper away from her.

"Seriously," I tried to convince her, "it seems like a great adventure, and we could save some good money." She disregarded me and carried on punching the keys on her keyboard. This was Carrie's way of preserving what we had created behind the picket fence, this was her way of keeping stability in a life, in a marriage where she didn't always know what was happening inside my head.

We agreed that I would apply for the job and see how the process unfolded. I think Carrie was secretly hoping that it wouldn't amount to much. Soon after submitting my application, I was called to an interview in London and three weeks after that, I received a call offering me the position. It was a two-year contract commencing the following January. With just over two months to go, we packed some personal goods and freighted them across to the island. We gave the necessary notices at our jobs and we found suitable tenants for our house—the house that we were so enjoying. Having strangers live in our little paradise was a bitter pill for Carrie to swallow.

WE ARRIVED IN Montserrat to sunny weather and even warmer hospitality. On that early Saturday morning in February, the world seemed crystal clear and navigable. The Director of Education met us at the airport and my new line manager escorted us up to our rented home. The island was beautiful and full of contrasts.

Once Jane and Kate were tucked into bed on our first night on the island, I walked outside to get familiar with the night-time in our new habitat. Crickets were screaming in the distance, but apart from them, the night was still. The Milky Way was splattered across the sky like a fragmented neon tube, and it looked like something that Vincent van Gogh might have painted with a luminous paint and frayed paintbrushes.

'What have you done?' I asked myself; the magnitude of arriving in the middle of isolated nowhere had just clobbered me. I had uprooted my three number ones and dragged them somewhere unfamiliar and unknown.

"What are you doing?" Those could have been my words, but instead they were Carrie's. She had made her way outside and walked up beside me and snuggled into me under that electric sky. "It's so beautiful," she said with sincerity as she gazed upwards.

"It is," I agreed, "more beautiful than I was expecting...a pity that the house is a bit shitty."

"I guess this setting makes up for it," Carrie retorted positively.

"It does," I replied feeling relieved that Carrie was doing her best to embrace the adventure.

Jane and Kate settled into school easily, Jane more swiftly than Kate. Carrie seemed happy and she began volunteering at their school, helping out with substitute teaching and also making the redesign of the school library her own project. I settled into work comfortably and was enjoying my new job: the people, the responsibilities, and the setting. Even our tiny house, peering down into the ocean, was also starting to feel like a space we could call our own. The isolation compelled a reliance between us, and the absence of distractions meant that we bonded and leaned on one another more so than before. We went on family walks most mornings and every Sunday afternoon. Jane, Kate, and I used to head out early on Saturday mornings while Carrie had her weekly sleep in. We would climb through fences, walk through forests and explore graveyards. We always finished at the small village shop where Jane and Kate had their eight thirty a.m. Saturday chocolate bar—it broke all of the sugar rules that were enforced during the week. We went camping, we climbed cliffs and we swam in the sea. These were some of the new rituals that we unwittingly established. These were rituals that made us stronger and that bound us together. We grew as a family, we counted our blessings, we connected more. We made boundless love—those chalices in our chests were overflowing.

MY 40TH BIRTHDAY came just two months after we arrived on Montserrat. We had made a small group of friends that we kept at a comfortable distance—some were expats and some were locals. On the Thursday before the birthday weekend, we had a scare in the Sterling household. Carrie's period was late, uncomfortably late, and we thought that number three might be in the making.

"Get it out," I yelled at Carrie. It was unfair and unkind, but the words were gone before I could recall them. Abortion would never have been an option for her anyway, but I wasn't interested in starting parenthood from scratch again.

"I'll buy a pregnancy test tomorrow," Carrie placated, offering a practical next step.

"Great idea," I replied, trying to undo my harsh words. We spoke about it for a while and Carrie was understandably emotional. The distance from home was no doubt a contributing factor. The next morning while I was at work, Carrie headed into town and bought the pregnancy test. First thing the following morning, as instructed on the packaging, she did the test. We waited together with bated breath. Only one blue line meant that the test was negative. I was elated, and I guess Carrie was as relieved even though I knew she would have been happy to find more love for baby number three. As pleased as I was about the result, I was still concerned because I had noticed that the test, like most things on the island, was way past its expiry date.

Later that day, I popped into the local supermarket during my lunch break. The friendly cashier, who I knew by face, but not by name, waved and smiled excitedly at me as I walked into the shop. I picked up some hooks that we needed for a shelf in the kitchen, and I also grabbed some paracetamol tablets which I realised were on the shelf above the home pregnancy test. I also noticed that the paracetamol tablets had expired some 13 months earlier. As I placed my two items down at the till, the lady with the welcoming smile, and with no name was eager to chat.

"Fancy seeing you in here today," she commented. "I served your wife yesterday."

"Now there's a coincidence," I replied with a smile, making the best effort I could at small talk given the new realisation that most of the island might already know that Mrs Sterling had taken a home pregnancy test.

When I got home that evening, Carrie was in a great mood.

"I have some good news for you," she exclaimed. Then she paused a while. The suspense was awful. "Granny came to visit today," she announced.

"Thank you, Jesus," I exclaimed, as I blasphemously expressed gratitude to that dude from my past. Saturday came and so did my party. Carrie and I were shattered from the stress of the week and it all felt like a bit of a blur. So much of my life has been a blur.

ACCLIMATISING TO LIFE on Montserrat was both exhilarating and daunting. Whilst we had come to a place where we could be free and where we could think; where we could be together and where we could be alone—the island could not offer anonymity.

Islands are fascinating places, their geographic separation from a mainland makes them complete and self-sustaining—and that's what had happened to the Sterling family, we had become complete and self-sustaining. On the other hand, islands are also heavily reliant on the outside world—but they have the safety of the water that separates them and allows them to control the level of support and interference from the outside. While on Montserrat, we could reach out across the seas for love and support, but always on our terms—because we could control the tempo and the dosage. The same applied to the boxes that contained the serpents in my head; the isolation and the distance helped me keep them closed and in place. This was partly because of the masses of water that physically blocked access to my temptations and desires, but it was also driven by the lack of anonymity that exists on small islands. Living on Montserrat was like living in a goldfish bowl, everybody knew your business. Islands are not places where you indulge your secrets. People and secrets become common property on islands.

I had spent more than 20 years of my life taming my flamboyance, hiding safely behind the guise of eccentricity. In the confined community of Montserrat, I felt the need to restrain myself even more—the next thing to tame was my eccentricity. I only realised that I was doing this once the process was fully in action, and it was toward the end of our first year on the island that I became aware of myself morphing into somebody who was more serious than I had ever been before. I had become somebody who didn't want to stand out in the goldfish bowl. The pressure of public life, being an outsider and the burden of my secret were stifling me. It shouldn't have been difficult or demanding—but it was. I had always been the ultimate great pretender, so tempering my behaviour and my actions should have been easy—second nature, but somehow, they weren't. I felt suffocated and I became aware of my emotions gripping my physical body. My larynx was under attack and I began to stutter badly. The muscles in my back were like sheets of twisted metal and my knotted stomach lost its appetite.

"Are you feeling all right?" Carrie asked as we were leaving for a Guy Fawkes function that Jane and Kate were so excited about going to.

"I'm good," I answered unconvincingly.

"You've been out of sorts lately," she noted.

"I'm really fine," I lied. "Work has just been crazy, I think we need our holiday—four weeks away from here is going to be a welcome break for all of us. I can't wait to be anonymous for a while."

"Tell me about it," she said with a sarcastic tone. Carrie had adapted well to life on Montserrat, she didn't complain much about the day-to-day—the good or the bad. She was loving the lifestyle and enjoying the love we shared. She was resilient in many ways—and very grounding for me.

We arrived at the sports field where the Guy Fawkes event was being held. There were lots of cars and lots of people. We made our way inside and we met up with Anne and Derek John. They had befriended us shortly after we had arrived on the island. Anne had been covering a maternity placement in my office for the first month that we were on the island. They were lovely people; warm, welcoming, and always available. Anne was always kind to Carrie and included her in many local events. Anne was slightly rotund and Derek was as skinny as a rake. In our family, we affectionately called them *Laurel and Hardy*. It was screamingly obvious that Derek carried a secret not unlike mine, and it always felt like we had identified it in each other. I just never dared to speak about it or acknowledge it. Coming out in an isolated goldfish bowl is almost unthinkable. The pain and shame must have been hugely burdensome for him, and I was sure that it was the weight of his secret that made him look so emaciated. I had an out. When I returned to the UK, I would be a nameless face on a busy high street. Poor Derek had to face his Mr. Evanses and his Uncle Bobs in close proximity for the rest of his life. If he had had blunders, like mine with Mario and the vicar—these people would be there on every corner to constantly remind him of his misdemeanours—and his secret would only be as safe as the tightness of their lips.

After a few drinks and a game of good old-fashioned skittles in which Jane had beaten all of us, we headed outside for the fireworks, the judging of the effigies, and bonfires. The proceedings were slow and by midnight Jane and Kate were exhausted. Kate was whining and Jane was repeatedly asking to go home. It was disappointing that they would miss the main event, but we had no choice but to head on home. I picked up Jane and Carrie picked up Kate. We both carried them straddled across our hips, their legs dangling, and their heads tucked into the hollow of our necks. The car park was now exploding with people and cars. Carrie and I had to make our way through a crowd that was lining the sand road that led to the entrance of the field. As we came close, the crowd went silent and the 500 or so heads that were out there in the moonlit night, followed the four of us in perfect synchronisation. At least 500 faces, holding at least 1000 eyes, moved in a smooth rotation movement from left to right, or right left—depending what side of the road they were standing on. It was eerie and unsettling. As we reached the end of the crowd, I could feel the movement and hear the chatter resume behind us. I looked at Carrie and I smiled.

"One day, we'll look back on these as our Brad and Angelina years," I joked. Carrie laughed with me.

"I think you mean Brangelina," she corrected. I chuckled and we joined hands with Jane and Kate dangling on our outer hips. They had missed the entire event.

CHAPTER TWENTY-SIX

DAD'S DEPARTURE

24 October 2011

DAD LEFT US all too soon; it was something he had warned us about since we were children.

"I'm not interested in living to be old," he would say. This would worry and traumatise us—especially my sister, Holly, who had a strong and inexplicable bond with him. He was her hero and she was his treasure. The thought of him not being around was inconceivable. Although not always easy, he was the light of our lives and he was loved by all. So, midway through his sixty seventh year—and true to his word—he surrendered to his secret battle with cancer and his lights went out. We all suspected that he was ill as he had lost a lot of weight and he had been way more irritable than we had always known him to be. He never mentioned being ill, but it was obvious. We learned of his cancer diagnoses the day before his operation to remove a bowel tumour. Emergency surgery, the doctor had told him. He never gained consciousness again. Five days later he was gone. We had all stood vigil with him until the vital signs monitor to which he was wired flatlined and made an ominous and painful sound, one that I had only ever heard in the movies.

There are no words to describe the empty feeling of standing around a bed that has timed out the man who gave you life. I was flanked by mum and Holly—and I had to be as strong as I could for them. His body was still plugged with life supporting tubes that no longer gave him life. His face seemed relaxed now and the muscles in his drawn cheeks had ceased to clench. His eyes were closed, his receding and thin hair was slightly rumpled, and his brow was still sweaty from the pain of crossing over. It seemed he was smiling. Looking at dad was like looking at an older version of myself, right down to the fingers and toes. We were similar in too many ways and that is what made us clash.

IF HIS ILLNESS was his secret, I was one step ahead of him—I wasn't taking my secret to the grave. I was sure that dad had many secrets. His childhood had been troubled—the battle between his parents who despised each other resulted in him and his brother being fostered by their aunt and uncle. Under the recommendation of a doctor, they were sent to a Catholic boarding school in Zambia where the air was better for their asthma. I always wondered whether one of his secrets, and the source of his contempt and impatience with the Catholic church, may have been rooted in some kind of abuse, when he and his brother were young and vulnerable and far away from home. Things were different in the 1940s and 50s; children had no voice. Perplexingly, dad loved Zambia and he would always tell us that one day he 'wanted to go home.' It was fitting that he chose the date on which Zambia celebrated independence from the United Kingdom to take another kind of trip to a different home.

Like me, dad lived in his head a lot. We were similar and we collided often. He had secrets—but if we knew them, they wouldn't be secrets anymore. Whatever they were, they weighed him down. Since having uncaged mine, I've learnt that a secret without a box has no power. Without it you are lighter.

Some nine months after my dad had crossed over, I found myself back online looking and searching. I registered a profile on a dating website, and I was eager to talk to somebody in a similar position to me—somebody like the vicar. It was as though dad's death had led to a new birth for me. Just the right amount of gestation time passed after dad's death before the difficult birth that would incarnate the authentic son that he would never know. A few months after coming out to Carrie I was talking to Avery, who was back in Canada, on a Skype call.

"Do you think you've come out now, because your dad isn't here anymore?" as always Avery was frank and direct.

"I hadn't thought of that," I replied, and I truly hadn't.

"Timing seems uncanny," she continued. "Must be some connection between the two," Avery added. She had a point and she wasn't the first or the last person to observe this. At a college reunion, Dean posed a direct question to me.

"Why'd you wait for your dad to die before you told the world you were a fag?" His mischievousness wasn't always tactful and it wasn't ideal that he asked me the question whilst standing in a group at the bar counter. The gathering included amongst others, Michael Carlson—who, disappointingly, hadn't aged well at all. A little flustered, I replied calmly:

"The old bugger would have loved me anyway...so not really sure why?" I joked and then I felt the need to let some long-held anger go. "I guess I just didn't ever feel the need to disappoint him by telling him I was a FUCKING POOFTER." My enunciated words were directed squarely at Carlson.

"Must be tough," Carlson noted swiftly, his face glowing at being reminded that he had been my primary school bully. "I'm sorry," he continued with some degree of sincerity, "I'm sure it hasn't been easy for you." It was good to hear my bully utter the word 'sorry', but I was left baffled by exactly what he was sorry for. Sorry for being a cunt to me for most of my time at school? Sorry for the death of my dad? Or sorry for the pain of my journey? I knew I needed to let it go. Times and attitudes had changed, and Carlson had probably changed too.

DESPITE OUR DIFFERENCES in opinions and the many fights that my dad and I had over the years, we shared a massive bond—I just didn't like him much toward the end. I loved him, but I didn't like him. I longed for the dad I knew when I was a child. Perhaps the fact that I had only come out after he died does tell a bigger story of fear and shame. It wasn't something that I consciously thought about—I guess dad and I were fighting our own struggles and privately dealing with our own demons. I never wanted to disappoint him.

Dad was a liberal thinker, he was also kind and jovial, he loved to pick up strays on the way, and come to think of it he wasn't homophobic at all. He would certainly have thrown the odd gay-bashing comment, like most people in the 70s and 80s, but his actions spoke differently. At Chris and Kai's wedding I remembered him voicing his support for love—all love, not only straight love.

When I was a student, my parents got a new set of neighbours.

"Seen the new fags next door?" dad asked. The question made me jolt and I had wondered if he was checking me for a reaction.

"No, not yet," I replied, hoping that I had been cool and calm enough in my response. I had also hoped that I wouldn't meet them because they may more easily spot one of their own kind and expose me to my parents. Hiding in the shadows, I felt so uncomfortable around gay people—but only because they might know my story. As it happens, I did meet the new queens next door. They became mum and dad's good friends and they seemed like a nice couple. I was intrigued, but I kept my distance; it was all a little too close for comfort.

IN 2018, SEVEN years after my dad had died, the movie *Love, Simon* was released. The story follows the life of a young closeted high school boy whose path was so similar to mine: he found an anonymous lover online; he was forced to balance his friends, his family, and his secret; and he was weighed down, tired and afraid. Simon's outing was more traumatic than mine in that he lost control of it to a two-faced friend who publicly outed him on social media. His father struggled to accept this news at first, but then, soon after, embraced him—secret and all. I felt envious at not having been able to go through that process with my dad. I felt robbed of some sort of rite of passage. In the movie, Simon's psychologist mum tells him:

I knew you had a secret...when you were little, you were so care-free. But these last few years, more and more, it's almost like I can feel you holding your breath. I wanted to ask you about it, but I didn't want to pry. Maybe I made a mistake.

These words reverberated in me and I broke down while watching the movie. I was surprised at how they unleashed my tears. I realised that only then—seven years after my dad had died and six years after officially coming out—that I also needed to breathe. I had held my breath for too long...fearful and guilty, morphing slowly toward my truth.

There is no doubt that dad would have accepted the honest and authentic me. He may have, like Simon's dad, struggled at first and then come around, but he may also have embraced it from the beginning. Whichever way it might have panned out, I have no doubt that he would have loved and accepted me. His shaky childhood had inspired him to make us a strong and unshakeable unit.

It has taken some time for me to accept myself. I know I am different and, scars and all, I am different for the better. I feel robbed that dad never got to meet the honest and true version of me, but I only have myself to blame for that. Was my decision to come out subconsciously initiated by his passing? Possibly—but whatever the reason, the time had come. 'Hey, my son-son,' he might have said, 'just breathe.'

CHAPTER TWENTY-SEVEN

COMPARTMENTS IN MY HEAD

28 July 2012

OUR SUMMER HOLIDAY to the Amalfi Coast in Italy and then to Dubrovnik in Croatia was a welcomed escape. The Croatian leg of the holiday was spent with our good friends, the Goldbergs. Spending time with the Goldbergs was always fun. They are authentic and accepting people. Being with and around them is always entertaining and just generally a happy and safe place. Vicky and Josh had been my friends since long before I met Carrie. I kind of knew that they knew of my secret, but like many, they respected the fact that it was something I needed to manage in my own time. Vicky, being as creative as she was, always gave me the odd opportunity to speak my truth—but I was never ready or brave enough to say it. The real complication was that the secret was something that I didn't particularly want to own or even acknowledge.

I TYPICALLY DIDN'T enjoy holidays. I know it sounds ridiculous—and almost ungrateful—as most people live the year out waiting for their annual holiday. For me, those times of rest, where I had time to think, were daunting and terrifying. Busy work schedules and the day-to-day distractions of children and homework and shopping and administration kept my mind preoccupied and focused away from dealing with the big issue in my life. These distractions were welcomed, because on the surface I was happy. I had two beautiful daughters, a doting and loyal wife, a house that I loved, an extended family who loved me and a career in which I was steadily growing and developing. But despite this, there were some serious cracks below the surface.

I had mastered the art of compartmentalising things and through some divinely inspired strength, I had sealed and wrapped my sexuality into a box and packed it tightly—for the most part—somewhere at the back of my head since I was a teenager. The box had been rattled from time-to-time. Sometimes unexpectedly by such things as the sighting of a handsome man while I was out and about, or by a movie or TV show such as Milk or Brokeback Mountain where the protagonists were good-looking gay men. It was always awkward being faced with these kinds of situations, especially when I had company. I would be aware of my eyes darting around, trying to not be conspicuous, doing all I could not to expose my homosexual thoughts and desires. Holidays were the time during which that tightly wrapped box took the biggest beating. Too much time to think and being exposed to anonymous people, who were also on holiday, were the perfect mix for my neatly packed boxes to become unsettled.

AFTER WE RETURNED from the holiday in Italy and Croatia something had happened inside my head and I still don't know what it was. It was certainly that I had too much time to think, but it may also have been that the liberating time with the Goldbergs in an anonymous setting had unfettered something inside me. The farce of not being my authentic self was eating at my core.

A few days after returning from the holiday, I found myself on the Internet—desperately seeking and looking for answers. I googled myself into oblivion—I found gay dad blogs and podcasts, academic articles and some support groups. However, no matter how much I searched or read, I couldn't find the answers that I needed to help me understand myself and the reality I had created. My searching led me to numerous dating websites—and whilst I had no urge to physically date anybody, I felt the universe was leading me to a place where I may be able to speak to another human being who might also be living and experiencing the pain of my compartmentalised reality. I was certain that I didn't want a repeat of what happened with the vicar some nine years earlier.

I nervously created a profile: false name, false email address and no profile picture. 'Dylan Johnson' was to be very cautious and strictly anonymous as he navigated his way through this unfamiliar territory. My *nom de plume* in this secret world gave me some strength and excitement—but while I was ashamed of him, I needed him to find some serious answers and gain some vital information for me. I was determined that I was not out for dating, nor was I searching for a life partner. I was simply looking for people in a similar position to me. I wanted to talk, to listen, to understand. I needed answers. Naively, I had no idea of the emotional enormity of what opening this can of worms would do to my world.

Once the profile was set up, I began my search...it felt odd describing an 'ideal match' but I guessed that doing that was the only way to be guided to the person I wanted to talk to. So, I began: must be married, must be between 30 and 60, must have children. Then I was asked to describe what I was looking for in respect of a partner: eye colour, hair colour, home language, smoker or non-smoker, income range...I didn't care about these. I just wanted to make contact with a gay and married dad who loved and respected his wife, his children and his family unit.

The initial search was frightening. I discovered that there was an underworld of sex and betrayal that existed right at my fingertips. It was all a little foreign for my Catholicized brain. Men who were sad or lonely or horny or dispirited—or a combination of any of these, were desperately trying to hook-up with somebody...anybody. The faceless world of underground dating was alive and not so savoury. It wasn't what I was after. I weeded through the many profiles and the countless offers for easy and quick sex in cars, parks, public toilets and hotel rooms. I was shocked at the secret underground world that I discovered.

In my daily scrolling, I kept being drawn to one profile in particular: Scorpion_D. This person ticked all the boxes: 41 years of age and married with children. Apparently with brown hair and brown eyes. There was something different about this profile and the veiled person inside it. The messages were gentle and inquiring with a lot of substance. Over the coming weeks, the highlight of my day was to log on to the site during the late afternoon or early evening and to read the next exchange with this mystery man. It was so good to hear that my pain and confusion did not just belong to me. Scorpion_D shared my fears and my pain and my guilt. He, like me, didn't want to cause any hurt or emotional trauma to those he loved the most in the world—his wife and his children.

Soon after, we moved the conversations over to email. No photos, no phone numbers—only email addresses for people who did not actually exist. Dylan Johnson told my story and my fears and he became the virtual friend of Dan B—aka Scorpion_D. Dylan and Dan shared epistles of their lives and their journeys. The process was cathartic and healing, but while it fed my need for answers, it was awakening something in me—yet I was not aware of it at the time.

Dan B was keen to meet for a coffee, but Dylan was terrified. A coffee meet was deferred to a later time. The exchanges continued and it became clear to me that the person behind the façade of Dan B was a real and genuine person. A person who was genuinely grappling with the pain and confusion of being a gay person, living a straight life. I came to understand that he was a person who shared similar family values and who saw the world a lot like I did. There was comfort in knowing that I was not alone and that—not too far away—there was another person, although without a face and real identity, who was walking my path. After two and half months of extended chatting, I agreed to a meet. It just felt like a natural progression.

So, after dinner on an evening early in October, I sent off an email suggesting a coffee meet at around 4:00 p.m. on the Monday or the Tuesday of the following week. I scanned my personal emails and closed my laptop.

"Want some coffee or tea?" It was Carrie calling from the kitchen.

"Coffee please," I replied. I felt sick. Agreeing to a coffee meet with somebody else felt like an act of betrayal. Although my intentions were innocent, there was a discomfort in my heart and in my stomach. I was planning something clandestinely and it went against everything I had been taught.

"Don't forget we have Jane's parents evening next Tuesday," Carrie reminded as she put the coffee down next to me. I looked at her hand within centimetres of my computer and felt uncomfortable at her proximity to my secret liaisons. Liaisons! That was an awkward word—but it seemed to be uncomfortably relevant.

"Next Tuesday?" I questioned.

"Yes, remember we spoke about it on the weekend," she replied. To be honest I hadn't remembered—but I was so often absent and preoccupied with my own thoughts. Physically there, but not present.

"Let me put it into my diary, before I forget again," I noted. "I'll make sure I'm back from work on time. What time do we need to be there?" I asked.

"Our slot is at four fifty" she replied. "Let's not be late, you know Mrs Smith can be a little tricky."

Suddenly I had two pangs of guilt to deal with—one: I had organized a secret coffee meet; and two: I had given that coffee meet preference over my daughter's parents evening.

"Are you all right," Carrie asked. I felt myself fluster as I sipped my coffee.

"I'm okay, just stressed at work at the moment," I replied. If only she knew, if only the world knew. There was some comfort in the fact that Dan B knew.

"It'll calm down, it always does," she said with a comforting smile on her face.

"I hope so," I retorted.

"It will," she called as she walked down the steps toward the bedrooms. I felt awful. I opened my laptop, logged into Dylan's email and wrote to Dan B:

> Hi
>
> Can now only do next Monday at around 4pm. Could that work for you?
>
> Cheers
> David

I had clicked send, before I realised I had blown my cover. I signed the message David—and not Dylan. Maybe this was a good thing, maybe not—but the time for lies and deceit felt like it was certainly over. I hastily composed another message:

Hi

My real name is David.

Cheers

David

CHAPTER TWENTY-EIGHT

THE COFFEE MEET

8 October 2012

DAN B REPLIED to my email and confirmed that he was available for the coffee meet that had been long in the making. As we were still anonymous and pseudonymized, our communications were strictly via unofficial email. As the email addresses were not our standard ones, exchanges were always a little slower and slightly more inconvenient. We had to constantly log in and out of our fake accounts to cover our tracks. After some to-ing and fro-ing, we agreed to meet at a small restaurant, slightly off the beaten track, that was somewhat central for both of us. With guilt and paranoia in the mix, it was clear we were both focused on managing the process tightly. Revealing our identities to each other was one thing, but what if we were spotted by somebody we knew? How would we explain that?

I arrived at *The Coffee Bean* at least an hour before we had planned to meet. I had an urgent work issue that I needed to attend to. I found a table that I thought was suitable and positioned myself for an uninterrupted view of the entrance. I took out my laptop, logged on to the wifi and got busy with the pressing issue. I became distracted with work and when I checked the clock at the top of my screen it was 16h06. 'Strange', I thought, 'no sign of Dan B'. I wondered if I might have been stood up. Could he have chickened out? I quickly logged into Dylan's email and discovered that Dan B had sent an email to me at 15h51 to let me know his last meeting had run over and that he was on his way. There was a second email sent at 16h02 to let me know that his ETA was 16h29. I replied to his message:

'Cool. I am sitting against the back wall working on my pc. I'm wearing a blue shirt and I have brown hair.'

I had made myself a sitting duck. I had another 20 minutes to sort out the urgent work issue. I returned to the Excel spreadsheet I was trying to decipher. I was both trepidatious and excited about this meet, but I was distracted by this unexpected work issue that hadn't been in my plan.

The next 20 minutes seemed to fly by and as I was nearing completion, I became aware of somebody approaching me from a distance. I looked up and we made eye contact. The person I assumed to be Dan B was still a good five metres away from me. I smiled and he responded by subtly, and slightly nervously, lifting his hand in a wave-like motion.

"David?" he asked, extending his arm for a handshake.

"Dan?" I retorted, offering my hand in return. His handshake was gentle—but not weak. It was as comforting as the many exchanges we had shared on email.

"At long last, a face to the mystery person," I joked.

"Ditto," he answered. It all felt so easy and natural. I felt like I already knew him, and in many ways, I guess I already did.

I knew his name was Dan. I may have worked his surname out from the clues that he had unwittingly given me in our various exchanges...if I was right it didn't start with a B. My Internet and social media stalking seemed to have paid dividends. I was certain that he was a financier, and I was pretty sure that I knew the name of the bank where he was employed. I had been nervous to follow this up with him, because my sister also worked at that bank. I knew that he had three children and it seemed his wife's name was Judy. I knew he was gay, that he pretended to be straight and I was feeling pretty certain that he was a decent guy. It was nice to have him sitting in front of me and to see for myself that he was a normal person—no weird clothing, no outlandish body piercings, and only one head.

The waiter disturbed our introductions and we ordered two cappuccinos.

"So," I asked, "tell me about the mystery Dan B." Dan smiled.

"He's as mysterious as Dylan...sorry David Johnson," Dan jibed. We both laughed.

"So, what is your real name?" he asked.

"It's David," I answered almost instantly.

"And your surname?" he asked, tilting his head trying to look a little coy.

"Sorry, can't tell you yet—it's too early for that." I felt uncomfortable saying it, but I was scared, and the truth was as much as my gut told me I could trust this man, I just wasn't ready to share personal information. He looked confused by my response. Wanting to immediately turn the attention away from me, I asked him a question.

"So, is your name really Dan—and does your surname start with a B?" He smiled, and he did have a lovely smile. Comforting and easy like the words in his emails.

"My name is Dan," he answered, "but my surname doesn't start with B." He smiled again. My obsessive research skills had taught me a lot about mystery Dan. His confirming that his surname did not start with a B told me two things: one, I was a pretty good researcher; and two, this man wasn't going to spin webs and lies around the friendship we had built over email. From my school days, I had a limited understanding of the Dutch language. If I had indeed worked his surname out correctly, I knew what it translated to in Dutch. I took a deep breath, because I knew this was a bold question for so early on.

"Is your surname Dutch...'*from the dike*?'," I asked. He seemed surprised, but was mostly calm and unphased.

"Impressive, yes, it is," he replied, scrunching his eyes. "You need to tell me how you did that." I smiled. It was time for me to get to know and understand Dan van Dijk, his world and his journey a little better.

The ice had been broken; it all felt quite natural and the conversation flowed easily. Sitting in the afternoon twilight, Dan's face was slightly silhouetted. He had dark hair which was short cut and brushed to the left.

There was some salt and pepper above each of his ears and his hair was receding ever so slightly. His big brown eyes were crowned by impressively thick eyebrows and his long eyelashes danced with every blink in the still of this momentous afternoon. The crow's feet that spread gently from the corners of his eyes told me that he had interesting stories to tell. His crimson lips, soft and gentle and his thin upper lip seemed to be the captor of his big and mighty secret. His face was gentle, and well proportioned—he was soft and strapping all at the same time. I savoured the enjoyment of being in his company. He was music to my eyes. Like the grown-up version of Chris—from Chris and Kai's wedding—prince-like, with less hair and more years.

'What are you doing?' I checked myself, 'you're not here for that!' But it felt like it may already be too late.

As we sipped our coffee, we reflected on some of the exchanges we had had to date and shared some of our guilt and confusion.

"You do know of the Kinsey scale, don't you?" Dan asked casually.

"Sort of," I responded vaguely, "can you refresh my memory please?" The truth was that I had never heard of it before. I had done work for the consulting company McKinsey and Company, but I wasn't sure what the Kinsey Scale was. Dan explained that it was a scale that placed people on a continuum somewhere between heterosexuality and homosexuality. A score of zero meant you were exclusively heterosexual, while a score of six meant you were full on homosexual. So, nothing to do with McKinsey and Company at all!

"It's easy," he explained. "Just go online and you can do the test for free."

"So, where would you put yourself on the scale?" Dan asked.

"I'm guessing I'm somewhere in the middle," I answered feeling a little unsure, "maybe about a three." Dan smiled. "Maybe, I'm bisexual," I offered, feeling uncomfortable.

"That's what many people like us say," he said. "We try to convince ourselves that there must be a logical reason for us being in the situations we find ourselves...married, supposedly attracted to our wives...and also secretly attracted to men."

"So, are you saying I'm probably just full on gay?" I asked. It was clear that Dan had done some extended reading and research on this topic.

"That's only for you to say," he answered. "Let me give you a scenario," he proceeded. "I'm here and Charlize Theron is here too—who do you want to get naked with?" I was taken aback by his bold question. Maybe he should have used Tom Cruise as a substitute for him in his scenario—but it emerged he was making a point. I thought for a minute and answered.

"Probably you," I offered.

"Point made," he noted with a cheeky smile. "I'm no oil painting but you chose me—you didn't choose Charlize, who is beautiful and rich and famous, with a perfect body—and who is lusted by men the world over because you are more attracted to the male physique and to male energy...simply put, you don't like boobs and vagina! You've convinced yourself that you do."

"Wow!" I exclaimed, "no beating about the bush then—I must be 100% gay!"

"Exactly," he stated. We both laughed.

The time flew by and before we knew it, it was heading for 6:00 p.m. We needed to leave. We both had a bit of a way to travel and we didn't want to raise any alarm bells on the home front. Well intentioned or not—it felt clandestine. Ridiculous as we had nothing to hide...or did we? I had enjoyed that meeting way more than I should have.

As I drove out of the parking lot, I pondered that it was October the 8th and if my memory served me correctly, this was the day that the Great Chicago Fire of 1871 had started. It is believed that Mrs O'Leary's cow had knocked over a lantern that had set the city on fire. I felt like that infamous cow—I feared I may have unwittingly started a fire that might burn out of control. I needed to get home to do the Kinsey test.

CHAPTER TWENTY-NINE

THE CAR PARK

4 November 2012

THE CHEMISTRY AND infatuation between Dan and I was all-consuming. I had a bounce in my step and the world seemed sharper and tantalisingly clearer. This was meant to be a friendship but it was morphing into something wonderfully and wrongfully wilder. The thrill of the chase and of being chased was exhilarating. Something was different...the daily WhatsApp exchanges between us were exciting and mildly flirtatious. There was no better sound than the 'ting' of my phone, and it all felt too good to be true. I found myself unwittingly in an emotional relationship with a man. I did feel sporadic pangs of guilt, especially on the days that Dan and I met, but the boxes in my head were now spread out like laundry at a jumble sale and I didn't want to fold or pack anything away for now.

Dan and I met for a second time, and a third, and then I lost count. I was demanding, I wanted and needed to see him every day. I needed my daily dose of my addictive new energy booster.

"I can't meet you every day," he told me as we sat down for another of our many clandestine coffees. "My work diary is crazy at the moment." I was too high on whatever I was feeling to consider his preposterous pulling back.

"I need to see you," I told him. "Maybe the urgency will subside in a few weeks," I suggested—but I hoped that it wouldn't. He scrunched his forehead and shook his head. He was enjoying it as much as I was, but his job didn't offer the same flexibility that mine did.

SUNDAY, NOVEMBER 4 was Dan's birthday—his 41st. Judy had arranged an intimate dinner for him on the Saturday evening before with a few of their closest friends. I had obviously not been invited, because I didn't actually exist in the van Dijk reality. During the festivities, Dan kept me as close as he could. He guardedly sent me some snapshots via WhatsApp—just as I had done for him whilst at my cousin's wedding two weeks earlier. I struggled not being with him to celebrate his birthday. I didn't like being the excluded outsider: positioned centrally to his thoughts—I had hoped—but physically far away. Later that evening, I was the first to utter the forbidden words. I had pushed send too quickly. 'I love you', the words could not be retracted. I knew they were premature, and that Dan may not actually believe them yet—but it was too late. They couldn't be recalled—but I didn't want to recall them. I believed them, wholly.

I was hardly awake on Sunday morning, when I sent Dan a birthday message. 'Happy birthday! I wish I could be with you', I wrote, 'I love you'. The forbidden words now twice. We exchanged a few messages and agreed to try to meet briefly later in the afternoon. Carrie was on the sofa opposite me and as much as I wanted this new distraction, I didn't want to hurt her.

"What time are you picking up your cousin?" she asked. My cousin Brian, his wife, Anna and their two children were visiting from the US for a week and because of this we were having the family over for lunch.

"I should probably get to Aunty Clare's place by around eleven thirty, to be back in time for an early lunch," I suggested to Carrie.

"Sounds good," she replied, giving me a peck on the cheek. Carrie had perfectly rearranged the yellow tulips that I had bought for her into a clear tubular vase which she placed at the centre of the dining table—extended and ready to seat the extra guests.

"They look good," I told her.

"Thank you, my darling," she responded, "I do love them." I glanced back at the tulips, glowing yellow like sunshine and joy, but also of coward-ice and deceit.

I set off to pick up the visiting cousin-crew for lunch. There were too many of them for Aunty Clare's small Uno. Aunty Clare and Uncle Hamish would drive across with their two grandchildren and I would ferry Brian and Anna to and from the luncheon in my car. Heading down the motor-way, I felt pangs of guilt. I knew that I was playing with fire and I didn't seem to care that I might get burnt. It was as though I was using Carrie's heart as collateral for my emotional adultery and if it got damaged, I would be wholly culpable. I knew I should stop, but I couldn't. Selfishly, I didn't want to. The flowers that I had bought her were a physical endorsement of our love and all that we had created: Jane who turned eleven just five days before Dan, and Kate who had turned nine at the end of May. These three beautiful women, our amazing home and the love we shared in it were my world and I didn't want to lose any of it—but I also wanted Dan. I wanted it all, but in reality I couldn't have it. I was playing baton relay again.

THE FAMILY GATHERING would have been fine had it not been for Uncle Hamish getting expectedly plastered. He managed to offend most of us with some outlandish racist slurs...something about the Nigerian football team. Ashamedly, we all blanked him out and let him get away with it. It was too exhausting arguing with a drunk—but Aunty Clare wasn't going to let him get away with it.

"You're a total disgrace to the family," stoic Aunty Clare reprimanded him publicly. It was all unnecessary and particularly damaging since one of his adopted grandchildren was of mixed race. Fortunately, the visiting chil-dren were playing with Jane and Kate upstairs at the time of the incident. After lunch, Uncle Hamish staggered back to the Uno and passed out on the back seat before they turned out of the street. Aunty Clare was not im-pressed. I shuttled everybody—including the children, who weren't allowed near their grandfather for now, back to Aunty Clare's place. On my way home I made a planned and secretive detour.

DAN AND I met at *The Plough* where I had impulsively met Mario on that shameful night nearly 19 years earlier. A lot had happened since. It wouldn't have been my first choice of venue, but Dan had suggested it as it was convenient for both of us. We met in the car park and we hugged awkwardly...trying to be a tad manly but aching for a little more body heat than would be considered usual.

"Happy birthday, handsome," I announced.

"Thanks" he answered, blushing ever so slightly; I was already learning that he hated the limelight. I was discreetly carrying a small gift for him. It felt sickly evocative of the night that I had carried Carrie's engagement ring onto the beach. I hated the connection that I had made. Dan and I entered the pub and found a table which was uneasily close to where Mario had convinced me to move our conversation to the sleazy B&B around the corner. I sat down and Dan walked over to the bar where he ordered two glasses of Merlot.

"Aren't I supposed to be treating you on your birthday?" I asked, as he placed the glasses on the table in front of me.

"You can get the next one," he responded with a smile, knowing full well that there wouldn't be a next one.

He opened his gift, which he seemed to really like—but if he didn't, he put on a good show. I had bought him a pair of brushed silver cufflinks on which his initials were engraved in a gothic style font.

"I have this insatiable urge to kiss you," I told him.

"What right here?" he asked with a sardonic smile. We both laughed.

"Well," I suggested playfully, "if you're too embarrassed to out yourself here, then let's go somewhere else."

"Are you serious?" he looked unsure.

"I sure am," I answered immediately. I stood up and put on my coat, gesturing for him to do the same. "Let's get out of here," I ordered as if in a kind of role-play as we made our way to his car.

We drove around for a while, looking for a quiet and secluded place to have our first taste of each other. The city was bustling for a Sunday evening, and it was difficult to find somewhere that was hidden from the public eye. After some time, Dan turned into the Writtle car park on the East side of the city and we found a relatively isolated spot. It was late afternoon and the light was dropping. This worked in our favour. The engine continued to idle and Rihanna's 'We Found Love', was serendipitously playing on *Heart Essex*. I leaned over across the centre console and met him somewhere on the driver's side. The kiss was slow and gentle and full of promise. I didn't want it to be over. I could have sworn he tasted like that delicious Abercrombie and Fitch eau de toilet he liked to wear. We leaned away slightly, and consumed each other with our eyes, then we kissed again and again.

Finally! It felt authentic and satisfying. Sorry Jessica. Sorry Gary. Sorry Carrie. Sorry for any pain I caused you—it was never meant to objectivise or hurt you. Sorry.

Dan drove me back to my car at *The Plough*.

"Enjoy the rest of your birthday," I declared as I gave him one last hug and clambered out of his car.

How naïve to think that what we were creating was sustainable.

CHAPTER THIRTY

DAYTIME HOTEL

20 November 2012

EVEN IN MY adult years, Chelmsford still felt small—this may have been because of my own perceptions and life-baggage. I felt stifled. I felt I should've moved away years ago, but I didn't and now it seemed too late. In many small towns, homophobic views frown upon same-love, and the down-low would be unthinkable. Surely, it shouldn't even exist. Well, that's what I thought until the online searching that led me to find Dan began— down-low was everywhere. I learnt quickly what the down-low was; and I had judged it to be dishonourable and shameful—perhaps even vile. It was something I would never partake in...unless of course, I actually did. During my online searching I received innumerable invites to do or be the down-low. I was never completely sure if down-low was a noun or a verb but either way it sounded dirty.

Although homosexuality expressed in private between two adult men had been decriminalised in the UK since 1967, the stigma, the guilt and the shame still kept expressions of lust or love clandestine. The down-low was certainly a carry-over from the days when homosexual acts were illegal. I assumed that it may be what repressed gay men who were hiding their secret did, to alleviate their urges. I had carried my urges since puberty, and maybe it was a good thing that my Catholic guilt had protected me from these dirty desires. Who knows how reckless I might have been in the 1980s and 1990s when AIDS was mowing down marginalised and terrified gay men?

I observed that the down-low has a straight cousin—the low-down—and that the low-down is not exclusively a gay thing, anybody can do it—just as Hugh Grant did. I felt sorry for him when he was caught with his penis in Divine Brown's mouth on Hollywood's Sunset Boulevard. It must have been around 1995, because I recall it being during my 'Jesus years' when I had been reeling from the guilt of Mario—and the fact that I had actually kissed and touched a man. I had always found Hugh Grant gorgeous and my perfect number one celebrity crush. His cavernous crow's feet and the deep and elongated dimples that spread across each cheek were strangely beguiling. I would have loved to have kissed and touched him like Divine did—but not on Jesus's watch. Hugh always wore a cheeky grin beneath his mop of bouncy, middle-parted hair, and he had an attractive vulnerability about him. After the tabloid press had made mincemeat of him, I wished that I could have held him soothingly and told him that it would all be okay. Whatever angle you looked at him, Hugh Grant was delicious: low-down or high-up.

THE YEAR WAS 2012 and times had changed, albeit slowly in Chelmsford. The 80s and 90s were long gone and I was braver, more inquisitive...and ready. Everything was perfect, except for the fact that I wore a wedding ring. I was about to go out on the down-low. Sitting at my desk, exchanging emails with Dan, I was ready for it. All that I hoped for was that it wouldn't be anything like what I had experienced with Mario.

"What time will you be home tomorrow?" Carrie unwittingly pricked my conscience.

"Probably around six," I answered. "I have a late telecon," I lied.

Dan and I had arranged to meet at a medical centre in London at 4:00 p.m. on Monday afternoon. We had chosen London because we wanted to be anonymous. Essex was big, but it was also small and we couldn't take any chances. We were scheduled to see a nurse for HIV tests at quarter past. A woman in a navy and white uniform approached us in the waiting area. We were both nervous about the whole experience.

"Mr van Dijk and Mr Sterling," she asked, with an outstretched arm to shake our hands. We shook hands and it felt like the entire waiting room was staring at us. "Right," she continued slightly officiously, "who is Mr van Dijk, and who is Mr Sterling?" In turn, we owned our identities. She resumed: "Mr Sterling, you're with me, and Mr van Dijk..." I cut her short, before she could finish.

"We'd prefer to go in together," I interjected. Her neck went pink for a moment—and so did Dan's face.

"I'm sure we can arrange that," she replied curtly after an awkward silence.

A few minutes later, Dan and I were both sitting opposite a more rotund nurse with a wide smile and even wider hips. Nurse Maeve Ryan, as her name badge stated, did the mandatory pre-counselling. Dan was first to go. He flinched as the needle pricked him and I felt his pain. Our four eyes were fixed firmly on the test as we waited for the non-reactive result. We wanted to see only one red line and that is what we got. I was anxious to see his results, but he knew he had nothing to be worried about. The same, in converse, happened for my test. The nurse concluded with the post-counselling, which she did with care and sincerity. I wondered what she made of our double-testing. I certainly wasn't going to offer an explanation. I should have known that she saw a lot of people like us. She walked us to the door of the consulting room and just before she opened the door, she looked up at us from her low centre of gravity.

"Now just be careful out there, remain faithful to each other," she instructed, "you're a lovely couple...treasure what you have." As we walked toward the Oxford Circus tube station, we were glowing with embarrassment and excitement. 'Lovely couple' she had said—wouldn't that be nice?

I arrived home shortly before six.

"How was the conference call?" Carrie asked.

"Long and annoying," I answered with suspicious hesitation. I didn't know if she was on to me or if she was being an interested and caring wife. I was riddled with guilt. The next day would be worse.

THE DAY AFTER our trip to the London medical centre, Dan and I had organised to meet at the Holiday Inn Express in Newbury Park. We chose Newbury because it was a safe and comfortable distance from Chelmsford and Margaretting where Dan lived. I had booked the hotel online and I was terrified that Carrie might spot the transaction on my bank statement. There would be no way to explain it away. I arrived earlier than was planned and completed the check in. I found a place in the bar area downstairs to do some work on my laptop. Dan was fashionably late but called me while on his way to update me on his progress. Communication was a lot easier since we had trusted each other with our mobile numbers. Once Dan arrived, we made our way up to the room. Instead of the lift, we took the stairs and the two flights seemed endless. Room 246 was right at the end of the corridor overlooking the BP garage at the back of the hotel.

"Perfectly romantic," I whispered sarcastically. But this was the down-low and I shouldn't have expected anything more.

"What was that?" Dan asked.

"Nothing," I replied with a nervous smile on my face.

The room was neat, white and clinically clean. It was almost too clean to host a down-low and it bore no resemblance to the room where Mario had taken me many years earlier. This was a fresh start, an action replay: new set, new actors and a new script. We closed the door behind us. We were both excited and terrified. Two deer staring into the headlights. I put down the small carry bag I was holding and I turned to kiss him. He reciprocated and pulled me in tenderly. We kissed numerous times and paused sporadically to look at each other, smile and to take proper deep breaths. He still smelt like *Abercrombie and Fitch* and I now knew that the fragrance was called *Fierce*. I savoured in recognising that this wasn't fierce or savage like it had been with Mario. This was gentle and respectful. I wanted more. He allowed me to unbutton his shirt and touched me tenderly while I did it. He dropped his shirt to the floor and I took my hands to his naked and manly chest. I was alive, I wanted to be one both physically and emotionally with this man who stood vulnerable and adoringly in front of me.

Next was my turn. He removed my shirt and tasted bits of my shoulders and my chest with his soft, crimson lips. I was hungry for him. I pulled myself closer and nibbled his left ear and then his warm neck. I held his hairy and manly arm against my face and savoured him using all of my senses. I took long deep breaths. This was like nirvana. I moved my hands to the stainless-steel buckle that hung below his naval like a padlock that was guarding something protected and sacred. His virtue maybe? I played with the buckle almost teasingly and when his eyes indicated that I had his permission. I loosened it, pulled his zip down—and his viscose trousers dropped like satin to the floor. His legs were strong and manly. Tight like pulled leather, but smooth like the words that Mario had used to lure me to that dingy room all those years ago. Dan didn't need my permission; it had already been granted. He removed my trousers and we stood there clad only in our underwear for some time. I slid my hand beneath the elasticated waist band of his designer briefs. I wanted to explore. He gasped and his chest heaved tightly upwards—and then immediately, he relaxed. We continued to kiss and touch and look—taking it all in. We had so many years to catch up on and so much to learn.

The lighting in the room was low and time was moving unhurriedly. I had wished for it to stop completely. It felt surreal and I hoped that it was dream-like for him too. I wanted all of him and I wanted to give all of myself to him. All that separated us from total vulnerability and surrender was one pair of Jockey scants, one pair of Calvin Klein briefs and two pairs of socks. We removed our underwear—and wedding rings—and climbed into the bed.

Removing my wedding ring was a guilt-stabbing reminder of my duplicity and it almost destroyed the moment. There was so much at stake. The sacred circle of promise was being compromised and another person had been invited into the ring. I regretted this, but I wanted it and I needed to do it. It took me a few minutes to recompose myself and I could see Dan was fighting the same dragons in his head. Slowly, we gained momentum again. We played and fumbled. We learnt about each other and we pleasured each other beneath those clean and crisp white sheets. It was getting late and I had to reluctantly release him so that he could return to his straight life, and me to mine. If this is what the down-low was, I wanted to stay down and as low as possible, forever.

We met on the down-low at least another three times. With each visit we got smarter—we undressed ourselves and placed our clothes neatly over any of the furniture in the room. Going home all creased up and smelling like soap was a sure give away. There was time pressure, there was emotional pressure, but there was also reward. Christmas came and we both departed on our respective family holidays. My family and I to Torquay to spend time with Carrie's parents, and Dan and his family went to Scotland for their family holiday. The digital chatting continued, but the distance and time apart was insufferable.

CHAPTER THIRTY-ONE

THE NUKE

7 January 2013

THE GUILT AND the shame were weighing enormously on both Dan and I. While our infidelity was grinding at us, the cold-turkey two-week separation over the Christmas holidays was also taking its toll. I missed him more than I should have, and I didn't seem to have any way of controlling those feelings. Secret WhatsApp messages and the odd sly phone call were exchanged between Torquay and Edinburgh. I loved to hear his voice. While visiting Torquay's Grand Flea market I stumbled across a *bric-a-brac* stall that had an antique map of the UK on display. I found myself staring at the vast distance between where Dan was and where I was...it was uncomfortably reminiscent of the distance that existed between Carrie and I when I went on my sojourn to Barcelona. The comparison jolted me and I, again, felt overwhelmingly sick and guilty about my desires and intentions.

Dan and his family returned from their holiday in Scotland on the Friday before schools opened. I had arrived home earlier in the week because of some pressing work commitments. It was comforting to know that for now, I would only need a map of Essex to gauge the distance between us. We had arranged to meet each other on Tuesday morning for a coffee before work, and it couldn't come sooner.

On Saturday evening, I became uneasy about how Dan might be feeling about me. Somehow, I instinctively decided to log on to the dating website where we had found each other some months before. I felt sick with anticipation as I completed the login process, and then my heart sank, and all of my senses froze. Scorpion_D was online at that very moment. Once the trauma of the revelation began to subside, I reached for my phone and opened WhatsApp.

"Aren't I good enough for you?" I typed and hit send. I saw that he read the message straight away.

"What are you talking about?" he replied. I was mad.

"Who else are you trying to get into bed with and how many other guys are you seeing at the moment?" I was fuming, confused and hurt. This time the reply took a little longer to come from him.

"I am committed to seeing how things unfold with us," he wrote. I was angry and unconvinced.

"If that is true, why are you looking for other guys RIGHT NOW on datingbuzz?" I pushed send and wrote another immediately. "I trusted you and you are the kind of fuck-boy that people like me are warned to steer clear of." I pushed send and his reply must have crossed mine in cyberspace:

"I'm just chatting to other guys, there is still so much I, and we, need to learn."

My second message had offended him and perhaps I had sent it off in too much haste, but I was hurt.

"Fuck-boy? Fuck you, buddy!" His message hit me hard and it seemed war had been declared. "Don't you question my integrity," came the second message from him. I should have learnt from the few months before that Dan was proud and hated his integrity being questioned. For this reason, he didn't take personal attacks well at all. I guess I didn't either, but the issue for me was that we were building a relationship on a questionable and shaky foundation. We both knew what we were capable of doing, and launching a relationship—or whatever it was that we had—from a low-trust base was not ideal for establishing trust, psychological safety and general peace of mind.

Another message came in from him. The man of few words was becoming verbose in his rage.

"I WILL CHAT TO WHOEVER I WANT TO," and then the next "WHENEVER I WANT TO." Now he was hot and angry. I tried to rein him in, putting my pride in my pocket, but I wasn't doing a good job. Probably because I couldn't condone or understand why he needed to talk to anybody else. I was his man. We were looping around and around, and we weren't making any progress in understanding the other's viewpoint or moving toward any possible solution. I could see that he had opened all of my messages except for the last one, which appeared to be undelivered.

I was completely distracted by his silence and the events of the evening. I could see Carrie was concerned for me and this made the whole situation worse—there was no need for her sympathy or concern. This was my problem, although the infidelity now belonged to both of us. My anguish was 100% self-induced and perhaps, the punishment that I deserved for breaking our marriage vows and for going against the cautious words in the book of Leviticus.

At around 11:00 p.m., I messaged Dan again.

"Are we going to sort this out?" I asked. It took him a while to answer.

"I don't think we can," he wrote. He was clearly still in a rage. Ten more minutes passed.

"Why?" I probed. I sort of knew why, but I didn't want to hear it. We were two men in our forties, but we were teenagers on the sexuality front. We had so much to learn and discover, we were naïve and vulnerable. My dad once told me that 'when you look for a house, you don't buy the first one you see—you need to survey the market'. He explained that this simple advice could also easily be applied to choosing a wife. His was conservative and heteronormative advice—but if you replaced 'wife' with 'life partner', surely the same principle applied? I was afraid that Dan and I may have found each other too soon. Also, apart from finding each other at the onset of our journeys, we were both still married and not actually legally on the market. We were each other's furtive pleasure and we were painfully growing something in the dark.

AT THE EVANGELICAL 'tent' I once attended, I heard Pastor Edwards preach a message, using fire and brimstone intimidation.

"Whatever lives in the dark, is evil and inspired by Satan," he cautioned. "It will surely be exposed by the light of the Lord—God knows everything." I had lived my life always fearing that I may expose my secret sexuality, and that it might ooze from my mouth, shine from my eyes, jump from my hands, or sway from my hips. More and more, I was beginning to fear my dark thoughts and acts being exposed by the light of the Lord.

Dan and I had been building something in the dark, and while I was grappling with my Catholic guilt, he was dealing with his guilt from the 'tent' where he worshipped from time-to-time. At the fire-and-brimstone church that Dan sporadically attended, Pastor Harold would shame and condemn homosexuality as an evil and dark act—a passport to an eternity in hell. Dan and I were living in that dark and we were all doomed to be losers: both him and I, and our faithful and loyal wives. It was all so messed up.

IT WAS CLOSE to midnight when I wrote to Dan again. He had not responded to my question about why he didn't think we could fix this situation.

"Let's meet for our coffee on Tuesday and talk about the issues," I suggested. I sent a second message—an 'x' to signify a kiss. I checked my phone numerous times until just after 2am to see if he had read my message or if he had responded to me. Carrie stirred and then she immediately settled. She had sat up a little dazed and confused, mumbled something in her sleep and then flopped back down and began breathing deeply. I was talking to my 'mistress' from my marital bed, right next to my wife, and in the dark—the dark that Pastor Edwards and Pastor Harold had warned us about.

I must have fallen asleep sometime after two and I woke up just before five with a sick feeling in my stomach that told me something was awry. I checked my phone and a long and painful message awaited me:

"This is not easy to write. I am riddled with guilt, I can't do this to Judy and the children. I feel like a fraud and I have a lot that I still need to work through. I can't give you the emotional monogamy you want at the moment.

I need to talk to other people to help me understand myself and my world better. Things have gone too quickly. I need to pull up the hand brake and I don't even know if this is what I want. I only wish you well. You are a great friend, and I hope you will still be willing to be my friend."

My heart felt like it was exploding in my chest as I read the message under the duvet to avoid disturbing Carrie with the light from the screen of my phone. I read the message again and again. I didn't want to believe the words that were jumping painfully out at me. I was devastated and in those early hours of 7 January 2013, I descended into the biggest downward spiral of my life. It was as if I had entered the aftermath of a nuclear explosion. Although what Dan and I had was hidden from reality, the nuking was real—it was gut-wrenching, and it was a significant loss. For a while, my head had no space to entertain the notion of guilt. I was shattered. I was devastated. I had been dropped. My heart was broken and I couldn't tell anybody. I wanted to tell Carrie, but obviously I couldn't.

Later that morning, I attended a colleague's birthday breakfast at work. I may as well not have been there—I could not focus. I messaged Dan one last time.

"Please can we talk?"

"The timing is wrong." His reply was quick. "Go well." It was a bombshell, my bombshell. I had been nuked and it wasn't open for discussion. I felt like I was suffering a pain comparable to the loss of my dad and gran who had gone two and eight years respectively before. I felt empty and I could not hide it sufficiently from Carrie. She expressed concern for me and all I could do was blame the pressure of work. More lies.

It was incredibly tough. Any hopes and dreams of a happily ever after with Dan were over. I had had a taste of who I really was and what I desired, and now—in a flash—it was gone. In times like these, I had a history of running to psychologists or to the church—brick and mortar or the evangelical 'tent'. This time I had no inclination. Me and the traditional concept of God were over. I needed more intuitive and divinely inspired advice and assurance from somebody tangible...I needed to see a psychic or a medium—or both.

I had always steered clear of psychics because I was scared that my concealed sexuality would shine brightly out of my chakras and into theirs. I could have been exposed, just from my energy. I had had a hard enough time trying to hide my dirty secret from the unintuitive world; it seemed foolish to present myself to somebody whose tarot cards, crystal ball, or intuition would out me. I wanted to control that process. In my devastation and need for guidance and affirmations, I decided that I didn't care. Dan knew my secret and maybe it was time to tell it to a psychic too...before they delighted in telling me. I made numerous calls to check out a few close-by psychics, their methods and their prices. I read their star ratings and consumed every comment I could find. Once my research was complete, I booked an appointment with Linda for the following Tuesday at 3:00 p.m.

CHAPTER THIRTY-TWO

THE ENERGY FLOW

27 February 2013

THE TUESDAY AFTER Dan had shaken my world arrived, and by quarter to three in the afternoon I was sitting in my car outside Linda's house. It wasn't in a great neighbourhood, but you could see that the residents cared for their homes as best they could with their limited resources. Linda's house was a little worse for wear and, as I waited in my car, I could virtually see the nicotine dripping from the yellowing and bedraggled lace curtains that hung across her bay window.

"This is going to be great for my asthma," I mumbled to myself as I knocked on her front door slightly before 3:00 p.m. Linda opened the door with a smile on her face and a cigarette in her left hand.

"You must be David," she said with a welcoming smile. She shook my hand and gestured for me to come inside. I smiled in return, took off my shoes as instructed and followed her into the front room. There were at least a dozen vanilla and cherry candles rigorously burning—but not strongly enough to hide the smell of nicotine and cigarette smoke that clung tightly to the living room walls.

Linda had stooped shoulders that made her neck shorter. Her eyes were blue, much bluer than Carrie's, and they looked reflective and shiny like chevrons on a winding road in the night. She didn't need a crystal ball, she had two, firmly perched on either side of her nose. They darted everywhere, not missing anything…taking it all in. I guessed that they must have been secretly and invisibly wired to her sixth chakra, the chakra that gave her all of the intuition and wisdom that she needed to help people like me.

Once I was seated opposite her, Linda asked me to shuffle the deck of tarot cards and then she instructed me to split the deck in a particular fashion. She asked me to select one of the piles and once I had done this, she flipped the first card over. This card, *The Tower,* didn't look like a good card to start with. The image on the card was dark and terrifying: a lightning bolt was striking the top of the tower, flames were belching out of the windows and two people were falling face-down toward the ground.

"Doesn't look like a good start," I gasped with a panicked voice. Linda smiled.

"It's not all bad," she explained. "This card can mean many things… danger, crisis and destruction…but it can also mean liberation and unforeseen change." I was feeling more encouraged by her use of the word 'liberation', but I was still apprehensive. "Let's see what the next card says," she continued, "we can't read the cards in isolation." I held my breath in anticipation as she flipped the next card. It looked like it was a lot worse. The *Death* card depicted a white stallion, ridden by a sombre looking knight in armour. He was holding an ominous gothic-style flag and riding over what looked like a multitude of dead people lying on a road.

"Oh dear," I exclaimed, "death doesn't sound good. Maybe I shouldn't have come here today." She smiled reassuringly and I felt slightly uneasy gazing into her all-seeing eyes.

"It's unlikely that this represents a physical death," she said, first pausing and then she continued. "It means something in your life is coming to an end. It tells me you need to become more self-aware."

"Self-aware," I repeated. "That's a big ask for where I am in my life at the moment." It was difficult for me to be even just a little bit self-aware given where I had allowed my world to spiral to: I had been dumped by somebody who embodied what I wanted in this life, and I was very close to hurting somebody else who I loved even more. The reading continued and I gave Linda the details of where my life was at.

"My fucking husband left me for a man about 25 years ago," she told me animatedly in her gruff smoker's voice. "We're best of friends now. He tells me all of his problems...but it took some time." I immediately felt relieved that I was in safe space, and I felt gratitude to the universe for sending me to somebody who would understand the complexity of this emotional journey. Linda listened attentively and gave me some reassuring advice. "Be calm and patient with yourself," she instructed. "Dan will come back to you, it all just needs time...he needs time...and you need time." It was what I needed to hear, it gave me some solace. I'm not sure why, because at that time it was one big fat pie in the sky: Dan and I were both married to women, we were both closeted and he wasn't even talking to me.

FROM MY POSTGRADUATE studies I had learnt that qualitative research should always be triangulated for reliability and validity. For where I was in that time and place, triangulation seemed too mild and timid. I needed to validate properly—and so started my psychic journey. If a thirty-sided polygon is called a triacontagon—then I triacontagulated. I was ballistic—out of control—but it gave me a thrill, kept me distracted and it gave me hope. No more churches, no more psychologists. I was communicating with the other side now. Every one of the psychics, mediums or clairvoyants that I found—whether close enough to see face-to-face, on the other side of the world by Skype or email, or via Internet forums—all corroborated Linda's story that Dan and I would be together. Well, nearly all—all except for Sam—who I saw in Cambridge, she told me there was no chance of us ever being together. Needless to say, I didn't see her again, nor did I recommend her to any of my friends. With hindsight, I will concede that seeking psychic guidance and insight—especially with the rigour with which I did—was over the top, but it fed me and gave me sanity in those dark, dark months. It felt safe, it was somewhat anonymous, it wasn't hurting anybody...except perhaps my wallet.

On the afternoon of 27 February, my internet searching led me to a new psychic. His name was Nuriel and he seemed to be exactly what I might be looking for. I gave him a call and explained my circumstances. His voice was calming, I felt I could immediately trust him. It was as though I already knew him.

"Please can you drop me an email," he requested, "I need you to give me the basic details and everybody's dates of birth." Sounded easy enough.

"Everybody's?" I asked a little confused.

"Yes, everybody's," he confirmed, "you and Dan, your wives and all of the children please." I found it an odd request but given where I was on my emotional roller coaster, I complied. I sent the email off and to my surprise I received a reply early the following morning. It was short and to the point:

Hi David

Thank you for reaching out to me.

I appreciate the information that you have provided. I have meditated on this and last night I communicated with my spirit guides. I feel confident that I will be able to direct you through this process.

I would prefer to meet you in person before we start working together. Please let me know when you would like to come and see me. I'm based in St. Albans.

Love and light

Nuriel

'Able to direct you through the process', I read the words in Nuriel's email a couple of times. I was excited and intrigued. I replied immediately and we set up a time for me to see him the following Wednesday afternoon. St. Albans was a bit of a trek for me, but nothing was going to get between me and this newfound guidance and promise of hope. Carrie thought I was at work and my boss thought I was working from home. More lies. I wanted to stop lying on my journey toward my truth, but it seemed I had a few more hurdles to clear before I could realise this.

Nuriel looked nothing like I expected him to. I'm not sure why, but I was expecting a small Jewish man with a balding head, dressed in gold jewellery and stylish designer clothes. Instead, I was met by a largish and slightly awkward looking man who was wearing a colourful and baggy oversized shirt that looked like it belonged on a beach in Hawaii. His jeans were tired, but his shoulders were proud. His eyes were deep and caring.

We met at a Starbucks, which was crowded and loud.

"Thank you for meeting me here," he said, "I know it's not hugely credible to meet clients in random public places, especially given the so-called 'questionable' nature of the work that I do."

"That's fine," I interrupted, but he continued.

"I had a bad experience once, so I prefer to meet where I feel safe."

"Understood," I smiled as he handed me his business card. Nuriel was easy to listen to, and maybe this was helped by the fact that he was telling me what I wanted to hear.

"I needed to meet you," he went on, "because I need you to understand this process clearly." I leaned in enthusiastically and he continued: "I work holistically with my clients when they, like you, have big issues to deal with. I am a psychic, I am an energy practitioner and, most importantly, I am a life coach. I use my intuition to guide you." He had me hooked.

"Can you explain what an energy practitioner is?" I asked with both intrigue and excitement.

"Rub your hands together—like this," he demonstrated, showing me how to create friction between the flat palms of my hands by moving them in fast circular motions. I did what I was told. "Now," he instructed, "hold your hands like this." He demonstrated that I should hold my palms about 3 inches apart. "Can you feel them pushing each other away?" he asked.

"Yes," I responded a little too loudly, excited by what I was experiencing. Nuriel went on to explain that I had just witnessed energy in action and that in his work as an energy practitioner, he worked with energy as tangibly as what I had experienced. I was confused—but invested. I wanted to hear more of what he had to say.

"I don't get involved with anything unless it is predestined and for universal good," he explained.

"So how do you know that what I want is for universal good?" I asked with trepidation.

"Easy," came his swift reply, "I have spoken to my spirit guides, who have spoken to yours." It all sounded way too easy. "I wanted to meet you to explain this," he explained. "I have never been more certain of success...more so than any of the other cases that I have ever worked with." Nuriel continued to explain that he would not be interfering in any outcomes or universal processes, he was only going to guide all of our energies to protect them, and to buffer us all toward a happy, positive and predestined outcome. He was clear in stating that I would still be at the steering wheel and that he would be focused on "cushioning everybody's energies." It sounded like it could have been far-fetched and crazy, but I was prepared to give it a go—there was nothing to lose, only love and protection to gain.

"So, how will this work?" I asked, feeling somewhat bewildered.

"Well," he continued, "we'll find a rhythm between us, but for starters, I need to talk to you twice a week—at a minimum—via Skype, and I'll also need daily updates from you." It all sounded easy enough.

Throughout the consultation something had bothered me. This man looked so familiar but I couldn't place him. Then, as we were finishing up, the proverbial penny dropped.

"Do you have a friend called Kevin?" I asked taking him off guard and taking a bit of a chance. He looked surprised.

"No, I don't," he pondered, "but...it must have been close to 15 years ago that I dated a guy called Kevin." Bingo, I was right. I went on to explain that my good friend Dean had a brother called Kevin and reminded him that—if he was the right person—he had been Kevin's partner at mine and Carrie's wedding in the autumn of 1999. I also told him that I felt sure that our paths had crossed once before that too—at Kai and Chris's wedding in the 1980s. He confirmed, with amazement, what I was suggesting. I found myself wondering why, if he was the psychic, he hadn't joined all of these dots?

"I'm sure your name was Martin in those days?" I phrased it as a question and comment all at the same time.

"Wow!" he exclaimed, "this is feeling quite freaky. Have you been stalking me?" he joked. We both laughed. He went on to explain that after Kai, and then Chris, had both died of AIDS in 2001 and 2003 respectively, he had decided to take his 'gift of guidance' more seriously. As part of that process, he had changed his name from Martin to Nuriel, which he explained meant 'fire of the Lord', or for him: 'fire of the universe.'

"Did your mother finally accept that you were gay?" I asked bravely. He looked startled. "You know too much about me," he laughed again.

"Universal synchronicity," I belted out, not knowing if the context was correct.

"She didn't," he said and proceeded to offload his journey of personal pain and trauma. "I got married and had three children and now I'm dealing with my own coming out...that's why your journey is important to me." He looked as pained as I felt in my heart. "The problem with us psychics," he pontificated, "is that we aren't good at working things out when we ourselves are involved."

Nuriel became my committed life coach—right up until the hours before I dumped my painful secret on Carrie, and then into the months and years that followed. To me, he brought some fire to my universe...burning out the decay and clearing a new path with an unknown, but desired, destination. He gave me the strength to own my truth.

CHAPTER THIRTY-THREE

LUNCH WITH MY SISTER

20 March 2013

MY WORLD WAS imploding. It had been just over two months since Dan had dropped me and only two days since he had sent me a birthday message. It hadn't been my birthday, but 18 March must have been the fake birthday that I chose for Dylan Johnston when I created him. Somehow, as technology does, it linked the information from my down-low yahoo email account and reminded Dan that it was my birthday. I didn't reply to his message—but the relief of hearing from him gave me hope.

Nuriel and I were in touch frequently, but I was getting despondent with the lack of progress. I was starting to think that he might be a fraud and that perhaps I had been a fool for believing his stories about energy and destiny.

"Just relax," he would say. "We need to keep things smooth and easy...if you are anxious, you will destabilise the process." There were many times I wanted to walk away from the esoteric journey I had embarked on, but it gave me hope where religion and psychology had let me down. The likes of Linda and her tarot cards, and Nuriel and his energy had kept me going through a dark and difficult time. The lack of progress with Dan was frustrating me, so I decided it was time to give Linda a visit again.

When I arrived at Linda's smoky house in the late afternoon, the crystal balls in the sockets on either side of her face were glowing with ESP.

"Your sister has been to see me a few times," she commented in passing. I thought that was strange, because although I had given Holly Linda's details, she hadn't specifically told me that she had been to see her—let' alone 'a few times'.

"She's seriously worried about you," Linda cautioned, "she thinks you're on the verge of suicide." I had been trying to hide my pain and fear from my family, but obviously not well enough. "Last time she came to see me," Linda continued, "she came specifically to ask about you and your well-being."

"What did you tell her?" I asked, worried that my secret might have leaked.

"Nothing," Linda replied calmly. "I told her that you have work stress and that she shouldn't worry." Linda smiled and handed me the deck of cards and asked me to shuffle them as before. While I was shuffling, she unexpectedly provided some psychic guidance.

"My guides are telling me that you need to tell your sister...it will be a burden off both of your shoulders." Her voice was calm and authoritative. I flinched. "Just relax," she lilted, "you are in control...you should do it when you have peace." I completed the card shuffling, split the deck and restacked it, before sliding the cards back toward her.

The first card over was the Ace of Swords. The card showed a shrouded hand holding an upright sword that pierced a crown bearing dangling willow leaves. It looked full of promise.

"This card signifies new beginnings and a breakthrough of sorts," Linda explained. "It means that you are embarking on a new journey, to better things...Dan is coming," she stated with confidence. This time I found myself clinging a little less to every word she said, I just wanted to know of the outcome.

"Okay," I hurried her slightly, "what does the next card say?" Linda turned the next card over, it was the Page of Swords.

"You will get what your heart desires," Linda told me with a glint in her reflective eyes, "but you need to be patient, you need to let the process unfold." At that point, I had heard enough, she was confirming what Nuriel had been saying all along. With the reading over, Linda walked me to my car. "Be kind to yourself," she cautioned, "and please, please share your burden with your sister."

EARLY ON THE morning of 20 March, I called Holly.

"What does your diary look like today?" I asked, trying not to show any emotion in my voice.

"Let me check," she answered, trying not to sound alarmed. "Looks flexible," came her quick reply.

"Any chance we can meet for lunch?" I asked. Without hesitation, she agreed.

"Sure. When and where?" she asked.

At 1:00 p.m., we were seated opposite each other at the Gaucho Argentine restaurant in Canary Wharf.

"Thanks for making time," I told her.

"No problem," she answered. "I've been so worried about you."

"Why?" I probed, trying to understand how I had let my guard down.

"You just look heavy," she signed. "Your face is distressed, and you look skinny...super skinny." She was right, I had lost at least 2 stone in the previous months, and I had taken to road running to deal with the madness in my head. I was very fit, fitter than I had ever been—I was literally running for my life.

"Well, that's why I wanted to see you today," I explained. "Things in my world are kind of imploding...but mostly in my head at the moment." Holly looked confused, and I began to ramble. "Things at home haven't been great," was where I started and I went around in circles, giving her some idea of what I needed to say—but I wasn't able to get the words out. I gave her enough clues for her to hazard an informed guess.

"Are you gay?" she asked, trying to take the stress away from me and helping with the words that I was unable to utter to her—my best friend for 18 months short of the entire span of my life.

"I feel sure I am," I replied. Holly's immediate response was to throw her head back and laugh—almost as if with some solace and intense relief.

"Is that all that has literally been eating you away for the past few months?" she asked with the relief still spilling off her face.

"It's more like the past 30 years," I groaned, "but it's come to a head in the last year or so." She leapt up, made her way around the table and hugged me tightly.

"I love you my gay brother," she declared with the same animated tone that you might use on a young child. "I will always love you, no matter what." She was sincere and appeared relieved.

Holly and I are like two peas in a pod. People often mistake us for twins—I'm the boy version and she's the girl. I'm not quite sure how it all works, because I am told that I look like dad, and she is told that she looks like mum—but mum and dad never looked alike. There's obviously something in the Sterling genes that makes us all look the same. Holly, like me, is highly strung and she always needs to be on the move. Her benevolent green eyes are always busy, always thinking, always darting, always looking for ways to be kind to others—people and animals alike. She was even always nice to Carrie's sister Abby, which always took some effort. Sitting opposite her in the Gaucho, with the soft shadows of the inside downlights flickering across her face, it struck me how she was looking a lot like mum, and a little like gran. Those Polish genes were strong—and kind.

"So, what happens next?" Holly asked, putting on her practical solicitor cap.

"I'm not sure," I answered. "I need to work out how to manage this with Carrie and the girls." I sighed. "It's more complicated than I've told you," I continued. Holly sat up, ready to hear it all.

"You mean there's more?" she asked.

"Not really, but sort of," I continued creating some unnecessary intrigue. I told her about Dan and of what had transpired since the previous July.

"You naughty diva," she joked, trying to put me at ease and instantly, without judgement, understanding the pain and the trauma of what I had been through.

"He also works at Barclays," I added. Holly's eyes grew wider. I could virtually see the cogs turning behind her corneas.

"Is he a CFO?" she asked cunningly.

"You should never kiss and tell," I joked, trying to protect Dan's veiled homosexuality.

"Is it Dan van Dijk?" she asked. The accuracy of her guess sent me off my stroke for a moment.

"How did you work that out?" I asked, forgetting to neither confirm nor deny.

"I just put two and two together," she replied both casually and matter-of-factly.

Holly had a few questions about Dan: "Was he married; Did he have children; and how had I met him?" Her nosey questions all came from a place of care and concern. Dan and Holly both held senior positions in the bank, they knew of each other—but they didn't specifically know each other. Dan knew that Holly was my sister, and now Holly knew that Dan was—like her brother—gay, and fearfully safe in his closet. They would be secretly eyeing each other out, watching closely—connected by me, even though I was currently disconnected from Dan.

"What about Dan then?" Holly asked soon after the waiter had delivered our cappuccinos to the table.

"I don't know," I contemplated, "but Linda says he is coming back...in his own time." Holly smiled and then I told her about Nuriel.

"Give me his number," she demanded. She was more of a psychic whore than I could ever be. When I spoke to Nuriel the following morning, he told me that Holly had made an appointment to see him later in the day.

"Via Skype?" I asked. "No, she's coming to see me in St. Albans," he replied. My mind began to race and I hoped I hadn't missed anything in Holly's empathetic eyes. Why would she need to see Nuriel so urgently? Was everything okay between her and Xander?

That evening, I felt at peace for having shared my secret, I didn't feel that I needed to worry about it now being uncaged and free. I trusted Holly more than anybody in the world.

THE NEXT DAY, probably as Holly was meeting with Nuriel, I met with Vicky Goldberg for a coffee in Brentwood, close to where she lived.

"Sorry Josh couldn't make it," she explained, "he's having a crazy day with some looming deadlines." It was good to be with Vicky—she was always a breath of invigorating fresh air.

"I need to tell you something," I blurted nervously. I wasn't afraid of her response; I was more ashamed that it had taken me so long to come clean with one of my closest and most trusted friends. A friend who had previously given me so many opportunities to speak my truth.

"Spit it out then," she coaxed, trying to make the words flow more easily.

"I can't say it," I replied stupidly.

"Yes, you can," she encouraged, "I know what you want to say, but I can't say it for you." I breathed in deeply and I exhaled heavily and then I said what I needed to.

"I think I'm gay," I declared for the second time in two days. Vicky smiled.

"Finally!" she exclaimed, leaping up and giving me a massive hug. "How many opportunities have I given you?" she joked.

"I wasn't ready," I sighed, grateful for this safe space.

"And you know we'll love you just the same," she hearteningly reassured. "We'll be here for you on every step of the way." Her naughty eyes were sincere, and her red lipstick told me that she was serious about her commitment. I told her about the preceding months, about Dan, about my fears, and about my hopes.

"One step at time, babes," Vicky reassured. We cried and we laughed, and then we cried and laughed some more. Oh, how I loved the Goldbergs.

CHAPTER THIRTY-FOUR

TELLING I'D TOLD

23 June 2013

FOLLOWING THE PAINFUL revelations earlier in the evening, Carrie was asleep in the bedroom. The sleeping tablet was numbing her shock and procrastinating the trauma that we had to navigate in the morning. I was in the lounge sipping my coffee, perplexed by the waning moon and feeling a multitude of unfamiliar emotions.

I was about to dial, but I was worried that Carrie may stir. I didn't want to disturb her, and I certainly didn't want her to hear me make this call. I unlocked the back door and walked out into the garden. Devious and deceitful again.

The ebbing moon was shining bright and the night was still. I felt exposed...not quite liberated yet—maybe a little numb. Happy and sad. I knew there was a long journey ahead of me...but I had taken the first step along this road less travelled.

Apart from doing this for myself, I was doing it for Carrie and the children—but mostly for Carrie. She would not have been convinced of this, so I didn't raise it in my revelation earlier in the evening. In the months building up to the coming out, I knew I needed to do this for Carrie. Keeping her trapped in a loveless marriage where she did not feel treasured and cherished was eroding her soul and destroying her confidence. It's not that the marriage was loveless, *per se*, because I did love her and she loved me— but the natural and basic instincts weren't there. Loving her like a man should love a woman didn't come naturally and I knew that my inability to satisfy her wholly—physically and emotionally—was hurting her immensely. I needed to break the cycle and set her free. I needed to nurture her back to independence and renewed confidence, to a place where she could find real happiness and fulfilment. I had eroded so much of who she was over time—and she had allowed me to. I felt guilty and I wanted to be part of the solution. I wanted her to be happy. As for our children, I wanted them to know their real and authentic dad. I wanted them to still love me and I wanted them to be proud of me.

Instead of calling, I sent a text.

"You able to talk?" It had just gone 10:00 p.m. and I had to be mindful of the circumstances on the other end. A message came back straight away.

"Sure, give me 5." I replied with a thumbs-up emoji. Time stood still as my mind raced ahead to scenarios of what the coming days, months and years might hold for me. I felt like a gambler at the roulette table who had just stacked his whole life's savings, his reputation and his heart on either red or black. The wheel was spinning, the stakes huge and the outcome unknown. My eyes were closed and that wheel was spinning...and spinning...and spinning. 'Ting!', my phone lit up and brought me back to reality. It was a text from Dan.

"Ready to chat when you are," he wrote.

I HAD INVITED Dan back into my life some six weeks earlier. With Nuriel guiding me, and my coming out to Carrie imminent, I contacted him to ask if he would like to meet up for a coffee. I was surprised at how speedily he accepted. It had been nearly five months since he had turned my world upside down, extinguishing me like a candle on a birthday cake. After a brief catch-up which was slightly awkward to start with, I told him that I was building up to coming clean with Carrie. He was shocked—almost stunned. His face drained of colour and he looked expressionless for a while.

"That's a massive step," he remarked, "you're incredibly brave." I remember it being amazing to be with him again and a compliment from him felt like a million dollars.

"I don't feel that brave," I replied, "I feel terrified."

I regaled Dan with stories of Nuriel, my loyal psychic life coach, and explained that Nuriel had been coaching and preparing me for this event over the previous months.

"Psychic life coach?" he questioned sceptically, pulling an unconvinced face—scrunching his forehead and pursing his lips. Dan is an accountant, an analytical, left-brain thinker and the word *psychic* and all its stands for goes against his logical grain.

"Take the 'psychic' out of it," I responded "and you have a life coach. He's been a lifeline for me, and he's kept me sane over the past couple of months."

Later that evening Dan messaged me: "Was great seeing you today. You are my hero." 'Hero?'—I pondered. I didn't feel like one, but I was flattered that he saw me in this light. Since that meeting, both Dan and Nuriel became my predominant lifelines—listening, encouraging and motivating. I was somewhat surprised when about a week later, Dan sent me a message.

"Please send me the name and number of your life coach," he asked. I read the message again and smiled to myself.

"Hmmm," I thought, "not such a rigid left-brain thinker after all."

IN THE QUIET of the night, I opened the contacts on my phone and I dialled Dan's number. He answered immediately and he was talking quietly.

"Hey, did you do it?" he whispered with trepidation in his voice.

"I did," I answered, reciprocating the whisper.

"And how do you feel?" he asked with sincerity.

"I'm not sure," I explained. "On one hand my heart feels broken, while on the other it feels like it may be able to escape its cage and all of its torture." Dan took a moment to answer.

"I'm sure it's not easy," he comforted, "but remember...like I told you, you are incredibly brave."

"Thanks," I responded. The truth was I didn't feel brave, I felt scared and had it not been for Dan on that moonlit evening, I would have felt very alone. His friendship was a huge comfort to me, but I wished more for companionship than friendship from him. He had told me before that I was not his type, and all of that aside, the timing wasn't right. We were both married—although as of about an hour and half before, I was on a steady slope down toward a divorce. There was so much to deal with—for now I only needed a friend.

"How did Carrie take the news?" Dan asked. I wasn't sure how to answer the question, I took a moment or two and described:

"First, she was shocked—then angry, and then she was sad. It wasn't pretty," I explained. "It was awful really, I struggled to say what I had planned to say, the words came out all wrong—not like I had prepared them. She asked me some unexpected questions."

"Like what?" Dan asked intrigued.

"Like, why did you get married? I didn't see that one coming." And I hadn't.

"What did you tell her?" Dan asked sincerely.

"I told her that I loved her and I thought I had overcome these gay thoughts and urges."

"Okay," was Dan's response.

"What would you have said?" I asked, not sure how to interpret his comment.

"Not sure, that's a tough one," he replied. A few seconds of silence followed, during which I became aware of the chirping of some nearby crickets. I usually found the sound of crickets irritating, but somehow the rhythm and song of these ones under the waning moon gave me some peace and comfort.

"Maybe," Dan continued, "I would have said the same, but perhaps I would have stressed that I have always loved her and that I still did—and that this big confession didn't change that." I thought Dan's response was pretty good, but I felt that in my own clumsy way I had sort of conveyed that to Carrie. Dan had another question:

"Did you manage to let her know that you would support her through this ordeal?" he asked.

"I think I did, but I don't think she believed me," I replied. "She's in a massive state of shock—and also, I think our trust of 15 plus years just flew out the window...I guess that's no surprise." Dan was silent for a few seconds.

"That's true," he reflected, "I hadn't thought of that."

TRUST IS SUCH a little word but it's massively complex and demanding. Over 15 years, I had presented myself as one version of David. This was the person that Carrie had grown to love, count on and rely upon. This was the person she doted on, the person she had built her reality and dreams around. The person she had made herself vulnerable to. Suddenly, she was faced with another version of David—somebody she didn't completely know. I guess I couldn't expect her to trust me unreservedly anymore. The reality was that I was still the same person—only with the secret spilled from my mouth. Without the emotion and the trauma, the reality was that she should be able to trust me more now...she had just been introduced to the true and authentic David—albeit a David that she did not know existed. The David whose hair she frequently cut—her scissored hands often uncomfortably close to the secret that lay hidden centimetres away from the hair that she snipped. But it was a lot more messed up and complicated than Carrie having to come to terms with the new David she had to face. A massive journey of pain and healing awaited us.

DAN AND I chatted more. I told him that I suggested to Carrie that she speak to Nuriel, who was on standby that night. I had introduced him as a life coach that I had on standby should she want to speak to somebody. She had declined the offer and instead opted for the sleeping tablet. Dan told me again of how in awe he was of me and this bold step I had taken. Talking to Dan and being in his company was always soul-satisfying. He had a calmness about him that was grounding and made things clearer. While I was very attracted to him, he was for now just a friend. And I needed a friend exactly like him. My decision to come out and to gamble so many things was not a coming out for him—it was a coming out for Carrie, for me, and for the children. I had to be clear about that—there were no guarantees.

Dan needed me as much as I needed him, he too had revealed to me at least three weeks earlier that Nuriel was now coaching him too, and that he was planning to come out to his wife, Judy in the coming weeks. I had suspected that there may have been an awakening of sorts happening within him, but I was still surprised when he made the revelation to me. He was moving at a pace much faster than I had expected. In the weeks that led up to this coming out, Dan had been incredibly supportive, always available and always genuine. As much as he was watching and learning from my initial steps, it was emerging that this was going to be a journey of mutual benefit and support. A mammoth journey had begun, and we needed to continue to be there for each other. It wasn't planned, but the universe was being kind—to both of us.

I was scared to end the call and of being alone.

"Goodnight, you've done good." Those were Dan's parting words. I needed to hear them because it didn't feel like that at all. The call ended and it was just the moon, the crickets and me.

CHAPTER THIRTY-FIVE

INVESTI-GAY-TION

24 June 2013

WHO WOULD HAVE thought that nearly fourteen years after saying 'I do', Carrie would find herself in a position where she would be 'investi-gay-ting' her gay husband and also exploring the unfamiliar and unspoken topic of homosexuality? She would be digging deep and ensuring that she did not leave anything unturned...snooping through physical evidence and combing intangible digital tracks.

The morning after I dropped the bomb, I woke up, as usual, at 6:00 a.m. It was a Monday, a new week and one filled with a huge amount of uncertainty. Carrie was still in a deep sleep and I didn't want to disturb her. The sleeping tablet was doing its job—kindly sparing her from having to deal with the aftermath of the previous night...for a little while at least. I climbed out of bed, showered and got dressed. While I was doing up the buttons of my shirt and putting on my tie, I synchronized my breathing with her loud and deep breaths. Her breathing was slow and calm, ignorant of what awaited her when she became *compos mentis*. I wanted us to remain aligned and, in some way at least, the breathing helped me connect with her. Together, we had created, experienced and shared so much since she had walked into the Nightingale staffroom some 15 years before. So much had transpired since then…some had been bad, but most was good. It may have seemed ludicrous given my nine-hour old revelation, but I needed her now as much as she needed me. She stirred slightly when I kissed her on her forehead as I left the room.

My drive to work was contemplative and sombre. I cried for much of the way. I cried for Carrie, for our girls, for our marriage, for broken dreams and for broken promises; and I cried for my shame and the shame I was about to cause those that I loved. I felt dirty. I composed myself when I arrived at the office and my day was relatively uneventful. I should have felt liberated and relieved, but I didn't. I felt heavy and concerned for Carrie and our girls, for our future and for how the Joneses might judge us. I wanted to see Dan, but I felt guilty for seeking support when I knew Carrie would be at home alone, for now at least, guarding my secret as securely as I had…basking in its shame and suffering in its torment.

I didn't see Dan, but instead, in a gesture of support, I arrived home early in the afternoon. I can't remember why, but schools were closed that Monday. When I arrived home Jane and Kate were watching TV.

"Hello daddy," they both replied in unison, almost as if they were led by the conductor of a choir.

"Mummy's not well today," Jane offered.

"Yes, she's got a headache and a very sore tummy," Kate added. I felt yet another wave of angst come over me. My stomach was in a knot too.

"Let me go and check on her," I suggested. When I arrived in our bedroom, it was icy. Carrie looked drawn and she was still in her red and white stripy pyjamas from the previous night.

"Stupid question," I blabbered, "but how was your day?" As I pecked her forehead she smiled—either at my kiss or at my attempt to lift her pain with my honestly phrased question. I wasn't sure. Maybe it was just because I was there.

"It's been enlightening," she explained, putting her iPad down next to her on the duvet covers. "I've learnt a lot," she continued. The iPad screen was still illuminated and it told me that she had been playing *Flow*, an addictive game that involved joining coloured dots to fill all of the blocks on a grid. We had all recently downloaded it from the App Store and it provided the perfect escape from reality. The entire family was hooked.

"Enlightening?" I asked quizzically.

"Yes," she answered sincerely, "I'm trying to understand all of this." She paused and sighed and then continued. "I've been doing a lot of research," she told me proudly. I knew, from the numerous blogs that I had read, that she was on a journey known as 'investi-gay-tion.' This term was an umbrella action for tracking down the activities and behaviours of a gay, or potentially gay, person. It could be used by a parent to try to ascertain if their child is gay, it could be used by a partner to confirm if their partner was batting for the other team—but as was the case in my new world, it would be used by the straight partner to uncover the length and depth of the betrayal. Some people, like me, outed themselves—others were outed by careless actions...but whichever way it happened, it didn't matter...'investi-gay-tion' was the art of uncovering the dirt and making sense of the lies.

Carrie had a million questions. In-between her hurt and pain, she seemed proud of the fact that she had taken the first steps to understand this unexpected reality.

"Maybe you could be bisexual," she suggested. I didn't know where to start and I didn't have the energy to explain all that I had learnt from Dan about the Kinsey scale. I also wanted to be kind. If I were bisexual—that was something for her to hang on to...for now at least.

"I could be, but I don't think so," I replied not wanting to entertain the idea too much.

"You must be," she insisted. "How could you have stayed married to me for so long if you were gay?" I was saved by Kate who came to the door to tell me that she wanted to have a bath. Once Kate left, Carrie continued.

"Some gay people, like you," she continued, "control their urges and manage to live a straight and happy life." I feared that her 'investi-gay-tion' had taken her to Christian family websites and I was worried that she might raise the idea of conversion or gay-cure therapy. Fortunately, the conversation didn't go there. She fired a lot of questions and offered much of what she had learnt during the day. I was impressed by the learning curve. That's why her early morning meltdown the following morning came sooner than

I had expected it to.

As the days went by, Carrie had more and more questions and it was clear that she was starting to try to tame the monster that I had unleashed on her. It felt like we were making progress, and we were—but then the 'investi-gay-tion' got majorly intense.

"Who is Linda?" she asked with venom in her voice. I was taken aback by her question. How did she know who Linda was? Then came the whopper, and it was delivered with more anger: "And who is Dan?" I was dumbfounded. I didn't want to dig any holes for myself, especially since I was thoroughly invested in wanting this story to have a happy ending.

"Tell me what you know," I probed trying to stay as calm as possible, "and then I will try to fill in the gaps for you." She flung a piece of paper at me and I nervously took it from her hand. It was an email that she had printed from my laptop—how and when she did it I will never know. I had sent the email to Linda shortly after my first reading in January. At the end of the session, she had suggested that I put some of my questions in writing to allow her time to 'meditate over them.' As a psychic medium, I would have expected her to have seen this one coming! In the email I had asked of Linda:

Is Dan happy?
Does he miss me?
Will he come back to me?

These were not easy questions to explain away. So, I had to come clean—well as clean as I could with Carrie sitting stone-faced and angry in front of me. I began with a half-honest confession. More lies or part truths. I explained that I had sought to find somebody to speak to who was in a similar position to me. I explained that it had been an anonymous email friendship that had developed into a few coffee meets. I explained that I was tempted to have an affair, but that I had chickened out. Lastly, I explained that once I had told Dan I didn't want to see him again, he had blocked me and that I was never sure whether I had done the right thing. Carrie lifted the corner of her left lip.

"Hmmm," she snarled. It was clear she didn't believe what I had told her. I had gotten off lightly—for now at least.

"Carrie," I muttered a little too softly, but it seemed to get her attention, "I don't want this as much as you don't want it." I felt myself choke up. "I have tried to get rid of it for years and I'm sorry you're in this mess with me." I wasn't looking for sympathy, but Carrie pounced.

"Don't expect me to have pity on you," she growled. Carrie's voice raised slightly and her face was cerise. "You are a liar and a cheat, David Sterling, and I've wasted too many years on you." I immediately thought of the years that she had had with Jim and how they had amounted to nothing, I had added another 14 and a bit to that—or had I really? We had shared rich experiences, exciting adventures, encouraged and nurtured each other and we had produced two beautiful daughters who would keep our souls bound, in some way for the rest of our days—eternity perhaps.

"I am sorry I have hurt you," I said. "I never wanted to do that." She grimaced.

"I think you know that it's too late for that," she snapped as she walked out of the room.

The following weeks and months were intense, Carrie was unearthing whatever she could. She suggested some hurtful things, but it was to be expected. She was vulnerable and exposed and the best form of defence was attack. My nerves were shot and I didn't want what had gone before to mar what could be. Sometimes her 'invest-gay-tion' led to things of substance, while at other times she was just pulling at straws. I had to give her credit, she was good. Very good in fact, although I was grateful that she never unearthed the stories around Mario or Graham or Gary. She only found the big one...the one that had real substance, the one that had shifted me and my world forward. The one that gave me hope.

CHAPTER THIRTY-SIX

THE PSYCHOLOGIST'S ROOM

25 June 2013

CARRIE AND I had both been sleeping badly since I had dropped the bomb. In the two nights since, we had found each other at opposite sides of our king-size bed. A strip of no-man's land had instantly formed down the middle of the bed. It wasn't declared, but it was tactically acknowledged, and it separated us as we lay on either side as if soldiers in our trenches. The atmosphere at home was understandably cautious and tense. Carrie was sad and had a lot of questions. Jane and Kate seemed ignorantly fine, but I wasn't totally sure. They didn't know any details, but they might have been susceptible to the sadness that loomed around us.

On the Tuesday morning following my revelation, I woke up sometime after half five with a sick feeling in my stomach. The bed was empty and I panicked. I rushed down the passage and found Carrie on the sofa in the lounge. She was having a melt down and it was painful to see. She had been seated there since around 4:00 a.m. and was in a downward spiral. The tears were flowing, and she could barely speak. The enormity of my revelations and how her life would be impacted had started to hit her hard. I held her tightly and she clung on to me. We both cried. I didn't want to cry because I needed to be strong for her, but I was also fearful—for her, for us and for our girls. So much was unknown and we were both petrified, for now, I was still her protector and ironically also her rock. A role that I no longer deserved.

"I'm terrified," she sobbed almost incoherently. I resorted back to operational solutions.

"We need to get you some professional help," I suggested with fear oozing from the back of my throat.

The next two hours felt like an eternity, and by eight thirty I was on the phone trying to secure an appointment with a private psychologist. On my sixth phone call, I was lucky to pick up a last-minute cancellation. We were scheduled to see Dr Ingrid Otis at eleven thirty. We arrived in time to complete the new patient forms and we were whisked through to Dr Otis's consulting room.

"Welcome," she crowed as she waved her arm, gesturing for us to sit on the sofa. The sofa was regal blue, large and rectangular and it had big square arms. The cushioning comprised deep buttons that formed triangular shapes. It was firm and hard and it felt like it had absorbed many tears. "What brings you here today?" Dr Otis asked. Carrie looked at me, her eyes welling up, then she looked down and began to cry. Dr Otis passed her a box of tissues. "Let it go, don't hold back," she encouraged annoyingly.

Maybe I had just had a bad experience, but I had become disillusioned with psychologists many years before. Dr Otis seemed to be cut from the same cloth as Dr Kessman who had been responsible for my previous disenchantment. Both women looked the same—short in stature, with long dark hair that needed a scrub. Both wore outfits that their grannies would have been proud to don—long unattractive skirts with thick elasticated waist bands, crowned by frilly blouses with floral patterns.

I had found Dr Kessman a week after I had allowed Mario to manhandle me in dingy room number 18. I was riddled with guilt and shame and fear and I needed to talk to somebody. I was also terrified that I may have acquired HIV, when logically I knew there was absolutely no chance that I could have contracted it. I visited her every week for at least ten sessions and every one of them was so predictable. I began to feel that I could pre-empt the questions before she even asked them: "Why do you feel like that? How did that make you feel? What could you have done differently?" Her questions were so tedious and I found no healing in them. That's why I turned to Jesus.

The air above and around the regal blue sofa in Dr Otis's consulting room was still and asphyxiating. Carrie was still sobbing and Dr Otis leaned forward, tilted her head and frowned in what appeared to be a gesture of concern—but it only made her look constipated. The silence continued for way too long and so I began to answer her original question:

"We're here," I told her, "because we've been married for 14 years and I have been dealing with my sexual identity." I paused.

"Relax...and go on...this is a safe space," she interjected, being annoy-ingly predictable.

"On Sunday, I told Carrie that I have come to accept that I am gay." Dr Otis appeared rattled, it was clear that my revelation was way beyond her frame of reference.

"How do you know this?" she asked. The stupidity of the question did not require a response. It was time to operationalise things again.

"I need Carrie to know that I am going to love and support her as best I can through this process. More than anything I want her to know that she and our daughters will be all right. I need Carrie to know that we will work through this together."

The remainder of the session turned into a fact-finding mission which was less irritating and more bearable. She asked questions like: "How would you describe your childhood? How many children do you have? What work do you do? Where do you live?"

I was excused toward the end of the session to give Carrie some private consultation time with her. Just before I left, we agreed that the consulta-tions would proceed twice weekly with Carrie—and that I would attend only when specifically invited. The drive home was lighter and we made a quick stop at a newsagent for some bread and milk. I even managed to convince Carrie to have a slab of chocolate and I also made her laugh at a silly joke that I cracked.

Although melancholy, the atmosphere felt strangely hopeful. Deep down, I knew that there was a long road ahead of us. I had told Carrie that

I would walk this journey back to wellness with her.

"Today," I noted, "we have taken the first step together." I wasn't totally convinced that it was the right step, but it was what Carrie wanted and I needed her to feel empowered and take back some of the power she had handed to me during the preceding years.

Carrie attended the sessions with Dr Otis religiously and I could see that they were giving her some degree of peace. At the very least they were a distraction for her and a place to offload. I never pried into the content of the sessions, I knew that I had no right to do that—but truth be known, I was dying to know. From time-to-time, Carrie would volunteer little bits and after about session five, she came home and seemed relieved to tell me some annoying news.

"Dr Otis says you are probably gay because you and your dad had issues." I could see that Carrie wanted to believe what she had been told because she needed answers. I didn't quite know how to respond to this exasperating assessment. I wanted to say: 'Tell Otis to go and fuck herself long and hard and then go back to psychology school', but I didn't.

"Why don't you suggest that she goes and does some reading up on Xq28," I suggested with a slight sting in my voice. Carrie didn't know what Xq28 was, but I did.

I had recently learnt from Dan that it was a maternally inherited genetic marker, which scientists were trying to link to homosexuality. There is no conclusive evidence, but research is ongoing. X chromosomes are inherited from our mothers, so if these studies proved successful, Dr Otis may have to concede that homosexuality is inherited from your mother and not your father—and by nature, not by nurture. My dislike for psychologists was further confirmed and growing stronger.

ON MY JOURNEY, I had discovered a different breed of psychologist. These, usually expert friends or friends-of-friends, enjoyed the drama of my coming out—the queer husband and all of the associated gay bashing. I found that these, were worse than those like Otis and Kessman who had certificates strewn across their walls. Our situation attracted a good deal of these would-be-shrinks. While Carrie, during her heartache, received support from her many girlfriends, some of the 'help' was not always helpful. Some of the advice was positively destructive. Stella, Carrie's over-the-top reborn Christian friend, who was grieving over the news of her brother's homosexuality, was a particular nuisance.

"Be careful, gay people are selfish," Stella cautioned, "it's always all about them...just them...nobody else." These were not comforting words to somebody who was vulnerable and at a huge crossroads in her life

I was struggling too, but I put on a brave face for Carrie and the girls—as well as for Dan who would be where I was in a few weeks' time. I walked alongside Carrie because I cared; I wanted to be there to nurture her back to the wellness that she deserved. I was willing to carry all of the pain—but I couldn't...because most of it was hers.

CHAPTER THIRTY-SEVEN

THE AFTERMATH

6 July 2013

THE DAY AFTER Carrie and I had visited Dr Otis's rooms, she seemed a lot calmer. She had bought a new A4 fabric covered journal when we stopped at the shops after the consultation. Dr Otis had encouraged her to write down her thoughts and feelings and she was furiously writing in her journal at every opportunity. It seemed to be helping her, a welcomed distraction at least.

It was clear that Carrie was in shock, and it was very upsetting to witness it—especially since I knew that I was the cause of her heartache. Her beautiful blue eyes were glazed and sunken, and they appeared lifeless. The trauma and the anti-depressant medication seemed to have disconnected her from the real world and from the agony of what she had to deal with. So, on the Wednesday evening, I arranged for Vicky and Josh Goldberg to come over for dinner. They were amazing friends who could always be called upon. They were good listeners and their presence offered a sense of safety. They were broad minded and offered no judgement. Vicky and Josh knew what they were driving toward when I called them at 6:00 p.m.

"Hello...we're on our way," she replied.

"Great," I replied, "but, that's not why I was calling, just checking if you're okay with take away for dinner."

"Sounds good," she replied, and then added: "We're about 15 minutes away."

Vicky and Josh arrived soon after I had called them. Carrie was writing in her journal and she seemed to be in control of her emotions, but the sight of our friends caused her to well up and the tears flowed. There was no need for words, only hugs and love and understanding.

"What can I do to help with dinner?" Vicky asked, filling the agonising gaps that lingered in the woeful air.

"There's nothing to be done," Carrie answered. "David is going to grab some take aways." Everybody decided what they wanted from the Nando's menu and Josh and I headed out, leaving Vicky and Carrie with a glass of gin and tonic in their hands.

"Carrie looks like she's handling it as best she can," Josh observed thoughtfully as we reversed out of the drive way.

"She seems to be more in control of her emotions since the trip to the psychologist yesterday," I explained. "But I'm still waiting for the big bang," I added, "I know that I still need to swallow some serious shit for a while." Josh chuckled.

"You'll take it in your stride," he comforted with his usual calming energy. The Goldbergs were so natural and easy to be around, sensitive and funny—always accepting. I was lucky to have them as my friends.

By the time we arrived home with the food, Carrie and Vicky had set the table and were seated opposite each other on the two sofas in the lounge, glasses of red wine in hand. Their smudged mascara gave away that they had both shed some tears. We all moved to the table where Carrie was portioning the chicken and salad onto everybody's plates. Vicky and Josh took their seats—Vicky next to me and Josh next to Carrie. I opened another bottle of Cabernet Sauvignon and filled everybody's glasses. There was nothing to celebrate and therefore nothing to cheers—except maybe the birth of my new life, but this certainly wasn't the time or the place. Vicky, true to her style and always looking for the positive in everything, raised her glass.

"Let's drink to love, survival and the preservation of friendships." We all raised our glasses and blinked to hide our tears. It suddenly felt good to have something to celebrate. The dinner was slow and cumbersome, something reminiscent of *The Big Chill*. There were silences and tricky moments, but all navigated well under the circumstances. Vicky was the driver.

"It would be easier for me if David was dead," Carrie's words hit me hard and almost took my breath away. I could have sworn that I heard Vicky and Josh gasp simultaneously with me. If the night was a festering wound, those words were the salt that stung—agonising and deep. In the research that I had done, I had been warned of the shock and the pain that would follow—but wishing me dead was totally unexpected. Nobody responded to what Carrie had announced. It was as though the words had never been uttered.

Carrie was subconsciously trying to frame what she was feeling, and it was clear that she was already working through the cycle of grief. The only problem was that the person that she was grieving—and the person that she wished was dead, was sitting diagonally opposite her and, he too, was also lost somewhere in that same cycle of grief. The initial shock of my revelation to her was over and for the first time since I had dropped the bomb, she was showing some real anger.

"How could he have done this to me?" Carrie directed her question at Vicky. I jumped in, trying to salvage things.

"Carrie, it's unfair to ask anybody else that question, that's a question for me." Carrie was quick with her retaliation.

"Don't you talk to me about FAIR?" she had raised her voice and she had a wild stare in her eyes. "There is nothing FAIR about what you have done to me." I felt guilty for having subjected our friends to this eruption, but I was pleased to have some backup in the trenches.

"Carrie," I countered, feeling the strain and some volume in my voice, "it's not fair what I've done to you, and it's also not fair to involve our friends."

"Sorry," Carrie retorted, directing her comments to Vicky and Josh, "just a rough week." Josh put his arm around her shoulder and instinctively gave her a squeeze.

"It's all going to be okay," he told her.

"I hope so," she crackled as she began to cry. "It doesn't feel like it right now." We finished the bottle of wine and our friends departed. I was grateful for their visit. The evening had been a bit of a mess, but it was progress none-the-less.

NURIEL HAD WARNED me of the grief cycle that Carrie would enter, and he had told me that he would work hard at buffering her emotions. He explained that he would do this 'to protect her from the overwhelming heartache, but also would allow her to feel enough so that she still felt and processed her pain'.

The following morning I had a scheduled Skype call with Nuriel. Our calls were more frequent that week because of the freshness of my coming out to Carrie. I gave Nuriel an update on the previous evening and he listened attentively.

"I need to channel a little more," he proposed. "I think we need some all-round protection," he added. I listened attentively. "Libra is ascending," he explained, "and this means that Carrie is susceptible to the opinions of others...we need to protect her." I was listening, hanging on to every word, but I didn't understand the mechanics. Nuriel continued. "Stay as close as you can to Carrie," he guided, "support her...talk to her...show her that you care about where things are at...keep people like Abby away...and...." The Internet connection dropped.

"Fuck!" I exclaimed as I redialled. Nuriel answered straight away and we had a much better connection. I could see his friendly and mystical face, his eyes as translucent as the day I had first met him at Kai and Chris's wedding all those years ago. With time, he seemed to have adopted his mum's Airedale terrier smile—but his was the more friendly version. He was wearing one of his trademark oversized and unstylish button-up short sleeved shirts; and a small blue crystal, too small for his solid neck, dangled above his top button.

"Should we still go away for the weekend we have booked on a farm in the Fens this weekend," I asked apprehensively.

"You absolutely should," he replied straight away, "Carrie needs to feel buffered and cared for during these early weeks…time away will be good for you all."

SO, ON FRIDAY afternoon after school, we all climbed into my Honda CR-V and we headed north toward Wimblington. The car was packed with food and snacks for the weekend, board games to lull away the time, extra blankets to keep out the chill of the flatlands, and a strange vibe that reminded us that we were and we weren't a couple. The girls were excited and that helped bring some ease to the air on the one and a half hour trip.

We arrived at Dawson Farm shortly after half five in the afternoon. The farm was set against a low knoll that was lined with windswept willow and alder trees. The twisted tree trunks leaned away from the slope of the hill as if their aching joints were suppressed by years of torment from the unrelenting winds. The farmhouse was a lovely old stone building, with larger than usual sash windows and a moss-covered slate roof. The doorway was small and disproportionate to the size of the house and the windows. It was as though a previous owner had been out to make a point when the window tax was repealed in 1851. The main bedroom and lounge looked out onto the meagre hill and the kitchen and the girls' room looked out onto a small pond which was adjacent to the long dirt track that led up to the house.

As soon as we arrived, Jane and Kate wanted to explore. After unpacking the car, we took a brisk stroll up the knoll and the girls climbed some of the tired and twisted trees. Kate called them 'nature's climbing frame'. Jane was more interested in two cows that we had stumbled upon on our way up. They had been blocking a dirt track like two policemen in the road. We stood for a while in front of them, as we looked at them and they stared at us with their big, sad, and droopy eyes.

"Why do you think they look so sad?" Jane asked.

"Probably because they're tired and they know they're going to get eaten when the farmer is hungry," Kate answered quite matter of factly. Jane squinted her eyes in disgust.

"That's why I think I might want to be a vegetarian," she announced. I was suddenly put off the barbeque that we had planned for later that night.

"I'm going to call this one Hot Chocolate," Jane stated with certainty, pointing at the darker of the two, "and this one will be Milk Slab," she announced gesturing toward the smaller and whitish one.

The girls were always at home in nature. Jane was ready to save the world and Kate was hot on her heels.

"Pick up those papers," Jane instructed her little sister, as she herself picked up some discarded and slightly rusted beer cans.

"We're going to leave this farm cleaner than we found it," Jane told me proudly. Amidst all of the chaos in our lives, it was good to know that I had got something right. Carrie was with us as we explored the farm, but she didn't say much. She just moved along with us, heavy and sad like a diesel tractor. It was clear that the pain of 'living one of the lasts' was eating at her. This would be our last family holiday, there were a lot more lasts to come—and we had already shared our last bit of intimacy, she just didn't know it at the time.

That evening we had our barbeque which was thoroughly delicious. As we ate our beef steaks and lamb chops, I tried hard not to think about Hot Chocolate and Milk Slab. Their big eyes, sad and forlorn, like Carrie's, pleading for mercy and love and hope. Like Carrie, they also had no idea of what tomorrow, the next day or next week might bring. After dinner, Jane and Kate roasted marshmallows over the fire, and they burnt sticks ends and wrote their names with the glowing embers in the dark—like shooting stars across the Milky Way. The evening was magical, only dampened by my revealed secret which had now contorted into a tangible shared pain for me and Carrie.

Once the girls were asleep that night, Carrie and I went to bed. She lay on her side of the bed writing in her journal. I read for a bit, but I was struggling to focus. After a while, I noticed that Carrie switched her journal for her iPad and she was playing *Flow*, mindlessly joining the dots that helped her escape her confusing reality. I put down my book which I wasn't enjoying, not because it was dull, but because my head wasn't in the right space to be captured by it. It was called the *Solitude of Prime Numbers* and it was about two kindred and damaged teenagers who find each other and then, by certain circumstances, are forced to separate. It was too heavy, I needed something light, probably something like *Flow*—something that would help me escape the pain of my awakening and the separations that lay ahead. I didn't need to be reading a book about separation—impending separation was all around me.

I reached for my phone and there were two WhatsApp notifications from Dan. One had been sent three hours earlier, and the other only a few minutes before:

"Have you guys arrived safely?"

"How are things going there?"

"All good," I replied. "The farm is lovely. So pretty. Went for a walk earlier and we had a barbeque for dinner." I pushed send.

"How is Carrie doing?" came his quick reply.

"She seems sad and not totally with us," I wrote back.

"Understandable," was his swift response. I stared at the phone for a while, aware of Carrie's eyes covertly darting between *Flow* and my fingers on the keypad of my phone.

"I wish I could fast forward all of this," I wrote and pushed send. I could see Dan immediately read the message and was typing a return message, when Carrie scowled.

"Who are you talking to?" She was abrupt and angry as she sprang to her knees and was facing me, sort of towering over me like a peacock that was ready to fight. "WHO? Who are you talking to?" she bellowed aggressively. I took a deep breath.

"I'm talking to a friend," I calmly answered.

"DAN?" she barked, tilting the end of his name upwards to turn it into a question. She was reminding me of what she had discovered during her 'investi-gay-tion' a few weeks earlier.

"It doesn't matter who I'm talking to," I responded as calmly as I could. Carrie was red-faced and angry.

"You've destroyed my whole life, and it doesn't matter who you're talking to?" her tone was angry and sarcastic. She lunged forward, ready for a fight. "Give me that phone!" she demanded. With her right hand she angrily clenched the top of the phone, trying to seize it from hands, and at the same time she sunk the long fingernails of her left hand into my lower right arm. "Give me the phone," she emphasised calmly through her gritted teeth.

"I'm not giving you the phone, Carrie," I countered with restraint in my voice. Her fingernails sank deeper into my skin and her grip on the phone tightened more. Carrie was angry and I had never seen her like this. It was frightening and confusing. She was quite literally fighting for her life and the anger was flowing from her eyes and out of her fingers.

"One last weekend with you, that's all I wanted, and you had to bring him along with us." Carrie was caustic and almost too cool. I managed to loosen myself from her vice-grip and leapt out of bed.

"Are you losing your mind?" I asked with some toxicity in my own voice.

"Maybe I am, David," she replied, spewing vitriol, "and I wonder why?"

CHAPTER THIRTY-EIGHT

THE COMING OUT TOUR

14 July 2013

As Dan and I began to grow our friendship during the coming out months, we aptly named the time of our secret liaisons during the latter half of 2013 'the dark ages.' Dan had told me that the David that he had met on the down-low during that time was not the David that he was coming to know and appreciate. He explained to me that during the dark ages, I presented a nerdy and terrified version of me, somebody who didn't have much confidence and who might be a little timid and reserved. This couldn't have been further away from the flamboyant version of myself that my friends and family knew. It told a story of the fear that I was doused in, even when I took those small, but brave and devious steps toward finding my truth. A deceitful truth, that was embedded in lies and was ready to let loose some serious emotional pain and trauma.

Dan was discovering the confident David, the exuberant David, and the animated David. The David that everybody else knew. The David that everybody loved. Dan labelled me as eccentric, and he identified my eccentricity as a mechanism that I used to both hide and display my homosexual flamboyance. It was a masquerade that I had created and one that I had unwittingly mastered throughout my entire life. Eccentricity was fun, but flamboyance was just queer. I was a pro at eccentricity. I did nothing in half measures. My coming out tour would be no different. All or nothing was my motto. Dan was to learn that too. My coming out tour saw the blending of my theatrical restlessness and my need to speak my truth. I needed to own my journey and I wanted the world to meet the new me. Above all, I wanted it to understand that I was not going to leave Carrie and the girls by the wayside.

For each sitting of my tour, I used a standard script that varied slightly from audience to audience, but it usually went something like this:

> *Things have been a little rocky lately with Carrie and I, and this is through no fault of hers. I have been grappling with my sexuality for many years now and I felt that I had to tell Carrie where I was at. I can see that my lack of interest and presence is hurting her, and I think it is unfair to keep her trapped in a marriage where she does not feel loved and cherished. We don't know where this will lead us, but I want you to know that I am going to do all I can to make sure that she and the girls are looked after.*

In most cases, I would sit alongside Carrie as I blurted these words out, sometimes I stalled with tears, and other times I stuttered and stammered. I would hold her and cry with her, and often we cried together with who-ever's turn it was to hear the news. It was a slow and emotionally draining journey, but we needed to do it—and we did most of it together.

First up were Carrie's parents, this would be the most difficult one. I had arranged for them to travel up from Torquay so that they could stay with us for a few days and be an emotional support to Carrie. I sat them down in the lounge. Carrie and I were on one sofa and they, opposite the coffee table and vase of daffodils, on the other. The daffodils looked tired and dreary in the afternoon light and they echoed my emotions on that day. When I finished blurting out my shocking soliloquy, Carrie's mother immediately leapt up and took me in her arms. I clung to her and we cried.

Carrie's dad was, by this time, consoling her. The room was heavy with pain—but also with hope. I was surprised by Carrie's mum's honest and supportive response, and I completely appreciated it.

"Don't worry David, we'll all get through this," Carrie's dad was warm and convincing. It all felt too kind, and I didn't feel like I deserved it—but I was grateful for their love and understanding.

Next up was my mum and then we moved on to Carrie's sisters. I was nervous to tell her youngest sister, Abby, because she was a fundamentalist Christian, living in fear and bound by what she called 'The Word'. Abby was the sort of person that you might find waving quotes from Leviticus 18 on big hate placards, lining the periphery of gay pride marches.

Abby came to our house on her own in order to hear what I needed to say. I was hardly finished with my prepared address when Abby unexpectedly took over.

"Why are you lying to me?" she shouted in a tone that might have demanded royalties from the likes of Billy Graham. I was confused and I could see Carrie was too. Before I could reply to say that I wasn't lying, she continued, first repeating her question again: "Why are you lying to me?" Then she wailed: "Because that is sin, a sin from the pits of hell," elevating her voice and gesturing with her arm and her hand in a way that showed that she was reaching deep—I guess somewhere deep into the direction of hell. Carrie and I were speechless but she wasn't finished. "When you were young," she continued, "Satan planted a seed inside your head and now it is growing." Her words were so loud that they echoed into the hall. Then suddenly there was silence, just when I thought the sermon was on its way to getting started, it literally fell flat and ended. Billy Graham would have been disappointed. The silence was so stunning that you could actually hear it. I looked at Carrie, who also seemed to be unsure as to what should happen next. I was floored by the extreme response from Abby, so what I managed to muster up may have seemed a little pathetic.

"Abby," I sighed, "I respect your religious beliefs, but mine are not the same." The rest of the conversation was a blur and Abby left soon after that. To this day she has thankfully remained silent in my world. Carrie's other sister, Chloë, and her husband were—to my great relief—reasonable and accepting of the news. They were also to steadily peter out of my life. It was easier that way and it left less of a sour taste in my mouth. It never seemed easy when Jesus was in the mix.

On another occasion, I sat with my cousin Brigette. Carrie did not join that meeting. Once I had shared my news, Bridgette broke down and cried. I was so confused. She and I had shared much of our early twenties partying and enjoying each other's company. Family politics had only allowed us to bond in our later years. Despite her late arrival in my life, she was in many ways like a sister to me—always available and always interested in my life. Once she had composed herself, with her husband Zac comforting her, she spoke.

"I'm so sorry David," she sobbed, "I had no idea, I really didn't." I tried to lighten the moment.

"Well...that's why I came to tell you," I retorted with a cheeky smile. She brushed over my response and continued.

"I am so, so sorry that I didn't know and that you have had to spend your whole life carrying this burden, living a lie...not being able to be yourself." She continued to cry. I squeezed her hand and smiled at her, she tried to smile back.

"It's been a little tough," I replied, "but the journey is unfolding."

"You know we're always here for you," she smiled reassuringly.

"I do," I answered, wiping my own tears away. "And that's why I am here tonight." Our tears dried up and Zac kept the wine flowing. It was good to share my secret with people who cared about Carrie and I and how we would navigate the future together—but apart.

Another big one for me was telling James and his wife Becky our shocking news. Many years had passed since our friendship had first blossomed at The Bonanza in 1987 and it had had natural peaks and troughs—but we always knew that we had each other's backs and that we could call on each other if we needed to. We were incredibly fond of them, and they of us. Telling them would not be easy. We broke the news to them toward the end of August, after what had been a painful meal out where Carrie and I wore brave faces.

"We need to have a serious chat with you," I said, as the last plates were cleared. Fear oozed out of my words. James and Becky looked immediately ashen.

"What is it?" James asked with obvious worry and some irritation. "Is it serious?"

"It's serious," I replied, "but not life threatening." I felt stupid as soon as I uttered the words, but they served their purpose. The gloom that hung over us was obvious enough to keep the waiter away for a while as I recited a version of what I had repeated so many times before in the previous weeks. The news was met with stunned horror and more tears, and we all cried together. Our foursome, something like the splitting of ABBA, had come to an end. I found myself apologising profusely to them and then again publicly to Carrie. It felt cathartic, but it hurt.

I reiterated, with them as witnesses, that I would love and support Carrie and the girls through this ordeal. The mood remained grim and we cried one last time before we said goodbye. The betrayal and the breakdown in trust for friends like James and Becky was too much to deal with, and our friendship entered a long and extended trough. I missed them immensely, but I had to concede that as much as the old David was dead to Carrie, he was dead to them too. This emerged as the case with many other friends on the way too. It was a bitter pill to swallow, but I came to understand that, like Carrie, everybody needed time to come to terms with what was perceived as a loss—and also a betrayal.

In contrast, I made a visit to Georgina to break my news to her. She had moved from Edinburgh to Nottingham to be close to her ageing parents. I spat my news out at her over afternoon tea at a quaint teahouse on the Royal Mile. She replied befittingly.

"Of course you are, Davey," she exclaimed, "you like soft furnishings, you sing show tunes and you love your mum…it's obvious!" I smiled in agreement.

"Always so easy with you, Georgie," I marvelled as I breathed in some of the positive energy radiantly illuminated at me by her warm smile. I wanted to explain more, but she stopped me. "Let's not talk about things that don't need justifying…knowing you," she continued, "I am sure that you will look after Carrie and that you'll continue to be the amazing dad that you have always been." I felt myself feel instantly grateful to the universe for sending Georgie across my path on that dirty corner in Aswan, Egypt all those years ago.

"That's the plan," I replied, already feeling more optimistic about my journey. I tried to explain and justify where things were at in my life, when she turned on her teacher voice that I knew all too well.

"Seriously, Davey," she commanded, "let's not give any airtime to rubbish." I took the instruction and we headed out for a Chinese meal where we spoke aimlessly about British politics and rich people's greed. It was a welcome escape and nice, for a change, to have the likes of David Cameron on the dissection table—where it felt I had been for the couple of months before.

Another significant stop on my coming out journey was at my dad's brother, Uncle Dave. He was married to an amazing woman called Gloria. Their home was always warm and welcoming. It smelt of intoxicating and exciting flavours that percolated from the kitchen from which they only served good wine. Their simple home oozed style reminiscent of Scandinavia in the 1970s. When you were with them you always felt like a million dollars. My news was met with love, affection, and acceptance. Uncle Dave immediately confided in me that my story was all too familiar to them. Their daughter had recently discovered that her husband was gay. He had left a trail of evidence that had led to him being outed by her, and things had gotten messy. She was obviously good at 'investi-gay-tion', I had thought, or he was careless on the down-low. So, for Uncle Dave and Aunty Gloria, I must have been a contradiction. On one hand, I was a victim of societal dogma, while on the other, I also represented the villain—the kind of person that inflicted pain, a pain that they themselves were dealing with at very close range. A pain that they nursed in the form of my cousin Gemma. Despite this complex situation, they continued to shower me with love and support, and for this I was grateful. Their walk alongside these two battles must have placed them in a variety of compromising positions: listener, informer, traitor, confidant and friend. Wherever I went on my journey, I seemed to create chaos and hurt—it was too soon for healing, yet those who loved me and trusted me, and those who believed in equality, stayed close to me, nurturing and guiding and acting as critical friends.

ON EVERY STEP of the way during the early days of my coming out journey, Dan, Holly, and Nuriel were there for me. Hands that guided and directed and hearts that loved. Dan was also learning: observing and listening, asking questions and reflecting with every stop on my tour. Nuriel had counselled me that, 'once you come out, you will never stop coming out...you will come out for the rest of your life'. And he was right, virtually every day of my life, I continue to come out in a world where my gender implies a certain stereotype and assumes a certain sexual orientation. I understand that it's probably most confusing for those who know me, I have two daughters and therefore I must be straight. And for those who don't know much about me, I'm a man who dresses relatively conventionally and therefore I must also be straight—unless, of course, their gaydar works.

My coming out tour was terrifying and liberating all at the same time. At the onset, I felt dirty from the years and years of guilty residue that had built up inside me like grease on a stove's extractor fan. Slowly, one coming out at a time, I started to accept myself more and the grease began to wash away. Removing grease takes time and a lot of effort. It requires hot water—boiling hot water, strong soap and daily scrubbing.

To this day, every coming out is another step toward self-liberation and self-acceptance. The fundamentalist responses, such as the ones that I received from Abby—and there have been at least 6 of those to date—have no hold or bearing on me anymore, I am too far down the road for that. But, for some reason, the silence and rejection from people like James and Becky—and others, who held a special place in my heart, still hurts massively. I guess the Abbys of the world need credit in so much that they spoke their mind, while the others left me guessing—which isn't helpful when you are on a personal journey of finding love and acceptance for yourself.

Apart from declaring my truth to Carrie, I felt I needed to also come out to the likes of the vicar, to Graham and to Jessica—because I had in some way, and to some extent, defrauded every one of them on the long road to finding my truth.

CHAPTER THIRTY-NINE

TELLING MUM

18 July 2013

GEORGINA WAS RIGHT, I did love my mum.

I loved my mum and I loved my grandma. I also loved my sister, Holly and I loved all the girls in my life.

I loved Carrie, but differently to the rest. I always tried to make her my number one, but somehow my secret separated us, and she felt it. The other women in my world came between us, she was understandably threatened by them, and I foolishly couldn't comprehend why.

I loved Jane and Kate. I love them more than words could explain— theirs was an all-consuming love—an overwhelming love.

The relationship between my mother and Carrie was always a little fragile. I could never understand why, until I started to unravel the world I was determined to fix. As part of this process, I began to consider and understand the juxtapositions held by the two main adult women in my life. Theirs was a complex mother-in-law-daughter-in-law relationship. Carrie had a vision of the picket fence, which she rightfully deserved, and because I wasn't always mentally and emotionally present, she didn't feel like number one. My relationship with my mum was always solid and as much as Carrie didn't like sharing me with my mum, my mum didn't enjoy sharing me with Carrie either. There was a silent competition that I never took any notice of. I thought I played fairly, but the bottom line was that my lack of physical interest and my emotional disconnectedness to her made Carrie feel unsafe and she was always left second guessing herself.

My mum's life was not too different from Carrie's in the sense that she was also often left wondering where she stood with my dad. His lack of interest in her as they got older, and as he became distracted with entrepreneurial ventures and friends, made her vulnerable and needy too. These unfortunate circumstances made them obvious scapegoats for each other, as they dealt with the pain inflicted on them by the Sterling men—both senior and junior. I was the go-between.

ONCE MY COMING out tour had hit the road, my mum was the second stop after Carrie's parents. I called her early in the evening.

"Hi mum, you all right?" I asked.

"I'm well, and you my boy?" came her reply.

"Do you mind if Carrie and I pop up and see you quickly?" I asked with a dry and hostile throat.

"Sure, is everything okay?" she asked apprehensively.

"All fine," I lied, not sounding fine at all. "We'll see you in about 10 minutes," I told her before hanging up. Carrie's parents were still in town and they came over to look after Jane and Kate while Carrie and I went out. We arrived at my mum's place about 15 minutes later. It was early evening and the afternoon light was orange and low in the sky. There were long shadows cutting across the living room and they made elongated and quirky patterns across the orange scatter cushions on the sofa. If I hadn't been as nervous as I was about this conversation, I might have enjoyed the show that the sunset had to offer.

"Coffee or tea?" mum asked.

"Just some water please," Carrie replied. She was softly spoken and fragile.

"Nothing for me, thanks mum," I added with some volume and lilt, trying my best to raise the tempo in the room. There was a radio playing in the background, softly whispering mum's insufferable country western music—probably Johnny Cash or Jim Reeves or something equally annoying like Dolly Parton.

Mum handed Carrie a glass of water and she sat down with her mug of tea. The long shadows and the even longer silence were both calming and forbidding. Carrie looked at me through the introspective afternoon glow which highlighted both the trauma in her eyes and the painful shadows beneath them. It wasn't comforting to know that I was responsible for this obvious torment.

"Mum," I gulped, "I needed to come here with Carrie to tell you something that you may have always known." Mum looked confused. I suddenly realised that I had deviated from the script that I had planned. This one was playing out differently.

"I'm not sure I know what you're talking about," mum responded as I started to recognise the anguish in her eyes. I offered more.

"I'm talking about something that I have known ever since I was teenager." I breathed deeply and I noticed that Carrie's wet eyes were darting between mum and I. "I've tried to overcome and fight this thing and I can't anymore..." I paused for few seconds, breathed deeply, and then finished the sentence, "I'm gay, mum." As I uttered the words, it felt liberating, as if my mother might finally know the *bona fide* David Sterling whom she had given life to and whom she had raised.

"Is that true, Davey?" she asked, looking slightly bewildered. Then before I could answer, she continued: "Because...if that is true, it's the best kept secret ever." It was a sweet, appropriate, and understandable response. What I had been processing internally for at least three decades, had now been delivered to her in just a matter of seconds. She would need time to process and comprehend it.

Carrie was sitting next to me on the two-seater and I was holding her hand as she cried quietly, tears were dropping from her cheeks. It seemed that she was about to speak, so I gently squeezed her hand and signalled with my mouth in a gesture that suggested that she should wait a minute or two. I could see mum was confused and she needed time to process. I also had no idea what Carrie wanted to say, but I suspected that she may want to offload some of her hurt and her pain. After what felt like a lifetime, but may have only been about a minute, my mum spoke.

"Well," she replied, "you're my son and I will always love you...no matter what." I could feel my heart dance with relief, but its pulse was still throbbing in my neck. Mum continued, now looking at Carrie: "I will also always love you, Carrie...you will always be a part of our family...and it goes without saying that I will always love my two beautiful granddaughters." I was incredibly impressed with mum's articulate and accepting response. Our entire life, she had been the abiding wife, the housekeeper and our caregiver. The woman who lived in her husband's shadow. We didn't know her as an articulate speaker and a pragmatic thinker. Since dad had died nearly two years earlier, we were getting to know somebody new, as mum evolved into more of an independent person.

Carrie cried more once she had heard mum's words. I held her tightly and I began to cry too. I noticed that mum had also begun to cry. Mum was the image of gran—only taller and slimmer. Her eyes were soft and caring. Mum's words, as kind as they were, indicated the end of something—something that Carrie surely knew was coming, but facing it and comprehending the reality of what it meant must have been so enormously overwhelming for her at that time.

The emotions in the room simmered down a little and mum turned to some practicalities.

"What does this mean for the two of you and for the girls?" she asked with genuine concern. I jumped in.

"We're not sure," I answered. "We're going to figure it out in the coming months." Carrie was still crying and I passed her her full glass of water and put my arm reassuringly around her bony shoulder. The stress of what I had done to her was quite literally eating her away. "My main priority for now is to make sure Carrie and the girls are fine," I added.

"Will you get divorced?" mum asked, opening a can of worms that I wasn't yet ready for.

"I'm not sure mum," I responded and then I clumsily added: "What I really want is for Carrie to find true happiness."

Carrie composed herself and after what was at least five minutes of silence she spoke. Her words were angry, and she needed to vent. She had to dump her pain somewhere outside of her body and if you were in David Sterling's camp, you were understandably more of a foe than you were a friend. The shadows were withdrawing from the room like tortoises pulling into their shells, hiding from the hurt and pain and the unknown that awaited us all. The light was low, hiding the pain in Carrie's eyes. Then, without warning, she lashed out at mum.

"And I want you to know," she heaved, "that David has destroyed my dreams of growing old with him...those dreams that I had of us getting older together in our rocking chairs—they are gone, forever!" I could see mum sympathise and understand her pain. She too had been robbed of a rocking chair retirement with the man she loved. For mum the thief had been cancer, for Carrie the thief was homosexuality.

"I am so sorry, Carrie," mum replied with genuine empathy and no more words. She got up, walked over to Carrie and they hugged and wept together. I sat and watched them, and I cried too.

Carrie left soon after and I stayed on with mum to provide more explanations and to answer some of her questions.

"Why didn't you tell us earlier," she asked.

"I never felt ready," I explained. "I felt dirty and shameful...I didn't know how you would all respond." Mum looked perplexed.

"We're your family," she sighed. "We could never not accept you." I wanted to be cautious about mum's religion, so I delicately delivered my next comment.

"The church hasn't made my journey any easier," I explained. "My whole life they taught me that this thing is bad." Mum was listening attentively, her soft eyes hanging on to my every word. Despite the fact that she had been crying, she still looked radiant. Her hair had recently been cut and styled into a layered bob that made her look younger than her 64 years. Her soft makeup was always classy and gentle. The lines on her face were classic and kind and told of a full life, with a few hiccups in the road.

"The church is completely fine with homosexuality," she offered.

"That's good to hear" I replied.

"Pope Francis has said it is fine," she continued.

"Not exactly," I responded kindly—having done my homework. "He has stated that if a person is gay and has good will and wants to seek God, then it is not his right to judge...he's not exactly saying it is okay." Mum didn't respond, instead she nodded her head in a motion of either processing or agreeing.

"Would you like coffee or tea now," she asked, shifting the conversation slightly.

"No thanks, mum," I replied, "I must get home to Carrie and the girls, I need to buffer them and make sure they are fine—things are rough at home at the moment. I think the girls might suspect something, but we haven't told them anything yet." Mum reached out for my hand.

"You'll always do what is right," she smiled with certainty, "you're a good person...that's why everybody loves you."

"Not Carrie at the moment," I griped, "and I'm not expecting that to change for the foreseeable future." Mum smiled.

"One small step at a time," she supported with a love akin to that of Simon's mum when she told him to 'just breathe' in that very emotional scene in the movie. I felt fragile, I wanted to cry. I was scared too, scared of the unknown and of the ramifications of my released secret.

"I'm going to pray for you, all of you." she declared.

"Thanks mum," I answered, as she kissed me on the cheek as I left.

LATER THAT NIGHT, mum called me to thank me for coming to see her and to ask how Carrie was doing. I told her that Carrie was doing better and that we were playing Monopoly to distract us all. I hated Monopoly, but the girls loved it.

"I called Father Walsh," mum added before ending the call, "and he confirms that the church embraces all orientations, cultures and races." Then out of the blue she revealed that he confided in her that he is gay and that because he is married to the church, he doesn't practice his sexuality. The news did come as some surprise. Father Walsh had chosen to be homosexually celibate—or had he? Perhaps he might be on the down-low with the likes of Vicar Gary Beltham-Smith.

"Interesting mum," I said, "let's chat more later in the week...love you."

CHAPTER FORTY

BARGAINING AND BATTLING

26 July 2013

IN THE MONTHS building up to my coming out to Carrie, I had researched *ad nauseum* what I might expect in the aftermath. I read books and blogs and articles—magazine and academic. I listened to podcasts and talk shows, and I watched YouTube, movies and documentaries. One book that I read that gave me some interesting insights was by Dr Bonnie Kaye and it was titled: *Gay Husbands/Straight Wives: A Mutation of Life*. If I recall correctly, Dr Kaye's husband had revealed that he was gay, and she had turned her loss and the healing that followed into therapy for others.

Dr Kaye wrote that even in this day and age we don't fully understand and accept the whole concept of what she called 'gayness'. She highlighted that even though we have exposure to gay people and lifestyles in our day-to-day lives or on TV and in the movies—we still find that we grapple internally when we have to face the gay in our worlds.

For Carrie, watching something like Brokeback Mountain or Milk would have been straightforward—those were gay people in another world. Watching those movies was my struggle, and I was acutely aware and fearful that my awkward body language and heightened interest might expose me. When Carrie had to deal with the gay in her world, she was shocked and repulsed...it wasn't meant to be like that. Gay movie protagonists were fine, gay at a distance was tolerable—a gay husband was not.

DR OTIS HADN'T warned us of the bargaining that would form part of Carrie's painful healing, but thankfully Nuriel and Dr Kaye had. After the initial shock and anger, Carrie moved—almost in textbook style—into the bargaining phase. The Dr Otises of the world create false hope for women—and men—like Carrie. Instead of counselling and supporting Carrie toward acceptance and healing, Otis planted false hope. She bandied that 'David might be bisexual', trying to convince Carrie that I may be able to control my urges and my preferences. The unrealistic expectations that Otis planted, quite literally, encouraged Carrie to bargain for her life, for her reputation and for her dreams of growing old with me. But worse than this, she made Carrie believe that if she fixed herself—made herself more beautiful, more sexy and more appealing—then I might choose to go with the heterosexual side of my non-existent bisexuality. Otis created in Carrie a hope that what we had could be salvaged. What she actually did was send Carrie into a deeper depression, thus slowing down the process of her own healing, and also *our* healing.

On the Friday evening of Dan's coming out weekend, Carrie and I spoke until after midnight at the dining room table after the girls had gone to sleep. It was one of our better talks, some of her anger was subsiding and a strategy of bargaining was taking over. It might have seemed easier to deal with than the anger, but it wasn't. It was exhausting beyond measure. It required calm and agility. It demanded quick thinking and honest and sensitive responses.

"Maybe I've not been a good wife," she blurted, the words almost winding me.

"What are you talking about?" I asked with horror in my voice.

"Maybe I've been too absorbed by the girls and I've neglected you," she offered. I was feeling exasperated, but I remained calm.

"If only it were that simple," I replied.

"Dr Otis says that you might be bisexual and that there are ways we could save our marriage." Her voice was sincere and desperate. Instead of responding in a way that came instinctively, I leaned back and offered her the space to speak some more. "If this is something that you need to get out of your system...I could turn a blind eye for a while—and then we could carry on like none of this ever happened." Carrie was steadfast in what she wanted to say, and so she went on unabated: "Or if you don't want me physically anymore, then we could agree that you do what you need to and we don't have to share intimacy anymore...we just won't tell anybody."

When she had finished offering her numerous cumbersome options— options that degraded her self-worth and made me hate Otis more than I did after the first session we had had with her, I leaned forward and held her two trembling hands in mine.

"Carrie," I agonised, "listen to your words...they tell me that you haven't grasped all of this fully and I don't think Dr Otis is being kind to you." She looked a little unhinged, so I squeezed her hands. "None of this is your fault," I added with gentle authority—but also with irritation for Otis. "This is about who I am, about how my brain is wired and about what I desire...it's about what comes naturally to me...you haven't failed at anything," I explained gently. Carrie was hanging on to every word, and she nodded her head to indicate her mild understanding. Soft and gentle tears were slipping painfully from her beautiful sad blue eyes, wetting her flushed and clenched cheeks. "You haven't done anything wrong," I reiterated. "I haven't been honest with you...or with myself."

Carrie let go of my hands to wipe her tears.

"Every suggestion," I continued, "that you have made so far has undervalued you, they are only bound to damage your self-esteem more...more than I already have." At that point, I began to cry and then we cried together. For a while there was no need for any words. The TV was droning quietly in the background and the warm summer air stood still around us, almost protecting us from all of the unknowns that awaited us. "You deserve more," I continued. "You deserve to be loved and cherished...you deserve to be desired and wanted in ways that I am incapable of." Carrie leaned backwards as if she was composing herself to take control.

"Maybe we can still come to some kind of agreement!?" she stated and asked at the same time. I knew I needed to be gentle and patient.

'You just need time," I offered. "We all need time."

NURIEL HAD WARNED that prolonging the bargaining would negatively impact Carrie's self-confidence and that it would also add more cata-strophic blows to her self-esteem which had already been severely ravaged.

"You need to constantly remind her that she deserves more," Nuriel told me in our Monday morning Skype call. "She needs to be constantly reminded that the universe will give her more...and I will take care of that," Nuriel added confidently.

"It's so tricky," I replied. "There are times that I just want to agree with her impractical suggestions, so that I give her hope and keep her go-ing...even though I know that they are not workable at all." Nuriel looked contemplative.

"Sometimes," he pondered, "you have to be cruel to be kind. Stay close to her, love her and support her, but we need to guide her into this new reality. Things will never be the same again...things can't be the same again."

I wanted Carrie to be all right, I wanted us all to be all right.

CHAPTER FORTY-ONE

ANOTHER BOMB IS DROPPED

28 July 2013

SINCE RE-ESTABLISHING CONTACT in the weeks prior to my coming out to Carrie, Dan and I stayed in constant contact. He was a lifeline to me. Our friendship was growing, and I continued to wish for more whilst he was firmly focused only on his next steps—breaking the news to Judy as sensitively as he could. I had learnt that there is no gentle landing for a bomb of that size. It lands hard.

More than anybody in my world, he knew first-hand of the pain and strife I was dealing with. He was also learning about Carrie's hurt and suffering, and I could see that he was carefully digesting and processing everything I shared with him because soon he would be dealing with similar circumstances. I had discovered that being the cause of another's suffering is incredibly painful and soul-destroying. There is nothing that you can do, except stay close to prove the re-envisioned model of your love, and even then, as I learnt from Carrie—sometimes you are wanted close and then at other times you are not wanted near at all. I allowed myself to become Carrie's punching bag. I needed to give her a place to release her hurt and her pain, but it wasn't always easy. It was sad and scary for both of us, but understandably I was the villain. I was five weeks ahead of Dan on this journey—and my journey contained valuable lessons for him. His task was to take from the good and to reengineer the bad.

The 28th of July was a busy day in the van Dijk household as it was Rachel, their youngest daughter's, second birthday. Amy, their eldest daughter, was nine, and Tom, who loved his Spiderman and Batman outfits, was six. Their home had been full that day with the entire family—at least 20 people over to celebrate Rachel's birthday. Dan had shared some photos with me via WhatsApp earlier in the day and it looked like a lot of fun. I remember studying the people in the photos closely, trying to work out who was who, and wondering if they would like me if Dan and I ever became an item. I was ever hopeful.

During the day, Dan had also told me that he was feeling distracted because he was stressed about the conversation that he was going to have with Judy later that evening. I was still shocked by his decision to come out to Judy so soon after my coming out to Carrie.

"I feel like I physically want to throw up," he told me in one of his WhatsApp messages.

"You need to breathe deeply and use every bit of energy that you have to visualise a happy outcome." I wrote in a coaching-like tone. He replied with a thumbs up emoji and I went back right away with another message:

"Keep the energy positive...work it!" Nuriel would have been proud of me. I saw that Dan read it immediately before he disappeared for an hour or two.

IN THE MONTHS and weeks before my confession to Carrie, I had continued to communicate with Nuriel at least twice a week, although it was often more frequent than that. In the weeks leading up to my dropping the bomb on Carrie, he probably became too much of a crutch for me. I knew it, but I didn't care, I was in survival mode, and I needed him to do some of my thinking for me. Since I had come out to Carrie, the frequency of mine and

Nuriel's interactions had decreased, but he was still steadily guiding me—focusing mainly on my communications and interactions with Carrie and Dan.

In the thick of it all, even I found myself questioning my own sanity and frequently asked myself what I was doing. To an outsider the story would have sounded ludicrous—I was working with a so-called energy practitioner who claimed to be psychic and who was guiding and protecting me as I plodded on with great focus toward something I really wanted badly—but which certainly seemed unattainable. I had decided that whatever it was, it was working for me and I fully subscribed to it. I saw it as Nuriel guiding and coaching me toward harnessing my own energy to manifest what I wanted. Essentially, it was quantum physics in action.

Dan hadn't ever actually told me that he was working with Nuriel in the same manner that I was, but I put two and two together: Dan had asked me for Nuriel's contact details and Nuriel had once said something to me that suggested he had spoken with Dan, after which he quickly and rather poorly tried to cover his tracks—all in the name of client confidentiality. I hoped that Dan had been fasting according to the same, or at least a similar, plan that Nuriel had given me in the week before the big event. I had found that the fast kept me focused and distracted all at the same time. From the WhatsApp photos that Dan had shared with me of Rachel's party earlier that day, I suspected that fasting might have been tricky—the food looked delicious.

At around 6:00 p.m., Dan messaged me.

"All the guests have left," he wrote. "Tonight's the night. I am terrified." I decided to send a light-hearted response.

"You'll be okay, just wear your big girl's blouse." He replied straight away.

"Ha ha," he wrote and then he went off the radar for close to four hours.

DURING THE WEEK before, I had moved into the downstairs guestroom, although Carrie, the girls and I continued to eat meals together as family. We had told the girls of the divorce but hadn't yet disclosed the issue of my sexuality. The transition was slow and difficult. Now alone in my new room,

I was incredibly anxious for Dan and wondering how his revelations to Judy had gone. Dan's coming out held no promises for me. He had been clear that I was not his type and also, I hadn't come out for him—we were two friends supporting each other through the most difficult event of our lives. All of this considered, I remained hopeful. For me it was written in the stars.

At twenty to ten, my phone tinged and it was a welcomed sound.

"We've finished chatting," came the message from Dan.

"And...?" I replied, feeling a little anxious.

"I couldn't do it," came his next message, "the words just wouldn't come out of my mouth," he continued. I felt my stomach sink.

"So, what now?" I wrote, feeling decidedly disappointed—for him and for me. He didn't read the message immediately and it must have been thirty minutes before I got a reply. It was a painfully long thirty minutes. He came back to me to say he had been joking about not telling Judy and apologised for disappearing on me. He explained that Amy had come downstairs to tell him that she couldn't sleep and that he had been lying with her for a few minutes.

"She must be in tune with the energy in the house," I noted.

"You're probably right," he wrote back.

Dan and I exchanged numerous messages that night.

"I'm sorry we'll have to just text," he wrote. "Talking is going to be dif-ficult tonight." Through the messages he told me that Judy's reaction had been somewhat different to what he had expected. "She was very supportive and understanding," came one of his messages. "We cried a lot together," came another. "We agreed that we will always put the children first," he shared.

"Brilliant," I wrote, feeling sorry that Carrie and I hadn't explicitly spo-ken about this; although I believed that we would instinctively do it anyway. Dan went on to explain that they had spoken a lot about the future and what that might look like. He said that he had been surprised that the conversa-tion even spilled over into sharing thoughts on what their modern blended family might look like. I was excited for him but given how things had un-folded for Carrie and I, it seemed like a little too much, a little too soon. I immediately hoped that I was in the modern blended family that he and Judy were beginning to visualise in their heads.

"I am so happy for you," I typed, "I hope the rest unfolds as easily as the conversation did tonight." He and I both knew from me being a few weeks ahead of him, that there was every likelihood of Judy entering the grief cycle. Nuriel had warned me in one of his sessions, that 'there is nothing more painful than grieving a person who is still alive.' From the pain I was witnessing in Carrie this seemed to be all too true. Tonight, Judy's journey of grief would begin, but it was too early for her to realise it.

"This is my turn to be proud of you," I wrote, "tonight you are my hero." And he really was. To be sitting opposite somebody you love, to shatter their hopes and dreams takes guts, but real heroes hang around for the whole of the bloody aftermath. I knew that he, like me, was committed to seeing the pain through to the end.

"Thanks," he replied. "Your friendship means the world to me." My heart warmed over pleasantly for the first time in many months.

We agreed to meet for a coffee in the week and then we said good night.

CHAPTER FORTY-TWO

UNIVERSAL SUPPORT

13 August 2013

NURIEL AND HOLLY were my lifelines, holding and carrying me when my transition out of my comfortable life became overwhelming. I was mostly strong, with a fighting spirit and had sheer determination to manifest what I wanted. I called on the Universe, I called on Linda's tarot cards, I called on Nuriel's energy manipulation, and I called on the collective efforts of everybody and everything in my world. I knew for sure what I wanted: I wanted Dan and I wanted everybody that we loved to be happy, safe, and protected.

Nuriel had taught me about quantum physics and the power of attraction. Every day of those long and painful months that I waited for Dan, I willed him into my world. Each day, I would chant to the Universe, over and over—in my head, and out loud when I was alone:

Powers of the Universe, pray listen to me-
if Dan is to be mine, please send him to me.

I was relentless. I knew what I wanted, I had known it from the day I had set eyes on him. My guardian angels were just faster off the mark than his were. Nuriel had explained to me that on a non-scientific, but purely psychological level, your mind and your thoughts affect your actions.

"It's basically about positive thinking," he had explained. "If you think the worst, expect the worst—but if you want something, then dream it, think it, and manifest it." It all sounded too easy, but I was on board. "Always visualise," Nuriel advised, "and don't focus on waiting for your goal to materialise, let it occur naturally." This was the hard part for me, because I became obsessed with looking for daily progress and my visualisation was taking its time to unfold.

"I'm trying," I explained, "but I'm impatient now."

"Energy can never be hurried," he cautioned.

Nuriel had also counselled that I should be cautious about who I shared my universal desires with.

"Bad and jealous energy can be like spokes in a wheel...be careful of who you share your visions with," he warned. My wishes were safe and what I wanted had only been shared with Holly, Vicky and more recently with another friend called Mark Musgrave. I trusted these three implicitly and I knew that they were seated firmly on my side of the universe.

MY FRIEND, MARK Musgrave, was the headteacher at Nightingale where Carrie taught and where I had been the Chair of Governors. All too tight and cosy for little Chelmsford. Mark and I had become friendly since his appointment at the school. We worked closely in our roles of headteacher and governor. His wife Eve and Carrie had become friendly—and the Musgraves became close house friends of ours. We shared some family weekends away and their friendship was interesting and refreshing. Eve was quite religious which always made me nervous, but she never pushed or shoved it on anybody else—in actual fact, she had made comments that suggested she was an ally of the gay community.

Mark was different to most friends that I had had before. He was a man's man—rugby loving, beer drinking and he'd been an excellent athlete in his earlier years. Rumour had it that he had been somewhat the ladies' man, strapping and handsome, when he was younger—but I couldn't see this. To me he was just a great friend and there was no physical attraction at all. Mark had cobalt blue eyes and his hair was thinning and receding on the top and at the sides. Middle-aged spread was taking its toll on him too, but he had a good sense of humour about it and he always drew attention to his expanding midriff. Humour was the tool that he used to deal with the loss of his youthful physique and his boyish looks. Mark and Eve had been one of the early events on my coming out tour. They had cried with me and Carrie and pledged their support—and they had followed through. Eve supported Carrie, and Mark supported me.

Mark would check in on me every day. He would call, he would pop around and he would joke with me about the person that I was becoming. His wisdom and his support were supernatural, almost unbefitting of his stereotype—masculine, straight and Christian. Late one afternoon, I stopped in at the school to sign some documents.

"What about boobs?" Mark asked with a straight face. "Aren't you going to miss boobs?" He phrased his question like there was a bereavement of sorts.

"Give me a flat hairy chest," I joked—but not actually joking, "...and I'm a happy man," Mark frowned. "No, Mr Musgrave," I continued, "I won't miss boobs, in actual fact I've never been attracted to them at all." He looked horrified.

One evening after a governors meeting, he walked me to my car and was curious to learn about Dan and our progress.

"This guy must catch a wake up," he demanded, "he doesn't know what he's missing out on."

"He should!" I cracked back. We both laughed. Mark was so incredibly supportive and encouraging. He was that one friend who I had trusted with my secret, and he was cheering me to the finish line.

As we arrived at my car, he pulled his winter coat open as if he was a flasher.

"So, David...tell me," he asked tongue-in-cheek, "am I your type?" With that he took a twisted stance and he pulled a face that made him look like his parents were related. I laughed out loud, the sight was too ridiculous for words.

"Sorry Musgrave," I rebuffed, "you're just not." He smiled.

"Damn it!" he cajoled, "I don't know what this Dan guy has that I don't."

"Maybe an interest in men," I suggested with a laugh.

"Probably," he replied, laughing with me.

The Universe had sent Mark to be my friend at the right time. It was as though he was lined up just in time and ready to swing into action when the secret escaped. He was kind and accepting, and he was a supportive listener, continuously coaxing me toward my dreams and the man that I wanted to spend the rest of my life with. Mark and I drifted apart over time—not because the strength and integrity of our friendship waned—but because as things progressed in my life, I needed to move out of Carrie's immediate space. I needed to give her room to heal. Moving away from people like Mark Musgrave were some of the sacrifices that I needed to make. These sacrifices were not always conscious, they happened surreptitiously over time, and I only realised some of them after the fact.

For many years before the likes of Mark Musgrave, the Universe had been working for me, with me, and alongside me. My family were my earliest gifts from the stars, and Holly was a cosmic gift bestowed on me 18 months into my life. Our childhood bonds were strong and through the trajectory of our lives we had come to learn that we could count on each other for anything and everything.

I KNEW THAT Holly always had my back, and I also knew that she was open-minded, accepting and non-judgemental. Telling her my secret had been tricky, but I had never feared rejection or retribution. She, like Mark Musgrave, became my confidant and champion. Since coming out to Holly, she had understandably become intrigued by Dan. Her interest was not so much in him as a closeted colleague whom she might accidentally pass in the passages at work, but more as the person whom her brother was fixated on. The person who unwittingly held her brother's heart strings.

"What is it about this guy that has you so hooked?" she asked.

"I don't know," I answered. And the truth was that I didn't know. For me, Dan was my destiny and I just understood and accepted that from the day that I had met him. There was no logic. For me, it had always been written in the stars. Neither Mark, nor Vicky, nor Holly could understand this, and I didn't really either—but I believed it.

Holly was showing more and more interest in meeting Dan. I guess she wanted to get a close-up glimpse of the man who was edging his way into our pod, but from the things she was asking, I detected that she was expressing some concern for him and the path that he was walking. Like me, he would also be terrified of the unknown.

One Saturday morning when we sat down for a coffee at *Pret a Manger*, Holly began to ask more.

"Who is he talking to for support?" Holly always looked at things from everybody's perspective. She was a fixer.

"Only me," I answered, "...and maybe Nuriel." Holly looked perplexed,

"Sounds like a lonely road...does he have brothers and sisters?" she asked.

"He does," I replied, "but I don't think he's ready to come out to his family yet." Holly took a sip of her cappuccino.

"I want to speak with him," she asserted, placing her cappuccino back on the table. Holly was as much an empath as she was determined. There would be no stopping her.

Later that afternoon, I messaged Dan.

"I've told Holly about you." The revelation was a few months late, but I hadn't told him to protect him and his sanity. I knew that I could trust Holly with both of our lives, but he had no basis on which to know this. The message went unread for a while and my heart was in my throat. I was watching a movie with Jane and Kate who were getting annoyed with me obsessively checking my phone. At least 40 minutes after sending the message, Dan replied.

"WHAT? Are you crazy?"

It was always difficult to read his tone in a text message—was he joking, or being dramatic, or was he angry?

"She's known for a while," I wrote back and held my breath.

"For how long?" came his anxious response. The time for cloaks and daggers was over, there was no more room for lies or half-truths.

"For about 5 months," I replied.

Jane and Kate were now harassing me but I needed to deal with this pressing issue that had the potential to implode.

"Push pause, please guys," I asked them, "I just need to go to the toilet." I hurried to the bathroom and locked myself in to finish the chat without interruption. By the time I got to the bathroom, Dan had replied.

"WHAT?" he exclaimed. My head was starting to zing.

"Sorry," I typed and pushed send, and then I typed some more: "Jane and Kate are waiting for me to watch a movie. I need to be quick." He replied right away.

"Should I be worried?" I typed as fast as I could, aware that time was not on my side, but also needing to pacify Dan as best I could.

"I would never compromise you. Holly is the most honest and trustworthy person I know. She wants to meet you. She's an ally. Stay calm. Chat later." I pushed send, turned my phone off and went back to the movie.

The following Tuesday afternoon, Holly called Dan. Apparently, she explained who she was and asked if she could pop over to his office. Dan was taken by surprise—but he agreed to see her.

"I'm on my way to see Dan," she messaged. Now it was my turn to be alarmed.

"WHAT?" I wrote. My message went unread and then an hour and forty-five minutes later a WhatsApp message came in from Dan.

"That was nerve shattering, but also liberating. I totally like your sister," he wrote. I had hardly finished reading the message when Holly called.

"I think I frightened him," she said, "but he seemed to relax after a while." My mind was racing with a million and one questions and so I fired the important ones first.

"How did he react to your call? What did you say when you arrived at his office? What did he tell you about me, his family, his journey?" Holly offered some information and then she got cagey.

"I can't tell you everything," she stated, "I need to establish some trust with Dan, but I want you to know that I really like him." It all felt like a bit of an anti-climax. I wanted to know more, but I was pleased that we were off to a good start—they were both telling me that they liked each other. That was progress. It was important to me that these two got on with each other, and Holly was taking good care of that.

SOME TWO MONTHS later when Dan and I were out for dinner, he took me by surprise.

"Tell me about your sister coming to introduce herself to me," he asked mischievously.

"What must I tell you?" I replied, a little confused.

"Did you send her with a mission?" he interrogated.

"What are you talking about?" I asked, still uncertain about where this was all going. "She initiated the whole thing...she was gung-ho about meeting you."

"Really...?" Dan pondered sounding unconvinced.

"I think she actually wanted to reach out to you to give you an outlet, and to offer support," I offered. These honest words seemed to provide Dan with the peace of mind he was looking for and his suspicions were laid to rest—for a while maybe.

"I think you're right," he agreed. "Holly did want to meet me, she did want to get to know me and she did want to offer me support on this journey...her actions over the last couple of weeks have proved that," he reflected.

"I told you she was an amazing and loyal person," I interjected.

"Hold on," he contemplated, "but she had a bigger mission, and I can see you are oblivious to it." I was confused.

"Are you saying she had ulterior motives?" I asked, becoming concerned.

"Not at all," Dan replied. "She needed to tell me what an amazing person you are...that you are one of the good guys...that you are a good catch." I couldn't believe what I was hearing.

"Are you sure?" I asked, feeling slightly puzzled at my sister's approach.

"Very sure," he replied assertively, "I wasn't sure then," he noted, "but now I know that she does tell the truth." We exchanged a smile and I felt butterflies dance in that golden chalice beneath my rib cage.

The next morning, I called Holly as bright and as early as would not be deemed antisocial.

"Morning," I lilted, a little like Father Ryan might have, and then I cut to the chase. "Dan tells me that part of your mission when you introduced yourself to him was to market me...like cheap perfume." We both laughed.

"I can neither confirm nor deny," came her cheeky reply, "but what I will say is that if somebody will not respond to the call of the Universe, my job is to loud-hail for the moon and the stars."

Gosh, how lucky was I to have an advocator as driven as my sis?

CHAPTER FORTY-THREE

THE ENERGY IN SYNC

9 November 2013

IT HAD BEEN a few months since Dan and I had both dropped the bombs, and things were progressing steadily and cautiously inside our marital homes and also between the two of us. A large part of each of our days was dedicated to dealing with the extreme emotions of our soon to be ex-wives. Dan with Judy and me with Carrie. The end of each day was always my highlight. For an hour or two before we went to sleep, we talked to each other—exchanging notes, offering support and listening and learning. It was uncharted territory, and as with the arrival of a baby, there were no DIY guidebooks. We were fumbling in the dark, each providing a little bit of light to the other.

The friendship between us was growing, and it was being built on a solid base with strong foundations. Our journeys and our shared stories gave us something bigger than we could ever have imagined. Dan, Nuriel, and Holly were there for me every step of the way and my Skype sessions with Nuriel were intensifying.

"Things are imminent," Nuriel told me earlier in the week. "On Saturday Jupiter is in retrograde and expansive energy will turn inward. The signal dropped for a few seconds which meant I lost some content, and then I heard: "…for a surge of energy expansion in one area of your life. After Friday's activation you will feel a pull of opposites." I didn't understand it fully, but it sounded positive. I was tempted to contact Linda for tarot card confirmation, but I didn't.

The months before had been good for mine and Dan's friendship, but my interactions with him were also emotionally arduous and hugely exhausting. I had previously declared my interests and he had stated his lack thereof. I lived in hope, waiting and praying that he would come to his senses, or that Nuriel's energy prediction would come to pass sooner rather than later.

"You can't rush energy," Nuriel always cautioned me.

Dan was back on datingbuzz, steadily searching for his new life partner, and I was his brave and jealous *fidus Achates*. It was painful. So, my retaliation, in true David Sterling style, was to do what he was doing—but tenfold, because that is how I do things. I also needed to look and see, and hopefully make him jealous too. I reactivated my online profile and I hit the digital dating airways. It was as scary as it had been just a year and a bit before. The pickings were few and I hoped that Scorpion_D was also experiencing the dearth of good men and the promise of everlasting happiness. I hoped that he might sometimes pause at my profile and feel a flutter or a pounding, but if he did, I never got wind of it. For every coffee meet that Dan had, I had multiple. I wasn't prepared to be left behind and it was a kind of rebound or rejection response. I hated doing it, but I couldn't help myself. I am pleased that I did because I met some interesting and damaged people on the way—sadly, or gratefully, no one with any kind of prospect for the long-haul.

Dan met one guy called Jeremy who seemed to tick all of his boxes. I already hated Jeremy and I had no desire to meet him. He lived in Glasgow, which was a comfortable enough distance away, but still too close in megabytes, gigabytes and airtime. Dan seemed one hundred percent smitten with his online gay bear, and I was struggling. Jeremy was making the trip down south to meet with Dan and it was almost as if the wedding plans just needed to be firmed up.

"Don't you worry about anything," Nuriel told me in our emergency Skype call.

"I hope so," I replied with distress in my voice. I had requested the Skype call because I was distraught at the prospect of what might transpire after Jeremy and Dan met on the weekend.

"It's not meant to be, but he needs to do this," Nuriel explained, "…at this time on Sunday, this won't even need to be a conversation," he concluded. Nuriel was calm and confident. Once I was composed and Nuriel had allayed my fears, I needed to ask something that had been in my head for some time.

"Can I ask you something out of the ordinary?" I probed.

"Sure," came his reply, sounding unsure of what was going to come next.

"Many years ago," I explained nervously, "I worked with a guy in Barcelona—his name was Lorenzo López." Nuriel interjected, he was slow and quizzical.

"Yes?" he drawled. The tone of his voice made me want to stop with what I had planned to ask. "Go on," he nudged.

"Well he's been on my mind a lot lately," I explained feeling slightly embarrassed.

"Yes?" Nuriel replied, drawling again.

"Does he show up anywhere in my future?" I asked.

"You mean, you're attracted to him?" Nuriel was blunt, but kind. I didn't answer. "He could," he answered contemplatively, "but that would be entirely up to you…he's a good guy…" Nuriel was quiet for a while and then he advised, "…but focus your energy on what you really want." He emphasised the word 'really' with some out of character volume.

Saturday night came and went and Dan messaged me early on Sunday morning. "Jeremy was a non-starter," he cut to the chase. I felt a massive sense of relief.

"Why?" I asked, pretending to be interested and surprised.

"Not my type, too queeny, too grubby and he was wearing too much *Joop*—it made me feel nauseous," he stated. I giggled. It was difficult to read the tone in his writing and I didn't want to entertain it much.

"Does that mean you're back on the market?" I jibed. It was a little bitchy, but it felt good.

"Guess so," came his reply.

"I have a coffee date tomorrow," I told him insensitively, trying to be one up on him. I should have been more sympathetic, but all I could feel was relief.

"Who are you meeting tomorrow," came his reply.

"He's Italian and his profile picture is delicious," I wrote. It was my turn to rub salt wherever I could.

"What's his name?" came Dan's reply.

"Donatello," I answered smugly, "he's a big shot at Deloitte and Touche." Dan was quick to warn me to stay away from Donatello. He explained that he had met him for a coffee a year before—a little while before he and I had met.

"He's a prostitute," Dan wrote.

'Sour grapes,' I thought. I didn't reply.

Monday afternoon came and I met Donatello for a coffee near his office at Canary Wharf. He looked nothing like the Enrique Iglesias look-alike profile picture. Instead, he looked like Danny DeVito, just with more hair and less height. His head looked like a rugby ball resting on a tee—waiting and ready to be converted for an additional 2 points. He spoke oddly out of the corner of his mouth, and only spoke about himself and the one hundred men that he had proudly bedded to date. Later that night, I wrote to Dan:

"Donatello was a non-starter," I copied his words.

"Why?" he replied almost immediately. I pondered on my reply and then I typed.

"No comment." I wrote and then I swiftly deleted those two words and replaced them with: "Because he wasn't you." I reread them. My heart was in my throat. "Fuck it," I muttered out loud and then I hit send. A few seconds later I received a smiley face emoji. 'Better than silence,' I said to myself.

The Saturday of Jupiter in retrograde arrived and I was excited to be heading off to see Dan after lunch. He and Judy had owned an investment flat, which they had made available and furnished for Dan's transition to his new life. He was starting to spend a few nights of each week there. The flat was in a building aptly named Soho in Brentwood. I arrived a little after 1:00 p.m., with a bottle of red wine and a corkscrew in hand. I knew from previous experience that wine made me brave…and amorous. This might not be a beach in Torquay, but Soho had a good ring to it. Our greetings had become slightly odd and awkward, we were never sure if we should shake hands or hug. I knew what I really wanted to do, but instead I gave him a kind of man shake—the sort where you simultaneously shake hands and bump shoulders. Dan showed me around the flat and then I opened the bottle of wine. It was a South African KWV 2010 Merlot, smooth, with soft tannins, cinnamon aromas, and tastes of nutmeg.

"Nice wine," Dan commented, "great aromas." I made a big swirl and took a deep sniff.

"Better than *Joop*?" I asked with a jestful sneer.

"Only just," he retorted.

The conversation flowed and before I knew it we were on glass number two. Then, somewhere between the cinnamon and nutmeg, I bravely leaned over and kissed him softly and gently. He reciprocated, pulling me in and holding me tight. It was so good to taste him again, and I didn't want that moment to ever have to end. I pulled off his t-shirt and he quickly pulled back the lounge curtains to block out the neighbours. It was good to touch him again. Next was my turn, he pulled my T-shirt over my shoulders and I removed my silver necklace that had carried St Christopher close to my heart since my confirmation many years earlier. I placed it on the footrest in the lounge.

Dan and I soothingly touched each other for a while, and I guess we both realised that we were also hanging on to each other for dear life. The trauma of the last few months had been tiring, and it felt good to be comforted and held by somebody who represented strength and safety. That moment, although incredibly satisfying, felt slightly marred by a multitude of concerns of where this might all lead.

"I'm happier when I'm with you," I told him as I left.

"Ditto," he replied, but he didn't sound hugely convincing. My heart was in a panic. I had to leave because I was meeting Holly at the Holy Rosary parish for the annual Catholic Church Carnival. Ironic that I was heading back to the church with my homosexuality now finally coming properly to life. On the way, I called Nuriel to give him an update. I was smiling from ear to ear.

"Energy never lies," he gloated. "Now go and meet your sister and rest easy." For the first time in months, I felt like I might be able to do that.

IT WAS, AS always, lovely to see my dear sister and her friends. She had surrounded herself with good, kind, and accepting people. They were like her, all from the same loving tribe.

"I kissed him," I told Holly excitedly.

"What? Wait, tell me more...," was Holly's enthusiastic response. I gave her the run down. "It's all going to work out," she reassured excitedly. Then she became distracted. "Now don't look at two o'clock," she added bossily, aiming her face downwards.

"Why not?" I asked, staring exactly where I was told not to.

"Jim Winterton, Nicky Thomson, and their whole family picnic," she exclaimed almost loudly enough for them to hear. Jim and I made eye contact, but I looked away to avoid any unnecessary awkwardness. Nicky walked over.

"You doing all right?" she asked.

"I'm okay," I answered, "I'm just worried about Carrie."

"We're all rallying around her," Nicky said offering some comfort, "make sure you also look after yourself too."

"Thanks Nicky, it means a lot," I replied. She gave me a hug and then made her way back to her cousin and the rest of their extended family. Nicky's words were comforting and a relief. Sometimes love, kindness and acceptance came from the most unexpected of places.

That evening, I messaged Dan somewhat apprehensively.

"How are you feeling about today?" I asked. His reply, with Jupiter in retrograde, came swiftly.

"I'm feeling very content," he offered. And so was I.

"God bless Nuriel and Linda and all universal energy," I vocalised and then I breathed in a big breath through my nose, heaving up into my chest and I instantly felt lighter. Then unhurriedly, I let it all out through my mouth and felt my lungs come to rest on my diaphragm, like a hot air balloon returning to its landing patch. "What a day," I whispered with light and bright energy oozing through my veins. I felt good. I had crossed a Rubicon, and it was time for some well-earned rest. I took off my shirt and reached for my St Christopher, "Oh shit," I exclaimed, "I left it at Soho."

I had, it seemed, quite literally dropped my religion in the name of what, only a year before, I might have labelled as my 'dirty and ungodly desires'. But now things were different. Very different. I had met my truth— and I had made it my own.

CHAPTER FORTY-FOUR

DAD'S NOT STRAIGHT

22 November 2013

WE HAD ALREADY told the girls that we would be getting a divorce, but Carrie wanted to protect the girls from the curse of the gay stigma that had arrived in our lives for a long as she could. It seemed that she needed to process it first before she was willing to share it with our children. Dr Otis wasn't helping with progressing things either. She had every reason to draw out the process for as long as she could. Every visit that Carrie made was another instalment from our pension fund into hers. Dan and Judy had been quick off the bat. They had sat Amy down soon after Dan had revealed his news to Judy and explained to her that mum and dad were getting divorced and it was because dad was gay. Straight to the point and nothing left to guess. Dan told me that Amy had taken it well and in her true direct nine-year-old style, she had responded:

"I'm not surprised dad, is that why you always watch Glee with me?"

Dan and I had developed a banter with each other where we would both try to prove that we were more butch than the other. Odd that we still found the need to be more manly than the gay man that we were starting to accept in ourselves. In essence it was mild gay-bashing—something that we had done so well in our closeted lives. Revealing that he was a Glee fan didn't do his street cred too much good, and I was one up on him. He called me *Queenie*, and I called him *Girlie*. Condescending and not very flattering at all, but they became terms of endearment and they worked. My title gave me more rank. I just never pointed that out to him.

"So, Queenie," Dan asked during one of our late-night calls, "when are you going to tell the girls that their dad is a homo?" His words were brash and also frightening. They reminded me that, after Carrie, I still had to do my second biggest reveal. I was waiting on Carrie because she had told me that she only wanted to tell the girls once the schools had closed for the holidays in December for the Christmas break. I was becoming impatient and I wanted to share my brave news with Jane and Kate. Carrie still seemed to need time—Otis time perhaps—before we divulged the facts to the girls.

"I'm working on Carrie," I replied, "I am eager to tell the girls." And I was, I knew that the bonds that I had created with them were strong and unbreakable. This was why I needed to be honest with them.

"My heart will be full of GLEE when I tell them," I joked, accentuating the show he had enjoyed watching with Amy.

"You're such a bitch," he replied with a chuckle. Later that night, when Carrie and I sat down at the dining room table, I raised the issue of wanting to tell the girls. To my surprise, she responded to my request positively.

"I think it's probably time," she agreed, "I'm feeling stronger now, so let's do it at the weekend."

In the build-up to Friday night, Nuriel told me that I would never regret telling the girls.

"Honest words and heartfelt listening," Nuriel explained, "will grow your bonds with the girls deeper. When they hear your honest revelations, they will instinctively trust you more...only because you're working from a solid base of trust." Nuriel always made things sound so easy, and even if they weren't, I have come to realise he was always setting up positive energy for positive outcomes. Throughout the journey he helped me constantly believe in and manifest the absolute best.

On Friday evening after dinner, I was ready to communicate the news as naturally and as simply as possible. I wanted to handle matters like Holly and Georgina did. I didn't want to make this an event, I didn't want to give it unnecessary power or credence—I wanted to convey it with love, safety and understanding. The plates were cleared, the dishwasher packed, and we took our bowls of ice-cream to the coffee table that sat between the sofas in the living room. Kate set out the Monopoly board and Jane gave us our starting bank balances. Carrie looked like she may have been struggling, but she was putting on a brave face and she played the game animatedly for the sake of the girls. They were none the wiser.

At one point in the game, I was sent to jail for landing on the wrong place on the board. While in jail, I took the opportunity to begin the revelation.

"Did you know," I asked, "that a long time ago people like Aunty Holly's friend Michelle and her girlfriend would have been sent to jail for being gay?" I looked at Carrie, she wasn't quite sure where all of this was going, and neither was I.

"What's gay?" Kate asked unexpectedly.

"You know," I explained, "like when two boys or two girls like each other." Jane jumped in to help her sister out.

"Like Cameron and Elijah," she offered. Cameron was the Goldberg's nephew—a brave young man who had been out and proud for at least half of his 28 years. Elijah was his kind and sweet partner.

"Yes, just like Cameron and Elijah," I confirmed.

"They're so cool," Kate commented.

"Especially Cameron," Jane added, "his jokes are kind of funny." It felt like things were progressing well and the gays were in favour. The time had come for me to cautiously release the bomb that I had been holding back from these two: my life, my joy, my everything.

"I'm like Cameron and Elijah," I said calmly, then I waited a second or two before adding, "that's why mum and I are getting separated." I still found it hard to say the D-word around Carrie and the girls. Divorce sounded so final, it reeked of finality and dissolution. Jane was the first to respond.

"Really?" she kind of asked with an inflection in her voice and then she added: "Why are you only telling us now?" It was clear that she was calmly trying to piece it all together.

"Mum and I wanted to make sure that you were ready," I explained. "We needed you to understand the divorce first." Jane was shaking the die in her hand while she replied.

"Hearing about the divorce was difficult," she noted with an advanced maturity in her voice, "but this news...you could have told us about it sooner." Kate joined the conversation.

"If you're gay, why did you marry mum?" she asked.

"Good question, Kate," Carrie interjected. It was a truth in jest comment.

"That's a long story—and maybe a story for another time," I retorted. "For now, we wanted you to know, and don't be afraid to ask us anything you want to know." We slipped easily back into the game of Monopoly and as with most games of Monopoly, we had to end it because it's one of those games that just never ends.

As we were packing the board game away, I wanted to provide a caution.

"Thanks for your understanding, my babies," I marvelled. Kate snuggled in under my shoulder and I kissed Jane on her forehead. "Now you probably don't want to be telling your friends about what we discussed earlier," I suggested.

"Why not?" Kate asked.

"It's nothing to be ashamed of," Jane added.

"I know it's not," I explained, "but it's your friends who might not understand it...and that's where there might be a problem." I felt immediately uncomfortable that I had just pulled them out of the closet with me and now I was pushing them back in. It's not that I wanted them to be ashamed—I wanted to protect them. I wanted them to be cautious. I only wanted them to share the secret with people who would love and support them without any judgement.

Before they went to bed that night, I went and lay with each of them. I read each a story and I reminded them that I was going to be there for them always. Then, before I kissed them on their foreheads, I told them that I was proud of them and that I was always grateful that they had chosen me to be their dad. It had all been much simpler than Carrie and I had anticipated. Children are resilient and mine were gun metal strong. Just before bed, I took out my phone and typed a message to Dan:

"Girls know their dad is a fag. It all went well." I copied the message to Nuriel too. They both came back immediately. Dan wrote:

"So pleased. Well done. I didn't expect anything different." Nuriel replied, true to his mystic style of coaching:

"I knew this already. Be grateful for your gifts, be thankful for every day. Keep loving everybody, with every step. Always be grateful to the universe." Nuriel was right, I had so much to be thankful for.

THE FOLLOWING MORNING, I went for a jog and I encouraged Jane and Kate to join me. When they ran with me, things were understandably slower. There was a lot of walking in-between which gave us the opportunity to talk. I explained that some people had issues with gay people and that it was usually to do with their religious beliefs.

"That's so stupid," Kate remarked supportively.

"It is," I agreed, "but unfortunately that's just how some people are," I explained. "And that's why I want you to be careful about who you tell...for now, at least," I urged. I needed them to come to understand this new development in their lives, I needed them to accept it and when they were more confident in it, they could take control of it. They needed time to start their own coming out.

The blogs that I had read and the podcasts that I had listened to cautioned how coming out was a never-ending process. This was more so the case in situations like ours, where our heteronormative histories assumed a mum and dad. When you have children, your partner is assumed to be a person of the opposite sex, and when you have a dad it is assumed that his partner will be a woman.

With time, they became proud of their gay dad and they became LGBT activists. Steadfastly and safely challenging phobias and fears in their little circles. When they joined events like Pride, they were out and proud—quite literally waving their rainbow flags for the world to see. With their friends, I noticed some caution, particularly in the spotty teenage years when they were dealing with their own sexual identities and complex teenage angst. Jane was always the most robust and unwavering—she never demonstrated any gay shame—she couldn't have cared less for the narrow-minded judgments of others. And she was right, we should all care less about what others think, and instead use what energy we have to respect ourselves and others more. The acceptance and love of my children made it so much easier for me to morph into my authentic self. It was as though the universe had engineered a plan to provide me with supportive soldiers who would mend and defend—validating my life, making the journey wholesome and worthwhile.

CHAPTER FORTY-FIVE

MEETING MY PREDECESSOR

1 December 2013

IT WAS LESS than three weeks after Dan and I were kind of—and sort of—officially an item. Things were going swimmingly. The energy was flowing and I had a bounce in my step. It looked like he did too. We had planned a week away to San Francisco, which was somewhat a reward for the trauma of the last year and also to celebrate 'us'. We chose San Francisco because it was a safe, gay friendly destination where we could finally be anonymous gays.

It took us a while to choose the location. We started with Edinburgh, and then somehow, we got to Rome, and before we knew it, we were planning a trip to San Francisco. By now, Judy knew about me, and Carrie knew about Dan. They understood each of us to be a friend, a support, and a confidant to the other. We weren't ready to share the progress that we had made at Soho a few weeks earlier. We were both excitedly planning what we called our 'liberation trip'. Dan and I were eagerly sharing screenshots of airfares and destinations with each other via WhatsApp. Unbeknown to either of us, the photos that I was sending were arriving in the van Dijk shared family photo folder. Judy discovered them and approached Dan. It was not the way we would have liked to have managed things—but it was too late. Judy was also proving to be a good 'investi-gay-tor.'

It seemed that for Judy, the intrigue had become too much. Her 'invest-gay-tion' skills, combined with the power of social media, must have already allowed her to put a face to my name—but it seemed she wanted to know more about the person who seemed to be whisking the stability out from under her feet.

"Judy's asked to meet you," Dan told me, kind of matter-of-factly over the phone during one of our late-night calls.

"Whatever for?" I responded, possibly a little alarmed. Dan paused and then explained convincingly that this was another piece in the big puzzle that she was working on to try to better understand where her world had spiralled to.

"I'm happy to meet her," I told Dan once he had sold the idea to me, "but please protect me if things get out of control, I have no idea of what I am walking into." Dan laughed, maybe nervously.

"It's all going to be good," he noted affirmingly.

Sunday morning arrived and we had agreed to meet at the Great Baddow Barn on the outskirts of Chelmsford. The pub had indoor play equipment which would keep the children entertained while we chatted. I was not only apprehensive to meet Judy, but also nervous to meet all three of their children: Amy, Tom and Rachel. I had arranged that I would take Jane and Kate, who came along with me begrudgingly. It was clear when we left the house that I had not left with Carrie's blessing. Meeting Judy for the first time was terrifying. I was facing another human being whose life, like Carrie's, had been thrown into disarray by an unexpected revelation a couple of months earlier. I was tired from carrying myself, Carrie, my children and Dan—I didn't know if I had enough energy for another.

The meeting with Judy went differently to what I expected. It was uncomfortable, but calm and easy. I was happy when it was over, but I understood her need to meet me. I watched her carefully assessing everything about me: how I made eye contact, how I composed myself, how I spoke, the way I moved and how I smiled. She was particularly observant when

Dan came near. She was weighing me up good and proper, and I was on my guard. At one point Dan disappeared, and I could see him with Rachel at the climbing frame a little further away. Jane and Kate had moved away with Amy and the three of them seemed to be getting on cautiously well. Tom was up and down in his Spiderman outfit, not anywhere at any given time. So, in that moment, it was just me—alone with my predecessor—at a pub table on the outskirts of Chelmsford and about 5 months on from her trauma.

"So..." Judy began and then paused. I was terrified that she was going to ask how long Dan and I had been together, or when we had met, or what our plans were for the future. I could feel my face begin to contort and glow and I was aware that I was clenching my fingers. "When did you realise?" she asked with sincerity in her voice. I was relieved.

"Realise I was gay?" I asked, double-checking the nature of her question.

"Hmm," she nodded, indicating confirmation.

"Probably since puberty," I explained vaguely, "but I guess I've just always known." Now that I was engaged one-on-one with her, I noticed that her face was friendly and framed by big dangly peach-tinted Swarovski crystals that swayed from each of her ears. She looked tired, as if the uncertainty of the last few months had taken its toll under her eyes and in her marionette lines. She, like Carrie, needed rest. The pain that Dan and I had caused these two women was permanent and everlasting. She interrupted my observations by calmly asking her next question:

"If you knew, why did you get married?" She was harsh and direct and it felt like *déjà vu*. Judy was asking the same questions that Carrie had asked me only months before.

"I didn't want this," I replied and took a slow breath before continuing. "I still don't want it," I concluded. She looked puzzled, but I continued. "This is not an easy path and I would rather not have it, but it won't go away, I've tried...I've had to accept that it's just who I am." She nodded contemplatively, scrunching her forehead, showing that she was digesting what I had just revealed. Then I realised that I hadn't answered her question. "So, back to your question," I explained, "I got married because I believed I had overcome those thoughts and those urges. I wanted a routine life...a wife and children...the picket fence...I wanted to be conventional." I could see that she was taking it all in and that it was helpful for her. It was also cathartic for me.

I was starting to wish that either Dan or one or more of the children would return to the table to disturb us. It felt like things were getting heavy and intense and I could see this was painful for both of us.

"Why don't I give you Carrie's number?" I offered, and then added, "I'm sure that she is experiencing a lot of the emotions and feelings that you are at the moment and it might be helpful for both of you if you chatted." Judy accepted the offer and she was punching Carrie's number into her phone when Dan returned to the table.

I hadn't had the opportunity to engage much with Dan's children and I wanted to get to know them—just a little at least. I also wanted him to engage with Jane and Kate because it was important for me that my children liked him and his family. Equally, I wanted us to be liked by them. I knew it was early—even premature—but it had been at least nine months since my first meeting with Nuriel, and eleven months since Dan and I had parted ways. I was impatient.

I got to interact with his children after lunch. Amy was confident and bright. Tom was sweet and transfixed in his world of superheroes, while Rachel was cutely oblivious to the world—all she needed was her blankie and her bottle and she was happy. Dan made an effort to talk to Jane and Kate and I could see that the conversation was about Kate's foot which was in a plaster cast.

"My granny drove over it with her car," Kate answered animatedly.

"So, tell me Kate," Dan inquired, putting his hand on his hip, "why did you put your foot in the way?" I saw the three of them laugh, and my heart smiled. This man was a definite keeper.

CHAPTER FORTY-SIX

ANOTHER PREDECESSOR MEETING

6 December 2013

A FEW DAYS after Jane, Kate and I had met Dan, Judy and their children at the Great Baddow Barn, Carrie told me that she would like to meet with Dan. I was worried about selling this request to him because it didn't sound like an introvert's idea of fun. In actual fact, both Carrie and Dan were more introvert in nature—I was the noisy extrovert that bounced between the two of them. So, instead of messaging him, I raised Carrie's request with him during our late-night chat. Casually and without too much emphasis, I conveyed it.

"Carrie says she'd like to meet with you, a..." Dan interjected and sounded immediately panicked.

"What for?" he snapped.

"I guess," I suggested tongue-in-cheek, "she wants to understand the big dragon in her life a little better." There was an extended silence and I could hear his TV playing in the background. "You still there?" I asked casually.

"Yes…yes, sorry, just processing this," he replied.

"I thought it might freak," I offered.

"It's only fair," he replied contemplatively, "everybody has met everybody and she's the only one who doesn't have a fuller picture."

"Thanks for your understanding," I proffered, and we continued to talk about our days, our challenges and the emotions in our respective households.

I was the go-between and liaised with Dan and Carrie for their coffee meet on the Friday afternoon. Dan had never been happy with me giving Carrie's number to Judy.

"It's too soon and too raw for communications to be productive," he insisted. Dan was convinced that they were already in contact—via WhatsApp at least, and that their collaborative 'investi-gay-tion' efforts would be focussed on trying to uncover as much as they could.

Our story was that we were friends—two guys who had sought to find somebody in a similar position, somebody to talk to, and somebody to lean on. We knew that Carrie and Judy did not believe us, and there was nothing that either side could do to prove or disprove the story. Dan and I were ashamed of what had happened in our dark ages and had made the decision to write that time in our lives off—like it never happened. We blocked and compartmentalised those months like we had done with much of our pasts. I had packed Scorpion_D far away in the back of my head with the likes of Mario, Jesus, Gary, and Graham. Dan and I were just friends—solid friends since a few weeks before I outed myself to Carrie.

Friday afternoon came and Dan and I made our way to the Chelmsford High Street. We were early, so we wandered around for a while. Dan was fidgety and I was doing all I could to distract him and calm his nerves.

"What if she asks me how we met?" he quizzed.

"Always short and sweet," I responded, "…we met online."

"Then why did we meet?" he was sounding a little frantic.

"We met because we wanted to meet and talk to somebody in a similar position," I explained. Dan sighed. "Danny," I continued "you are overthinking this…we've already agreed the dark ages did not exist." The problem is that Dan is a terrible liar. He would never be the sort to inflate an insurance claim or call the office to say he was ill when he wasn't. The grey areas in our story were distressing his moral obligations to himself.

We arrived at Costa before Carrie. We sat down and didn't order anything until Carrie arrived.

"Just relax," I coerced, as I leaned over and squeezed his left hand that was lying idly on the table. Carrie arrived soon after. The salutations were awkward. I kissed her on her cheek and gave her a hug. For Carrie and Dan, it was a soft and awkward handshake for now. I arranged drinks—one flat white for Carrie and two cappuccinos for me and Dan. I felt myself having to work hard to keep the energy and the conversation flowing, but I might have been responding to my own anxiety. The conversation was light and it brushed over the real issues; we could have been three strangers talking on the platform at a train station. I was the nervous passenger trying to keep the other two off the tracks—and on track. Carrie had told me that she would prefer me not to be there when she spoke to Dan. This is what had made us both nervous—especially me. It had unsettled Dan. He had no idea of where things would go and what Carrie hoped to achieve from the meeting. His biggest fear was that she might want to throw a lot of her pain and anger at the closest people to the situation—that included him. When my drink was finished, I excused myself.

"I should go now," I suggested, "can I get you two anything else?" I bought two bottles of water and put them on the table on my way out. "See you later," I said, with a fake jovial tone.

I walked up and down the high street to pass the time. This time, I was the distracted and agitated one. My mind raced with what it might be that Carrie wanted to say and then I dreamed up a million scenarios for the ramifications. I kept reminding myself that Carrie was a level-headed and rational person so it was unlikely that this meeting would have any negative outcomes.

In my surfing of the high street, I walked past the Costa shop window three times during the hour after I left them alone. Each time, I saw Carrie and Dan engrossed in deep conversation. They were seated at three o'clock and nine o'clock—opposite each other at a small round table. My empty cappuccino mug still sat at six o'clock, marking a clear divide between them in my absence. The first time that I walked past, Carrie was leaning forward and explaining something to Dan with an intensity that seemed to spill from her index finger that she was tapping on the table. When I walked past again, both Dan and Carrie were leaning in, Dan with his elbows on the table, like a couple quietly sharing a secret. The last time that I walked by, Carrie was leaning backwards in her chair and Dan was still tilted forward with his elbows on the table. To the onlooker, they would have looked like a couple sorting out an issue or navigating a dilemma—and in many ways they were, only with me—the third wheel—in the middle, wedged between them.

After an hour, I thought that I should return to them to see if they had finished. I also thought that Dan might have had enough by then. I had no idea if the meeting had been good or bad, whether it had gone well or whether it had been uncomfortable. I made my way toward the table. I stood at six o'clock waiting for Carrie, who was midsentence, to acknowledge me. She didn't. She finished her sentence, and then she looked up at me dismissively.

"We're not finished," she insisted, "we'll call you when we're done." So, like a scolded child, I found my way back to the high street. I was more distracted than ever now. I had no idea of what was being discussed around that table and how it would impact my reputation and my future with Dan. It was brave, or stupid, or both, to allow my outgoing partner to engage with the incoming. About 35 minutes later, Dan called me.

"We're done," he stated enthusiastically. I made my way back to the Costa, where Dan and Carrie were standing outside. The farewells were easier. Mine was the same as when we had arrived, but I noticed that Dan and Carrie hugged each other. 'Progress,' I thought, 'an Eskimo party!' Carrie looked at Dan with noticeable sincerity.

"Thank you," she said, "that was really good for me—and I hope for you too." Dan smiled and nodded. I think in agreement.

Dan and I started to walk toward the station.

"And...?" I probed, "what did she say?" Dan remained mum and had a big grin across his face. "Come on," I nagged.

"In case you hadn't noticed," he retorted, "that was a private conversation...you weren't invited—in actual fact you were asked to leave." I rolled my eyes and told him not to be ridiculous. He could see that the suspense was making me agitated. He smiled and then provided a sensitive explanation.

"Carrie did most of the talking," he offered. "I think she needed me to understand what this has been like for her." We arrived at the station and I could see Carrie walking toward platform 1 in front of us.

"Let's hold up a little," I suggested to Dan, "probably best if we get the next train."

"Sure," Dan replied. "She seemed to find comfort in sharing her feelings and her emotions with me," he explained. It was interesting that Carrie was brave enough to go to the core of her pain by wanting to meet Dan. "She is a strong woman," Dan commented. "She is going to survive." Dan shared a few more details about his exchanges with Carrie and he seemed positive about the meeting. I hoped it would have been good for him too. If this was all going to work out, we needed everybody to survive. Our dream of a modern blended family would never be realised if we didn't establish mutual respect and strong psychological safety. We would all need to listen, and we would also need to hear the hard truths. "Oh, one last thing!" Dan cheekily added, "she kind of warned me about the fact that you aren't the easiest person in the world." I responded quick off the mark.

"And I'm probably not, but I'm brilliant in bed, and I'll be a very loyal husband." We both laughed, I pecked him on his cheek and jumped off the train as we had reached my stop.

CHAPTER FORTY-SEVEN

ANONYMOUSLY GAY IN SAN FRANCISCO

14 December 2013

If you're going to San Francisco
Be sure to wear some flowers in your hair

I couldn't get the words of that Scott McKenzie song out of my head. They played over and over again, sometimes silently and at other times they boomed from my mouth with gusto. The song was unrelenting, I hated it, but I loved it. It was liberating, it was tantalising and its connection to my upcoming trip with Dan embodied so much of what I had always dreamed of wanting and being.

It might have seemed premature that we were going on an overseas holiday a few weeks after we had become an item—but for me it wasn't at all. This was close to 18 months in the making...perhaps even more like 30 years. For three decades this had been brewing in my head. Dan and I had passed the first couple's test—we had successfully agreed and planned our first project together. As much as we were aware of how difficult this sojourn would be for Carrie and Judy, we selfishly needed to do it. I didn't care that Judy's 'investi-gay-tion' had uncovered our holiday planning, and I cared less that she had used Carrie's number, the number that I shared with her in the name of goodwill and healing—to report her findings to her new sister in grief.

"I told you from day one that it wasn't a good idea to put them in touch with each other," Dan's words were somewhat scolding, but also kind.

"I thought it would be good for them to have somebody to lean on, somebody who is walking the same journey...a bit like us," I explained.

"I get that," Dan, went on, "but ours is a story of joy and finding, theirs is of heartache and loss—it's too soon for them...they need time." And Dan was right, they needed time. Time knows no unit of measurement when love is involved, it can fly by and it can also stand still. Hours and minutes and seconds mean nothing. When pain is in the mix, more time is always needed. Somehow, we become aware that time is different, we're taught that it's eternal, but the reality is that it is not. There never seems to be enough of it, not for working, or relationships, or sleeping, or loving, or healing, or anything.

Dan and I met at the Virgin Atlantic check-in desks at Heathrow's Terminal 3 at 8:00 a.m. for our flight at half ten. It was a feeling beyond description. It was as satisfying as our devious down-low meet at the Holiday Inn Express in Newbury Park just over a year earlier. But this time it was different, it had substance, it had light. It was real and tangible, and it existed in the public eye, validated by real names on airline tickets and on our burgundy passports issued by Her Majesty's Identity and Passport Service. During the online check in which I had done the previous evening, the system had asked me to supply the name of a next of kin in case of any emergency. I knew he would be travelling with me, but that didn't make any difference. 'Dan van Dijk', I typed in the designated window, feeling proud of the progress I was making in my world. Unlike Judy and Carrie, I didn't need time. The only time I needed was the amount of time that Carrie needed to heal. As we were standing in the boarding queue, Dan suggested we take a selfie.

"I think it's called an *usie*," I joked.

"What do you mean?" he asked looking confused.

"A selfie is a photo of yourself," I explained tongue-in-cheek, "so if it's a picture of more than one person, it's of us...it's called an usie." He rolled his eyes and then, humouring me, he retorted.

"Okay then, let's take an usie," he said with a smile on his face. Dan took out his phone, flipped the camera and held up his arm. "Ready?" he asked and then he took the photo.

"Let's see," I chortled as he brought his arm down. It was a lovely photo, the first one of the two of us. Now we existed digitally too. Not ready for social media but ready for the gay capital of the world. Naïve, perhaps, of what awaited us, but in love or in lust—or something. Whatever it was, I liked the feeling. The only thing that was certain at that very moment was that very moment—and there was something special in the air.

We arrived at our first hotel, the amazing Casa Solstice Spa Hotel in Sausalito, which was across the Golden Gate Bridge from San Francisco. Dan had chosen this hotel for us and it ticked all the boxes: gay friendly, indoor pool, close to restaurants, and within walking distance to public transport. We arrived at the reception and were met by an outrageously camp young man—too girly to be considered hot, but with Italian features and jet-black hair. He looked a little like Double L.

"How can I help you?" he asked in a squeaky, condescending voice.

"We're here to check in," I responded politely.

"Last name?" he asked. He was impatient and with a curt sting in his voice, one so common in a lot of gay men.

"Sterling," I announced, "David Sterling," trying not to give rise to my temper. His fingers rattled on the keyboard in front of him.

"Yes, we have you here in the system," he suddenly sounded kinder. "I see it's a king-sized bed, is that correct?" he asked. He scrunched his brow over the thick square frames of his glasses that were hanging off the end of his nose.

"That's correct," I whispered, feeling like the entire reception was now staring at Dan and I. Dan glowed pink, I might have too. We had come here to be anonymous gays in rainbowville, and we hadn't been prepared for this curveball. Our guilt and our shame had followed us.

"Maybe it's just a standard question," Dan suggested, as we made our way to our room.

"I'm sure they don't ask it to the straights," I snapped and was sure that I sounded as angry as the Italian gay boy with the gelled back hair.

Not far from where we were staying were the consulting rooms of a certain Dr Alan Downs. Dr Downs is a well-known therapist who has counselled gay men for some 25 years. He is, if I recall correctly, HIV positive and many of his patients also carry what the gay community call 'Aunty Aida'. Much of his work focuses on supporting his clients through the emotional struggles of dealing with the day-to-day challenges of being gay. Just before I had dropped my bomb on Carrie, I had stumbled across his book and ordered myself a copy from Amazon. I found it incredibly riveting, helpful and healing. I read it secretly in the downstairs guestroom where I had moved—hiding it like a teenager hiding a pornographic magazine that they shouldn't have had. The book, titled The *Velvet Rage*, identifies that anger and sting—so often prevalent in gay men—as *velvet rage*. It is that same sting that Dan and I had witnessed in that complex and angry young man at the hotel reception. That same anger that led people like James's friend Peter and I to gay-shame the very people that we should have been striving to protect. Dr Downs describes how this *velvet rage* is rooted in shame and guilt, and that it manifests as anger. Anger at the world and anger with oneself. It is a battle for acceptance by society and a battle to be at peace with your own mind, body and soul. The guilt and shame stem wholly from the dirty societal stigma associated with homosexuality.

Apart from the guilt and the shame, if I had to use one single adjective to describe how I felt about myself in the weeks and months following my revelation to Carrie and the world—that word would be 'dirty'. I felt so incredibly dirty as I hung out my lifetime of laundry for all to see. I felt dirty for the sin of Leviticus, I felt dirty for the shame I brought to my family, I felt dirty for the embarrassment I had and would continue to cause Carrie and our beautiful daughters; and I felt dirty for the world knowing I was a queer man who liked men. Just as Lady Macbeth had repeatedly washed her hands to erase the figurative murderous blood that stained them, I too wanted to repeatedly cleanse myself, washing away the evidence of my now untamed secret, set loose like a deadly virus—with no means to reel it in.

Now, far away from home, at the start of a new chapter, Dan and I were still looking squarely in the eyes of guilt and shame—and somehow, we had come to realise that like Judy and Carrie, this all needed time. We all needed time. We were to learn that it takes time to scrub away the guilt and the shame, and the residual dirt that grows from that.

We didn't see Angry Italian Boy for the remainder of our time at the upmarket Casa Solstice Spa, and we ended up having a fabulous stay. The comforts were plush and posh, and the staff were all welcoming and hospitable. We grew quite fond of a young woman who served us in the dining room at dinner time. Her name was Angel and she truly was one. Her heritage was Bolivian, but she was third generation American and proud to be a citizen of the USA. Her veins ran red, white and blue.

"If you don't mind me saying," she blurted out of nowhere, as she placed a bottle of Chilean Terra Noble 2009 Merlot and two glasses onto the table, "you guys are such a cute couple." The moment had the potential to become awkward, because we simply needed more time, but it was refreshing. I decided to play along, much to Dan's amusement.

"Thank you," I replied, "we try to put up with each other," I joked. It felt so natural. Some people might have called my whole life a charade—so I decided, in that moment, to indulge myself some more.

"You remind me so much of my Uncle Herando and his partner, Blake, they are so happy...just like the two of you seem to be."

"How nice," I exclaimed, gesturing to Dan who was nervous to play this game with me.

"How long have you been together?" she asked. I sneakily decided to turn the weeks into years.

"Coming up for six years." I answered. "Is that right Dan?" I asked indifferently, trying to lure him into my roleplay game. To my surprise and delight, Dan joined in.

"Sounds about right," he confirmed with some degree of conviction. I smiled at him.

"That's amazing," she commented.

"I've tried to leave him," I added jokingly with a straight face, "but I can't seem to shake him off." There was a brief silence.

"True story," Dan was straight-faced and then a massive smile cut across his cheeks. His dimples and his crow's feet were gorgeous when he smiled. Angel left us alone to finish our meal and Dan and I discussed how liberating it was to talk freely about who, and what, we were. We needed to find more safe spaces where we were surrounded by like-minded and progressive thinking people. We needed to find more Angels, the world needed more Angels.

For the last three days of our holiday, we moved to the Club Donatello Hotel just off Union Square in downtown San Francisco. The hotel was basic, clean and comfortable, but nothing as outlandish as the spa. Once we arrived in our room, Dan and I had somehow ended up talking about homosexuality and the Bible. Out of the blue, I asked him if he knew the story of the wedding at Cana. Dan seemed to have some vague recollection of it.

"Okay," I signed abruptly. "Let me explain...you're supposed to bring out the good stuff last." Dan looked confused. "This is a downgrade from the last hotel," I noted, "at Cana Jesus bought out the good wine last." He looked unamused as he drily picked up his iPad.

"I'm going to look for a show for us," he said, "one that tastes like good wine." It was my turn to roll my eyes and look unimpressed.

In many ways, we did save the best for last—each day on our journey we became more liberated and increasingly brave. I started to link arms with Dan as we walked down a street or through a park—subtly and cautiously, always releasing him for oncoming traffic, but it was progress. Baby steps.

With each conversation and each action, we began to establish trust, learning to be more open, confident, and comfortable with each other. We learnt a lot about each other: our shared values and the number one place that our children occupied in our lives. We learnt about our similar tastes and our love for wine and pizza and chocolate. And we learnt about our warped and similar senses of humour. There was so much in common to join us, and there were also so many opposites to keep us attracted. We were starting to reveal the real Dan van Dijk and the real David Sterling to each other. We both needed to unearth the person that we had hidden beneath the shame and the guilt, and we also needed to come to understand the person who would emerge from beneath those layers over time. We needed to introduce both versions of ourselves to each other.

Our time in anonymous San Francisco was a priceless launching pad toward our authentic being and the lives that we aspired to live. The physical distance from home made it easier to relax and feel less dirty. The emotional distance from Carrie was a welcomed respite. I returned from San Francisco with a new vigour—it was as if somebody had opened the pressure valve and a whole lot of steam had blown away. There was one thing I knew for sure...I wanted to keep those flowers in my hair.

CHAPTER FORTY-EIGHT

THE BIZARRE BARBEQUE

27 November 2013

DAN AND I had returned from San Francisco in time for Christmas. After the joy and excitement of the holiday, and having had a taste of the life I was aspiring to, I had to face the reality of my first Christmas without my children. I found it painful. Carrie, her parents, the girls and I visited my mum early in the morning for a light breakfast and to open presents. After that, Carrie and the entire gang left for Abby's house where the Durhams would spend their Christmas together. Leviticus would have been invited, but not his abominators.

Dan was at his mum's house, having spent the morning at his marital home with his children opening presents and pretending that the world was normal. It was a warm and dry morning that turned cold and damp with my mood just after midday. It felt like a pity party, but I was indulging myself. I felt as if I was entitled to it. Mum, Holly, Xander, and their son Luke all went out of their way to lighten the mood. We laughed and we cried, and we missed dad. It was our third Christmas without him. I tried to be present, but I felt estranged from my nuclear family and from myself. Despite the love and acceptance from the people that were my tribe, I wanted to be with Dan. I was separated from my children and from the security of a life I once knew.

Over the previous couple of months, I had ridden—and mostly survived—a roller coaster of emotions. The sentimentality and the traditionality of Christmas day whacked me hard. It was unexpected. The absence of my girls made me feel notably fragile. I also missed the familiarity of Carrie, and the picket fence stability of the life I had surrendered for the sake of my truth. That was the first day I questioned whether, if I had the choice, I would have used the rewind button had it been an available option. It was only the allure and the love I was nurturing for Dan that kept me sane and focused.

ON THE DAY after Boxing Day Judy had invited us—the Sterlings—to their house in Margaretting for a barbeque. The van Dijk house was modern and ostentatious, not my taste or style. Too modern, with too much glass. There were expansive entertainment areas and an over-the-top kitchen that opened into an indoor entertainment area equipped with a barbeque and a heated jacuzzi.

We had all previously met one another, except for Judy and Carrie—the two homosexual widows—both working at their own pace through the painful cycle of grief. A macabre grief where they faced their morphing partners daily—watching them slowly become more liberated and less guarded.

Judy was a confident and welcoming host. Carrie seemed shy and uncomfortable in what was essentially the house of her successor. Likewise, I was uncomfortable in the home of my predecessor.

As far as everybody was concerned, Dan and I were just friends, we hadn't disclosed the developments that had taken place at Soho some seven weeks earlier. The San Francisco holiday would have already raised suspicions. It was in everybody's best interests, especially ours, that they were not shared—for now at least. I was feeling happy and content, but equally vulnerable, knowing that Dan could flush me away at any moment—as he had done nearly a year previously. There were too many unknowns in this big turning machine for any of us to feel safe or certain about anything. We were all sitting ducks with our hearts vulnerable and exposed to the world.

I guess it was probably for this reason that Judy had bizarrely brought in her reinforcements for the day—and they were indeed an interesting and peculiar back-up crew. First up was her single and stocky lesbian-looking friend, Jolene, who was there with her three odd looking children. Then there was her cousin Ethan, who looked like he might have specifically been there for some coming-out advice. The conversation was stilted in the unfamiliar territory. We were strangers forced together and bonded only by recently disclosed secrets and the pain that had grown out of them.

The children all seemed to be getting along well. I was starting to see the sweet and gentle side of Amy, who was playing with Jane. Kate had taken an interest in two-year-old Rachel and was entertaining her by building Lego models and reading her a story from a dog-eared copy of a Noddy book. Tom had changed his Spiderman outfit for Batman, and he was acting as a superhero to Jolene's atypical children who were seemingly mesmerised by his antics.

"Lovely to see the children getting on so nicely," Judy commented confidently and slightly awkwardly as she approached me holding a glass of wine. Any onlooker would have thought that we were old family friends.

"It is," I responded, unsure of how to answer. We smiled awkwardly.

"You all right, Carrie?" Judy asked, trying to draw Carrie into the conversation.

"I'm all good," Carrie answered, not sounding good or looking comfortable at all.

"Carrie's not been feeling well," I explained. "She was up most of last night with a bad stomach." I didn't divulge that it might have been from the stress of dealing with the unknown of the upcoming day. Judy offered Carrie some medicine to settle her stomach and they began to talk.

The two wives, bound by the pain of loss, the unknowns of their impending divorces and by the shame of their gay husbands, were finally standing face-to-face. They were searching for meaning in the eyes of another who might understand their suffering. I had always felt that it would be helpful if they, like Dan and I, had had somebody with whom to share their thoughts and their fears. Somebody to report on progress to, and somebody to ask for advice. Somebody who wasn't a Dr Otis or a Dr Kessman sitting in pristine consulting rooms with fancy sofas, exchanging words for money—shallow words, textbook scripted words that failed to comprehend the realities of which neither had first-hand experience.

I moved away from Carrie and Judy to allow them time to bond and to share and to grieve. I approached Dan, who was turning the meat on the gas flamed barbeque. He was oblivious to what was happening behind him. It was his way of coping and, as I was already learning, he preferred not to have to deal with unnecessary social interactions.

"Everybody okay?" he asked with a smile as my interruption pulled him back to reality.

"Think so," I answered, "it's all just a little bizarre." Dan nodded his head in agreement and then I began to ramble.

"Carrie's miserable, and like you, doesn't seem to want to talk too much...Judy is trying way too hard to make us all best friends...her moral supporters don't seem to be much help...but then again, maybe they are silent motivators...it's just weird..." I grumbled.

"I think," Dan interjected, "it's probably all pretty normal for this unchartered space...we're all stabbing in the dark." I thought about it for a second or two.

"So we're just navigating blindly trying to survive these troubled waters?" I asked.

"And doing the best as comes naturally to us," he added.

We were interrupted by Jolene, who clumsily came between our philosophical words.

"You boys nearly done?" she asked, and then maladroitly added, "or should I say girls?" It wasn't funny, but I filled the awkwardness with a cumbrous laugh that sounded fake from the moment it left my throat. Dan smiled nervously.

"Boys, girls...we're all the same," I offered, subtly acknowledging Jolene's possible secret, and maybe even offering her a safe space to be the lesbian she might always have wanted to be.

"I just want to let you know that I have no problem with gays," she added. It was an odd comment but befitting for the day which had been curious beyond measure.

Carrie and I left around five, and as we hurtled down the A414 toward our fractured home, I used the silence in the car to reflect on the day. As bizarre as it had been, it was all part of our greater vision...the first steps toward what would be first prize at the end of the trauma—a modern blended family where this would all be possible and natural. The only missing guests were the straight men that Carrie and Judy still needed to find.

CHAPTER FORTY-NINE

PIZZA IN EALING

4 January 2014

SHORTLY AFTER DAN and I returned from San Francisco, I arranged for a big 'family and friend' get together. I was eager to introduce him to everybody who mattered to me. In hindsight, it was enormously brave—or stupid—and perhaps a bit of both. One thing for certain is that it was a little premature, too much, too soon.

What I hadn't realised while I was in that frantic space was that many people who loved me were also dealing with their own grief related to my world. The pristine picket fence was in tatters, and it was as though a drunken driver had mounted the pavement, ripped up the lawn and mowed down the fence—stopping very close to the front door. What I learned over time was that many people mourned Carrie, not specifically as my wife, but as a person they had come to love, others mourned the unit that was our family and feared what this meant for Carrie, Jane, and Kate.

I guess to the onlooker, it might have all looked reckless—it had been just 6 months since I had disclosed my secret to Carrie and to the world, and things were raw. Amidst this fresh wound, I had brought a new person into my world. Somebody who nobody knew, somebody who didn't have the 14 plus year track record that Carrie had.

I also learnt quickly that Dan is more introverted in nature and that social gatherings can sometimes, like they are for most introverts, be quite overwhelming. So, before our weekend getaway to London early in January 2014, Dan was stern with me.

"You can have one social engagement while we're there...that's it," he ordered. There were so many people that I wanted to introduce him to and to share him with. We had a busy schedule while in London Town, and we needed to use our time efficiently. We were going to see Billy Elliot, we had a trip booked on the London Eye and I wanted to visit Kingston for some shopping. If time allowed, I had also hoped to fit in a visit to Hampton Court.

With limited time and having been restricted to just one social gathering, I decided to make it one big bash. Dan and I, my sister and my mum, Uncle Dave and Aunty Gloria, Dean and his wife Peggy, my friend Emma and her husband Ben, my cousin Bridgette and her husband Zac, and my younger cousin Cara and her boyfriend Justin. Fourteen of us altogether. I booked a table at Carluccios in Ealing because it was close to Uncle Dave and Aunty Gloria's house and as Uncle Dave hadn't been well, it seemed like a good idea that he be close to his home. Everybody, including Dan, came wearing their brave faces. It was an exciting evening, but it was a difficult one. I had been oblivious to the deeper emotions in the room because I was excited about where my life was at. The support and care I was providing to Carrie didn't hide the fact that family and friends were grieving her absence.

It was the first time that Dan met most people, including my mother and some of my cousins. Mum seemed to warm to him rather quickly—she always spoke to everybody and is a good judge of character. I could see that she liked him and that was consoling. It was the first time that I had seen Dan and Holly interact and they seemed quite comfortable around each other. Topics such as work and broader office politics kept them chatting for a while. They seemed to get on swimmingly. The success of these family relationships were important to me—family has always been paramount in my world.

For an introvert, Dan was doing well—I could see that the flowing wine was easing his social anxiety. My cousin Bridgette, who a few months earlier had cried with me about the pain of my stunted living, regaled Dan with stories about me that made me sound like a king and a saint. She could have been my agent, and certainly a very invested one. My younger cousin Cara, who is sweet and clever and wise beyond her years, came over and whispered in my ear.

"Be good to this one, he's a keeper." These small and powerful validations were so important for me in that particular time and place.

In hindsight, I have come to realise that that evening was almost superficial. An onlooker wouldn't have picked up anything jarring, and to be honest I was oblivious to this on that cold and windy January night. Carrie was the elephant in the room and Dan was a reflected manifestation of that elephant. He filled the space and he was under the scrutinous eye of everybody there. Even with love and good intentions, they were weighing him up, watching his every move and trying to determine what this one was all about.

Uncle Dave and Aunty Gloria observed him closely, and I could see them mentally making comparisons to the reality that had recently unfolded in their worlds. I hadn't considered the pain that the exposure to my world might have caused them. I hadn't clearly thought this through, and it reminded me of the time I took my gran to Auschwitz on a pilgrimage back to Poland. In my naivety, I had thought that facing her demons would bring liberation and healing, but I was wrong. When we arrived in the first hall, the pain of her childhood and the loss of her family members in Siberia must have overwhelmingly come flooding back.

"Take me back to the car please," she insisted. Her pitch was painful, and her tone was full of authority. I complied.

"Are you okay gran?" I asked as we walked back toward the car.

"I'm fine," she replied curtly, but I wasn't convinced. "I just don't want to see all that nonsense." I held her hand, which was as cold as the pain in her heart. Perhaps I was pulling people like Uncle Victor and Aunty Gloria into their own Auschwitz. We all carry pain and loss and heartache. Some of us are more adept at hiding it than others. Facing our pain or seeing its reflection can sometimes be more distressing—especially when it arrives unexpectedly. As much as I wanted the approval of my aunt and uncle, I needed to realise that the pain that I had inflicted on Carrie was all too similar to the pain that their daughter was experiencing at that time and in that moment. My cousin had recently caught her husband with a man, and it was all too fresh. That was why she hadn't joined that night.

I was desperate for Dan to be loved and accepted by the family, I wanted them to approve of him and I wanted him to feel the same—but the reality was that love and trust and acceptance would take time.

The following morning, I was feeling somewhat uneasy about the flow of the previous evening, so I called Holly for an autopsy.

"Was last night maybe just a little bit odd?" I asked.

"Not really," she responded, and then with a cheeky tone she added, "maybe just for the odd ones." We both giggled. I explained that I had felt the evening slow and disconnected, and while everybody had made an effort, there was something hanging in the room that left me feeling uneasy. Holly heard me out and then she responded with some pearls of wisdom.

"This is your journey," she reassured, "not anybody else's—invite them to be a part of it, but don't let them detract from it." It took me a few seconds to think about her comment before I responded.

"But, I want them to walk it with me," I retorted with some desperation in my voice.

"And you've given them that opportunity," Holly replied, "it's up to them now—just give them time." Holly was right, but my impatient nature and my need for acceptance were still such huge obstacles for me. When we ended the call, Dan, who had been listening to the conversation, added his bit.

"Relax, Davey," he soothed. "You're expecting too much." And he was right. Those words were so incredibly reassuring as part of my anxiety was rooted in the pressure that I had placed on him too.

"Thanks beautiful," I said, turning to him with a smile. We shared a comforting and solid hug.

"Cara's right," I mumbled, "you are a keeper."

"What are you babbling on about?" he asked, only half interested as he peered over his iPad.

"Nothing," I mumbled, "just happy to be keeping you."

CHAPTER FIFTY

DIVORCE DAY

15 February 2014

DESPITE CARRIE'S EARLY bargaining, in the months that followed she came to accept that divorce was inevitable and that staying in the relationship would damage her soul and douse her fire. She needed to use the divorce and what came after it to reignite the remaining glow of her tired and struggling embers. I wanted to be a part of that journey, but only Carrie could decide if I would be allowed to journey with her.

An important divorce conversation involved breaking the news to Jane and Kate. I was invited to one of Carrie's sessions with Dr Otis to talk about breaking the D-word to the girls. I went begrudgingly because my experiences of Otis weren't pleasant ones, and the feedback that Carrie gave me from time-to-time always made me flinch.

On this occasion I was pleasantly surprised. I decided that she was probably a better divorce therapist than she was in matters of homosexuality—where she had proven that she was clearly out of her depth.

"This is how I always encourage parents to break the news," she explained, taking out a sheet of paper from the printer behind her. Clutching a pencil, she drew an odd-looking three-legged cauldron. Her artistic skills were poor, but the explanation that followed was ace. "I find this analogy works well with children," she explained. She then began to describe that we should explain to Jane and Kate that the pot represents mum and dad's marriage. "It is," she explained, "filled with all sorts of wonderful things: children, a house, dogs, a cat, lots of love, etcetera...you can add any ingredients you wish," she suggested. Otis went on to explain that next we should tell the girls that the pot has three legs. One is for love, one is for trust and one is for respect. She suggested that we should tell the children that these are three things that hold the pot and everything in it upright and safe. Next, she scribbled a deep and almost unpleasant line at the top of where one of the legs joined the pot. "Then," she added with dramatic pause, "you should tell them that when one of the legs is broken, the pot cannot stand up properly." It all seemed easy enough. I was about to ask a question when she continued: "You need to explain that in your case the trust leg is broken, and that sometimes when things are broken it is very difficult to fix them...a broken pot cannot be used," she kind of lamented. Carrie leaned forward, her shoulders somewhat hunched over and clearly showing her pain:

"Do we actually say the word 'divorce'?" she asked.

"You can," Otis replied, "but take the lead from the children, try to be calm and natural...they will give you natural clues." When we left Otis's rooms, Carrie was quite upbeat. She usually was after her sessions with her. Carrie and I agreed to have the 'cauldron talk' with the girls the following evening.

After dinner on the Thursday, we all sat down in the lounge. Carrie made us four mugs of hot chocolate and she had sprinkled them with miniature marshmallows that were soft and fluffy—floating with purpose...trying their best to offer protection from the news that awaited the girls.

"Jane," I asked, "please can you grab a pen and paper for me—mummy and I want to explain something to you and Kate." Jane returned with an A3 piece of paper from her art folder—bigger than I was expecting—and a black Biro. I followed Otis's instructions to a tee. Jane and Kate were seated on the sofa on either side of Carrie. She had her arms around both of their shoulders, and she was pulling them closely toward her—in a manner that looked like she was exercising her instinctive maternal protection. I could see her lip was quivering and her eyes were glazed. I had to switch my emotions off because I could feel that I was spiralling. I had become good at that. The proverbial rug that I was about to pull from beneath my children's feet was trembling in my own hands. The room was full of pain, but it felt like a strangely odd rite of passage—one that nobody wanted to be a part of.

As I was nearing the end of my explanation—the point at which I explained that the trust had been broken. Kate jumped to her feet, releasing herself from the grip of Carrie's bloodless hand.

"Are you getting divorced?" she bellowed from her gut, her anguish coming from the depths of her stomach. It was raw and distressing.

"We are," I choked, pulling her into my chest and clutching her tight, "but not for while," I added clumsily. The pain in the room had been ignited like the act of an arsonist. Kate sobbed, I sobbed, we all sobbed. Jane's and Carrie's arms were entwined on the sofa and Jane, who always shared her emotions sparingly, was as distraught as her sister. It was as unpleasant as my coming out to Carrie had been some months earlier. Again, I had inflicted more pain and uncertainty on the three women that I loved most in the world. I wished I could douse the fire, but I no longer had control over the flames that grew out of the revelation I had made to my two babies. Once the emotions had simmered a little, Carrie and I tried to console the girls as best we could, but they needed time to process the bombshell. We concluded the evening by snuggling together on the sofa, eating popcorn and watching Dr Seuss's The Lorax. A happy family, for a short while longer.

A few days later, Carrie and I approached Holly's husband, Xander, who was a solicitor, and we asked him to assist with our divorce contract. The atmosphere in his meeting room was sombre and my brother-in-law had suddenly become the officiator of the unravelling of our marriage.

"This isn't a complicated case," I suggested, "Well, at least I don't think it is." Xander was calm and sympathetic to Carrie's obvious emotions.

"Let's hear how you want to do things," he asked with compassion and kindness in his voice. I looked at Carrie:

"Okay if I explain?" I asked.

"Sure," she replied with a nod, her eyes already welling up.

"Basically," I proceeded—wanting to get the business over, "we just need a simple contract...I will buy Carrie the house that we've found for her and I will use our savings and all of the capital available in our current mortgage to fund it. I will take over that debt." Xander was scribbling away, and he dropped his head in a gesture that showed us he was listening to all I was saying. "Then," I continued, "I will buy Carrie a new car, we've been looking at different options at the moment." Xander carried on writing and Carrie was crying. I leaned over and squeezed her hand before proceeding: "Carrie will have all of the furniture and household goods, I would just like to keep some sentimental pieces that I have inherited from my dad and grandparents." Xander lifted his head.

"I'll need you to list those for me," he instructed.

"Then finally, we need something about custody and access—anything standard should work," I suggested. I looked at Carrie prompting her to talk, but it was clear she was too upset to participate. I continued: "I know that Carrie and I will always jointly parent and I can't imagine that access would ever be a problem. We've already agreed that the girls come first." Xander finished jotting down his last notes and then he spoke.

"It all sounds very amicable, which is a great start," he noted, "but there are so many unknowns, so it's always better that we put everything in writing." I explained that we didn't want to reduce our separation to legal clauses and technical jargon, but Xander cautioned that the possibility of new partners who brought new perspectives and influences, coupled with the unknown that lay ahead made it wise to have a definitive contract in place. I wasn't fussed with a contract, I wanted Carrie to be happy and I wanted us all to survive this ordeal—happy and loving and still friends on the other side of it. It was amazing that even in the springtime of my new life, when I was discarding and releasing so much: secrets, friendships and belongings—all I wanted to clutch on to were my children and a few heirlooms that connected me to my past—my happy but cloistered past.

AT OUR LATE-NIGHT dining table talks, Carrie and I spoke about the girls and how we would work together to make sure that they remained our number one priority. We pledged that we would always ensure that everything we did in our new lives would consider the girls first. They would never be pawns in any disagreements. With each conversation, I could see that Carrie mostly believed my promises, but it didn't help that friends of hers like Stella had labelled gay people as 'selfish'. Time was the only ingredient that would show Carrie that I was serious about my long-term commitment to her and the girls. It felt so frustrating that I needed to prove it—but there was no other way. The trust scale was bottom up, rather than top down.

While Carrie and I were talking about what our future might look like, Dan and Judy were having similar conversations in Margaretting. Their approach was to develop a handwritten pact that signed and sealed their commitment to giving their story a happy ending. The covenant outlined how they would preserve their friendship, jointly parent their children, and always look after the children's best interests. 'Children first' was the theme of the treaty that they signed with their broken hearts and with lots of love. It was a goodbye letter with the promise of an eventual return. It was the kind of letter that a soldier left for his wife when he departed home to fight for his country—it told of love past and present. It bade a temporary farewell to love in the hope that the horror of the war would be kind enough to let everybody return and have the privilege of loving again. They sealed their pact with love and yearning. Its success would be determined by their commitment and the arms of time...which can turn very slowly or be as fleeting and as fast as a broken promise.

OUR DIVORCE DATE was set for 15 February. Ironically, our love story clocked out the day after the world celebrated love and union. As the plaintiff, I had to appear in court with my solicitor, Xander. We arrived early at the courts and sat in one of the back benches. It was intimidating and *infra dig*. I felt like I was on the set of something like Judge Judy or Judge Rinder. Xander had briefed me of what to say when I was called up.

"Don't mention your sexual awakening," he jokingly cautioned, "some judges will want to send you for therapy and counselling." We both laughed. "You just say that your relationship has broken down beyond repair," Xander explained. He then told me, if prompted, I should describe how the trust had been breached, and it could never be regained or repaired. "Keep it simple and uncomplicated," he advised. My case was called up, Xander did the legal introductions and it was all over in three minutes.

As we walked out of the courtroom, I was unsure of what to feel. I felt empty, I felt like something was missing and I should have felt liberated— but I didn't. It was an eerie and melancholic experience. So much invested and then annulled with one bang of a magistrate's gavel. I looked down at my left hand and my wedding band was boldly staring up at me. I surreptitiously slipped it off my finger and put it into my wallet. The game was over and I wasn't sure if I was the winner or the loser.

I had arranged with Mark Musgrave to collect Carrie from school once I had finished at court. He had agreed to arrange cover for her classes. We drove to a nearby coffee shop that we frequented often. The atmosphere was understandably gloomy and despair hung in the air. We ordered some coffee and some cake. Carrie chose the signature carrot cake, and I opted for a bran muffin. The conversation was not easy. Next to me on the floor I had been hiding a gift bag that I had prepared for Carrie. I lifted it up and handed it to her.

"I know it's probably unusual to have a divorce coffee meet and to receive a divorce gift" I explained, the pain evident in my voice, "...but this is for you." Carrie managed to squeeze out a tired chuckle. She pushed the white tissue paper aside, reached into the bag, and pulled out an olive-green box that lay at the bottom of it. She placed the box squarely on the table in front of her and sprung it open. I could see her sad eyes glimmer in the reflection from the light on the gold bands that lay in the box.

"What are these?" she asked.

"Those are three gold bracelets," I offered, "one to represent you, one Jane and one Kate." Tears were rolling down her face and I was also starting to choke up. I composed myself and continued. "They represent my promise to you and the girls that I will always be here for the three of you as we all find our ways in this new reality...today isn't the end, it's just the beginning of something new." My collectedness crumbled as we sat across from each other, our hands clenched across the table—my hands above hers, her left in my right and vice versa. We simultaneously laughed at our lack of composure and we cried for our loss.

CHAPTER FIFTY-ONE

A MAN IN MY BEDROOM

22 February 2014

IN THE WEEK before Dan and I left for San Francisco, Carrie and I sat down for what had become our usual evening chat. The girls were asleep, and Carrie and I were seated facing each other, from opposite ends of the dining room table. Carrie had her schoolbooks in front of her, and I was working on my laptop.

I was never sure why we took our work out, because we seldom did any of it—we just spoke. As much as I recognised the cathartic and healing value of our talks, I had grown to hate them. They had evolved into sessions where Carrie would bounce between various stages of her grief and loss. On some evenings she was angry, on others she was sad. Then there were times when she would bargain prolifically, and others when she seemed to accept where our worlds were headed.

On this particular evening, Carrie was edgy, and I knew that what I needed to tell her wouldn't be well received. I had thought long and hard about when I might break the news to her, and I had pretty much decided that there would never be an opportune or good time to convey what I needed to. I had considered not telling her at all, but I wanted to foster open communication and transparency as we transitioned into our new and unfamiliar reality. The time for lies, deceit and omissions were over. Going forward, I had decided to be honest with Carrie, Jane, Kate and myself—no matter how uncomfortable it made any of us. So, with not much warning, I took the bull by the horns:

"After you've moved out at the end of January," I wavered, "Dan will probably move in sometime after that...maybe early March," I added vaguely. Carrie's face was instantly red, and for the first time ever, I became aware of the veins in her neck. They were taut and prominent. I was about to witness a rage in Carrie, such like I had never seen in her before.

"OF COURSE HE FUCKING IS!" she bellowed, as she slammed her flat palms down with a thunderous clap onto the polished and exposed surface of the Rhodesian Mahogany table.

"Carrie," I mouthed, half whispering, "the girls are asleep." Carrie's eyes were in a rage, her pupils were dilated and the veins in her temples were protruding.

"I don't fucking care," she vociferated: "How dare you? How dare you bring somebody into my space? How dare you bring somebody into my house? Into my bedroom?"

"It's not like that, it's..." I tried to explain, but she wasn't having any of it.

"How many blows do you want to throw at me?" she blasted sarcastically. I knew that I needed to hold back and let her blow off her steam, but the truth was that I was afraid. I had never seen Carrie as angry as this before.

Once Carrie had calmed down a little, I tried to provide an explanation.

"I know that this is a bitter pill for you to swallow, but we need to be practical." Carrie's eyes swirled and twisted again.

"Practical about what...about fucking up my life?" she barked. I felt myself sigh. "Carrie," I went on, "I don't want to hurt you anymore than I already have, and the fact that I am here swallowing this shit night after night should show you that I am owning this mess...I want us to survive this and I want our friendship to persist." These words seemed to give Carrie some solace, but I knew that they would never be enough for her aching and broken heart.

The truth was that I deserved all that she threw at me on those long and arduous evenings—but I was also tired, and I was also in pain. Once Carrie seemed to calm down a notch or two more, I tried to provide more explanation.

"We need to be practical," I reiterated. "I've begun the process of making sure that you have the home and safe place that you want. It was your decision not to stay here. Judy, on the other hand, wants to stay in their house. Dan needs to move out. We're both financially stretched at the moment, so it makes sense that he moves in here. That's why I made the offer...it will help both of us financially. I've told you over and over that I will make sure that you are looked after, but I have limited resources." Carrie seemed happy with my explanation, but she was still struggling with the idea of Dan occupying her space.

"It's not easy David," she replied, sounding calmer and more in control. "This is our space, we have created many happy memories here, it's hard to walk away." The tears welled up in her eyes, I wanted to hold her— but I was uncertain if she would welcome any comfort from me.

"Would you like a cup of tea?" I asked, as I made my way to the kitchen where I cried alone.

Carrie and the girls moved out on the first of February and it was more earth shattering than I could ever have imagined. Although there had been a lot of transition in our home, in our hearts and in our heads, the act of them not physically being there anymore was overwhelmingly painful. I loved Carrie, but Jane and Kate were my world and suddenly they were gone. Just like that. In the few weeks that I lived alone, I loathed being at home and I hated heading home after work. I was either submersed in solitude or I was heading toward it. It was a seclusion and a loneliness that I had created for myself—all in the name of personal liberation and authentic freedom. And the truth was, I didn't feel liberated or free, I felt heart sore for the absence of the love, and the voices, and the steps of those two little human beings who were the joy of my life. I panicked that maybe I had made a mistake. I was having a taste of the loss that I had inflicted on Carrie. Knowing that Dan would move in in the weeks that followed was all that kept me afloat.

I began to prepare Jane and Kate for Dan's arrival.

"You know my friend Dan?" I asked them at the dinner table when they were with me one Wednesday evening.

"That nice guy with the big house?" Kate candidly asked back.

"Yes, that one," I responded. "Well, he is going to be moving in here in the next few weeks," I concluded.

"Cool," Jane replied. It was all going easier than I had anticipated. So I continued by explaining:

"His children will come like you guys do on Wednesday and every second weekend." They exchanged a glance with each other, and Kate proceeded to assign rooms to everybody. There were only four bedrooms and there were seven people. She pretty much assigned the three of us our historic rooms, and placed Dan and his three children into the spare room.

"I think that's going to be a bit of squash," I suggested. "I think it should be you guys in your rooms, Amy and Tom in the spare room and then Rachel can have a small bed in the big room with Dan and I." Jane seemed unphased, but Kate needed clarity.

"So Dan and you will sleep in the same room? she asked slightly hesitantly.

"That's right," I answered coolly and calmly.

"In the same bed?" she asked confidently and clearly seeking absolute clarity.

"That's right, my baby," I answered with a smile and then asked her to pass me the salt. By not giving credence to the shame or the awkwardness, I felt like I was adopting Georgina's approach—and it felt good. "Any other questions guys?" I asked.

"Not for now," Jane answered pragmatically. Kate nodded in agreement with her sister.

"Pass the tomato sauce please, daddy," Kate asked, almost seeming like she was unphased by the discussion and her intense questioning.

Dan moved in on Saturday, 22 February and it was exciting. I had been with him at Soho on the previous evening helping him pack his final things and I had returned home later that evening; I was unable to fall asleep. I was like a child on the eve of their birthday party—ready for the excitement, for the surprises and for the unknowns. Finally, at age 43, I would have a taste of the life I had always dreamed of—a life that only months before had seemed like an impossible dream.

I returned to Soho early the following morning and arrived just before the removal company. Dan was in high spirits and it was good to see him as excited and as upbeat as I was. The arrival of the removal truck signified the beginning of our real union. Our compatibility with, and our tolerance for each other were going to be tested in ways that would either bind us stronger—like Nuriel and Linda had predicted; or drive us apart like Sam— my least favourite psychic from Cambridge—had implied. I am always the eternal optimist, and I had invested too much in this not to believe that it could be anything but amazing. Besides, under the tutorship of Nuriel, I had manifested this, I had made it happen, and I was going to enjoy and savour every moment.

It was remarkable how smoothly Dan settled in and how we comfortably found our groove. It was young love and young love is always compromising. Although we shared a young love, we were also seasoned partners— not spring chickens, and we knew of the struggles associated with finding balance in a relationship. We understood the need for the gentle give and take that is essential to any relationship. Somehow, it all flowed easily, it didn't feel like hard work, we were both comfortable with giving. Taking was secondary.

The concrete merging of our worlds didn't only comprise Dan and I and the physical building that we lived in. It was much more complicated than that. It involved the entwining of the complex personalities of the little people in our lives; and it involved the homogenising of the value systems of two families who saw the world rather differently.

Just as Carrie had previously voiced her dissatisfaction with Dan occupying her emotional and energy space, Jane and Kate had equal difficulty in accepting Dan's children into their safe and familiar space. There was an unwritten acknowledgement that Amy, Tom, and Rachel were camping on Jane and Kate's turf and this made things tricky some of the time. Levelling the playing fields required constant attention and nurturing. Dan and I remained focussed on letting all of them know that all of us were equals. The natural pecking orders in each sibling arrangement were destabilised in our developing blended family. The biggest tensions were between Jane and Amy and these seemed to be about dominance and control. Both were the eldest in their straight homes, but with the gay dads,

Amy was now the middle child of five.

OUR ENTIRE WORLDS were about adjustment. Nuriel had warned that the blending would not be plain sailing.

"Blending isn't a pretty verb," he warned. "It involves chopping and dicing and cutting and then throwing things together to mix them up at high speed and with sharp spinning blades...you never know what you will get out at the other end, and it never looks like what you put in at the beginning." And he was right. The process was messy and Dan and I made it up as we went along, always with the best intentions. Love and mutual respect was what we strived for. We wanted our children to like, and even love, one another, but we couldn't force it. It needed to work itself out over time. They needed time to learn to understand one another. All that we could do was establish a sense of family, create memories, build trust and show love...the rest would follow...hopefully and wishfully.

What Dan and I hadn't realised at the time was that for our children, our union was a tangible and visible manifestation of their homosexual fathers. They were on their own coming out journeys and they had their own fears to face. This was unchartered territory and they were all trying to make sense of their new and unusual realities. It might have been easier for little Rachel, who was easily contented with her bottle and her blankie—but she too would have felt the separation from her mum when she was with us—and that would have been confusing for her and the routine of what she had come to know in her straight life.

We had disrupted their simple, straight worlds. We had shaken them up and they were adapting and surviving as best they could. With the love and support of all of us—their dads, their mums and their extended families, they put on their brave faces and they valiantly took on the challenges that we had thrown at them.

The new siblings in their lives were tangible and blatant artefacts that told the world that their dad had a partner, and because the partner was a man, these siblings indiscreetly exposed that their dad was gay. Stepfamilies are always complex and, to some extent, their new stepsiblings became their baggage. Only queers had boyfriends—special friends who they shared a house and a bedroom with. Sometimes dads were queers. It wouldn't always be easy explaining this to their friends.

CHAPTER FIFTY-TWO

NEW CONTRACTS

18 March 2014

IN THE MONTHS after we had told the girls that we were getting divorced, we began to deal with some of the practicalities required for the separation. Carrie's decision not to stay in the family home triggered an extensive house hunt. It wasn't long before Carrie carefully chose the house where she would lay new foundations and reconstruct her life. The house stood on a quarter acre stand, nestled at the centre of a well-established garden. It had expansive rooms with high pressed ceilings and substantial cottage pane windows that peered out into the lush garden. It was the perfect place to start over. The walls breathed hope and the trees whispered love—and the combination of these two made the promise of happiness. By pure chance, the house was on the same road as our marital home, where I would continue to live. Close enough for comfort, and just far enough to re-establish independence. Carrie and the girls moved to their new home at the end of January.

The weeks that followed focussed on getting them settled and preparing for Dan to move in with me. Dan and I started to explore other accommodation possibilities for us. We knew that him moving in with me was a short-term solution and it was exciting thinking about and planning our futures together. Dan had stumbled across a new housing development in Wickford, which seemed idyllic. The homes were contemporary and built in a modern barn style, with five bedrooms. The development was on the edge of the village—so semi-rural with amazing views and with the convenience of the local shops and a train station that provided an easy commute to London, only a short walk away. Wickford was almost equidistant from each set of our children—about a 15-minute drive in each direction—so it seemed like the perfect location.

Four weeks after Dan moved in, the two of us took a drive out to Wickford to have a look at the development. The town and the high street were bog standard small English town, but the rural location of the development, which stood on a portion of a subdivided farm, was beautiful. The houses were sensitively scattered across the pasture and they blended into the landscape—like structures that belonged there. The brook that ran along the periphery of the estate and the horses that grazed upon its banks completed the picture-book image. All that was missing was Henri and his horse, Onyx. Dan and I were awestruck, we knew immediately that this was where we wanted to write our story.

"I love it," I exclaimed.

"Me too," he responded with more emotion than he usually did. This was a sure sign that Dan was keen.

"I'm not sure we can afford it," I suggested in my usual cautious style.

"We need to look at the numbers more closely," he suggested optimistically. We went away to think about it, to do some sums and to research the area and the bus and rail connections into the city.

By the following Monday, 18 March, we met the agent to sign an offer, ironically at the same coffee shop where Dan and I had first met, and on what was Dylan Johnston's non-existent birthday. The following morning, our offer was approved, and that evening called for a celebratory dinner. Things were happening at pace, but it felt good, and I didn't want it to stop.

When I had come out to my boss some few months earlier, he had jokingly responded:

"Just be careful, gay people can be very unstable." Although stereotypical and probably not funny, I had found it hilarious. Anybody looking from the outside in might have thought that the pace at which Dan and I were working may have slightly hinted at instability. We knew that it would have looked hasty, but it felt right, and we were over being concerned about what others thought. That ship had sailed. The guilt and the shame were subsiding. We immediately began working with an architect to finalise the internal design of the house. This was more than about just building a house; this was about building a relationship and building a future with the man that the universe had sent to me and that it had made me wait so patiently for.

I was amazed at how Dan and I could so swiftly complement each other. We were an instant team: me the negotiator and he the number cruncher, me the soft furnisher and he the technical designer, me with OCD and ADHD, and he with a calm presence and a lack of respect for obsessive neatness.

The project was going swimmingly, and we had been given a move-in date of September when we got some unexpected and some mind-numbing news. There had been some undisclosed issues with council approval for the development, and all building works were immediately suspended following an upcoming investigation. It was the first blow that we faced as a couple and it was a big one. This project signified more than just bricks and mortar, it was the merging and creation of us: The Vanlings—a combination of our surnames and the name of our family WhatsApp group. We were the Vanlings—modern and blended, and now potentially homeless. We were, however, fortunate that the investors were decent. We were given the option to hold out or withdraw from the purchase with no financial loss. We decided to withdraw because there were too many unknowns.

WHILE I WAS possibly on the biggest high of my life, Carrie was in her doldrums. Adjusting to her new life was proving difficult for her and seeing me happy didn't seem to help. I tried to hide it from her, but it exuded from every pore of my body.

I had the children for my birthday weekend at the end of March and

Kate had forgotten her iPad at Carrie's house. I called Carrie to ask if I could pick it up and I popped up to her house to collect it. One look at me set Carrie off. Her eyes were dead, and her face was drawn with loneliness. She looked bereaved. If it was gut-wrenching for me to witness, it must have been a hundredfold more agonising for her.

I climbed out of the car and gave her a peck on her cheek and a comforting hug. She held on tight, almost as if a dead weight—and she wept. Her body was heavy and tired, and she needed reassurance.

"I can't do this," she wailed.

"You're going to be fine," I answered calmly, rubbing her back with my flattened hand to soothe her.

"I'm lonely and I'm scared," she said, her voice crackling with honesty and terror.

"I'm sorry," I said, holding her tighter. "You're an amazing and strong person. You are going to be okay," I told her with confidence. We stood there for a while, the happy bird song from the trees above unable to lift the mood—even a little. After a few minutes, Carrie seemed to compose herself and she released herself from the comfort of my hug.

"Thank you," she quavered, "thank you for still being here." I smiled and my heart ached for her.

"I'm always here for you," I offered, knowing that I would leave in a matter of minutes. She gave me the iPad and we stood talking for a while. We spoke about insurances and Internet service providers, and we spoke of some of the other practicalities of life. I left soon after.

As the months and then the years passed, Carrie reclaimed her confidence and she needed me less and less. I missed her friendship, but this equation required sacrifices from all of us. One of my many sacrifices was to let go of her as she moved further and further away from her state of depression, slowly but surely toward an acceptance of her new reality. I hoped she would come back for me when she had found some peace.

AT THE BEGINNING of December, Dan and I moved out of my house and into rented accommodation that was, like Widford, almost slap-bang between both sets of our children. We had changed the arrangements slightly and the children now came to us every Thursday night and every second weekend. It worked well, because if it was our weekend, we got them for a nice chunk of time—from Thursday through to Sunday. Moving away from my house and into the rented accommodation was the best thing that we ever did—but there had been an unpleasant catalyst that had driven us to that point. Which only proves that unpleasant events can lead to happy and prosperous outcomes.

The new house changed the dynamics in the family. Suddenly, we were all equals, the playing fields had been levelled and we were all the same. The tricky dynamic associated with the van Dijks being on Sterling territory no longer existed. A lot of angst evaporated, and territorial behaviours disappeared. We were all almost instantaneously happy and we were all equals. Love and interdependence were the replacement, and positive emotions. The house itself was ugly and it lacked flow and simplicity. It was kitsch and clumsy with too many Italian finishes. The living area was only partially separated from the dining room and kitchen which meant that the TV blared everywhere you went in the house. But, for all of its design flaws and the architect's obvious lack of practical taste and style—the house was beautiful for the fibre of the Vanlings. It drew us together.

Each new home we moved to solidified Dan and I more. More than the buildings, the love that we shared, and the love that we made under those roofs were what created our memories and bound us together more and more strongly. On every step of the way, I learnt more about Dan and I learnt to love him more. There were times when I wanted to kill him, but more than that I wanted to continue to hold him forever.

Each time we signed a new contract for a new home, we combined our signatures and we made a pledge to the owners, to the agents and to each other. These were important bonding milestones on the road toward everlasting love and commitment. The sun, the moon and the stars remained our constant witnesses as we journeyed along and pledged, with each new day, more and more of ourselves to each other.

CHAPTER FIFTY-THREE

EARLY BLENDING VICTORIES

15 June 2014

DAN AND I were finding our groove. I was more in love with him than he was with me. It was obvious—and if that wasn't the case, he simply wasn't expressing his love in words or actions. I was always the initiator and it was becoming frustrating. He was slow and pragmatic, waiting to see if it would all work out. I had already waited for him for much longer than I thought I should've. I knew from the first day that I met him that it would work out. For me it was already working out. I needed to reconnect with Nuriel for advice and direction.

Every day that passed was another opportunity for Dan and I to learn more about each other. Every Thursday night and every second weekend was an opportunity for the Vanlings to discover more about one another and to slowly and cautiously start to connect and interlock. The process couldn't be rushed and as with any process of change it was messy and unpredictable. It was a blank page and we were its authors. There were things to do and there were also many things to undo in the process of merging our different worlds. It was reiterative, it required constant reflection and it demanded quick thinking. Dan and I were dancing together—on our toes, mostly. We also danced with our five children and we danced with the outside world.

AUNTY CLARE, WHO had fully embraced her new gay nephew and his evolution, invited us all around to her house for Easter lunch. It was bound to be an interesting day. Uncle Hamish was sure to be drunk again and if Aunty Clare was a TV character, she would have been Hyacinth Bucket from Keeping Up Appearances—bossy and pretentious, but kind and always interested.

"Now give me your mobile phones," she iron-fistedly barked at the tweens. Jane, Kate, Amy, and Luke—Holly's son who is the same age as Kate, all handed them over to her with enough resentment to fill a football stadium. I wanted to intervene, but I didn't know how. "It's Easter Sunday," she grouched, "you should all be outside on the grass and under the trees—none of this technology nonsense." Uncle Hamish jumped in.

"Clare is right," he told the children, his words starting to overlap one another from his whisky, and then he turned to address Aunty Clare. "Sometimes," he mumbled, "you're an interfering old bitch." Aunty Clare's face was instantly red and her eyes were large—like Buckets.

"Just you shut your drunken face," she shouted at him as if she were on the Jeremy Kyle show. The children began to giggle, and I was trying to silence them with my frown and the whites of my eyes that were now bigger than Aunty Clare's.

"What's a bitch?" Tom innocently asked, looking at Dan right in the middle of a perfect silence. Dan hesitated, not aware that what was happening was pretty standard for an Aunty Clare and Uncle Hamish affair.

"It's a...it's a girl dog," he replied, stumbling over his words.

"Yes, that's what it is Tom," Aunty Clare was back in the conversation.

"Well," replied Tom with five-year-old perspective, "you don't look like a dog, except, maybe your hair at the back." Everybody laughed, even Aunty Clare. Tom had salvaged the Easter hunt and Uncle Hamish was rescued too. The Easter hunt was a success. Aunty Clare had drawn up clues that the children had to solve. My mum had to read them out and Holly, Dan, and I were appointed to monitor certain sections of the garden.

"Only one egg per child per section," Aunty Clare officiously instructed us, with the confidence of Mrs Bucket. Holly rolled her eyes and Dan grinned nervously. After the hunt, we were served her signature 'no-bake fridge cheesecake', after which the children were reissued their mobiles with a smug smile from Aunty Clare and we all headed home.

"How dare she take our mobile phones away!" Jane was first off the mark

"Yes!" interjected Amy.

"I don't want to visit them again," Kate complained, "except maybe for the cheesecake." Dan and I laughed. The children didn't—except maybe for Kate. There is nothing like a common enemy to bind you closer. Aunty Clare had done a good job—the food, the hunt, the mobile phone confiscation and common irritation. We loved her, but she was hard work.

EVERY SHARED EXPERIENCE and event tethered the Vanlings more and more. It was as though we were all stood around a potter's wheel—any combination of up to fourteen hands shaping the clay at any given time. Each hand taking its turn to sculpt and mould what we were collectively making. The final product was unknown, but the investment of time and commitment were immense. Seven people brought, quantumly together, by predestined love and by the powers of the universe. What was shaping was beautiful.

FATHER'S DAY WAS on Sunday, 15 June and it was the first time that we were officially out and proud gay dads. We were proving every day that we were dads and not just fathers. It felt good, but it also felt odd to be a dad in love with another dad. It was exciting to share the double dose of Father's Day elation, but it was unsettling to know that Carrie was a little way up the road, feeling the inverse of the joy that was being celebrated in the house that she had occupied only six months earlier.

Kate took it upon herself to use their dress up box and her imaginative mind to organise an interfamily games day: the Sterlings versus the van Dijks. The van Dijks didn't stand a chance. There were four of them and two-year-old Rachel and five-year-old Tom didn't have the dexterity required to be of any help to Amy and Dan as they tried to master Kate's complicated tasks. The Sterlings were the champions on the unlevel playing fields. We won the sack race, the egg and spoon race, the running race, the three-legged race and the flour in the face game. I tried hard to be slow to give the van Dijks a spitting chance, but Jane and Kate's competitive spirit made it difficult for me to be as slow as little Rachel. I managed to, thinking on my toes, build in a handicap system into the rules, that was linked to age, and it meant that we finally shared the Father's Day trophy. It was a horrible plastic imitation cup that I had won some 15 years before in a road race. The gold paint was peeling off around the handles and Kate had blu tacked a label over the original inscription. It read: 'The Vanlings—2014 Father's Day Award'. We all held it up and we cheered—out and proud. Collectively we were all victorious.

CARRIE'S DEPRESSION SEEMED to grow as the months ticked away. Seeing and hearing of the activities of our new blended family were painful and difficult for her. She became less patient, less flexible with me and just generally trickier to interact with. Her sadness made her difficult, needy perhaps—it was an unpleasantness that I hadn't anticipated. Her grief pattern was proving to be unpredictable. It wasn't linear; it was like a flashing headache that darted madly across the cortexes inside her head. To her it seemed that my world was perfect, yet it wasn't. I yearned for Dan to tell me that he loved me, but he seemed unable to say the words. The absence of those three magic words began to eat at my heart. Needing to hear them became my obsession and Dan would not or could not be hurried.

Carrie's manic sadness evoked more guilt in me and to compensate I gave her some of my time with the girls. The time wasn't mine to give away but I did it because I didn't want her to be alone. From whichever way you looked at it, we were all losers somehow—but I couldn't see any other way of trying to hold her heart together.

CHAPTER FIFTY-FOUR

PSYCHIC AND CYBER INFIDELITY

29 August 2014

DESPITE THE IMPERFECTLY perfect picture that we were all painting, adjusting to our new lives was not simple. I wanted open and honest accountability and Dan didn't want to be controlled. We had, by the way we met, proven to each other that we were both very capable of infidelity—and we knew that we did it well. Nobody knows your propensity for a secret liaison quite like your mistress—and that's what we had been to each other at some past point...mistresses. Adultery is adultery—regardless. Sexuality and secrets don't legitimise anything about it.

Our sordid history, coupled with Dan's inability to confirm his love for me by something as simple as uttering those three magical words, were making me anxious and hysterical. I felt unloved and I felt vulnerable. I wanted to be wanted, I wasn't feeling it. I would interrogate him about his daily activities, and he would tell me that I was jealous and possessive. Our words clashed like psychedelic colours on a black backdrop. The more we clashed, the less he told me. The less he told me, the more unpleasant I became. We were in a downward spiral. In my efforts to foolishly make myself feel more secure I engineered ways to find and access the information that I needed. I would find it—the good and the bad...but it never made me feel any better. I became obsessed with wanting to hear him say that he loved me. The scales were out of balance and we were both feeling the lack of equilibrium.

"Just calm the fuck down," Nuriel uncharacteristically told me. But I was struggling to do it—even with him channelling the right kind of energy in my direction. One evening, Dan arrived home later than usual from work. After dinner he needed to do some work, so he sat at the desk in our room and I lay on the bed behind him.

"Can I use your phone to listen to some music?" I asked, with no real intention of wanting to listen to music at all.

"Sure," came his reply, "the code is 0411." He tossed his phone over to me like he was spinning a frisbee upwards and it landed solidly on the duvet next to me. I opened the music app and started to shuffle Celine Dion's *Loved Me Back to Life* album. Then I began my 'investi-gay-tion'. First, I opened WhatsApp and looked for Nuriel. I saw that Dan hadn't been in touch with him for nearly a year. Next, I looked at his private Gmail account and I saw that he had arranged a sports massage for late that same afternoon. That explained his late arrival home.

"I see you had a massage this afternoon," I growled without strategy and with a lot of fury.

"Yes," he confirmed, turning his head and peering over his glasses, his face reddening up like mine.

"Why did you feel you could hide it from me?" I scathed.

"Because I can't tell you anything without you getting weird or jealous," he retorted with restraint in his voice.

"Maybe," I began, "if you made me feel more secure and didn't go around looking for happy endings behind my back, I'd be more receptive to your need for the millions of massages that you need for your constantly aching back." I was sarcastic and I knew that I had crossed a line, but I was too mad to care.

"Fuck you!" he belted—with calm and force.

"No fuck you—you deceitful son-of-a-bitch!" My words were not calm or controlled, I was mad. I felt unloved and I felt as if I had nothing to lose. The argument escalated and we screamed and threw our disrespectful baggage at each other way into the early hours of the morning. The neighbours must have been very entertained or incredibly annoyed. Dan tried to escape to the spare room, but I followed him where I continued my ranting. He eventually gave up and returned to our bed. By around 4am, we made passionate make-up love, and then we got in an hour's sleep before the alarm woke us up for another day on our fragile journey.

The passion between us was intense but we both had our own myriad insecurities to deal with. There were many more evenings like this one to follow, they all had different triggers—but for me they were all rooted in my need to know that Dan loved and wanted me, that he was invested in me for the long-haul. I should have acknowledged that something as clear as him coming home to me every day was progress, but I needed more. I would tell him that I loved him, and he would look at me with his beautiful eyes in shock and terror. Like a deer in the headlights, his pupils dilated and he would say nothing. In those moments, my heart began to feel like his empty eyes and my mode of self-preservation was to attack. It was an unhelpful downward spiral.

I called on Nuriel for support and I began to unload all of my pain in my interactions with him. I sent him daily emails in which I dumped my heartache and my irritation with Dan. I felt taken for granted and I was struggling to see any good in where our relationship was. Dan was hurting me and I didn't know what to do next. I might have been hurting him too, but I was looking at things through my lenses and through my pain and my insecurities.

"Just take it easy," Nuriel would say, "this is going to make you both stronger." It didn't feel like it.

As the intensity of arguing increased between Dan and me, so did my intuition. My hunch was that Dan was considering his options and I had this feeling in my gut that he was back on datingbuzz, checking out who was out there. I set up a new profile and designed it to appeal directly to Dan. My profile name was RecentlyOut, and my buy line was: just a decent dad with children. I made myself 6 years younger than I was and I loaded a silhouetted photo of a dark-haired man that I found on the Internet. I scanned, in detail, the active profiles on the site and I identified the ones that I thought might have been him. Over a few days, I narrowed my list down to only five. Next, I tracked the online activity and frequency of each of my shortlisted candidates. For example, one morning, I saw that Stud-Guy was last online at shortly after 9:00 p.m. the previous evening. I knew that that couldn't have been Dan because we were out to dinner at that time. Using the same technique over the next two weeks, I eliminated, Lone-lyHeart57, FarmGuy, and JustLooking7111. Only one profile remained on my devious shortlist and this veiled person marketed themselves under the profile name of JustinCame. They did not have a profile picture and I was sure that this was Dan. It also helped that JustinCame signed his messages with an 'M'.

On Friday, 29 August I was up before Dan because Jane had an early start at school. The Year 6s were having an entrepreneur's day and I needed to help her set up the pancake stall that she and friends were going to run in the school hall. While Dan was in bed, I was in the kitchen preparing school lunches for the girls. I was also on the datingbuzz app, continuing a conversation that JustinCame and I had started the previous evening. JustinCame wrote:

> *Hi. Do you still want to meet up today?*
>
> *M*

I replied:

> *Really looking forward to it. Let's meet at Pret A Manger—opposite Patisserie Valerie inside the St Pancras Station. Hope 3pm is still good for you. I will be arriving at the office shortly so probably won't check the app again. I'll be wearing blue jeans and green Polo golf shirt. I'll try to get a table outside.*
>
> *Ben*

I hit send with my heart in my throat. I didn't want it to be him, but I felt sure that it was. I hurried to the bedroom, and when I approached him to kiss him, he abruptly turned his phone face down onto the bed.

Jane, Kate, and I left for school. The previous evening's planning made the setting up of the pancake stall quick and easy. Jane was happy, and that meant that I was too. I left school and drove back to the house. I was hurried and unfocussed, in a mild state of trauma. Dan and I passed each other in our cars toward the top of the cul-de-sac. We stopped, opened our windows and we smiled. My smile was more a grimace—tight, painful, and angry.

"Have a nice day," he said with a small amount of guilt in his voice.

"You too," I replied. Dan started to drive away, and I called him back. He stopped and reversed back a little toward me.

"What now?" he asked with a playful look on his face.

"Nothing" I scoffed, "just wanted to tell you to please send my regards to Ben." I stayed a second or two to see the shock in his face and then I accelerated home.

I arrived home and my adrenalin was pumping at the top of my head and in the base of my throat. I felt sick. Dan was hot on my heels. He walked into the living room, his face sallow, and his eyes told that he couldn't defend his actions. He had been caught.

"How do you know?" he asked.

"Do I look like a fucking stupid cunt?" I clamoured loud enough to re-engage the neighbours. He remained gentle in his tone, trying to calm me. The conversation took a while to simmer down and he tried to defend his actions. He explained that all of our recent arguing had created a niggle in him about whether we were right for each other. I wasn't impressed with his approach and I told him so. We made some progress, but the relationship was on a knife's edge. I needed to see Nuriel—and I needed to see him soon. As soon as Dan left for work, I called him. I cancelled some meetings for the morning, and I got on the road to St Albans.

We had the children with us that weekend, so it was difficult to be overtly unpleasant to each other. The children saw us mildly fight for the first time that weekend and it was clear that it was distressing for them. I wanted to see Dan's datingbuzz profile and I also wanted to see the email account linked to it. He complied and gave me all of the login credentials. It was painful to navigate, and my body shook more and more with each click. My throat was dry and I was terrified by what I might discover.

His messages, although undeniably deceitful, seemed to focus on the need to converse with others. I didn't find any that suggested he was looking for the down-low, and if he was, he hadn't left a digital trace of it. Dan wanted to see my accounts too. My datingbuzz account only showed my trail of 'investi-gay-tion' which would lead to my catching him out. There was nothing else there for him to find. He did however catch me out on my linked email account. It was the account that I used to send my daily missives, and complaints about Dan, to Nuriel. The contents of my emails were painfully honest, sometimes bitchy and unkind, and they were unnerving for Dan. They revealed private details about him that he wouldn't have wanted anybody else to know, let alone Nuriel, whom he had recently decided was a charlatan. My words were harsh, but they told of how exposed and scared I felt. Dan became instantly angry, unsettled and embarrassed. He was vulnerable. Yet, somehow the state in which we found ourselves had all fallen on my shoulders. I was the instigator...I had caused him to have to double check if this was the right relationship for him. I had made him feel unsafe in my home. He wasn't taking any responsibility. He named me the crazy person. It was all bullshit. Gaslighting.

His instinct was to flee. The only way to keep him was to run with him. I needed to decide if I was willing to do that. I wasn't sure if this investment was paying the right dividends.

CHAPTER FIFTY-FIVE

THE BRAIN BLEED

29 October 2014

IN THE WEEKS following the explosion of infidelities, Dan and I began to heal. It was stiff and uncomfortable at first, but we soon found our mojo again. We looked for a new property to rent and the joy of the hunt brought some of the magic back. We had also decided that we needed to buy a bigger family car. Nuriel was right, our pain did make us stronger. I had recalled, from my last call, that Nuriel had explained to me that I would need to be patient with Dan because as much as I was expressive and outgoing, he was not.

"Dan is reserved and shy," Nuriel explained, "and his emotions are blocked from the deep-seated shame of his secret...he needs love and he needs time." I wanted to speak to Nuriel more about this insight, but I dared not.

AFTER WORK ON Wednesday, 29 October I had arranged for us to view a white Hyundai H1 van. It was basic but it was in good condition. It had low mileage and came with a full-service history and a warranty. We told the salesman that we would confirm if we definitely wanted it the following morning. After the car viewing we headed out for dinner. We ate a curry at our favourite local, which was adjacent to The Bonanza where my mum and dad had always loved to eat and where Holly and I had had our first jobs. The curry was average, but the company was way more than that.

Everything we had been through had taken it out of me, but somehow this man always replenished my soul. I was addicted to him—the good, the bad and the ugly. The flickering light from the candle between us was dancing on his face. His eyes glowed with depth and honesty. Things felt different, almost as if there was an awakening in him. Had he had the time that Nuriel suggested he would need to overcome his past and endorse me as that special person who was central to his future? I wondered and I hoped.

When we got home, the mood of the dinner table followed us into our bed. We danced beneath the sheets like the flicker of the candle in the warm restaurant light. Just like the curry house, things were hot and spicy and there was a lot of passion. The lovemaking was the most passionate and intimate it had ever been. It made me feel alive, like the version of Dan's eyes I had seen earlier that evening—and also like the first day that I had met him. By around midnight we were spooning lovingly in bed and the light was out. The evening had been magical.

I lay there for a while, but I couldn't fall asleep. I had an intense headache that seemed to originate at the base of my cerebellum, and the pain sporadically pulsated to the roof of my head with short sharp knife stabs. Dan was snoring, oblivious, and I was pacing up and down trying to relieve the unbearable pain in my head. At around 1am I took two paracetamols which seemed to help. I lay down again and fell asleep quickly—but only until just after 2:00 a.m. When I awoke, the pain was too much to bear I placed a cool damp flannel across the base of my neck and lay down again. A few minutes later, I woke Dan.

"Danny," I whispered, "I have a really bad headache." Dan stirred and was a little dazed and sleepy.

"What's wrong, Davey?" he asked worriedly. Even in my agony, I knew that I loved it when he called me Davey.

"I don't know," I answered, "I'm in a lot of pain and I don't know what to do." Within minutes the pain had escalated, and my fingers were tingling. "I don't know what's going on," I panicked, "I think you need to take me to the hospital." Dan leapt out of bed realising the severity of the situation.

"Are you sure, Davey?" he asked with obvious anxiety in his voice. "That sounds quite extreme." I was sure, and within a few minutes we were heading to the hospital in Dan's car.

On the way to the emergency room my hands went numb, and by the time we arrived there 10 minutes later, I couldn't feel my face. I was feeling delirious and things were hazy. Dan took care of the admission admin while I was triaged behind the port-holed doors. When a doctor arrived a short while after that, I was vaguely aware of being wheeled into an MRI machine. A friendly nurse was trying to converse with me in my hallucinatory state, but it was hopeless. My eyes darted around for Dan at every stop, but he was nowhere. I wanted to ask for him, but the medication had sedated me enough so that I couldn't talk.

When I awoke from my drug induced sleep in a ward bed later that morning, Dan was sitting patiently beside me looking shaken by the trauma of the previous night. He looked harrowed and exhausted.

"I'm sorry you did it all on your own," he apologised. "They wouldn't let me come with you." I was still struggling to focus. "They told me that because I wasn't your blood relative, I couldn't be with you," he explained.

"Cunts," I muttered, my voice still groggy.

"If we were straights," he complained, "they would have let me in."

"Probably" I replied—drowsy, but sad and angry.

A young doctor arrived at my bedside.

"Hello Mr Sterling," he said, "looks like you and your friend had a rough night." His name badge read Dr V Pérez, and he was almost too handsome to look at. His eyes, his smile, and his jet-black hair reminded me of Double L. I wondered if Lorenzo and Stefano would be married—or still married? Dr Pérez pulled me back from my thoughts.

"It will be difficult from here for a while," he explained in his thick accent, "although you're going to be okay, your brain tissue is going to need about 6 months to heal."

"Sounds like a long time," I noted without much emotion.

"You've had a subarachnoid haemorrhage," he continued, "but luckily there was no intracranial aneurysm picked up by the MRI." His technical jargon had lost Dan and I and he seemed to notice. "Basically," he explained talking in layman's language, "you burst a vein in the base of your head and that's better than bursting an artery—we need to keep you in for seven days to observe you." It sounded like a long time. Dr Pérez nodded his head as if to say goodbye and he moved on to his next patient who was in bed directly opposite me.

"Danny," I asked, "I need you to please call Nancy Reynolds, the HR manager at my work, and also my mum and Holly...and Carrie." I could see Dan twitch nervously at the thought of making the calls, but I was already feeling tired and my eyes were closing heavily. I drifted back into a deep sleep.

Dan was left alone to make the calls and so began my outing at the office, where my 'so-called-friend' called in to report my illness. After calling mum and Holly, Dan made his first post-divorce communications with Carrie. By 9:00 a.m., my mum arrived at the hospital with Father Finnigan. He was friendly and jovial, and I was semi-conscious. It was hard to make out what was transpiring, but he was reciting something which sounded like he might be reading me my last rights. I was too delirious to know exactly what he was up to—but if it made mum happy, I didn't mind.

Carrie arrived at the hospital with Jane and Kate a little after 4:00 p.m. that afternoon. They all look worried. Carrie looked particularly concerned. She sat beside my bed, while Dan took the girls down to the shop for a treat, and she cried many tears. She didn't have to say it, but we both knew that this haemorrhage was the one that would heal us. This one would have a reverse effect; this one was here to remind us that we didn't always have the time that we thought we had. We need to use all of the time that we have wisely. I leaned over and held her hand.

"Thanks for coming," I said, "I'm going to be fine," I added without certainty. She smiled.

"I hope so," she replied. "The girls need you—and I need you."

IT WAS JANE'S 13th birthday on the Saturday that followed. So just after visiting hours started on the morning of her birthday the whole crew arrived: Carrie, Jane, Kate, Carrie's parents, my mum, Holly, and Luke. True to the rituals that we created, we sang 'Happy Birthday' as many times as we could. Jane glowed, like any embarrassed teenager would, each time we sang it. We ate cake and Jane opened her presents. She was growing into such a beautiful, confident young woman. Both she and Kate astonished me beyond words. They were resilient warriors and I could be nothing but proud of them. They were surviving all of this with us.

Everybody left at around half eleven, overstaying the visiting hour by half an hour, but the staff seemed relaxed—perhaps because it was a Saturday.

It was too premature in our relationship for Dan to be there for the birthday celebrations. He wasn't ready to make small talk with my ex-wife and my ex-parents-in-law. He brought his children to the hospital for the afternoon visiting session at 3:00 p.m. He had arranged for Holly to bring Jane and Kate for birthday party round two. We had a lovely afternoon in ward 3. The Vanlings, mum, Holly, and Luke. We ate more cake, we sang again, and Jane opened more presents. The NHS wasn't going to put a dampener on my daughter's 13th birthday celebrations. Jane was glowing with love and she was revved up with the excitement of becoming a teenager.

At the end of the visiting hour, Holly took the children home with her, and Dan sat with me for at least another two hours. It was blissful and it felt like what might have been borrowed time. I wanted the clocks to stand still. We spoke about the deep stuff—our lives, our fears, our ambitions and our wishes for our children. Our meaningful conversation was halted by the ward sister who politely asked Dan to leave as visiting hours were long over and dinner was about to be served. Once he had compliantly put on his jacket, Dan leaned over and kissed me sweetly on my forehead.

"I love you, Davey," he whispered with a sincerity that touched my soul.

"I love you too," I replied, and I began to cry silently on the inside. In a fleeting moment he was gone, but my heart was full.

THE JOURNEY OF healing and growth continued. I was banned from psychics and Dan agreed to communicate his movements more openly with me. We journeyed on, wiser, safer, more content and falling more in love. Both of us this time.

CHAPTER FIFTY-SIX

EXTENDED AND BLENDED

31 October 2015

TWELVE MONTHS ON from my brain bleed and my head was feeling clearer than it ever had. The compartments in my head were virtually box free and the serpent that had once slithered between them had been cast into a faraway pit for ophiophagous birds to feed on. The world was less clouded, and it felt sharper. Everything was coming into focus. For the first time, ever, I was beginning to breathe and savour the small moments, just as Simon's mum had beckoned him to do in the movie. I was finally moving toward the present where I was aware, and where I could feel my body. I was grateful for Dan, for the Vanlings, for my family and for my friends— well, at least for those who had clambered the rocky journey with me. I missed Carrie, I missed her parents and I missed James and Becky.

Dan and I periodically met our exes for coffee to talk about their lives, the children, to offer support. The conversations were mostly calm and civil, but they could also be tricky and angry when the pain felt like it was too much to bear. We had accepted that we needed to own the product of the pain that we had inflicted, and within reason, we took our punishments. The long-term goal was forgiveness, healing and friendship. We were unapologetic about wanting it all and there was only one way to get there. Soldier on and never give up. We didn't.

Apart from some tricky cross-border meetings in the passages at the hospital a year back, we had had no interaction with each other's ex-spouses. The one-on-one meets and the bizarre barbeque were a distant memory. Carrie and Judy were the elephants in our world. They were there but also, they were not there—sort of semi there, and it was always tricky. It's difficult to dance with an elephant, especially when you cannot see it.

Our blended family encompassed more than just the Vanlings and the mothers of its five children—it extended to both of our own mothers, our siblings, our in-laws, our nieces and nephews, and our aunts and uncles. The whole shebang. We wanted extended and blended.

As our lives merged, he continued to meet a few others on the way. I needed to meet his family too, so a few weeks after Dan moved in with me, we had a big family lunch at what was now *our* house. It was the first time that I was to meet most of his family, and it was also the first time that our families were all meeting one another. Everybody was acclimatising and now they had to come face-to-face with the 'boyfriend'—and his family—to confirm all of the recent revelations and progress. Everybody was lovely, kind and relaxed and they all made an effort—surveying and sounding out. All drawing their own cautious conclusions.

AT AROUND THE time of her birthday in May, Carrie had begun cautiously dating Kurt. I arranged to meet her for a late afternoon coffee on the afternoon before her birthday. It was so good to see her looking alive again. Her beautiful eyes were sparkling in the afternoon light. Her face was radiating with second-chance hope, her shoulders were back, and I could see that she was breathing deeply again.

"I need to tell you something," she declared with anticipation.

"You're pregnant?" I teased.

"Now that would be an act of God," she replied wryly with a smile.

"Just kidding," I replied, "go on..." Carrie confided that she and Kurt had met for coffee on a few occasions and then a few times after for dinner.

"It's going really well," she enthused with some passion in her voice, "and I think we're probably an item by now." I was genuinely excited for her, and I didn't reveal to her that Kurt had called me a few days earlier to tell me the same thing.

Kurt and I had been friends since we were about 12 years old. He hadn't been one of those friends that I had secretly crushed on—and just as well, as that would've added a whole new and complicated dimension to this crazy new Jerry Springer reality. It was all very close—I had been at his wedding before I met Carrie, and he and his ex-wife had been at mine and Carrie's. Kurt had been divorced for a few years and was eager to settle down again with somebody that he liked more than his ex-wife.

"I'm so incredibly happy for you," I told her, leaping up and hugging her.

"It's all a bit weird and close," she expressed optimistically. "Only David Sterling would have this kind of luck." Carrie smiled contentedly.

"What do you mean?" I quizzed.

"A replacement for him that he knows," Carrie replied. "And somebody who he would trust whole-heartedly with his ex-wife and his children." She was right, it was ideal. I knew Kurt and I liked him. We had been family friends after we got married. Our families and children knew one another. He was a decent human being.

Soon after, Dan got to meet Kurt at Kate's school prize giving. Initially, Carrie was tense at what I assumed was the public display of Dan and I in her proximity. Having Kurt in the picture seemed to relax her. It was as though he was peeling her pain away, gently and slowly—and one layer at a time. Carrie glowed with love and healing and her face told of new beginnings and of new hope. She was metamorphosing into a stronger and more independent woman—a better version of herself—and it was beautiful to see.

At the same time that Carrie was settling in with Kurt, Judy had been gaining in strength too. She was experimentally swiping left and right on Tinder and had met somebody who she had seen a couple of times over a few weeks. She messaged Dan to tell him of what was transpiring in her life and said that she would like to introduce him to Dan and me. Her messages highlighted how it would give her peace of mind if Dan met and was comfortable with this new entity in her life: the person that she was keen to introduce their children to, and the person that she hoped to build a new future with.

We met at Pastasciutta at the High Chelmer Shopping Centre. It was a lovely restaurant that had a family-owned charm about it. The couple who ran it always went out of their way to make you feel like you were all that mattered. Dan and I arrived before Judy and Jason. We sat down at the table that Judy had booked and we ordered two glasses of the house Italian Merlot. Dan looked flustered.

"You okay?" I asked, taking hold of his thigh under the table to offer him some kind of comfort and support.

"Social events aren't my thing," he answered, "but I know this is important." Judy and Jason arrived just after our drinks and Judy had also brought little Rachel along as Amy and Tom were both out at birthday parties.

The introductions were falsely overzealous with animated handshakes and maybe too much interest shown in one another. We were back in uncharted waters and we were making it up as we went along—perhaps overcompensating in interest. The conversation flowed and Rachel was a welcomed distraction for anybody who wanted to opt out for a while. Jason was under mine and Dan's scrutinous eyes. We watched his every move and we analysed his discourse and his actions. He was pleasant, open and chatty, and way younger than Judy by at least 10 years, maybe more. He had a boyish enthusiasm about him and way more testosterone than Dan and I combined. He seemed nice enough, but only time would tell. The evening ended well with the promise of another gathering sometime in the not too distant future.

IT WAS TOM'S birthday the following month, so Dan and I headed over to his marital home in Margaretting for the party. It was also Judy's birthday. She had arranged a huge party at the house. There were at least thirty children and probably as many parents; Tom's friends and Judy's friends. Tom had three dads and one mum at the party, but he was unphased.

Spiderman and Batman were being traded for Minions and other things Universal Studio and Disney on this, his 8th birthday.

Dan and I mingled, and we felt welcome, but we also knew that we were being given the beady eye from some quarters. We remained unvexed. This wasn't about the judgers and the shamers, this was about us, our children and their mums. This was about our new family. Our vision was taking shape. Hard work always pays dividends. The ice had been broken and we had started making a point of engaging more frequently with the elephants in our lives...dancing cautiously, always keeping our eyes on our feet and on the prize. An elephant on your foot is bound to be painful.

SATURDAY, 31 OCTOBER was Jane's 14th birthday. The children were with their gay dads for that weekend and it was a happy one. Birthdays were always happy times, and our exuberance for them stretched them out happily. We had arranged a family breakfast to celebrate and it was another blended function: Dan and I; the five children; Carrie and Kurt; Carrie's parents; my mum; Holly, Xander and Luke; and also Jane's boyfriend Dean. We set the table for 16. It was a bit of a squeeze, but we made it work. Ten was comfortable, 16 was a squash—a happy squash. Dan and I had fried up a big breakfast: eggs, bacon, onions, mushrooms, potatoes, tomatoes, cheese, and some toast. We set the food out buffet-style and everybody helped themselves. The children helped pour mimosas for the adults and non-alcoholic versions for themselves. I clucked my teaspoon three times toward the rim of my mimosa glass and the hustle and bustle ceased.

"Happy birthday to our beautiful Jane," I announced. Jane glowed teenage red. "We're all so proud of everything you do," I continued, "we love you and hope that this next year is better than the last 13." I looked at Carrie. She looked fragile. Happy fragile perhaps. "Anybody else want to say anything for our beautiful Jane?" I asked. I was looking at Carrie but kept the pressure off her by opening the question to everybody. Carrie shook her head indicating that she didn't want to. Her eyes welled up with sentimentality. Kurt put his arm around her and pulled her close to him.

"We want to say something," Amy offered, speaking on behalf of herself and Kate.

"The stage is yours," I gestured, rolling my arm out like I was completing a circus act. Kate and Amy stood up and moved to either side of Jane.

"We have written a poem for you," Kate told Jane.

"So, we're going to read it to you together," Amy explained. I glanced over at Tom and Rachel, their eyes were bursting with intrigued excitement. Kate and Amy began in unison:

A poem for our big sister:

Jane, you are finally fourteen,
Although you're kind—you can be mean.
You like to dance and you can sing,
The kitchen's where you don't do a thing.
Your style is cool and you know how to dress,
But your bedroom is always one big mess.
You drive us crazy and that is true,
But one thing's for sure, we'd never swap you!

There was rapturous laughter at the end of each stanza; everybody seemed to enjoy every single word. Amy and Kate gave Jane a kiss in stereo on either side of her head at her temples.

"Great effort," Dan shouted across the table.

"That was amazing girls," Aunty Holly added. Carrie was back in control and she was smiling and laughing.

Kurt and Dan began talking across the table about the latest Range Rover Evoque model. Carrie moved to occupy the empty seat next to Holly and they were talking about the release of the much talked about Fifty Shades of Grey. Carrie's folks and my mum were chatting like the old days and they were reminiscing about the births of the girls. Xander was entertaining Tom and Rachel by asking them silly animated questions which they loved. The other children disappeared upstairs.

I was preparing the coffee and teas in the open plan kitchen and I was deep in thought—savouring the extent of how far we had come.

"Hi David," a voice pulled me back to reality—it was Carrie's dad.

"Hello grandad," I replied and gave him a big smile.

"This has been wonderful," he retorted.

"It has, hasn't it?" I asked rhetorically.

"Thank you, David," he stated with unexpected candidacy and sincerity. "You have dealt with and managed all of this so well." I smiled again—both proud and a little embarrassed for all the pain I had caused to everybody. Then he added "...and we know it hasn't always been easy for all of you...you've been as dependable as you promised." I could feel myself welling up, but I wanted to stay strong for this honourable man. He had every right to hate me for the immeasurable pain that I had inflicted on his daughter and on all of their worlds—but instead he recognised our collective pain and the journey of healing that we had walked together, but also apart.

"Thank you," I responded, "I've tried but there have been some cracks along this rocky road." He smiled.

"Life is full of cracks," he corroborated, "it's how you fix them that counts." Grandad Durham has always been a true sage. Kind and forgiving, patient always and wise. Accommodating, too, but never anybody's fool. He will always be an important part of my life.

For me, there was no higher affirmation of a race well run than what Carrie's dad said to me in our kitchen on that perfect and pivotal autumn day. The respect was mutual, and the love had endured. It always does when everybody's well-being is part of the equation.

CHAPTER FIFTY-SEVEN

NEW YORK, NEW YORK

12 October 2015

AS IN ANY relationship, we had our bumps in the road. Some days were angry growly ones, but most were happy. The few months after the brain bleed were difficult because my hearing was sensitive, my attention span short, and my fuse even shorter. Together we managed it and the safety that had grown between us made it easier. We seemed to become more patient and kinder with each other.

SOMETIME EARLY IN May, Dan and I were out for dinner at our favourite curry house. It was the first time we had returned there since the near-fatal brain bleed evening the previous October.

"Here's to good health," Dan saluted raising his glass of Israeli Tishbi Ruby Cabernet, which was delicious beyond words.

"L'Chaim," I replied, clinking my glass on his and trying to keep the

Hebrew theme going.

"It's been a rough couple of months for you Davey," he reflected with real care and reflection. "So," he continued, "I think we need a holiday." My eyes lit up.

"Where did you have in mind?" I asked.

"Nowhere really," he answered. "I thought we could decide together...how about New York, London, Paris, Munich?" he asked, almost breaking into the famous song. I jumped in to help him finish the lines from the 1979 song by artist M:

"Everybody talk about pop muzik...talk about pop muzik...." By the time I got to the end of the chorus Dan and I were both singing and beatboxing and the couple at the table next to us looked a little uncomfortable. When we got to the end of the chorus, we both laughed at our silliness.

"Freak!" he exclaimed, forgetting that he was just as involved in the song as I was.

"New York doesn't sound too shabby," I stated cheekily, ignoring his 'freak' comment.

"Let's do it," Dan agreed without hesitation and he raised his hand to high five me. The following day the tickets were booked, and we were due to fly to the Big Apple on October 12. Maybe my boss was right when he had told me that gay people could be impulsive and unstable, but if this was what instability was—I was fully on board.

In the same way that I, nearly two years earlier, had sung about flowers in my hair for the San Francisco trip—I now sung New York, New York in overdrive. Ol' blue eyes would have been proud of me:

Start spreading the news
I'm leaving today
I want to be a part of it
New York, New York...

I sang the lyrics over and over so many times—far too many times... everyday...nearly all of the day—but only the two verses that I knew. I was on a high.

"Start spreading the news..." I would erupt with vigour and rigour and Dan would roll his eyes.

"Here he goes again," he would predictably chant. I was incorrigible.

"If I can make it there, I'll make it anywhere..." There was no stopping me, and I probably could have come up with a song for any of the other cities named in artist M's song. My friend Gail had once told me that there was a song for every occasion and every event—and she was right, there absolutely was!

Dan and I landed at JFK in the early afternoon and we took an Uber to our hotel in Hoboken just across the Hudson from Manhattan. The Modern Settler Hotel was contemporary and chic, but not quite as beautiful as the Casa Solstice Spa Hotel that we had stayed at in Sausalito on our previous escape. We had decided to stay awake into the evening to alleviate jet lag and to smoothly adjust to East Coast time. We freshened up and we took a walk around the neighbourhood. It was beautiful and it was again liberating to be anonymous gays in the land of the free, with Lady Liberty not too far down the water.

"Let's go singing and dancing," I suggested impulsively.

"What? Now? Right now?" Dan asked not sure how committed I was.

"Yes," I retorted without hesitation and then I burst into song.

"Because...if I can make it there, I'll make it anywhere...," I lamented. Dan looked exasperated.

"Why not?" he sighed and jested all at the same time. I was surprised—and equally excited—that he had given in so easily. So, within a few minutes we were on the train to Greenwich Village. I had done a lot of pre-holiday research and I knew that Greenwich was bustling with gay piano bars. I had visions of Dan and I cosying in around a grand piano and singing those show tunes that Georgina had pointed out I liked to sing.

First we headed to *Smalls Basement Bar*. It was a cute place—a bunch of queens huddled together and singing, just as I had imagined. We joined them and their theatrical pianist, who was disappointingly playing an upright piano. The crowd were singing various Andrew Lloyd Webber songs and one or two songs by ABBA. The singing was fun, but the crowd was cliquey and us new gays were being suspiciously eyed out.

So, after our second drink, we headed to another bar called *The Duplex*, where there was a grand piano and the words of the songs were displayed on a big screen—karaoke style. The place felt upmarket and the crowd was fun. It was so good to be amongst our own. The throng was warm and welcoming. Dan and I sang and we danced, and I kissed him in public for the first time. It was adventurously risqué. We were like sexual teenagers—testing boundaries, excitable and learning more each day. We drank too much and after midnight, we returned to the hotel and continued our teenage explorations.

The next day we hired bicycles and cycled across the Manhattan Bridge toward Brooklyn. We ate horrible food at a quaint vegan restaurant and we drank Corona beer—which is apparently also vegan, unlike Guinness which is apparently not. The waitress told us the Guinness manufacturing process involves the use of isinglass which is made from the swim bladders of fish.

By the end of the meal, we were drunk enough to know that we should not ride our bicycles again, so we decided to walk back to the hotel. As we headed for the Brooklyn Bridge, I held Dan's hand.

"I need to tell you something very important," I told him, "and it's not about singing New York, New York," I drunkenly joked.

"Thank God, so tell me then," he jibed. I made a dramatic pause which made him laugh.

"This has been in my head for a long time..." I began and then I paused for effect again.

"Spit it out," he instructed, showing concern about the potential seriousness of what I was going to tell him.

"As I said," I recommenced, "this has been in my head a long time...and after visiting that shithole gluten shack, I need to tell you something really important." I was struggling not to laugh.

"What is it, Davey?" Dan asked in a joking, patronising tone.

"Okay, I'll tell you," I answered with dramatic authority. "I think," I pondered, "... now please don't be alarmed..."

"Spit it out, damn it," he interjected.

"Okay," I abided, and then announced: "...I think I am gluten intolerant, intolerant." The alcohol in our veins made us laugh out loud at my stupidity.

"You're a nutter, Davey," he managed to squeeze out between his laughter.

"Takes one to know one," I replied, as I pulled him closer and surprised him with a kiss on the Manhattan side of the bridge.

"Not in public, you loony," he bellowed, pulling away and wiping his mouth.

"Well then let's get out of public," I countered. Ten minutes later we were sitting in a Starbucks, drinking cappuccinos—with sugar—to try to sober us up. "I love you," I told him.

"I love you too, you old queer," he replied. It was so nice to be immersed in each other's company and to make happiness and love which seemed to overflow from the chalices locked behind our rib cages.

A few days later we visited the *Top of The Rock* to get a view of the city from above. We queued for a long time, and we used the time to reflect on our world. We spoke about a lot—but mostly we spoke about each of our children and their place and their needs in the Vanling family. We spoke of buying a new home and we spoke of what our future together might look like.

After we visited the top, we had lunch at *L'Avenue At Saks of Fifth Avenue*. We sat at a window table that allowed us to look over at the neo-gothic and stunningly decorated Cathedral of St Patrick. The church was beautiful, but it reminded me of the pain and judgement on the road I had walked: my emotional pain and my self-judgement—and not to mention the pain of Jesus who, was no doubt, hanging inside that beautiful façade with nails hammered through his flesh. Apparently to save the sins of this world.

I DIDN'T NEED to be saved. I had already saved myself—from the church and from the judgement of my secret. I was in the Big Apple with the man of my dreams. I was having the time of my life, and 'if I could make it there, I could make it anywhere'. I was learning to love my holidays, I was learning to love myself, and Dan and I were loving each other more...and more every day.

CHAPTER FIFTY-EIGHT

TEARING DOWN

30 May 2016

IT WAS A Sunday afternoon and Dan and I popped over to his mum's for afternoon tea. He was helping her with something on her PC in the study, and I was standing in the passage admiring a curatorship of decorative plates that hung in the space between the study and bathroom doors. There were at least six or seven of them in a range of blues and cyans that all complemented one another beautifully. Each plate was a different shape and size and the configuration in which they hung was pleasing to the eye.

One particular plate caught my eye, and I was intrigued with the story it told. It was an oval Willow Pattern plate, its blue print was faded a little more than similar ones I had previously spotted in charity shops along Chelmsford's High Street. It told the story of an eloping couple who were transformed into a pair of doves and who found everlasting happiness across the bridge of their dreams. The winds of hope—and of change—were captured in the static movement of three willow trees that were whimsically placed slightly off centre and to the right.

While closely observing it, I noticed the plate had been glued together. Pretty well I thought, but still noticeable from close up. Rather ironically, the three fracture lines merged at the bridge of dreams, where a small chip in the plate identified where the epicentre of trauma must have been. The fine repaired lines told of pain and of injury, but also of repair and renewed hope. The plate told me that sometimes things had to break a little so that they could become stronger. It told me that scars try to hide, and that they point—as gentle reminders—to the past. They are lessons learnt. Breaking and fixing is not always bad. Stripping things bare creates a new canvas and a fresh start. Dan and I had learnt that all too well over our traumatic psychic and cyber infidelity weekend.

OUR WICKFORD DREAM had fallen through some two years earlier and if we were to look for a cause, we need look no further than attributing it simply to bad planning. Not ours, as much as the developers—but we should have been more vigilant in our purchase. My dad always said that if something sounds too good to be true, then it probably is. Our naivety with the Wickford barn development and proven him right. He would have been watching closely from wherever he was, appreciating that it needed to be a lesson and relieved that we hadn't been hit too hard by it. He might also have been disheartened that we had fallen for the nonsense, but I don't think he would've been disappointed with Dan. I'm sure like cousin Cara, he would've also called Dan 'a keeper'.

The time had come for us to invest in a home that would bind us and our lives together—ever stronger and more committed.

We began the search for our house after Christmas and I was in top OCD form. I registered with every agent in the area and I viewed at least one house each evening after work. When he could make it, I dragged Dan along too. If he couldn't come and I liked the house, I would drag him to see it as soon as was possible. Every agent in the area knew me and my brief was clear: off street parking, three reception rooms, five bedrooms, two bathrooms (at least) and a garden—with grass. We were happy to do some work, but the floorplan needed to lend itself to alterations that wouldn't be too costly. We wanted to live between Carrie and Judy—and public transport to London needed to be easily accessible. Our budget was up to five hundred and fifty thousand pounds.

After a mammoth two-month search, we made an offer on a property in the village of Widford. The offer was accepted by the vendors on the same day and as there was no chain involved, the transfer proceeded swiftly. Completion was expected by the end of March and as the property was vacant, we arranged to move in on April Fool's Day.

The house was a large and inviting three-storied orange brick Victorian semi. It was set on a sloping stand, which meant that the drive was on an incline and there were some steps up to the front door. Behind the beautiful Oregon stained glass front door, there was a small vestibule that led into a hallway which opened into three reception rooms: a lounge, a dining room, and a large space off the modern, but badly executed, kitchen. The living spaces had potential, but they needed to be better configured. On the first floor there were three bedrooms and two bathrooms, one *en suite*—both needed to be redecorated. In the loft, there were two additional bedrooms and a small box room that had the potential to be converted into a small bathroom. There was some work to be done, but our plan had always been to make the house that we bought our own. Buying our first house together was monumental. It wasn't just about purchasing a physical building. More than this, it represented the continuous construction and investment we were making into our relationship, into each other, and into our modern Vanling family.

Dan employed his creativity before we moved in by designing numerous options for the redesign. Night after night we discussed them, prodded them and tweaked them. It was an exciting time, planning the investment in our home, but also strengthening our relationship on the foundations we had already been laying with love and dedication over the preceding years. To give us a more realistic perspective, we agreed to live in the house for at least two months before we started any work. We had a great canvas to create new memories on, but before we could build and flourish, we needed to break things down. We wanted to make some practical changes and we wanted it to tell our story. We wanted to fix it, just like Dan's mum's repaired Willow Pattern plate. We wanted to make the house more functional. Better and stronger: the walls, the energy, and the love. The house needed to become an extension of ourselves; we needed it to flow with us—and us with it.

We were eager and impatient, so four weeks after moving in we finalised the plans with the architect. Much to our surprise, planning permission was granted within three weeks—so, we sprang into action. Kate had a few friends around for her thirteenth birthday, which fell on the last Friday in May, and then the builders arrived—jackhammers and all—on Monday the 30th. We were ready to break down and to build up again. Most of the furniture was put into storage. Dan and I moved into the smaller room in the loft, and the five children shared the bigger one on the nights they spent with us. It was a squash! On the landing outside the bedrooms, we set up a makeshift kitchen that comprised a fridge, a microwave and a kettle; and we all used the bathroom on the first floor. The situation was far from ideal, but demolition is never pretty. It's raw and it's painful and it exposes what lies beneath the surface. Ask Carrie and Judy...they knew about demolition all too well!

The build would put Dan and I to the test.

Two months into the build and things were going awry.

"What the fuck have they done with this extension?" I yelled unnecessarily at Dan at the end of a long day at the office. I needed to vent my anger somewhere and he was the safest place to do it. It wasn't fair.

"I don't know, Davey," he murmured calmly, trying to sooth me. After a short pause, he continued: "Didn't you tell Max that the window needed to be set nearer to the kitchen side?" I knew he was just trying to make me think rationally, but I was beyond that.

"Can't Max read a fucking plan?" I exclaimed.

"Don't you take your fucking stress out on me!" Dan retaliated.

"It's a little difficult," I replied, unrepentant. "I've had enough of this builder, and I don't trust him and somehow," I snarled, "this building project has become *my* problem." Dan walked away.

Later that evening, after yet another repugnant microwave dinner, Dan and I got into bed with our laptops to look at the building budgets and Max's draw downs.

"Something isn't right here," Dan commented reflectively. "He's drawn too much money and he's behind on his deliverables." Dan was peering over his glasses that were halfway down his nose. We both knew it, but we had been too terrified to acknowledge it. The house was a shell and it was pretty much stripped bare.

"How much ahead is he on payments?" I asked.

"About £15 000," came Dan's frightening reply. The words were hardly out of his mouth when my phone rang. I didn't recognise the number.

"Hello, David speaking," I answered.

"Hello David, this is Carl," came the reply. "I work for Max, you've seen me on site a lot."

"Yes, Carl...are you the guy with the shaved head?" I asked matter-of-factly.

"That's me," he answered, still sounding nervous.

"What can I do for you Carl?" I asked almost officiously, which seemed to make him stutter.

"I probably shouldn't be making this call," he almost stammered, "but I need to let you know that Max is taking you for a ride." I listened attentively and Carl continued: "Yesterday, he made a comment that he is going to sabotage this project...he thinks he underquoted and now it's not worth his while." I wasn't surprised at the news.

"Fucking cunt!" I exclaimed almost involuntarily. Dan looked at me, startled.

"What's going on?" he mouthed. Instead of whispering back, I replied with fury and volume.

"It's Carl—he's Max's foreman. He's phoned to inform us that Max is out to fuck our project up." Dan squinted as he tried to process it all.

"Please David," Carl interjected, "please don't let him know I told you." I took a grip of myself and responded to Carl by thanking him for his call and I reassured him that I would treat what he had told me with utmost discretion.

The next morning when Max arrived fashionably late with his crew, I met them on the back lawn, I was calm and collected.

"Max," I droned with a flat and unemotional tone, "we find you insidious, we don't trust you and your work is substandard." Max was too shocked to respond and so I continued: "We have reviewed our contract with you and I'm sure that I don't have to tell you that you are in breach and you have also pretty much stolen money for time that you haven't given us." Max was getting edgy, but I wasn't finished. "Dan and I," I said, as if speaking for two made my voice stronger, "have decided that you don't work here anymore—so please arrange to remove all of your equipment by close of business today." Max was red in the face and the veins in his neck were raised.

"If that's what you want," he replied calmly, "then so be it, but you haven't heard the last from me," he threatened as he started to make his way to the side gate that led to the street.

That evening, I called Carl and asked him if he still wanted to work on the site as the foreman. I became the project manager and Carl my right-hand man. The house was a damaged shell. It was reminiscent of a church that had been bombed by the Germans in the Second World War—wailing to be mended but searching for its soul, its innards exposed and crying desperately for help. Max had left behind some seriously bad energy there, he was our very own Luftwaffe pilot with a mission to kill. Dan and I needed to reclaim the space—physically, spiritually and emotionally. We needed to restore the soul of number 4 Clifton Park Road. We needed to inject new energy in our home, our relationship and our lives. It felt good to be in control again. Dan and I made the decisions, I executed them with Carl and we never heard from Max again.

The progress on the build gained momentum and we doubled the workforce to speed up the completion. Six months on and the children were incredibly claustrophobic in their one-bedroom huddle. Dan and I were tired of instant dinners and of the dust that enveloped us—our hair, our clothes, our towels, our bed and our relationship. There was no escaping it. My lungs rebelled and my underlying asthma became chronic—something else that needed to be fixed. Simon's mum was right, I just needed to breathe, and I was finding that very difficult.

Carl and his team finished up two weeks before Christmas. The finished product was beautiful, more than we could ever have hoped for. Grey and mushroom tones and large panes of glass bought the outside in and took the inside out. The remodelled lounge was modern and sleek. Its central feature was an eye-level wood burning fireplace with a large railway sleeper mantelpiece. It jutted out into the room and stared across at the beautiful bay window that peered onto the street. The rest of the downstairs had been stylishly converted into an open plan kitchen, dining room and informal TV lounge—all part of the extension to the back of the house.

Straight lines and contemporary finishes gave the room a classic and modern feel. Large industrial black I-beams offered support where walls had once stood. The large grey aluminium sliding doors opened onto an inviting entertainment area that enticed you into the summer garden. On the first floor, all the bedrooms and bathrooms had been revamped. Our master bedroom overlooked the back garden, while Tom and Rachel shared the room above the lounge below. The small room became our study. In the loft, we pulled the dividing walls out and had converted the space into a massive room for the three teenage girls. The small box room became their shower room

The children loved it and so did we. Having been so close to the build, I had seen and been aware of the defects and flaws up close. I knew they were there when others didn't. I knew what lay behind the perfect façades and I had seen first-hand that it wasn't always pretty. It took me a while to accept that the house was perfect, only because of its imperfections—but I learnt that surface beauty can hide the scars, the pain and the trauma.

MINE AND DAN'S lives were no different to the plates that hung so perfectly in Dan's mum's passage. Each plate represented a different entity: Carrie, Judy, the house, our relationship, our children...each of these fragile and each with their own cracks. In the case of Carrie and Judy, Dan and I had caused those cracks and we remained committing to mending them. We wanted to be the superglue. Concurrent with our building project, our ex-wives were building things in their lives too. Things with Kurt and Jason were progressing with Carrie and Judy respectively and they were both looking happy and radiant again—cracks and flaws and superglue...the lot.

WE SHOULDN'T ALLOW imperfection and pain to distract us, because it can overtake us. We need to learn to stand back a bit and look at things from a greater distance. It gives us a better view and it obscures the fracture lines beautifully. We're all damaged, but we can all work again—just like those plates that hung in Dan's mum's passage. We can all be fixed and our scars and imperfections *can* make us stronger.

Perfection doesn't exist. Dan and I needed to learn that. Carrie and Judy had learnt that the hard way. Scars and all, we all managed, in our own different ways, to soldier on. Apart, but coming together. Till the day we die, we are *all* a work in progress.

CHAPTER FIFTY-NINE

A CRUISE ON THE MED

11 April 2017

DAN AND I had had our jollies across the pond and now it was time for a holiday abroad with the children. Two dads, five children and lots of love—with a few arguments and fights in-between.

We ended up revealing the holiday plans to the children over Christmas lunch in our newly renovated and extended home at 4 Clifton Park Road. The children spent Christmas Eve with their mums and we collected them midmorning to have lunch with us. The following day, we were going to hit the road bright and early as we had a few nights planned in the Cotswolds between Christmas and New Year.

"When are we going to go for a holiday on an aeroplane with you guys?" Kate was never one to ask indirect questions.

"Yes," interjected Amy, who was as brazen as Kate, "you're taking us to some village in the Cotswolds, but we actually want to go somewhere serious." We chuckled, embarrassed at our children's entitlement.

"What does 'serious' mean?" Dan asked Amy with a sardonic tone.

"Like Kate said," Amy replied without hesitation, "somewhere on a plane that's not in England...or Scotland." Jane who would usually have been the first to lead on these kinds of conversations was slow to join.

"Rachel and Tom?" she called with a conniving smile.

"Yes," they replied in unison as if not wanting to upset their big sister. "Would you two like to go on a holiday—far away," Jane asked, "...where you can sleep and eat on a plane?" The sale didn't need much convincing.

"Yes!" shouted Tom.

"Yes, yes!" squealed Rachel. Jane turned to Dan and I.

"Well." She commented with a coy sneer, "I'm in with the other four— so that would make it five votes to two!" The others cheered. "You two lose," Jane added. We all laughed at her strategy and wit. It was all getting a little tricky as we actually did have a surprise for them, but we had planned on telling them when we were up in the cottage for our short holiday in *Stow-on-the-Wold* in the coming days.

"Should we tell them?" I asked Dan animatedly, building up some excitement in the room.

"I think we should," Dan replied, bursting with excitement himself.

"Are you absolutely sure?" I seriously double checked with him.

"Let's just do it," he affirmed.

"Okay," I announced, "we have something important to tell you, but let's grab the puds first." Everybody dished up as fast as they could and then were all eagerly awaiting my proclamation.

"Please just tell us," Kate ordered.

"So..." I announced dramatically with volume and pause once everybody was seated back at the table, "if, between the five of you, you can find at least five five penny coins in your puddings, we have a big surprise for you."

"Urgh, gross," Rachel shrieked animatedly, "why do you put money in the pudding?"

"Apparently," I explained, raising one eyebrow, "it brings good luck to the person who finds it." Rachel didn't look convinced but she was going to give it a go. The three big girls were mowing their puddings down, chewing carefully to make sure that they didn't bite a coin. Rachel and Tom weren't enjoying the tippled pud and had resorted to using the spoons and then their fingers to find the elusive coins.

"You guys find them and clean them, and then bring them back to us," Dan instructed. Dan and I watched the frantic activity. They only found four between them, so I had to tell them to excavate the remaining portion in the kitchen to find the last one.

Once all had been found—and cleaned, I told the children to stand in a circle. I had quickly prepared seven pieces of paper and wrote one word on each of them:

Venice
Genoa
Sicily
Malta
Barcelona
Marseille
Rome

I placed the papers face down and asked Dan to randomly hand them out, without revealing what was written on them.

"Okay, you guys," I instructed, "turn your paper over—read it and show it to everybody." The big girls read each piece of paper—including the ones that Dan and I were holding. Jane took the lead in reading the word on each piece of paper out loud. Amy was first to guess.

"We must be going to one of these places?" she suggested with an excited voice. Dan and I shrugged our shoulders.

"Interesting," I mused, "which one do you think it is then?" The five of them began to randomly make guesses and Kate was doing all she could to help Tom and Rachel read the names of the places which were now displayed on the ground in a relatively straight line. They were struggling to reach any kind of consensus.

"All right then," Dan announced, "give us a shortlist of three." There was much debate and consternation and finally they presented us with their shortlist: Venice, Rome and Barcelona.

"Interesting selection," I noted, trying not to give anything away. We interrogated them as to their choices and we tormented them a little. "What if we told you that we were going to all of these places?" I asked with pan face.

"I'd say you were lying," Jane immediately retorted. The rest of the children agreed with her.

"Well," Dan offered, "we are going to them all...it's a cruise with some extra stops in Italy before and after." There was stunned silence in the room.

"Are you serious?" Jane replied, sounding slightly shocked—and almost overwhelmed.

"As serious as a dad can be gay," I replied. All five of them screamed with delight and they hugged us like we were movie celebrities.

After lots of planning, three and a bit months later, we set off on an Alitalia flight from Gatwick to Rome. Our early arrival on 11 April was to a pretty and slightly chilly spring morning. As soon as we landed, we took a train to Venice where we spent a few nights. After that we travelled across country to Genoa where we embarked the ship for the cruise.

We had previously had a few short local holidays with the children at home, but this one was different. It was to be a 'real' holiday, where the children felt deeply invested in and included in a part of our lives in a way that they hadn't been before. Perhaps they also found solitude and excitement in the safety of the anonymity—much like Dan and I had sought when we visited San Francisco and New York on our previous trips. Somehow crossing the channel with the children nucleated us. It strengthened us— fun, laughter, arguments, fights and all. There were lots of laughs and lots of irritations too. Separation by water does strange things to the mind. Those taken across the water, bind together, stronger—but they also yearn for those left behind. The children missed their mums.

It's as if there are fibres across the water luring you back, but those same fibres can bind you happily with the people you love and who are with you in your temporary foreign space. Carrie, the girls and I had learnt this all too well during our time on Montserrat.

AFTER A HAPPY three days in Venice, we took the train to Genoa, changing once in Milan. It's no small feat getting seven people and fourteen pieces of luggage up one flight of steps and down another when there is no escalator involved. It was an even bigger mission getting the seven plus fourteen from the train station to the hotel across from the port where we would board the following day. Five tired and hungry children between the ages of 6 and 16 are not fun to drag around, and so on the way to the hotel we found a quaint Italian restaurant to drink Coca-Cola and to eat pasta. It was a delightful little place under the trees where there was a gentle breeze and lots of love and wine. We even allowed the teenage girls to drink some Italian grapes with us. Our waitron spoke no English and we didn't speak any Italian, but we got by with the help of pictures on the menu and some very enthusiastic gesturing.

The next morning, we excitedly boarded the MSC Magnifica. Our Vanling crew made up a measly seven of the 3010 people on board—but we felt like kings—and maybe also like queens—ready to sail the Mediterranean. We were literally in the middle of the world. That's what Kate had told us Mediterranean meant—the middle of the world. We felt on top of the world, ready to make memories and to have fun.

First stop was Palermo in Sicily. We had been warned that it could be very unsafe, but our experience was quite the opposite. We made our way from the port into the little town and found a picturesque Sicilian café off Piazzetta Franscesco Bagnasco. The children had milkshakes in a range of flavours and Dan and I had cappuccinos that were way too strong to enjoy. The waitress was rude and snappy, but we excused her on the grounds of the language divide that existed between us. Sicily was the first day that we weren't all squashed up in train, or a hotel or a cabin—so it should have been a day to unwind, but instead it wasn't. It was the day when all of the pent-up emotions and frustrations of the previous five days exploded. Mostly between Dan and I, and the children saw it all—they became casualties in the crossfire. Two dads flapping like angry old queens on the edge of the Piazza. Growling and shouting and f-bombing like chavvies from Essex. Which was literally too close to our homes for comfort. And all of the fuss was over something as trivial as an issue with Facebook. It wasn't actually the reason; it was just the unsuspecting trigger, the pimple popper. We ended up separating for the day—Dan and the little ones, and me with the three big girls. We met each other back at the cabin later. We were all fresher and with clearer minds. Sometimes small gaps are good for your soul and for the love.

Sometimes we need to be islands, even be it for a short while.

By supper time the tensions had dissipated and we had apologised to each other and to the children for our outbursts. It's a curious truth that warring brings about peace, sometimes more peace than before—because much of the nonsense is mowed down in the crossfire.

We had a few happy days at sea and a stop in Malta before we reached Barcelona. Arriving in Barcelona, I was riddled with mixed emotions. It was the place where I wooed Carrie via snail mail, it was the place where we spent a few months after we got married and it was the place where I had met and crushed on Double L. I had contemplated trying to track Lorenzo down, but it seemed inappropriate.

I was certain that I wanted to visit *Palau Güell*. I was excited at the prospect of being able to be my authentic self in the city that I had previously been in love with. Barcelona, as before, was immediately alluring and inviting. It told you to be yourself and it told you that you were enough. Maybe that was why I always hoped to return. I had spent much of my life trying to prove that I was worthy and enough. Different and unconventional perhaps—but with purpose, like the Pollard Plane trees which lined the streets of Barcelona. They look like the Trufulla trees in Dr Seuss's The Lorax—whimsical like the city, like Gaudi, like Picasso, like me and Dan and the Vanlings and others who are square pegs in round holes. Their fuzzy hairdos and gnarled exposed roots made them unique...almost a little crazy—like the city, like the world and like many of us who live inside it.

After *Palau Güell*, Dan wanted to visit the Sagrada Familia church—the iconic and controversial building which was scheduled to be completed a century after its architect died. The design of the church was phenomenal, the façade was lined with scenes of the nativity, scenes of the fructification, goblins and gargoyles and kings and saints. The electivity of the unconventional church pretty much mirrored the world that Dan and I had created: different but pleasing—and oozing love and commitment. Dan and I were mesmerised.

"This is boring," Tom niggled.

"I don't have any wifi," Amy complained. Jane and Kate joined the protest.

"Looks like we're being forced to head off," I told Dan.

"Probably time to go," he replied.

"Come on guys," I shouted, gesturing with my hand as we headed back toward the port.

We finished the day up at a tapas bar close to the port. The children snacked on small tapas bowls—but nagged for burgers. It was a toss-up between burgers and wifi—and the wifi won. Barcelona had been lovely and so was the following day in Marseilles.

On the night we sailed out of Marseilles, we went to the main deck to feel the wind and to smell the spray of the surf.

"What's been your favourite part of the cruise?" I asked the children as we were all leaning onto the railing at the front of the ship. They all seemed to be processing their responses when little Rachel—all six years of her—responded with honesty and without inhibition:

"That we've been together as a family," she said with a coy smile. It was heart-warming and it summed up what we had wanted to achieve on our holiday—and on our journey. The other four children were off the hook, their answers were all summed up in Rachel's honest and heart-warming contribution.

EVERY DAY WAS a new adventure for us, and time and experience bound us together more and more. Dan was big on the idea of making memories and we had all got incredibly good at making them. Dan and all of the children taught me that living in the present was where you created memories that you could watch later in your head and share with your words. I had never been any good at living in the present and through the magic of this world that I had manifested, the present had become my favourite place to be. Me and my Danny and our beautiful five—all living together in the present.

The pain was fading and the focus was very much on the future. We were all feeling alive—moving onward and forward.

CHAPTER SIXTY

I Do

1 July 2017

IT WAS A big day and we had some distance to travel. We left home just after 3:00 p.m. and arrived at the venue slightly before four. The venue was charming and quaint—picture postcard perfect. There was a large barn, beautifully set up for the reception party. The long end of the barn was fitted with large aluminium framed glass doors that gave it an industrial feeling. The doors opened to a steel-railed balcony that dropped to lush lawn which inclined down to a small pond. Beyond the pond there was a small wooded area, with a path that led to a clearing where the marriage service would be conducted.

Dan and I arrived in the parking lot at the same time as Judy and Jason and Dan's three children. They were all smartly dressed and incredibly excited to see their dad. We made small talk as we meandered down beyond the pond and into the woods where there was a hive of activity underway.

There were a lot of familiar faces in the clearing in the woods and people were mixing and mingling. There was an electric buzz in the air. A lot of the old Nightingale crowd were there, but I noticed the absence of James and Becky. Somehow, they had slipped away permanently, like wet fish that had never been there to start with. Sometimes change and lending support are too painful for onlookers, perhaps they too grieve the event and what existed before it themselves. Sadly, they miss out on the acceptance that comes at the end of the long and painful grief trail. My dad had always taught me that good friends may laugh together, and they may cry together, but one thing's for sure—they are always there for one another. Some friends had proven that they had never been friends at all. Carrie and Judy were finally recognising Dan and I as dependable friends—those that don't go away...we had no plans of going away.

"The bridal party has arrived, will you all stand please," boomed an all too familiar voice from the public address system that was clear and crisp in the outside air. It was Nicky Thomson, not looking a day older than she had at Nightingale School some 20-years earlier. We all rose from the wooden benches that had been placed in a fishbone formation with a gap down the middle—just wide enough for the bridal party. The rocky clearing in the woods provided the perfect backdrop for an intimate wedding. A beautiful place for two to become one.

The ivory 1963 Austin Princess Limousine pulled up leisurely to the sound of the rustling leaves in the trees that enveloped us. As the limo came to a stop, the violin and piano of the Josh Groban version of 'You Raise Me Up' took over from the rustling trees and sent chills down my spine. Tears ran down my face. I hadn't heard the song since my dad's funeral.

The chauffeur leapt out of the car and opened the back door of the limo, which led to the red carpet that sprawled all of the way through the fish bone to the makeshift rustic altar at the front of the open-air chapel. All eyes were on the beautiful bride and the two gorgeous young women who flanked her. Carrie looked radiant and beautiful. Her off-white dress was classic and timeless with a beautiful bodice of delicate pearl beads. Her hair was styled in a half-tied French braid with gentle locks that hung on either side of her face. Her face was alive, her beautiful blue eyes were shining again, and her make-up was soft and natural. Jane and Kate looked radiant too, both in off-white dresses, bespoke to their personalities and styled to complement Carrie's. They were the princesses and Carrie was the queen.

As the three of them proceeded down the aisle, Jane and Kate linked arms with their mum as she held her spectacular and simple bouquet of arum lilies in her hands. The girls' outer arms flanked the procession with simple and stylish bunches of purple heather.

As they passed the row where Dan and I were standing, Carrie's eyes darted sideways toward me as if on purpose. I smiled reassuringly, and my heart cried for her happiness. Today, all of the tears would be tears of joy. And if I was meant to feel awkward or ashamed around the guests—many of whom had been at mine and Carrie's wedding some 18 years earlier—I didn't. Instead, I felt proud that I had released Carrie from a marriage where she had not been cherished and I was comfortable in being my authentic and constantly emerging self. The judgers had no more power over me. Carrie and I, and Dan and Judy, were all free. Free from one another and free to find happiness. Also finally free to be friends.

Kurt stood at the end of the aisle waiting for his gorgeous bride. His shoulders were back and his smile covered his entire face. He looked like a proud peacock. I felt many eyes turn to me, I guess trying to assess my emotions at handing Carrie over to him—like a relay baton in a 400-metre track race. They didn't get it. The tears I shed were for joy and for new birth. Rebirth perhaps. I felt an ache in my heart when Jane and Kate stepped back and Kurt took Carrie's arm. He smiled graciously at all three of them and then spoke softly.

"Thank you, girls," he offered, "I promise to look after your beautiful mum." His words choked me up because I was relieved for the security that this marriage signified for Carrie—a security that she deserved and that she had desperately yearned for since I had taken her safety away from her some years earlier. I was also emotional because I realised that the girls had to share their mum with this new person. I wished for all four of them, all the love in the world.

The service was light and happy. Jesus was invited, but he didn't overtake the proceedings. We sang 'Guide Me, O Thou Great Redeemer' and we listen to Bryan Ferry's 'Shakespeare's Sonnet No. 18' while Carrie, Kurt and their four children completed a candle lighting ceremony to signify their collective union. It was beautiful and poignant. It did feel strange that my children were part of a new union that didn't include me—but I understood it, and I acknowledged that I was the root of its creation.

While Carrie and Kurt were exchanging their vows, I happened to glance at Judy, who was with Jason one row in front of us. She was leaning in toward Jason and resting her head on his shoulder. I couldn't see her face, but it seemed to me that she was savouring every word, breathing them into her soul and imagining the happiness that awaited her and Jason somewhere further down the road.

Later that evening, after the speeches, Dan and I were outside sipping champagne with Holly and Xander under the soft orange spray of the evening sky. Mark Musgrave and his wife, Eve, joined us and we reminisced about the highs and lows of mine and Carrie's journey.

"Might be you and Dan next," Mark joked. We all laughed, but I was ready to commit to spending eternity with my Danny. The moon's waxing crescent was rising in the twilight to the sound of the string quartet playing Ed Sheeran's 'Photograph'. I felt like I wanted to sing along, especially the part where he says 'loving can heal, loving can mend your soul...I swear it will get easier'. Loving had certainly healed and mended me...and it was definitely getting easier. Clearly for Carrie too.

BLUE GIN, ORANGE skies and a waxing moon—the universe was signifying the beginning and the end of enormous things on this beautiful and momentous summer's evening. Carrie and I were free. Free from the pain of our pasts, and free to love each other unconditionally again as friends. I felt certain that Nuriel would be tuned in and smiling at the manifestation of this impossible dream.

Later, loud and familiar 1980s dance music started to bellow out from inside the candle-lit barn, drowning out the string quartet who played on relentlessly. The different music genres, and the red wine made the evening long and satisfying.

"Let's take a walk down to the water," Dan suggested, "looks like it will be a little while before dinner is served." We strolled down to the small pond where the ducks and geese had already roosted for the evening, disturbed only by the flood lights that shone across the lawns from the barn above them.

"It's been an emotional day," I said, taking his hand and feeling the warmth of his love. "But for all the right reasons," I contemplated.

"It's been amazing," he reflected, "another piece in our nearly completed puzzle." I leaned into him and held him tightly to my body. The familiar smell of *Fierce* by Abercrombie and Fitch radiated from his neck and it smelt like the sweet smell of victory.

"We've done good Danny," I whispered, "the universe has been kind to us, all of us."

About John Thurlow

Born in Zimbabwe and raised in Zambia and then South Africa. John now lives in Henley-on-Thames in the United Kingdom.

John started out his career first as a primary and then as a secondary school teacher. After 12 years of teaching, he moved into the education development sector where he continues to manage a variety of education programmes that support teaching and learning in underprivileged communities. He holds a PhD in Education.

John loves chocolate and he loves travelling... sometimes he likes running and walking. He always likes telling stories. The characters in his stories are based on his own personal experiences and interactions. Human relationships are super important to him and his family is the centre of his universe.

Email
johnthurlow@yahoo.com

Facebook
www.facebook.com/john.thurlow.7

Twitter
@johnthurlow29

Instagram
www.instagram.com/johnthurlow

CONNECT WITH NINESTAR PRESS

WWW.NINESTARPRESS.COM

WWW.FACEBOOK.COM/NINESTARPRESS

WWW.FACEBOOK.COM/GROUPS/NINESTARNICHE

WWW.TWITTER.COM/NINESTARPRESS

WWW.INSTAGRAM.COM/NINESTARPRESS

CPSIA information can be obtained
at www.ICGtesting.com
Printed in the USA
LVHW082336170922
728630LV00008B/121